"TUVOK!"

The lights were gone, only the emergency illumination remaining, but it was enough to let Deanna see that the Vulcan was sprawled motionless on the floor beneath the office table, his head coated in something dark and glistening. She couldn't see color, but she knew it was green. "Oh, God." She struck her combadge. "Medical emergency, Counselor Troi's office!" *Maybe emergencies,* she thought as she felt her insides heave and she vomited up her last meal onto the carpet. She couldn't tell through the inner turbulence if the baby was still kicking. "Sickbay, acknowledge!"

Nothing. "Computer!" She began dragging herself toward Tuvok. "Where are you, you stupid computer?" But that voice, the one that reminded her so maddeningly of her mother, remained silent. "Somebody!" she yelled. "We need help in here!"

Finally she reached Tuvok and began pulling him toward the door. Her muscles, overtaxed from months of service as a walking baby carriage, strained from the exertion. It felt like that wasn't all she was straining. "Dammit, Tuvok, wake up! Help me out here! I'll leave you here if I have to!"

Now her own voice was starting to remind her of her mother's, in attitude if not in timbre. *So be it,* she thought. *Lwaxana Troi's sheer cussedness got her through the occupation of Betazed in one piece. And kept her baby boy alive.* She'd never been more glad to be that woman's daughter.

Finally she reached the door, which shuddered halfway open—better than nothing. Forcing it the rest of the way, she channeled her mother's sheer vocal volume and began screaming for help.

Other *Star Trek* Novels by Christopher L. Bennett

Star Trek: Ex Machina

Star Trek Titan: Orion's Hounds

Star Trek: The Next Generation—The Buried Age

Places of Exile
(from *Star Trek Myriad Universes: Infinity's Prism*)

Star Trek: The Next Generation—Greater Than the Sum

Short Fiction

"Aftermath"
(from *Star Trek Corps of Engineers: Aftermath*)

". . . Loved I Not Honor More?"
(from *Star Trek: Deep Space Nine—Prophecy and Change*)

"Brief Candle"
(from *Star Trek: Voyager—Distant Shores*)

"As Others See Us"
(from *Star Trek: Constellations*)

"The Darkness Drops Again"
(from *Star Trek: Mere Anarchy*)

"Friends Among the Sparrows"
(from *Star Trek: The Next Generation—The Sky's the Limit*)

More Novels

X-Men: Watchers on the Walls

Spider-Man: Drowned in Thunder

STAR TREK
TITAN™

OVER A TORRENT SEA

CHRISTOPHER L. BENNETT

Based upon STAR TREK® and
STAR TREK: THE NEXT GENERATION®
created by Gene Roddenberry

POCKET BOOKS

New York London Toronto Sydney Droplet

Pocket Books
A Division of Simon & Schuster, Inc.
1230 Avenue of the Americas
New York, NY 10020

This book is a work of fiction. Names, characters, places, and incidents either are products of the author's imagination or are used fictitiously. Any resemblance to actual events or locales or persons, living or dead, is entirely coincidental.

First Pocket Books paperback edition March 2009

POCKET and colophon are registered trademarks of Simon & Schuster, Inc.

For information about special discounts for bulk purchases, please contact Simon & Schuster Special Sales at 1-800-456-6798 or business@simonandschuster.com

Cover art by Cliff Nielsen; cover design by Alan Dingman

Manufactured in the United States of America

10 9 8 7 6 5 4 3

ISBN-13: 978-1-4165-9497-0
ISBN-10:   1-4165-9497-3

To absent friends

HISTORIAN'S NOTE

This tale's prologue begins in the latter half of February, 2381 (over a week before the epilogue of *Star Trek Destiny, Book III: Lost Souls*), and concludes at the end of April (about two weeks before the end of *Star Trek: A Singular Destiny*).

The rest of *Over a Torrent Sea* unfolds between July 1 and August 4 of the same year.

I am the daughter of earth and water,
And the nursling of the sky;
I pass through the pores of the ocean and shores;
I change, but I cannot die.
For after the rain when with never a stain,
The pavilion of heaven is bare,
And the winds and sunbeams with their convex gleams
Build up the blue dome of air,
I silently laugh at my own cenotaph,
And out of the caverns of rain,
Like a child from the womb, like a ghost from the tomb,
I arise and unbuild it again.

—Percy Bysshe Shelley, "The Cloud"

PROLOGUE

We will not shrink from the challenge of raising back up what the Borg have knocked down. We will honor the sacrifices of all those who fought and died to defend us, by committing ourselves to repairing the damage that's been done and creating a future that they would have been proud of.

... More important, though Starfleet is needed for the recovery and reconstruction and to render aid, we will renew our commitment to its mission of peaceful exploration, diplomatic outreach, and open scientific inquiry. The *Luna*-class starships will continue—and, in the *Titan*'s case, resume—their missions far beyond our borders: seeking out new worlds, new civilizations, and new lifeforms and offering, to those that are ready, our hand in friendship.

> There are those who might doubt our ability to do all these things at once. To them I would say, don't underestimate the United Federation of Planets.

> —President Nanietta Bacco,
> Stardate 58126.3 (February 16, 2381)

UTOPIA PLANITIA ORBITAL SHIPYARDS, MARS

Captain William T. Riker did not underestimate the United Federation of Planets. After the decisive victory it had achieved over the Borg Collective the week before, Riker wasn't about to put anything past the Federation at this point—even if he, as one of the people directly responsible for that victory, did say so himself. But just because he believed something *could* be done didn't necessarily mean he agreed it was the best option.

"The Federation needs every able-bodied person it can get right now," Riker argued as he paced in front of Admiral Masc's desk. "I want to be part of that effort, Admiral. And so does my crew."

"I understand, Will. Believe me." The elderly admiral folded his hands, his normal Denobulan cheer subdued by recent events. This was a man who had carried heavy burdens before, including his failed effort to prevent Betazed from falling to the Dominion, without losing his customary aplomb. He had remained an optimist despite everything, spearheading Starfleet's ambitious *Luna*-class program as a symbol of the Federation's commitment to diversity and peaceful exploration. But the devastation the Borg had inflicted over the past month and a half—including the complete obliteration of Deneva, Regulus, and other major worlds and massive destruction across the faces of Vulcan, Andor, and Tellar—would take the rest of his career, if not his life, for the Federation to recover from. "But the decision is made. Do you want President Bacco to back down from her promise?"

"She doesn't have to, sir," Riker said. "There are still ten other *Luna*-class ships out there. They can continue the mission without us."

"The president mentioned *Titan* by name."

"So this is politics?" Riker stopped pacing and leaned over the desk. "Admiral, you're going to have to give me a better reason than that. Something I can take to my crew, that will convince them. Otherwise you're going to be looking at a lot of transfer requests. Maybe including mine."

Masc examined Riker patiently. He may not have been as cheerful as usual, but he wasn't prone to anger. "I would have thought you'd be glad to get back to exploring. I remember Admiral Akaar telling me how unhappy you and your crew were when your Gum Nebula survey was postponed for the Romulan diplomatic mission."

"I don't have to tell you how different the situation is now, sir. I'm still an explorer. But I'm also a patriot."

Masc finally smiled. "Will, you and your colleagues have already done the Federation a service we can never repay you enough for. Think of this as your reward."

"I don't want a reward, sir. With all due respect. I want—my crew wants—to be useful."

"And you will be." Masc rose from his desk and turned to the window, the ruddy glow of the Martian surface reflecting off his bald, textured pate, highlighted by the multi-colored lights of the orbital shipyard complex surrounding them, where *Titan* herself was currently undergoing repairs after its confrontations with the Borg. "We've been through so much this past decade," Masc went on. "After the Dominion War, we thought we'd weathered the worst crisis our civilization would ever face . . . and then, just a few years later, the Borg come roaring in and make the Dominion seem like the warm-up act. We're wounded, Will. Not just physically, but in our hearts and souls. The people of the Federation need hope. They need inspiration. The president knew that—it's why she mentioned your ship in her speech. *Titan* helped save the Federation. It's the most famous, most admired ship in the *Luna* fleet. That's why we need you out there at the vanguard. To give the people something they can feel positive about. To show them we're not giving up who we are."

He held up a hand before Riker could speak. "And no, that's not all. There is a more tangible goal you can achieve out there. If the quantum slipstream drive the *Aventine* is testing proves practical, then Starfleet is going to begin questing much farther out into the galaxy, much faster than ever before."

"Then doesn't that make us obsolete, sir?"

Masc smirked. "Only until we can retrofit the *Luna* ships with slipstream drive. But that's probably years from now; the Federation will need to devote its resources to reconstruction for a long time to come, so we can't make propulsion upgrades a priority. In the meantime, though, it's in our best interest to have advance scouts out there, getting at least a basic picture of the terrain, both astrographic and political. Better to send crews like yours out to make initial contacts before we erupt into the wider galaxy at slipstream speeds. Ideally to make new friends, of course . . . but also to identify and assess potential threats."

Riker studied the admiral in a new light. Masc may have been renowned for his optimism, but he was too much a veteran not to be a realist. Especially now.

"That's been part of our mission all along, hasn't it, Admiral?" Riker said. "Laying the groundwork for future slipstream vessels."

"Not a formal part," Masc replied. "You would have been told if it had been, of course. But as the slipstream research proved more promising, it became a larger factor in Starfleet's considerations."

Riker nodded to himself. It explained a lot. When *Titan* had entered the space bounded by the Gum Nebula, a region vaster than the Federation and all its neighbors put together, it had been with the expectation of spending years there. Indeed, it would take a hundred ships centuries to make a thorough survey of such a region, and Starfleet had assigned only two—first *Titan* and *Ganymede*, but after the latter ship had taken damage and needed to return temporarily to port, *Charon* had been reassigned to cover its survey zone, an assignment that had unfortunately led to its destruction at Orisha two months later.

And yet, with only *Titan* remaining to survey the nebula interior, Starfleet had soon ordered the vessel to head out beyond it and probe past the inner edge of the Orion

Arm. The rationale had been that the star charts and databases that *Titan* and *Charon* had obtained from regional civilizations such as the Pa'haquel, the Vomnin Confederacy, and the Gam-Pu Star Command had provided Starfleet with sufficient information on the nebula's interior. Riker hadn't quite understood Starfleet's haste. Even a well-populated, well-explored region could still turn up surprises; space was so vast that even now there were star systems less than a hundred light-years from Earth that Starfleet had never sent a crewed vessel to explore. Starships racing outward to get the big picture were bound to skip over a great many discoveries. True, Riker had once declared that *Titan* would always go forward, but he hadn't meant it to be in such a rush.

"To be frank, Admiral, I'm not sure I'm happy about being just the advance scouts for the real explorers."

"Nobody's saying that, Will. Yes, you've been . . . encouraged to quest outward as far as possible, but you haven't been prevented from doing real science. It's just that your goal is to seek out the most significant discoveries, to hit the high points. Every mission has to prioritize."

"With all due respect, Admiral, our last mission before the Borg invasion was charting an extremely dull, empty sector of the interarm expanse."

Masc quirked a smile. "Which is where you stumbled upon the key to solving the entire Borg crisis. You never know what you'll find until you get there, Will. Sometimes you lose the gamble, but sometimes it pays off hugely."

Riker conceded the point. To be honest, now that he thought back on the discoveries *Titan* had made over the past year, he was beginning to feel renewed excitement about returning to an exploratory mission. "So where will we go next, sir? Back to the interarm expanse? All the way to the Carina Arm, perhaps?"

Masc chuckled. "Ohh, I think we can strike a better balance between distance and thoroughness. If anything, it's probably best to keep you *relatively* close to home, so there's not as much delay in getting your mission reports to an eager public. But far enough out to be interesting, anyway. I can't tell you more just yet; we're still working out how best to redistribute the *Luna* fleet. Your sudden return home has left yet another gap in our coverage. We'll let you know when we have your new course.

"For now, though, you and your crew are entitled to a long vacation. Besides, *Titan* still needs plenty of repairs. Not to mention a new set of upgrades. If she's to be the flagship of the fleet, she needs the newest and the best we have to offer. And, uh, she needs to be made as durable as possible, since you're going to be far from any repair bases. Goodness knows, we built all the *Luna*s to be as resilient as we could, but after *Charon*, we don't want to take any chances."

"My crew and I appreciate it, sir."

Masc quirked a brow. "I'm sure you and Commander Troi want your daughter to be as safe as possible."

Riker fidgeted. "Of course, sir, I wouldn't let my concerns as a father interfere with my duties . . ."

Masc waved him off. "Don't worry about it, Captain. Honestly, right now I can't help but feel that a child would be safer out there on the frontier than here in the Federation. We tend to present a large target, and a stationary one."

After a somber moment, Riker asked, "And what if, while we're out there, sir, we stumble across the next Borg or Dominion?"

The admiral smiled, but it was cheerless. "Try not to tell them where we live."

VULCAN, STARDATE 58239.3

She found him in the desert just beyond the city borders. It had become his habit, in the weeks since they had returned home for their extended leave, to come out here to meditate—if meditation was indeed what he did. T'Pel knew that Tuvok had found it difficult to reach a meditative state in recent times. The cumulative traumas of his years in Starfleet had undermined his control, and T'Pel understood that he came out here not merely to seek an outer calm and quiet he could attempt to emulate, but to avoid the embarrassment of exposing his lack of control to their neighbors.

Tuvok's difficulty with meditation troubled T'Pel, for it impeded his process of coping with grief. T'Pel's grief at the loss of their youngest son, Elieth—who had died at Deneva with his wife Ione, staying behind to help others evacuate before the Borg laid waste to the once-bustling Federation colony—was as deep as Tuvok's own, if not deeper, given the greater time she had spent with her son over the course of his life. There was no shame in that; Vulcan philosophy acknowledged grief as a valid response to loss. "I grieve with thee" was an ancient formula which Surak himself had refused to renounce. While Surak had cautioned against succumbing to the debilitating emotional effects of grief, and most especially against the tendency to transform grief into a desire for vengeance and violence, he had nonetheless taught that even the most logical, dispassionate civilization must cherish life and the ties of family and community, and must acknowledge and reflect upon the great cost incurred when a life, particularly that of a kinsman, was lost. Otherwise, he had written, that dispassion would become callous self-absorption, nullifying the bonds that enabled individuals to function as part of a greater whole.

But T'Pel was able to manage and process her grief through meditation. It was true that, deep within, she experienced a great sense of emptiness and a profound pain. It was still difficult to process the reality that she would never see her son again, never hear him speak or share the preparation of a meal with him or argue with him over his career choices. But she was learning to accept these things as new facets of her being, integrating them into her psyche in a way that minimized impairment of her function and stability.

Tuvok, however, was having a much harder time. As he heard her footfall and turned, she noted the inflammation around his eyes. Although the desert air had swept away the proof, she knew he had been weeping. Wordlessly, she extended her paired fingers to him, and he returned the touch. Distantly, she felt the turmoil that raged within him. She braced herself, allowed it to buffet her, remaining strong and serene as an anchor for him. She accepted the gratitude and love he projected as stoically as the rest.

"My husband," she said. "Starfleet has sent a revised estimate of *Titan*'s launch date. We are to report by stardate 58260.0 . . . or issue a transfer request by 58245.0."

Tuvok nodded. A number of *Titan*'s personnel had already requested transfers, wishing to participate in reconstruction efforts, like Chwolkk, Okafor, and Roakn, or to return home to their families, like Bohn, Ichi, and Worvan. Although T'Pel suspected that a few had perhaps left because they had found *Titan*'s exceptionally diverse crew too difficult to adjust to. Both Fo Hachesa and Kenneth Norellis had exhibited difficulty in broadening their minds to accept other cultural viewpoints, whereas the herbivorous Lonam-Arja had never been comfortable serving alongside obligate carnivores. In T'Pel's judgment, their departure from *Titan*'s crew would not be a grave loss.

"It is now 58239.3," she reminded him. "That leaves us little time to decide."

"Us?" Tuvok countered, his voice rough. "I know you wish to remain aboard *Titan*."

"Indeed. I have a responsibility as caregiver for Noah Powell and Totyarguil Bolaji. And once Commander Troi gives birth to her child, I am certain I could be of assistance in her upbringing as well." Tending to *Titan*'s small complement of children had enabled T'Pel to make renewed use of the skills she had not needed since their youngest child had left home. It brought her satisfaction to be useful once again. "But in my absence, another caregiver could be found. And the Borg invasion left many orphans; my skills as a caregiver could be employed here as well." Inwardly, she contemplated the question of whether adopting a war orphan, or perhaps more than one, might give Tuvok new purpose to help him through his grief.

"The key issue for both of us, therefore, is whether you believe you are ready to return to duty as *Titan*'s tactical officer."

"Then that is a problem. For I do not believe I am."

T'Pel nodded in acknowledgment, if not acceptance. "Please explain the logical basis for that conclusion."

"I am not convinced I have sufficient emotional stability to perform in that capacity."

"That logic eludes me. Was not your predecessor in the post Commander Keru? He is an emotional individual, from what I have seen. And he experienced the loss of a life partner some years prior to taking the post."

"Conceded."

"Commander Vale was previously the tactical officer aboard *Enterprise*. She is human, and therefore highly emotional."

"I concede this as well."

"Moreover, was not her predecessor in that post a Klingon . . . ?"

Tuvok cocked a brow at her. "Not her immediate predecessor. I do take your point, my wife. However, you know that as a Vulcan, I must be held to a higher standard. Our emotions are too volatile to be unleashed."

"More volatile than those of a Klingon?"

"Other species are accustomed to utilizing their emotions. My lifetime of training is in their discipline and restraint. That is the way I know how to function."

"From our encounter with the star-jellies onward, you have been endeavoring to learn how to integrate your . . .

less restrained emotions into your normal functioning—to at least manage them with logic if you could not cast them off in its favor. You proved able to function effectively for most of a standard year."

"Until I was forced to cope with an emotion as profound as this," he said. "My grief at the death of my son. My . . . regret at not being with him at the end, having so many things to say that will never be said. What if it were you, T'Pel? If we returned to *Titan*, and I lost you . . . I do not believe I would be able to function. As an officer . . . or as a man."

Again she touched her fingers to his, acknowledging his admission. "Husband . . . this is a concern that all married crewpersons must face. It is one Captain Riker and Commander Troi no doubt consider every day. If they can function in the face of that risk . . . if individuals such as Commander Keru and Nurse Ogawa can carry on even after losing their life mates . . . then how can we, as Vulcans, expect any less of ourselves?"

She faced him squarely. "I asked you, my husband, to inform me of the logic underlying your decision. I have not heard logic. I have heard fear. Refusal to undertake a task because of speculation about possible negative results is not logical. Not unless the probability of such negative outcomes can be demonstrated to be unacceptably high. I am not as trained in risk assessment as you; can you demonstrate this to be the case?"

Tuvok's lips narrowed. "No. I cannot. Clearly my judgment is still impaired."

"In which case, you would no doubt benefit from further counseling by Commander Troi. She has been of considerable assistance in helping you to adjust this past year." *And in helping me adjust*, T'Pel added to herself. Though she was completely committed to her husband, his increased emotionalism did sometimes prove . . . difficult to live with. Difficult to respect. Counselor Troi was the only person T'Pel had been able to admit this to. "And since Commander Troi will be remaining aboard *Titan*, it follows that it would be in your best interest to remain aboard as well."

Frayed discipline or not, Tuvok still retained the ability to make quick decisions when needed. After a few more moments' thought, he nodded. "Very well. We shall report aboard *Titan* by stardate 58250."

"We have until 58260," she reminded him.

"Indeed. But as second officer, I have an example to set."

Her fingers brushed his once more in approval. He was starting to sound like his old self again.

U.S.S. TITAN, STARDATE 58327.6

"I can assure you, Counselor Troi, that there is no need to worry."

Somehow the reassurance was less convincing coming from the knife-toothed mouth of a predatory sauroid. Deanna Troi knew it was unfair to Doctor Ree to perceive him in that way, but convincing her mercurial hormones was another matter. "Doctor, I collapsed in the middle of a briefing."

"That is a bit of an overstatement. 'Swooned' would be more accurate. Your electrolytes are simply low."

"And you're sure it's nothing wrong with the baby? This pregnancy feels . . . different somehow."

"At the risk of sounding insensitive, considering how your last pregnancy went, I would consider that a good sign." Deanna winced at the reminder of the miscarriage she had suffered last September. Even though the Caeliar had healed her fetus's damaged genes, it was hard not to fear a repetition.

"In fact," Ree went on, "your daughter is developing relatively more rapidly than usual. At this rate, I would estimate she will come to term in no more than three months." Deanna's eyes widened. That was a month early for a human, two for a Betazoid. "Possibly even less. No doubt her accelerated growth is making increased demands on your metabolism, which is why your electrolytes are so depleted. I will prescribe a more robust diet and plenty of fluids."

"Why didn't you mention this before?" she asked with a trace of heat. "Could it be a sign of some problem? An aftereffect of the Caeliar treatment, maybe?"

"I was not yet sure. The gestation rates of humanoid hybrids are often unpredictable, especially in cases where genetic therapy is performed to enable the hybridization. It is possible that the Caeliar treatment had some effect, but it could simply be the vagaries of a mixed human-Betazoid biology." He laid a scaly hand on her shoulder. "Rest assured, there is no risk to you or the baby. Indeed, the Caeliar restored you to the peak health of a woman two-thirds your age. You should be able to handle an accelerated pregnancy with relative ease—with the proper diet and hydration," he stressed.

Once she left sickbay, now fortified with a sports beverage and a vitamin shot and carrying a padd containing the doctor's new dietary recommendations, Deanna felt embarrassed at her anxiety. Now that her emotions were settling, she was able to recognize how irrational it had been. She knew she and her baby were in extraordinary health—"obnoxiously good health," as Christine Vale teasingly described her post-Caeliar condition—and that the doctor would not keep the truth from her if anything were wrong with her pregnancy. (She had had more than ample proof of that back in February, when it had seemed they would lose this baby as well.)

In truth, she understood, the anxiety she felt was not entirely hers. Just before the briefing, she had been counseling Tuvok. His profound sense of loss resonated strongly with Deanna's own grief at the loss of her and Will's first unborn child, still a knife in her soul after nearly seven months. That pain had been so overwhelming that when Ree had informed her that the daughter she carried now was doomed as well, she had been unwilling to terminate the pregnancy even though the alternative was her near-certain death. She had simply been unable to face the prospect of losing another child. Even after the Caeliar had saved her daughter, even with the joy she and Will had felt as this robust new life grew inside her, the memory of that anguish still lingered within her. When she counseled Tuvok, when his own parallel grief fed into her, it tended to amplify her own anxieties.

Sometimes she wondered if she should ask Haaj or Huilan to take over Tuvok's counseling; perhaps she was too close to the matter to be objective. But as an empath, she couldn't accept that being able to identify with a patient's traumas was intrinsically a bad thing. As long as she kept a check on her own judgment and continued to receive regular counseling from Haaj, she believed she could manage. And ultimately it was Tuvok's choice. She had raised the matter with him before, and he had insisted on keeping her as his therapist. The two of them had a good, established rapport, a bond forged during their encounter with the Pa'haquel last year, and it would be difficult for him to open up to another counselor.

Lost in thought, Deanna almost collided with another woman who was rounding the corner at some speed. "Oh! Excuse me, Counselor. I wasn't watching where I was going."

"It's all right," she said automatically. It was one of the new enlisted security guards, Ellec Krotine—a lean Boslic with bright cherry-red hair. Deanna had seen much the same color on Christine Vale a while back, but she believed Krotine came by it naturally.

"I guess I'm distracted by where *we're* going," Krotine added. "Just another two days, and we're into the unknown. I can't wait." The golden-skinned young woman's angular brow ridges gave her an elegantly hawkish look—and indeed the trifurcated indentation in her forehead resembled the track of a bird of prey—but she was quiet, even-tempered, and inquisitive, even her expression of excitement sounding casual and laid-back. Despite her security background, her time aboard the *U.S.S. da Vinci*—one of the Starfleet Corps of Engineers' top "troubleshooter" vessels—had awakened in her a fascination with discovering the unknown and solving scientific and technical problems. Though she wasn't formally trained in those fields, she had told Deanna in her initial interview that she enjoyed participating in them vicariously and picking up what knowledge she could in the process.

"Anyway, I have to go," Krotine said. "Commander Pazlar is giving a presentation on the sectors ahead. I love stellar cartography on this ship. Isn't the microgravity great?"

Deanna made a noncommittal noise; she vomited quite enough these days in normal gravity. But she smiled and told Krotine to enjoy herself, and basked in the wave of confident good cheer that came with the Boslic's gentle grin.

Indeed, as she moved through the corridors and extended her senses, she felt Krotine's eager anticipation reflected in most of the minds around her. *Titan* was finally about to cross into uncharted territory once more—the Canis Major region this time, out beyond Adhara and Muliphen, between the Gum Nebula and the Orion Reach. Right now they were just within the fringes of the Kavrot Sector, a territory charted by the Klingons' Chancellor-class fleet four or five years back—and naturally Pazlar's cartography teams were taking extensive scans, for the Klingons had been more interested in prospective conquests than pure science. But even so, it was still charted territory. In the wake of the Borg invasion, the Klingon-Federation alliance was stronger than ever, so much so that a Starfleet vessel could travel through space claimed by the Empire without being challenged and gain access to the Klingons' cartographic data without going through a lot of noise about imperial secrets.

To be sure, these were interesting times for the Federation and its neighbors. The Borg onslaught had shattered their political, economic, and social stability, and the consequences were just starting to be felt. Deanna regretted leaving that behind; not only could her skills as a diplomat prove useful in coping with those crises, but it would be fascinating from a sociological perspective to experience how the civilizations of known space adjusted to their new reality. Would they fragment still further, or come together as never before?

But in her heart of hearts, she was an explorer, and so was Will Riker. And she shared this vessel with three hundred and fifty other explorers, all ready to quest into the unknown. True, it would not be easy for many of them to shake off the baggage of the recent past. Most of them had suffered some loss in the invasion, or simply been wounded in their souls by the profound destruction and death. That would linger with them for a long time to come. But *Titan*'s crew was ready to face ahead once again.

No matter how much they'd lost . . . there was always something new to be found.

CHAPTER ONE

"We call it Droplet."

Melora Pazlar tried to rein in her enthusiasm about the small blue-white dot that was displayed behind her on the holographic viewer in *Titan*'s main briefing room, the best view the sensors could get so far of the fourth planet of UFC 86783. The rest of the command crew didn't yet know what was so exceptional about this planet, so she didn't want to go overboard. Of course, she was here to convince them that this world, out of all the current candidates, should be the vessel's next destination. But it wasn't in her nature to broadcast her emotions too openly, even among people she knew as well as this crew. As a fragile, low-gravity Elaysian living in a high-grav environment, she didn't like to feel vulnerable.

Deanna Troi leaned forward, no doubt sensing the excitement Melora held in check. She couldn't lean forward too easily, since she was huge now, looking as though she could give birth any day. She had long since eschewed a standard uniform for loose maternity dresses in the blue and green shades of her department. It suited her, Melora thought. She found it odd the way humans talked about pregnant women having a "glow" about them, but Troi did seem to have a certain radiance these days. "A water world?" the counselor asked.

"More than that," Melora responded. "A classic Léger-type ocean planet, class O, subclass L1. About three times the mass of Earth, nearly half of it water ice. Slightly lower than Terrestrial gravity due to the low density."

"So what makes it interesting?" asked Ranul Keru. "We've charted plenty of those." The large, bearded Trill had been a stellar cartographer once, but his priorities had shifted since his move to security. At the moment, he was preoccupied with this morning's update from Starfleet about the developing situation with the newly emerged Typhon Pact. As if the crew hadn't felt guilty enough about flying off into the unknown while the rest of the Federation dealt with the aftermath of the Borg invasion, the existence of this new rival power had been revealed mere days after *Titan* had crossed into uncharted space. Eight weeks later, it was still unclear what the rise of the Pact meant for the Federation's future, and there was nothing the crew could do but watch and wait.

"Yes, but they're usually not inhabited."

Keru blinked. "And this one is?"

"Undoubtedly. We thought the oh-two levels might be from water vapor dissociation, but there's a strong ozone line in its spectrum too, meaning the oxygen has to be biogenic. Plus there's a substantial chlorophyll signature. It's hard to get more detailed readings at this distance, due to the sensor interference." As she'd mentioned at the start of the briefing, UFC 86783 had an unusually dense disk of asteroidal debris for a system of its age, one rich in exotic minerals and radioisotopes that interfered with scans. "But we've managed to cut through the interference enough to get dynoscanner readings suggesting abundant higher-order life."

"On an L1? You're certain?" Melora answered Keru's question with a nod, smiling. He definitely wasn't dwelling on the Typhon Pact anymore.

"Maybe you could remind the rest of us," Captain Riker said, "why that's so unusual."

"Because an ocean is basically a desert," Melora said. "Life needs water to survive, but it also needs mineral nutrients. On a class-M planet, life in the oceans is richest where there's mineral runoff from the land masses, and fairly sparse elsewhere. A Léger-type class O has no land, no minerals anywhere near the surface." She worked the controls to display a cross section, the trim antigrav suit she wore making it easier to lift her arms against an artificial gravity dozens of times that of her native world. She'd mostly given up the holopresence system that Xin Ra-Havreii had designed to let her interact with the crew from her microgravity haven in the stellar cartography lab, since it had been making her too isolated from the crew. But this antigrav suit—the latest gift from Xin, who gave out brilliant inventions as romantic gifts the way other men gave jewelry—was an improvement over the motor-assist armature she'd used for most of her Starfleet career, and over the cruder, bulkier antigrav suit she'd tried briefly last year. "Droplet, for instance, has a metal core thirty-seven hundred kilometers deep surrounded by nearly three thousand kilometers of silicate rock, and above that is a mantle of high-pressure allotropic ice over four thousand kilometers deep. The outermost ninety kilometers is liquid water, an ocean a hundred times greater in volume than Earth's. But on most planets of this type, the ocean is virtually barren. Whatever minerals get delivered by meteor impacts are barely enough to sustain a limited microbial population, and the minerals tend to sink to the bottom of the ocean, where the pressure is too great for most forms of life to survive."

"What's more," Keru added, "without deep-sea volcanic vents, there's no mechanism for conventional life to arise in the first place."

"Except seeding from space, whether by natural panspermic bombardment or alien intervention."

Riker perked up. "Could the life on Droplet," and he smiled a bit at the name, "be evidence of alien intervention?"

"Or perhaps a colony," Commander Tuvok suggested. "Six years ago, on stardate 52179, *Voyager* encountered an artificial ocean in space created by unknown builders. It had subsequently been colonized by travelers from elsewhere."

"Monea, yes, I read about that," Melora said. "But we're picking up no signs of artificial power generation. At least, as far as we can tell. But we were able to get those biosigns on the dynoscanners. Power readings would most likely be easier to detect."

"You said meteor impacts could deliver minerals to

the ocean," Christine Vale said. This month, the deceptively slight first officer's hair was tinted a rich, deep blue with aquamarine highlights. Melora hoped that was a sign she'd be receptive to exploring this ocean world. "Could the bombardment rate here provide enough minerals to explain the life readings?"

Melora shook her head. "Not in these abundances."

Riker's smile widened. "Sounds like it might be worth checking out."

"You sure you don't want to follow up on the video broadcasts from the Oraco system?" Vale asked.

"We just surveyed a pre-warp industrial society last month, back at Lumbu," the captain replied. "And another the month before at Knnischlinnaik. Aren't you ready for a change of pace?"

"But this one seems more advanced. And those signals are thirty-four years old—the Oracoans could be in space by now."

"Creating a greater risk of our accidental discovery," Tuvok pointed out.

Riker nodded. "We can continue monitoring their broadcasts from a distance, send out a probe to intercept more recent signals." He looked around the room. "Any negatives about Droplet?"

"The density of the asteroidal disk would pose a hazard to navigation," Tuvok answered. "Once in the system, the sensor interference would be amplified, impeding our ability to chart the trajectories of potentially hazardous objects."

"We'd still have optical imaging," Melora replied. "It

would take a lot longer to do a thorough survey, but we could see anything immediately dangerous soon enough to get out of the way."

"It looks like the planet has a pretty strong magnetic field too," Keru put in.

"That's right. Its core is unusually hot; it probably contains many of the same radioactive elements we see in the system's debris disk, like plutonium and pergium. That makes for an active magnetic dynamo with some unusual energy patterns."

"And that field," Keru said, "would interfere with sensors, communicators, and transporters."

"We'd need to use shuttles anyway," Vale said. "After all, where would we beam down to?"

"Indeed," Tuvok said. "There would be many difficulties involved in surveying this planet."

Riker was grinning widely now. "Come on now, people. The first generations of space explorers didn't have transporters or subspace sensors, but that didn't stop them. Personally I'd relish the chance to do some old-school exploring. And when has this crew ever backed down from a challenge?"

The rest of the senior staff was smiling now, catching their captain's enthusiasm—all except Tuvok, who merely sat back with a stoic lift to his eyebrow, satisfied that his concerns had been voiced. Xin rewarded Melora with a more personal smile, congratulating his lover on her success in selling her case. She smiled back, and Xin turned to the captain. "Shall I begin converting our multipurpose shuttles to aquatic configuration, sir?" he asked.

"As many as you can by . . . what's the travel time, Commander Pazlar?"

"Three days at warp five, Captain."

"All right, then." He hit his combadge. "Riker to Ensign Lavena."

"Lavena here, sir," came the response, the Selkie pilot's voice filtered through the hydration suit she wore.

Riker's grin grew even wider. "Set a new course, Aili. You're gonna love this one."

STARDATE 58506.3

Captain Riker had been right; Aili Lavena's pulse was surging with excitement as she flew *Titan* into the UFC 86783 system—or New Kaferia, as the stellar cartographers had dubbed it, for the star was a virtual twin of Kaferia's sun Tau Ceti, a smallish yellow-orange dwarf with a dense debris disk around it. Except Tau Ceti's disk was sparse compared to this one. Aili was as energized by the navigational challenge of reaching Droplet as by the prospect of getting to dive into its oceans. Although she was a pilot by training, she knew she'd be at the forefront of this survey, for her aquatic physiology would let her explore this planet's depths in ways no other member of the crew could.

But the true depths of this planet, she reminded herself with a slight shudder, were far more profound than even she could plumb. Below ninety kilometers, the pressure became so great that water itself was crushed to solidity, forming exotic crystalline phases with names like ice-seven and ice-ten even at temperatures she would consider boiling hot. At best, she would be able to descend a tiny fraction of that depth before the pressure exceeded even a Selkie's tolerances.

First things first, though. She brought *Titan* into the system at a sharp angle to its ecliptic plane, coming "up from below" to avoid the worst of its debris disk and give the sensor techs a good overview of its asteroid distribution. Their estimates of the asteroids' courses, a constantly updated file of which was tied into her nav computer, were necessarily inexact, limited as they were to optical imaging; more accurate orbit plots would require observing their motion for weeks, as early astronomers had needed to do in the days before subspace-displacement motion sensors. But the rough data she had were enough to let her skirt around the probability cones of any hazardous bodies.

Droplet was in an unusually wide orbit for a habitable planet around a star this cool. With an endless supply of water to vaporize, Droplet had a considerable greenhouse effect, plus the convection in its oceans brought some heat up from the planet's interior; so the surface was balmy and tropical. Aili had been glad to hear that; though her body was well-insulated and able to adjust to a wide range of water temperatures, she liked it warm. And land-dwelling humanoids definitely liked it warm, which would be a plus if the away team included anyone she wanted to invite for a private skinny-dip. She smiled to herself at the thought.

As the ocean world loomed larger on the viewer, it looked almost like a Jovian; without land masses to break up the airflow, the weather patterns were very regular, with parallel bands of clouds circling the planet, most solidly concentrated around the equator. But as the angle changed, allowing the bridge crew to see around the curve of the large globe, the cloud bands around the equator broke and swirled around a more circular pattern—one which Aili soon realized was an enormous hurricane. "Don't tell me," Riker said. "Hurricanes break up when they hit land. No land means they can get . . . that big."

Beside him, Troi's eyes widened. "Some Jovians have standing storms that last for centuries."

"Like Jupiter's Red Spot or the Eye of Vetlhaq," Vale said.

Riker was grinning now. "How long do you suppose this hurricane has been around?"

"There's no way of knowing," Pazlar answered. "I'd just recommend that we avoid getting too close in our shuttles. There's some ferocious lightning in there."

As the planet drew still nearer, more detail began to appear. The pole they could see was wreathed in a bright ring of auroras, lost in the blue of the lit hemisphere but vivid and alive against the night side—the visible evidence of the powerful magnetic energies emanating from this planet. Much of the ocean surface was hidden under the clouds, but in the exposed portions, shadings of green were visible. "Algae blooms," reported Chamish, the Kazarite ecologist, from the secondary science station.

"But where are they getting their nutrients?" Pazlar wondered.

"Any sign of mineral concentrations?" Riker asked.

"With the sensor interference, the blooms themselves are the best sign we're getting," the Elaysian science officer replied.

"Wait," Troi said, trying to lean forward with little

success. "This can't be right . . . but I could swear I'm seeing islands!"

Looking up from her board, Aili saw faint specks dotting the ocean surface. When Riker ordered magnification, they came into view more distinctly. The most prominent feature from this angle was a small polar icecap, but hundreds of other bright specks dotted the ocean surface around it. "They could be icebergs," Vale suggested.

"Not bergs, ma'am," Aili told her. "Those break off of glaciers, which need land masses to form on. Here, you'd only have flat ice sheets and floes. And they couldn't survive very far from the poles, not if the ocean's as warm as Commander Pazlar says."

"She's right," Pazlar confirmed. "And some of them are too large anyway. Look here." She magnified a portion of the screen, centering on what seemed to be a cluster of islands, each one either a single light-colored disk or a cluster of multiple disks of similar size.

"There's no way you could've been wrong about there being land, is there?" Vale asked.

Pazlar shook her head, studying her readouts with a slightly dazed expression. "Those aren't land. Not the way we think of it. They're moving, sir. They're drifting in the current."

Riker was out of his chair, his hand on Aili's seat back as he took a closer look at the main viewer. Glancing up, she saw he was grinning like a kid at his birthday party. "Floating islands? Tell me you're not kidding!"

"I swear it. I wouldn't care to speculate about what they are, though."

Chuckling, Riker turned to Vale. "What was that you

were saying about not having any place to land? I think we've just found our first touchdown site."

Christine Vale looked on with a stern expression as Riker's eyes roved over the shuttlecraft *Gillespie*, now refitted into a full aquashuttle configuration. Half of *Titan*'s eight shuttles were designed to be reconfigurable for multiple mission profiles, and Ra-Havreii's engineering teams had managed to convert all four of them in time for planetfall. *Gillespie*'s nacelles had been lowered and modified to serve as pontoons, equipped with stabilizing fins and linear induction thrusters. Searchlights, undersea sensor suites, and extra structural integrity field generators had been added to allow the shuttle to function as a deep-sea submersible. In lieu of the manipulator arms of old submersibles, an undersea tractor-beam rig had been installed below the nose, with a pair of emitters that together would focus the tractor effect at the desired distance, with the individual, unfocused beams exerting minimal effect on the intervening water. All in all, it looked like one hell of a boat, and Vale was looking forward to taking it for a spin.

Assuming the gleam in her captain's eye didn't translate into action. "Don't tell me you're thinking of going down yourself, Captain," she said, hands on hips.

His eyes turned to her, the gleam giving way to wistfulness. "Don't worry, Christine. Just an idle thought." He sighed. "Time to put those days behind me now. I have to be a responsible captain *and* a responsible father. You won't have to argue with me about who leads the away teams anymore."

Vale studied him, knowing that he wasn't too unhappy

about it. He and Deanna had been through a rough time after deciding to conceive a child: first a long, unpleasant set of treatments to overcome their cross-species compatibility issues, then the miscarriage, then the near loss of their second unborn child. It had put a strain on their relationship, but they had come through it stronger and more committed to each other—and to their little girl—than ever. She knew that at this stage of his life, Will Riker was happier to be by his pregnant wife's side than to go gallivanting around uncharted planets in souped-up shuttles. But there was still a part of him, she knew, that felt nostalgia for that freedom and excitement.

She laid a hand on his shoulder briefly. "Don't worry. I promise to bring back plenty of holos."

Most of the team was already present. Aili Lavena was running preflight checks, no doubt eager to get down to a new ocean. Melora Pazlar and Lieutenant Kekil, the Chelon biologist, were loading equipment and sample cases. That left only Ranul Keru, she thought—until she heard a familiar soft whirring sound and turned to see Ensign Torvig Bu-kar-nguv approaching. "Permission to join the away team, Captain?"

Vale did a double take, followed by Riker a second later. Both of them had long since grown accustomed to the appearance of the young Choblik: a meter-high mammalian with a cervine head, ostrichlike body, and long slender tail, but augmented with bionic implants. The surprise was that those implants had changed. The cowling that protected his skull and snout had been modified with a more streamlined prow, his deerlike ears swept back into recessed nooks. His robotic arms appeared to have been modified to fold up flush against his ventral plate, which had been also been reshaped for streamlining and even given a slight keel. His foot-claws had been replaced with paddlefeet, and the extra handlike manipulator at the tip of his tail had been replaced with a structure like a Japanese fan. A dorsal fin rising from his spinal armor completed the ensemble.

Riker finally found his voice. "Ensign. I see you've . . . dressed for the occasion. How, uh, how long did this take? You really should've consulted me before making any major modifications . . ."

"Oh, it didn't take long, sir. I was due for a regular swap-out soon anyway, and I figured I might as well . . . Hm. I suppose it would be literally true to say I decided to make myself useful." The little engineer seemed pleased by his wordplay, but more in the way he took quiet pleasure in any new discovery than out of full-fledged humor.

"And . . . how hard would it be to change back afterward?"

"It wouldn't pose any difficulty, sir. I have the necessary equipment in my quarters." He tilted his head, his mechanical irises widening in realization. "I apologize for not making a formal request, sir. I just got so interested in the project . . ."

"Say no more, Ensign." By now, everyone knew how Torvig was when he got intrigued by a new project. Although he wasn't highly emotional by humanoid standards, he was a creature of pure impulse when it came to intellectual curiosity and experimentation.

The captain turned to Vale. "Christine? It's your mission."

"Well, Vig, um . . . I wouldn't want all that work to

go to waste . . . but Droplet doesn't seem like the kind of planet where we'd need an engineer along."

"Oh, I've uploaded the xenobiology and planetary science databases into my memory buffer, Commander," he said. Much of the Choblik's intelligence was assisted by the bionic implants that some unknown benefactors had given them millennia in the past; without them, Torvig would be only a fairly bright woodland animal. He thus had the ability to upload new knowledge at will, though it took his organic brain some time and practice to process it. "Besides, the aquashuttle systems are largely untested, so it might be a good idea to have an engineer along. And I don't take up much room, ma'am."

Vale chuckled, conceding the point. "Okay, okay. If nothing else, you can keep us cool with your, umm, fan there."

"Thank you, Commander. I *am* a fan of yours."

"Oh, no," Vale whispered to Riker as the Choblik clambered aboard the shuttle, stumbling a bit on his newly enlarged feet. "Now that he's discovered puns, he's going to be 'experimenting' with them for weeks and driving us all out of our minds."

"Look on the bright side," Riker replied. "Down there, he won't take it badly if you tell him he's all wet."

CHAPTER TWO

DROPLET

The away team's first destination was a small cluster of floating islands at a high southern latitude, comfortably removed from the equatorial storm belt. The winds on an ocean planet built up swells that never broke against land and thus could grow to mountainous size. There was wind at these latitudes, of course, the same steady, predictable circulation patterns that could be found planetwide. But sensors showed no major swells heading toward this grouping. Swells of such size could be fairly gentle and would pose no risk to the aquashuttle; but until the nature and behavior of the disklike islets were determined, it was better not to take chances.

Melora Pazlar gazed out the forward ports with fascination as Aili Lavena brought the aquashuttle down to a flight trajectory just a few kilometers above the waves. "Astonishing," she said. "I don't think I've ever seen so much water at one time." Since the planet was so large, more than half again the radius of a typical M-class world, the horizon was unusually distant, all but lost in atmospheric haze. It was easy to imagine the water stretching to infinity. It couldn't have been more different from Gemworld, the artificial crystalline planet where her Elaysian species resided. But then, her world was different from any other world in the galaxy, so that wasn't much of a standard of comparison.

"I know," Lavena replied. "It's gorgeous! I'm going for a swim first thing once we land."

"Hold on there," Commander Vale said. "Before you do that, I'd like to get a little sense of what the ocean's like. With the interference, we should double-check our scans of its chemistry, make sure there's nothing toxic. And there's no telling what kind of sea monsters might be lurking down there."

Pazlar threw her an amused look. "Do you suppose that's what these islands are? Some kind of giant turtles or something?"

Torvig turned to Kekil. "Relatives of yours, perhaps?" The pale green Rigellian Chelon, so called because of his people's somewhat turtlelike appearance, simply ignored him.

Soon, the cluster of islets was in naked-eye range. The sight left no doubt that they were floating atop the water, rising and falling with its slow swells. The larger clusters flexed and warped somewhat as they rode atop the changing surface, but their saucerlike components remained connected. They were a pale yellowish white around the edges, with darker soil and assorted vegetation covering them farther "inland." The larger clusters had the most abundant vegetation.

"Set us down by the nearest single islet," Vale ordered. "Let's not complicate the variables."

"By it, ma'am?" Lavena asked. "Not on it?"

"Just to be on the safe side. We're not sure how buoyant those things are."

"Aye, Commander," Lavena said, looking happy to touch down in her native element.

Pazlar, aware of the Selkie pilot's skill, was expecting a smooth landing. But the *Gillespie* hit Droplet's surface with a bit of a jolt, rocking her in her seat. "A little overeager there, Ensign?" she asked.

"What? Oh, no, ma'am. I just eased back the inertial dampers a bit. We're diving into a new ocean—it seemed right to feel the splash."

"Just take us in to the nearest lone islet," Vale ordered.

When the shuttle bumped against a solid surface, Lavena programmed it to keep station with the islet and popped the hatch. Vale led the way out of the shuttle, with Pazlar following. The air was warm and almost stiflingly humid, a shock after the controlled environment of the ship and shuttle; but there was a steady cooling breeze blowing from the west, carrying the fresh, wet tang of ocean air along with other exotic scents.

They waded across a few meters of shallow water— also unexpectedly warm—before climbing out onto the gently rising shoreline. Pazlar sized up the weight she felt, or what fraction of it was filtered through her antigrav suit's field. She knew it was a few percent below standard, but she couldn't feel the difference.

Once Torvig had clambered onto the shore, he jumped up and down a couple of times. "Well, it isn't rocking," he said with his usual straight face. "Commander Keru, maybe you should try it," he said, looking up at his burly Trill friend, who outmassed him by about three to one.

Keru just rolled his eyes and bent down to examine the waterline. "No obvious edge. Looks like it extends several meters under the water before dropping off."

"It looks like an island," Vale observed. "Soil, plants, some treelike things . . . and I think I can hear insects, or something like them."

A fuller survey of the islet revealed nothing particularly striking living here beyond what her eyes and ears had revealed. There was no sign of avian life, though *Titan*'s optical sensors had sighted flying creatures in Droplet's skies. Though it seemed reasonably habitable, the islet was simply too small to support much of an ecosystem. Some of the larger clusters visible in the distance bore thicker vegetation, however, and Pazlar thought she could see birds or the local equivalent flying around their treetops.

Meanwhile, Kekil knelt and ran his tricorder over the soil, taking a handful and kneading it with his broad, webbed fingers. "Very rich. It's mostly organic decay products; minimal silicate content, as you'd expect."

"Ah," Keru said. "A connoisseur."

Everyone (save the solemn Kekil) seemed to be in a playful mood today. Perhaps it was just the enthusiasm at setting foot on an intriguing new planet, particularly a tropical paradise like this. Droplet's star was of only moderate brightness and more distant than was typical for an M-class world, but that only served to soften the light, letting Pazlar gaze out at the sun reflections dancing on the waves without being blinded by glare, as she had been looking out across San Francisco Bay in her Academy days. If anything, it made the warm, sunny scene even more inviting. But the oxygen content of the air, she reminded herself, was a little high; she was feeling a bit lightheaded from it. Something to watch out for. Fortunately, the high water vapor content of the air discouraged breathing it too deeply; Vale had tried a moment before, and was now coughing from the aspirated moisture.

"I'll have to make a more thorough analysis to be sure, of course," Kekil added as he placed some of the soil in a sample container.

"Dig down some," Vale ordered. "I want to know what the island's made of. Torvig can help you. Meanwhile, I want to check out the flora and fauna."

"I could check out the underside," Lavena called hopefully from the shuttle door.

"Not yet, Aili. Run a scan first." The Selkie sulked her way back inside. No doubt she was eager to get out of her hydration suit when there was a whole planetful of water to flow across her gill crests and keep her skin moist. Melora could sympathize; she wouldn't mind getting out of her tight antigrav suit and letting the water buoy her up. She was slender, but her bones and muscles had low density, so she figured she could float all right in the moderately saline water at these latitudes—though perhaps not nearer the equator, where the constant rainfall diluted the upper ocean with fresh water. But of course Vale was right to exercise caution.

"Commanders?" Torvig called, not having to shout too loudly, for they couldn't get more than eighty meters apart. "I think you'll want to see this!"

Pazlar followed at her best pace as Vale jogged over to him and Kekil. At the bottom of the hole they had dug was a hard, light-colored material that appeared porous and slightly sparkly. "It looks almost like seashells," Vale said.

"Not dissimilar," Torvig said. "It's largely keratin. However, there are silicate spicules interwoven inside, increasing its strength, analogously to fiberglass. And there's a fair amount of calcium carbonate as well. Odd to find heavier elements in such concentration in the native life."

Pazlar knelt and took a closer look, activating her own tricorder. Then she looked up at Vale and smiled. "It reminds me of a reef structure, like Terran coral or Pacifican *si'hali*."

The human's eyes widened beneath her fringe of midnight blue hair. "You think this whole islet was grown, like a coral atoll?"

"Exactly. Though I'm not quite certain why it's light enough to float. It would have to be very porous."

Vale pondered. "Let's get back in the shuttle. I want to take a look underneath."

"I could swim underneath," Torvig said, sounding as eager as Lavena.

"You heard what I told Aili," the exec replied. "For our first dive, I'd rather be inside a shielded duranium hull."

They returned to the *Gillespie,* and Lavena wasted no time taking it down. The gentle curve of the islet's surface continued for just a bit below the waterline, then suddenly increased. The sides ran roughly vertically for a few meters before curving inward to form a convex lower surface. The soil and surface plants, naturally, did not extend below the

waterline, so the bare surface of the islet was clear for them
to see. But this surface had one significant difference from
the one Torvig had excavated—for out of every one of the
thousands of holes which riddled its surface extended a
small set of tendrils.

"It's alive," Lavena breathed.

"Take us in closer," Vale suggested in a similarly
hushed tone.

As Lavena complied, the surface resolved itself into
a large number of individual units, each one a few centimeters across—an attribute which had been blurred up
above by erosion. There seemed to be one set of tendrils
for each of the distinct cells of limestone.

"It's a colony of polyps," Kekil observed, sounding
intrigued.

"Like a coral reef," Vale said.

"Yes, although the individual polyps are larger here."

"And reefs usually lead a more sedentary existence,"
Pazlar remarked.

"It's as busy as a reef, though," Lavena observed. At
this range, they could see numerous smaller life forms
either attached to the underside of the floater or swimming
among its tendrils. Stalks of seaweed resembling attenuated broccoli hung down for several meters. Between the
widely-spaced stalks scuttled a number of small crusta-
ceans not unlike yellowish, four-legged tarantulas, clinging to the underside and using elongated mouthparts to
dig out organic debris in fissures between the polyp cells,
interestingly leaving the actual polyps alone. Turning her
eyes in another direction, she saw a more open patch along
which crawled several six-pointed starfish with snaky

limbs and feathery tendrils. And swimming amid the broccoli seaweed were creatures that appeared very much like fish, although they bore clumps of small tentacles around their mouths and exhibited shifting color patterns on their smooth skins. She couldn't tell whether they were vertebrates or invertebrates.

"Naturally," Kekil said. "These floating colonies would be some of the few sources of shelter in this ocean, the few places where life could concentrate and have solid support."

Torvig looked up, his ears flicking forward the way they did when he had an epiphany. "That could be why the polyps have so much calcium and silicon. As numerous other organisms live and die on them, minerals and other nutrients would tend to accumulate on them in greater concentration than anywhere else."

"Good call," Pazlar said. His ears perked up happily, and she resisted the urge to give him an approving pat on the head. "I wonder how it gets its buoyancy. Not to mention how they get into this form, how they start out, their whole life cycle."

"Take a sample," Vale suggested. "A living polyp for study."

"Aye, Commander." She reached for the tractor beam controls. "But considering that they live in this collective form, maybe I'd better take five or six of them."

"Agreed."

Pazlar focused the beams and delicately worked a small cluster of the polyps free of the mass. Sensing the disturbance, the polyps in and around the cluster yanked their tendrils back inside. But she ended up dislodging a chunk a good three times larger than she expected. As soon as she pulled it free, a stream of large bubbles erupted out and upward. "Whoa," she cried, staring as the outrush of air continued unabated.

Vale gently tapped her shoulder. "Umm . . . Melora . . ." She pointed upward. Pazlar raised her eyes—and saw that the islet was starting to list to one side.

"Uh-oh."

"Ensign?"

But Lavena was already spinning the craft around. Pazlar barely managed to retain her tractor grip on the sample as the aquashuttle shot away from beneath the sinking islet. Once they had resurfaced, Lavena turned the shuttle so they could watch. Soon the bubbles stopped rising and the islet began to stabilize—but about half its previous surface was now below the waves. Much of its soil was already washing away, staining the surrounding water.

Pazlar gave Vale a sheepish look. "Sorry. I didn't mean to do that."

"Don't feel bad. It was almost a galactic first."

"How do you mean?"

"A wrecked island setting down on a ship."

"*Now* can I go in?" Aili Lavena asked, trying with little success not to sound like an impatient child. Her scans had shown the water chemistry to be safe, and at Pazlar's suggestion, Vale had allowed her to pilot the aquashuttle to a fairly empty region of the ocean, one which the interplay of currents had left essentially devoid of dissolved iron, without which there was little phytoplankton and thus hardly any of the higher life forms that would be sustained by it—or by each other. It was as safe a spot for a first swim as any.

Vale threw her a look, amused at her tone. "You remembered to wait an hour after eating, right?"

"That's a myth, ma'am. Especially for a Selkie."

Finally, Vale grinned, letting her off the hook—so to speak. "Okay, Aili. But don't swim too far from the shuttle."

"Thank you, ma'am!" Aili was already out the door, standing on the short platform that extended from its base (which Keru had dubbed "the plank," for some reason). She was eager to get out of her hydration suit, but had to wait until it had drawn its water supply back inside its storage capillaries, for she would need that water once she donned the suit again. Once that was done, she hastened to shed it. She could survive in the open air for a few minutes at a time, as long as enough moisture remained in her gill crests. She couldn't take in a breath of it the way she could have back in her amphibious days, since her lung had now closed off and become a flotation bladder, but she opened her mouth to taste the breeze. Its flavor was strange and alien in many ways, yet there was the familiar salty tang, the fresh, wet flavor of ocean air. *Oh, how I've missed that.*

Once out of the suit, she transferred her combadge to the front of the brief, backless undergarment she wore before tossing the suit into the shuttle. Her preference right now would be to strip fully nude, but Starfleet had its standards of decorum. This would have to do for now.

A sense of ceremony made her pause briefly, but eagerness overcame her. She dove into the water as though it pulled her into itself. For several moments, Aili remained completely immersed, her nictitating membranes shut, reveling in the too-long-missed sensation of diving in the open ocean. The confines of the glorified fishtank she called her quarters were nothing compared to this. Here, currents wafted across her smooth blue-green flesh like cooling breezes, carrying exotic, information-filled flavors to her tongue and scents to the receptors in her gill crests. Distant sounds shivered through the water, resonating through her body—the low ostinato of wind playing percussion on the waves, the chirp and chatter of distant schools of fish, a hint of distant moans and creaks that could be larger life forms. Land-dwellers had the bizarre notion that the sea was silent; in reality, being out of the ocean was like being deaf for her. Out there, sound was a thing of the ears, a tenuous disturbance in the air; down here, it was a tangible thing that permeated one's whole being. She was made mostly of seawater, closely matching its density and chemistry, and sound waves passed through her as though she were part of the sea, her flesh resounding in tune with the rest of this great instrument.

She opened her eyes now for the complete experience, for up here near the surface, the sea was alive with light as well. She bathed in the rain of gentle yellow-orange sunlight as it danced across her limbs, adding its own intricate marbling to the mottled blues and greens of her flesh. She observed the shifting patterns of the light as it illuminated the water, her practiced eye discerning information about the wind, currents, and purity of the sea around her. As expected, this stretch of ocean was largely barren of algae or plankton, giving her a clear view for hundreds of meters around and below her.

But what was this? Near the limits of visibility, she saw a glint of movement. She tapped her combadge and spoke softly, needing no breath, for muscles vibrated her larynx. "Lavena to *Gillespie*. I think I see something swimming nearby. At your five o'clock low," she added, checking the position of the aquashuttle above her. "I'll try to get closer."

"Acknowledged. But be careful."

"Don't worry, it looks small."

She began swimming slowly at an oblique angle toward it. As she drew closer, she began to discern its appearance. It was another of the tentacled fishlike creatures, but its head seemed to consist mostly of an enormous pair of forward-facing eyes, its tiny mouth tentacles barely visible below them. Eyes that seemed to be watching her. Soon she had no doubt: the grandocular piscoid was gazing directly at her as she approached, yet not fleeing. Was it simply unsure what to make of a form as alien as hers?

Taking a chance, she kept coming closer, but slowly, doing her best to appear unaggressive. She halted her approach a few meters away from it, letting it get a good look at her. It swam around her, scooting sideways as it kept its gaze locked upon her, surveying her from all sides.

Belatedly, Aili remembered her wrist-mounted tricorder, and deciding that turnabout was fair play, she switched it on. But no sooner did she begin the scan than the piscoid abruptly darted away, heading for deeper waters. Determined to get the scan data she should have collected already, she impulsively swam in pursuit.

Her combadge soon crackled. *"Ensign, you're ge . . . ng too f . . . ay. Los . . . gnal . . ."*

"I'll be fine," she called back. Vale could be such a worrywart sometimes. She was enjoying the chase, enjoying the freedom of this vast ocean, and there was certainly nothing dangerous about the little bugeye fish she was pursuing, nor was there likely to be much of anything else inhabiting this barren stretch of ocean. The bugeye must have wandered off from its school and lost its way. It was probably half-starved.

Though it did seem to have plenty of energy for swimming, she realized after a while. They were getting deeper now, not too deep for her body to adjust quickly, but enough for the light to begin to fade, along with the susurrus of the wind upon the ocean's roof. She began to notice a high-pitched piping coming from the bugeye piscoid, almost beyond her auditory range, and probably beyond that of most humanoids. *A distress call?* she wondered. She was no expert, but that suggested some sort of social structure. But what could it be calling to?

But there were other sounds down here, Aili realized—not echoing from afar, but nearby, in the direction the piscoid was swimming. Whistles and creaks and low, guttural groans, coming from multiple sources. She slowed her descent and checked her tricorder. Its sensors had limited ability to penetrate the water, but it was able to register a number of large shapes, maybe four meters long. What were they doing here? There was nothing to eat, save the lone bugeye.

And a lone Selkie.

She decided to change strategy, halting her pursuit and instead trying to boost her tricorder gain. The picture on its tiny screen couldn't give her nearly as much information down here as her full suite of senses could, but a later analysis of the data could be informative. From what she could tell, the creatures had fairly streamlined, torpedo-shaped bodies, but with several tentacles extending from the front, or what seemed to be the front. Their calls were growing closer now, and seemed to intensify in response to the bugeye's keening—perhaps a hue and cry after prey, but it almost seemed like . . .

A new reading caught her eye. In her preoccupation with the large creatures ahead, she had been slow to notice the faint life reading registering behind her. That was puzzling, but such a weak reading was probably distant enough not to require her immediate attention, at least until she'd gotten a full scan of the creatures ahead.

Or so she thought until a tendril of fire tore across her thigh and she began to pass out. . . .

"Aili? Wake up."

She found herself deaf again, back in the confines of a tiny sheath of water with only the dead dryness of air around it. Weight pressed her against a hard surface. She was back in her hydration suit, back in the aquashuttle. Her vision focused on the burly figure above her—Ranul Keru, who was packing up a medkit. As chief of security, he was a trained medic.

"What happened?"

"Something stung you," Vale told her. "When you suddenly swam off, we submerged and came after you. We saw you get attacked by some kind of jellyfish."

"Jellyfish?"

"More or less," Kekil said. "A large spherical scyphome-dusan form with tendrils extending in all directions." Now that the details of her last moments of consciousness were coming back, Aili realized that the weak life signs behind her had been due to the tenuousness of the creature, not its distance. The tricorders would have to be recalibrated.

"Venomous?" Aili asked.

"Not to worry," Ranul Keru said. "Thanks to differences in biochemistry, the venom wasn't as harmful to you as it probably is to the native life forms. And it only stung you a few times."

"You stopped it?"

"We didn't have to," he replied, looking a bit nonplussed.

At her puzzled look, Vale elaborated. "We were trying to get to you, readying the tractor beams to pull it away, when a large, very fast fish of some sort dashed in straight as an arrow and gobbled the jellyfish thing right up."

"And didn't get stung?"

"There are aquatic species that are immune to jellyfish stings," Kekil said. "Even some which take the stinging barbs and integrate them into their own anatomy as a defense. Obviously this fish was a natural predator of the medusans. It's just lucky for us it came in at just that moment."

Aili noticed Vale's uncertain expression. "Commander?"

"Call me a cynic, but I'm not one to believe in luck. It's an anomaly, like the presence of so many life forms around here where there's nothing to feed on, nothing to draw them."

"Except us," Lavena said. "The fish with the large eyes certainly seemed curious."

"Maybe," Vale replied. "Anyway, Ensign, you should rest. Not enough you had to be the first person to go swimming in Droplet's oceans, you had to be the first one to get attacked by a native critter too. Try to stop hogging all the excitement in the future, okay?"

CHAPTER THREE

"So how's the fishing?" Chief Bralik asked as she settled down at the Blue Table with a drink and a bowl of tube grubs. Naturally the science department's weekly informal gathering was filled with chatter about the discoveries on Droplet over the past few days, but Bralik had been kept busy surveying the rest of the system. The Blue Table gatherings were a great chance to take a break from one's own, often insular work and connect with other points of view on the universe. Bralik was thus a regular member of the sessions, always keeping her ears open for new knowledge that could profit her and her fellow Ferengi.

"They aren't fish," Lieutenant Eviku told her. "There are no true vertebrates on this world."

"Really?" Bralik leaned forward curiously. The Arkenite exobiologist's bald, tapering skull and large, backswept pinnae appealed to her sense of aesthetics, so she enjoyed flirting with him, though he remained completely unaware of it. She wasn't sure whether it was because Arkenite and Ferengi sexual cues were mutually unintelligible or if it was simply that Eviku was charmingly naive. But she chose not to press the issue. Like many in the crew, he had borne a deep sadness since the Borg invasion. He spoke of it to no one, but no doubt he had lost loved ones and would need time to heal.

Now, though, he had science to talk about, so that kept him engaged. "There isn't enough calcium in the eco-system to allow for full bony skeletons," Eviku explained to her in his slow, thoughtful voice. "The highest life forms, including the piscoids, are chordates with cartilaginous pseudovertebrae. The majority of forms are invertebrates of various types, though. Even many of the chordates have tentacles or chitinous exoskeletons of the sort generally seen in invertebrate species."

"What about the floating islets?" Bralik asked. "They're made partly of calcium carbonate, aren't they?"

"Yes. We've also detected small concentrations of calcium in some other creatures, usually in cutting or grinding mouthparts."

"Teeth?"

"Hard to call them that exactly, since they're not set in jaws and not made of dentin. More like chitinous beaks or plates strengthened with calcium."

"But the floaters have the highest calcium levels we've found in any organism here," Melora Pazlar put in. Eviku turned to face her politely, his gaze not lingering on Bralik. She took it in stride and simply appreciated the elegant taper of his cranial lobes. "We're pretty sure it's for the reason Torvig proposed, that they collect and concentrate decayed matter from the other life that lives on them."

Ensign Vennoss, a Kriosian female from stellar cartography, asked, "What have you learned from the sample you collected?" Bralik grinned, recalling the amusing account of how the sample had been obtained. In all her years as a geologist, she'd never sunk an island.

"Well, first off," Pazlar said, "after collecting the sample, we took a look at the insides of the, uh, wounded islet. It was made up of polyp shells all the way through, but the interior ones were empty except for air. It seems the living creatures' bodies form an airtight seal that's lacking in the dead shells further inward."

"Except there are some airtight walls," Eviku added, "dividing the interior into about a dozen air chambers. We believe that evolved so the islets don't sink fully when there's a breach in the outer layer of live polyps."

"So how did the air get there in the first place?" asked Zurin Dakal. The young Cardassian ensign had been a regular at the Blue Table from the start, even though he had spent most of his tour aboard *Titan* in operations. He had been included as the protégé of Jaza Najem, *Titan's* now-departed science officer. Jaza had been lost to a time warp over a year ago, and Dakal had subsequently decided to honor Jaza's wish that he switch his specialty to the sciences. After months of study aboard *Titan* and a post-invasion leave spent taking crash courses at Starfleet Academy, Dakal was now a sensor analyst.

"Same way it gets into Lavena's swim bladder," Eviku told him. "It's extracted from the water by the gills. It then gets pumped into the shells of the dead inner creatures and keeps the whole thing afloat."

"But there are still gaps in what we know," Pazlar said. "For instance, we observed some smaller floater colonies living beneath the surface, more active and motile than the large ones. So why do the large ones rise to the surface, when it kills off all the polyps that end up out of the water?"

"What we're trying to do in the lab is to recreate the conditions of their spawning season in hopes of accelerating our sample's growth," Eviku said. "It's a challenge figuring out what those conditions are." Bralik enjoyed the smile he gave, even though it was directed at the exciting mystery rather than the exciting Ferengi female seated across from him.

"Sounds like you're in the same boat I am," Bralik said, undaunted. "So to speak. This whole system is a mystery."

"How so?" Chamish asked.

She kept her gaze on Eviku as she replied, though. "All this clutter of asteroids. Normally in a system of this age, most of it would've been cleared out by now, condensed into planets or flung away by their gravity."

"That's if there were large Jovians in the system," Pazlar replied. "New Kaferia only has a couple of Neptune-sized ice giants."

"Which is part of the mystery. This system is loaded with heavy elements, including all those stable or semi-stable transuranics—yurium, celebium, rodinium, timonium. Most systems with that much heavy stuff produce big, heavy planets, superterrestrials and superjovians. The planets in this system just don't fit its mineralogical profile."

"Could the abundance of water in the system be a factor?" Dakal asked.

Bralik shook her head. "Water's common in any system. Beyond the snow line, out where the star's heat doesn't dissipate it, ice is one of the most abundant minerals you'll find."

"She's right," Pazlar told him. "Droplet must have formed in the outer system as another ice giant, then migrated inward, losing its hydrogen and helium. It's not uncommon. But," she went on, nodding in Bralik's direction, "that kind of migration should have cleared out some of the asteroidal debris."

"Any evidence of past artificial intervention?" Dakal suggested. "Could there have been a planet that was blown apart?"

Bralik shook her head. "The geology of the asteroids we've been able to scan isn't consistent with that. If they'd been part of a planet, they would've differentiated—they'd show the signatures of the different planetary strata they'd been part of, like some being pure metal and others pure rock. At most, some of these asteroids were parts of bigger asteroids."

"You look disappointed, Ensign," Pazlar said to the Cardassian youth.

"No, it's just . . . it would have been interesting to find signs of intelligence."

"We can't find intelligent life everywhere we look. And we've got enough interesting puzzles to solve here even without intelligence being involved."

"Besides," Chamish said, "we haven't ruled out intelligent life on Droplet. Our shuttles' audio sensors have recorded some intriguingly complex calls, though nothing the translators have been able to interpret yet. Ensign Lavena suspects they come from the large tentacled animals she detected on her initial dive."

"Perhaps," Dakal acknowledged. "But at best, they would still be smart animals. Technology is impossible on a world like this."

Eviku threw him a surprisingly cold look. "Are animals only of worth if they build tools?"

"I didn't mean that."

"Then what did you mean?"

"Simply that a technological species would be a more interesting find."

"You mean you have no interest in life too dissimilar to your own. I had thought that by now this crew had moved beyond such divisions."

"I resent your implication. Sir."

"Hold it, both of you," Pazlar said. "There's no sense in fighting over something that's still strictly hypothetical. At worst, you have a philosophical difference. Just let it go."

Dakal and Eviku both mumbled chastened acknowledgments, but neither offered an apology. Bralik felt Pazlar had been a little harsh to Eviku, but she said nothing more about it, in the spirit of the Thirty-third Rule of Acquisition. "So," she said, hoping to get things back on track. "Anyone up for a new round of drinks?"

Deanna Troi sat on a coral beach, watching the undulations of an endless ocean and contemplating the strange sensation of the ground beneath her rocking gently like the deck of a large ship. Will Riker's arms went around her from behind, hands resting atop her ever more ample belly. "Aren't you glad we came down here after all?" he asked.

She turned to smirk at him. "What, down to the holodeck?"

He gave her a rueful look. "I was just trying to get into the spirit of the illusion." He turned to the others with them on the beach. (Could it be a beach, she wondered, without sand? The surface below her was somewhere between coral and chitin, but ground down by the action of the waves.) "Not that it needs my help," Will went on. "It's remarkably convincing. This is a real-time feed?"

Doctor Ra-Havreii nodded. "From the surface station's sensor feed." The away teams had established a base camp on one of the planet's larger floating islands, a cluster of over two dozen disk-shaped floater colonies fused together, part of an archipelago (or school?) containing multiple such large clusters—suggesting that its latitudes had been fairly calm for some time, devoid of any massive swells or storms that might break up such a large cluster and endanger an away team and its supplies. "I've adapted the same software I used to allow Melora—Commander Pazlar—to interact by holopresence with the crew." He nodded at Pazlar, who stood next to him. Their hands brushed together discreetly, but Deanna sensed the mutual warmth that passed between them. "So it's highly detailed and current. The only difference is that you have no holo-avatars on the surface, so any change you make in the environment will be simulated only. But I've been working on a prototype for a compact mobile emitter robust enough for away missions —"

"Thank you, Doctor. We can discuss that another time." Underneath Will's reluctance to sit through another of the Efrosian chief engineer's ivory-tower technical lectures,

Deanna sensed, was a distaste at the idea of replacing live explorers with simulations, even ones operated by telepresence. It would be safer, certainly, but it grated against Will's explorer spirit.

That thought led him to gaze out at the ocean, and she felt his wish to be down there for real, without technological intercession. "So what do you think the odds are we can see some squales from here?" he asked.

"Given how imager-shy they are, sir," Pazlar replied, "I wouldn't bet on it."

The squales had become as much a running joke over the past few days as a source of genuine, growing curiosity. Multiple explorer teams had reported sensor readings of moderately large chordates in groups of six to twelve, built something like large dolphins or small whales but with several large tentacles toward the front and a cephalopod's ability to flash vivid colors on their skin. They seemed to be a match for the creatures Aili Lavena had glimpsed on her first dive. These "squid-whales," a nickname soon shortened to "squales," repeatedly showed up at a moderate distance from the away teams, hovering in the vicinity, but at every attempt to approach and investigate them more closely, they donned camouflage colors—suggesting their skins contained color-changing chromatophores like Terran cephalopods—and retreated in haste. Optical scans from *Titan* showed pods of them traveling on the ocean surface, suggesting they were air breathers, yet when approached they dove deep and seemed able to remain submerged for hours. The biologists believed they had a dual respiratory system like the Argoan sur-snake. Bugeye piscoids had repeatedly been detected at the same times as squale contacts, suggesting they were associated somehow, like pilot fish and sharks.

"But you do think they're the source of the complex calls we've been hearing?" Riker went on.

"There does seem to be a correlation with their proximity."

Will nodded. "Very well. Keep me posted. Dismissed."

Ra-Havreii and Pazlar exited together, holding hands, and Deanna felt their amused approval at how their captain and diplomatic officer presumably intended to make use of the simulation. Lovemaking while extremely pregnant was difficult but not impossible, and being in the water—or a force field facsimile thereof—increased one's options.

But for now, Will was still busy taking in the sensory experience of Droplet, and she was content to share in his feelings. Yet there was a bittersweet tinge she couldn't ignore. "You wish you could be down there for real, don't you?"

He cradled her against him, a hand atop where their daughter rested in her womb. "I am exactly where I want to be, *imzadi*. Now and forever."

She showed her appreciation for his sweet talk, but then said, "It's all right, Will. You don't have to reassure me of your commitment. But that doesn't mean you can't have regrets. I miss beaming down to new worlds as much as you do. I understand perfectly."

He threw her an uncertain look—more puzzled than skeptical. "Do you really? To be honest, I'm not sure when the last time was you went on an away mission. It's been months."

"I suppose it has. This pregnancy's gone by so fast I guess I lost track."

"But you didn't have to give it up so soon. That contact with the Chir'vaji a couple months back . . . there was no medical reason you couldn't have gone yourself."

"I figured Christine could use the diplomatic practice."

"But the way they revere parenting, I was surprised you didn't take advantage of that."

"It wasn't necessary. They were agreeable enough without it." He just looked at her, *felt* at her, until she relented. "Fine. Okay. I've been erring on the side of caution. Can you blame me, Will? I don't want anything to happen to her." Deanna's hand moved protectively over their child.

"I understand that," he said, his voice breathy. "You know I do. But the Caeliar healed her. They healed you. You're both as strong as an ox. As . . . oxen. Anyway . . ." They shared a chuckle, defusing the moment. "I just worry that you're living too much on the defensive. You can miss out on so much that way."

She considered his words. "I know that's true. But sometimes, up to a point, a little extra caution isn't a bad thing. Will, we've all been through hell. Not just you and me—the Borg took so much from everyone. It's instilled all of us with a keen awareness of . . . of loss. And if we need a little time to deal with that, to retreat into our comfort zones for a little while, that's simply part of the healing process. It's not healthy to stay there too long, but it shouldn't be rushed through either."

"And you're picking that up from the whole crew," he said with deep sympathy. "Carrying that for all of us."

She clasped his hand. "I'm trained to cope with other people's negative emotions. Not to let them get confused with my own. But it can be . . . saddening." She reflected on some of her most troubled patients over the past few months. Lieutenant Kekil had lost most of his family when the Rigel Colonies had been attacked, but his natural pride and stoicism made it difficult for him to face his grief. Pava sh'Aqabaa from security had a triple burden to deal with: not only the loss of kinfolk in the bombardment of Andor, but post-traumatic stress and survivor's guilt after coming back critically injured from the joint raid on the Borg reconnaisance probe—a raid that the other five members of her team had not returned from at all. And then there was Tuvok, who still struggled with depression over the loss of his son. That tragedy had undone all their work together to build new methods of emotional management to replace the Vulcan control that his years of cumulative cerebral injury and strain had left in tatters. They had needed to begin again from the ground up, and it was slow going. Even without Vulcan discipline, Tuvok's natural stubbornness was fully intact.

"So I think I'm entitled," she went on, "to want to stay within my own comfort zone for now. I'm enjoying the sense of being . . . cocooned with our baby. Being together with her, and with you, in a place of safety, surrounded by friends. Where I am right now, that's enough for me. Visiting new worlds on the holodeck is all the adventure I need." She gave him a lopsided grin. "After all, we're both in for plenty of adventures after What's-Her-Name here comes out in a few weeks."

He studied her for a moment, and she felt his concern giving way to mischief. "So, you're saying you're not interested in excitement of any kind?"

Her grin reflected the mischief she felt in him, and his own soon matched it. "Well, now, I didn't exactly say that. It *is* getting awfully humid here." She began to pull off her maternity dress. "I, for one, could use a swim."

"You seem bittersweet," Ra-Havreii said, stroking Melora's cheek as they strolled down the corridor from the holodeck toward her quarters. They always made love in her quarters rather than his, since he could adjust to her gravity far more easily than the reverse. "Aren't you happy we were able to assist our commanding couple with their love life?"

"Hey, Xin, that's none of our business. Certainly not for public dissemination," she hissed, glancing around at the passersby.

He chuckled. "An ironic choice of words, etymologically speaking. But I was asking about *your* business, my dear. Which I believe I am entitled to consider mine, wouldn't you say?"

The corridor was empty now, so she sighed and answered. "It's just . . . seeing the captain and Counselor Troi so happy together . . . it just reminded me that I can't have kids as long as I remain in Starfleet. An Elaysian fetus couldn't survive the gravity. And I couldn't wear this antigrav suit for eight months straight."

She realized that Xin had stopped walking two sentences back. She paused and waited for him to catch up, though he wasn't as close as before. "Ahh, why would you be thinking about . . . conception, Melora? I thought that what we had was mutually understood to be . . . well, more than recreational, of course, but not . . . I mean, you know that Efrosian males don't participate in the rearing of our biological . . ."

She let him squirm on the hook of her gaze for a few more moments, then relented and laughed. "Don't worry, Xin. I'm not overwhelmed with an urge to return home to spawn. I'm just . . . contemplating future possibilities."

He didn't seem reassured. "Including the possibility that your long-term future might not include me?"

"Why should that bother you? If you Efrosian males never involve yourselves in family, I mean?" There was still amusement in her tone, but there were barbs beneath it.

"My dear, I thought we were both in agreement about the loose nature of our association. I thought you were satisfied with that."

"I didn't say I wasn't. Don't overreact to this. Like I said, I'm just considering future possibilities." She stared at him. "And if you're so determined to keep our 'association' so loose, why are you acting so threatened by the idea that it might not be permanent?"

Efrosians were a highly verbal people, their mastery of speech and language exceptional among humanoids. But right now, Xin Ra-Havreii was at a complete loss for words.

Chapter Four

DROPLET

"Ohh, this is nice." Commander Pazlar had finally followed Lavena's lead, stripping out of her antigrav suit and allowing the buoyancy of Droplet's ocean to shore her up against its gravity. She'd needed Aili's support to reach the water once she deactivated and removed the suit, and Aili knew how reluctant she was to let anyone see her as weak. The pilot was touched that her superior had trusted her enough to let her help. Perhaps it was because they were kindred spirits of a sort, both dependent on all-encasing technological aids to survive aboard *Titan*, always set slightly apart from the rest.

Now the two women, Selkie and Elaysian, floated together in their undergarments a few meters offshore from the floater island that housed their base camp. Pazlar had ordered the rest of the team to stay in the camp or on the far side of the island for the duration of her swim, although

Commander Keru had insisted on standing by within shouting distance in case some large sea creature found them appetizing. Pazlar had acceded, perhaps in part because Keru would *not* find two scantily clad women appetizing.

For a while, they just floated there, gazing up at Droplet's night sky. The persistent cloud bands that obscured much of the view during the day tended to dissipate somewhat at night, so they could see a wide swath of stars as well as two of the planet's four captured asteroidal moons, while colorful auroras wafted and flickered to the south. Aili had always loved staring up at the stars in her youth. But unlike then, she now had the comfort of knowing she would be back out among them in a week or two. Still, she had greatly missed the sensation of being in the sea, and this sea was far more comfortable than her own, for there was no family, no peer group to look on her with disapproval for failing to live up to her culture's expectations.

"So what progress are you making with the squales?" Pazlar finally asked. Her tone made it sound more like casual conversation than a command to deliver a report.

Aili responded in the same spirit. "Well, they've been getting closer, and letting me get a little closer to them. I think they're acclimating a bit. But they still retreat every time I switch on my tricorder."

"Incredible hearing."

"Not for a sea creature."

"I'll take your word for it."

"Without my tricorder active, they've let me get close enough to see them relatively clearly. They have four large tentacles at the front, but they can fold them back along the body and flatten them out for speed. The mouth is beaked, and has two large eyes behind and above it. They have some vents that I've seen them expelling bubbles from; I think they can function like a cetacean blowhole but also as a kind of jet thruster for maneuvering."

"But not for propulsion?"

"No, they're too massive for that. They have strong tails with four flukes. They can oscillate them in either direction, using one set of flukes or the other for thrust. I think it lets them switch from one set of muscles to the other, giving them more endurance."

"I don't suppose they've let you observe much of their behavior."

"Not visually, but I can hear them talking to each other."

"Talking? Don't jump to conclusions, Aili."

The use of her given name instead of her rank softened the chastisement. Still, she knew better than to respond in kind. "That's the feeling I get, Commander. They're constantly exchanging elaborate vocal signals through the . . . the deep sound channel, like my people do back home, or like the humpback whales on Earth." She'd almost called the deep sound channel by its Selkie name, the *ri'Hoyalina*, before remembering to use its Standard name. The channel was a region of the ocean, about eight hundred meters deep here, where temperature, pressure, and salinity conspired to produce the lowest speed of sound. Since any wave passing between two media was refracted toward the one where its speed was lower, the DSC tended to confine sound waves inside it as solitons, much as light was trapped within the opti-cable inside *Titan*'s consoles and computers. Since the waves propagated in only two dimensions instead of three, it took their energy longer to disperse, so sounds emitted in the DSC could travel thousands of kilometers if loud enough. "We've recorded hundreds of distinct sounds being used."

"Sounds the translator hasn't been able to find any definite meaning in."

"That could just be because they're so alien. The translator couldn't handle star-jelly communication either. And we know *they're* highly intelligent."

Pazlar nodded at the reminder of their encounter last year with the vast, jellyfish-like spacegoing organisms. "True, but we can't jump to conclusions. For one thing, if the squales were intelligent, wouldn't they be more curious about us? Their avoidance suggests an instinctive fear reaction, one that isn't being overcome by intellect."

"Maybe." Aili sighed. "And they won't let Chamish get close enough to get an empathic reading."

"That wouldn't really prove anything, though. If he couldn't commune with them, it could be because they're intelligent." For some reason, Kazarite psi abilities only worked with subsapient animals; higher cognition interfered with them in some way Aili couldn't understand. "Or it could be because of some other factor, like the way Betazoids can't read Ferengi brains."

"Too bad our most powerful empath is too pregnant to come down and get a read on them."

Pazlar's silence gave agreement. They stared at the stars a bit longer. "And if you're right," the Elaysian went on in time, "if the squales are sapient, then we've got a Prime Directive problem. We'd have to avoid further contact. In fact, I have to wonder if we should be erring on the side of caution—looking for ways to study them that don't let them see or hear us."

"Oh, that would be a shame. They're so beautiful. The way their song resonates through me . . . I'd hate to have to observe them only from a distance, through a probe or something. Besides, with the sensor troubles we have down here, how could we study them remotely?"

"Well, Xin's been talking about his mobile holo-emitters. Maybe we could disguise some probes as holographic sea creatures."

"And control them how?"

"Let them function autonomously and then return to base."

"That's so limited."

"It might be all we can get."

Aili let her head sink beneath the water for a moment, letting the immersion refresh her, then lifted it again so she could hear Pazlar's speech clearly. "Doesn't it frustrate you sometimes? Coming out here to meet new life forms, but having all these rules limiting how much contact we can make?"

"And how much damage would we do without those rules? Or how much damage might be done to us? Making contacts . . . connecting with other beings . . . you can't be careless about it. Can't let yourself get too close too fast . . . not until you're sure it won't hurt . . . somebody."

Aili frowned. "Are you still talking about the Prime Directive? Or are you trying to give me some kind of relationship advice?"

"What?" Pazlar let out a brief, breathy laugh. "No,

I'm sorry. Believe me, I'm the last person who'd have any meaningful insights about relationships."

That drew a sympathetic look. "Did you and Xin have a fight? Ma'am?"

"I'm not even sure of that, really. And I don't think I want to talk about it. Not unless you managed to glean the secret to understanding Xin Ra-Havreii during your past liaisons with him."

"Umm, sorry. The main things I learned about him were physical and . . . logistical. He's very creative, but I assume you know that." Aili smiled. It actually wasn't as hard for her to make love with an air-breathing partner as most people assumed; her quarters did have about sixty centimeters of air at the top, and she could function with her head—or other body parts—out of the water for a fair amount of time so long as most of her gills remained wet. Some of the maneuvering to keep her partner's head above water could be strenuous, but the principle was straightforward. But she enjoyed playing up the sense of mystery involved, in order to make herself seem more impressive and intriguing to the rest of the crew—and to pique the curiosity of those who might like to try it for themselves. "That, and we talked a lot about language and music. We enjoyed connecting in body and mind, but the heart never came into it."

Pazlar frowned. "I'm not sure if that makes me feel better or worse."

"Because you're worried he can't love you?"

"No . . . because I'm worried he can. I'm not sure how I feel about being that . . . unique to him."

Aili thought it over. "I don't know if it's my place to offer advice . . ."

"Go ahead. What the hell."

"You're better off letting him go. Letting him get back to being the man he is. He's a theorist—he indulges his curiosity, but he doesn't want to move out of his ivory tower. Maybe the right woman could make him into something more . . . but if you're not sure you're happy with the idea of him loving you, then it's probably more trouble than it's worth. There's got to be someone better out there, if commitment is what you want. And if you're just interested in having fun, well, sometimes it's best to move on before things get stale and complicated."

"Uh-*huh*," Pazlar said at length. "Thanks for the input. I'll give it the thought it deserves."

Aili looked at her, but the Elaysian's face gave nothing back. "Well, you asked."

"I did." After a moment, she smiled. "It's okay. I appreciate the effort. It's not your fault that I don't have any answers yet."

"Thank you."

"Sure."

They floated together in silence, gazing out at the stars. But soon Aili noticed something impinging on that silence, just barely at the edge of her awareness. "Wha . . . ?" She ducked down beneath the roof of the sea, flipping upside-down, and listened for a moment. Soon she felt a tap on her ankle and looked up to see Pazlar looking down at her quizzically. She started to speak, but remembered the sound wouldn't pass through the water-air interface well, so she surfaced. "I thought I heard something. Just a moment, please." Pazlar nodded, and she dove back down, listening intently. Sure enough, there in the distance was a shrill sound—no, several overlapping sounds, piercing, rising in pitch, growing in loudness. She breached the surface once more and described what she'd heard. "It's the squales, I think! It sounds like it might be a distress call. And they're heading this way, a whole pod."

Pazlar hit her combadge. "Pazlar to *Gillespie*. Lavena says she hears a pod of squales approaching. Anything on sensors?"

"We have a sonar reading," came Torvig's voice. *"Too much interference for other sensors to clarify, but there are multiple four-meter bodies heading in your direction, emitting sounds consistent with squale calls. ETA two minutes at this speed."*

"Are they attacking?" Keru called from the shoreline. Aili could see him coming forward, drawing his phaser as his eyes scanned the area around them.

"Why would they give a distress call, then?" Lavena responded.

"We don't know that's what it is," said Pazlar.

"Maybe it's a warning." Lavena ducked down and surveyed the area. Her wide eyes were more sensitive in this darkness than anyone else's would be—except probably Torvig's—but she saw no sign of predators. The only thing in their immediate vicinity other than the floater island was a chunk of dead floater polyps, about eight meters across, that drifted nearby a few meters down. Young floater colonies had been observed at various depths—apparently they only surfaced once they reached a certain size—but she could tell this one was dead because it was irregular in shape and didn't spin like the live juveniles did.

Just to make sure, she swam around it to see if there was something hiding behind it. Nothing was there, so she returned to the surface, hovering just above it as she called to Pazlar, "No sign of anything."

"Still, we should get out of the water just to be —"

Too late. Something wrapped around Aili's leg, stinging her. She cried out and tried to pull off the stringlike tendril. But more of them wrapped tightly around her, stinging her, pulling her, and she was yanked beneath the waves as Melora cried her name. She twisted around to see what awaited her.

Hundreds of writhing tendrils had shot up from the holes in the clump of dead floater coral. Dozens of them now gripped her, burning her exposed flesh, although her minimal clothing provided some protection. She struggled to free herself, straining toward Melora—only to feel her heart tighten in horror as she saw that the fragile Elaysian was being pulled down by the tendrils even faster than she was, having no strength to resist.

A phaser beam cut through the water, blinding Aili, and she felt a tremor transmitted through the tendrils. When her vision cleared, she saw Keru pulling a limp Melora to the surface, alongside a trail of large bubbles rising from the coral clump. It was sinking, and pulling her down with it. The stings of hundreds of tendrils were making her numb, unable to fight. She could only strain to stay conscious as the darkness grew more profound. She felt the pressure beginning to rise, and realized that there would be no end to it, not for another ninety kilometers. Even if she survived the stings, she was being dragged down to depths where there would be no life, no dissolved oxygen for her gills to extract. At least she would be gone before the pressure crushed her into pulp . . .

But then there was light. And movement. Something darting across her fuzzy vision, multiple somethings. She felt the tendrils snapping, giving way. Something caught hold of her, pulling her free, supporting her. She forced her eyes to focus. Before her was a pair of large, disk-shaped eyes, reflecting the glow from the bioluminescent piscoids around them. A sharp, elongated beak, four strong tentacles, a streamlined chordate body with four tail flukes.

It was a squale. And another one held her in its grasp.

Her rush of adrenaline countered the numbness from the tendrils' stings. Forcing herself to focus, she sensed herself rising, the pressure diminishing. The oxygen-rich water rushing across her gill crests helped revive her. Regaining her presence of mind, she struck her combadge to activate its translator function. "Can you . . . understand . . . ?"

But the squales convulsed as if badly startled. The one holding her released her and retreated, swimming backward; luckily her own buoyancy supported her now that she was free of the tendrils. "Wait!" she called weakly. They stopped and watched her warily from a few meters away, but there was no indication that it was in response to her plea.

"Keru to Lavena! Come in!"

"Here . . ." She tried to say more, but the venom was taking hold, making her laryngeal muscles sluggish, along with her thoughts.

"Hold on, we're almost there!"

She heard the aquashuttle in the distance, saw the squales retreating at top speed. "No, wait . . ."

Aili tried to reach for them, but she had no more energy. She thought she saw the light from the shuttle, but just then darkness overtook her. . . .

She awakened to see Captain Riker looking down at her. "Welcome back, Aili."

Her wide eyes took in the surroundings without her needing to turn her head; her peripheral vision was greater than most humanoids'. She was in sickbay, but not in her hydration suit; she floated in a bathtub-sized tank that had taken the place of a normal sickbay bed. This was one of the upgrades Doctor Ree had insisted on before *Titan*'s relaunch: using replicator and transporter technology, several of the surgical and recovery beds in sickbay could now be dematerialized and reconstructed in specialized forms to accommodate crew members with unusual physiological needs. It was something she wished she'd had last year, after she'd been injured in an attack by rogue Fethetrit.

"Captain," she said. "Glad to be back."

"You gave us quite a scare."

She laughed weakly. "I gave *you* a scare?" She stretched her limbs, which seemed to have been healed of the burning welts left by the tendrils. "What the Deep was that thing?"

"A colony creature," came another voice. Lieutenant Eviku came up on her other side, and she smiled at the sight of him. The Arkenite xenobiologist came from semi-aquatic stock himself, so the two of them had bonded, both as friends and occasionally on a more physical level. There had been none of the latter since the Borg invasion, however; he had become closed off, outwardly sociable but not letting anyone get closer, except presumably his counselor.

"We got a sample of the portion Mister Keru blew off . . . it was still clinging to Commander Pazlar when we rescued her. Each tendril and its base is a complete organism in itself, but they all work collectively. They apparently take up residence in the empty shells of dead floaters, use them as camouflage. They engulf prey that passes too close, and slowly"—he hesitated—"release acids to dissolve it. The . . . biomass is absorbed into the tendrils, through tiny pores."

"What we're more interested in," Riker said in a gentle but authoritative tone, "is how you got away from the tendrils, Aili. It was hard to get good readings, but the sonar showed what seemed like squales . . ."

"They saved me," she said. "I don't know how . . . something else cut the tendrils . . . but they were there. They tried to warn us about the tendril trap, and they . . . they buoyed me up once I was free."

"Something else?" Riker asked. "Another species?"

"Something small and fast . . . and there were luminescent creatures too. I'm sorry, my memories are vague. But it was like . . . they were working with the squales."

Riker frowned. "We heard you trying to talk to them over your combadge."

"I thought . . . maybe this proved they were intelligent. I was trying to communicate." She lowered her head. "But they just ran away. Like Melora . . . Commander Pazlar said, if they were intelligent, wouldn't they be more curious?" She strained to remember details from her rescue. "I don't know, sir . . . I'm not sure I wasn't delirious. I can't be sure what was real down there."

He patted her hand. "It's all right, Aili. The important thing is that you're still with us. You just rest now."

"Thank you, Captain."

Eviku lingered for a moment, and she read sympathy and sadness in his eyes. "I'm fine, Ev," she told him, reaching to stroke his hand.

He just nodded and smiled, not resisting the touch but not returning it. "I'm glad."

"If you want to stay and talk . . ."

"No . . . the captain's right, you need your rest." He nodded farewell and departed.

But she couldn't rest. She had finally seen the squales up close, *touched* them, and still been unable to bring back any answers. They had saved her life: was it the instinct of a social animal, or the act of a sapient, ethical people?

She had to know. Somehow, she had to make contact with them again.

It took some time for Tuvok to answer the door after Ranul Keru signaled. Keru was just about to try a security override when the panels finally slid back, revealing a tired-looking Tuvok in a disheveled uniform. "Mister Keru. Is there a problem?"

"I just wanted you to know," the Trill replied in an easygoing voice, "that you missed the start of your shift again. I had to cover your asteroid-deflection drill."

Tuvok straightened. "My apologies, Mister Keru. I . . . lost track of the time. I will see that it does not happen again."

It was a rather transparent excuse; either the computer or T'Pel could have reminded Tuvok, if he'd been in a condition to listen. But Keru let it slide. "It's all right, Tuvok. I don't mind the extra work. I carried both our jobs for a while, before you joined the crew. Not that I'd want to do it full-time again, mind you. At least this way I get some time off. So I'm hoping to see you back in full swing before long. But until then, I want you to know I have your back."

Tuvok lifted a brow, and for a moment Keru expected a dose of boilerplate Vulcan literalism in response to the idiom. But that was the sort of banter Tuvok engaged in when he was in a good mood, or so it seemed to Keru after serving with him for a year. Right now, he didn't have it in him. "That will not be necessary, Mister Keru. Any further dereliction of duty on my part should not be tolerated. The captain—"

"The captain understands. So does Commander Vale. I made sure of it." He forestalled another protest, saying, "Listen, Tuvok. I know what you're thinking. It's been five months, you should be moving on with your life by now. But that's not how it works. I was in grieving for years after Sean died. I wasn't able to let him go until *I* nearly died in the Reman attack last year. So if anyone can understand what you're going through, Commander—"

He broke off, since what he saw in Tuvok's eyes gave him a keener understanding of just what it was inside of Vulcans that was so frightening that they felt they had to keep it buried at all costs. "With all . . . due respect for your loss," Tuvok said stiffly, "it is not comparable. You did not lose a child."

"It's not a competition, Tuvok," Keru said, his tone as placating as possible. "Every loss is different." He sighed. "But it's still loss, my friend. That's a universal."

Tuvok was silent for a time. Finally, he said, "How were you able to do it?"

Keru blinked. "Do what?"

"Let him go."

It was a while before he could decide what to say. "I just . . . let it happen. Eventually. I think . . . at first, when you lose someone, you don't want to stop thinking about your last memories of them, no matter how much it hurts, because it's all you have left of them. But there comes a time when you try to relive those moments and it starts to slip away. And you don't want it to, you try to cling to it. But I think . . ." He swallowed, clearing his throat. "I think your mind knows when it's ready to start healing. So when you try to dwell on those memories, it resists, because it needs to start moving on. If you fight that . . . if you keep on clinging to it . . . you end up getting stuck, not moving on with your life the way your loved one would want you to. But once you realize your mind is trying to let go, to move on . . . once you let it . . . it just sort of happens. Not quickly; the sadness doesn't go away anytime soon. But . . . it doesn't *trap* you anymore. You miss him . . . but you live your life, and start to feel normal again."

Tuvok took it in and thought about it for some time. Keru stood patiently, the gift of a security guard. "An interesting insight," Tuvok finally said. "I do not know, however, if it is applicable to me. I do not believe I have yet reached that state of readiness—if I ever will."

"I think it takes longer for people like us." A brow went up, inquiring. "People who never got to say good-bye. Who never got to prepare for the end, to say the things that went unsaid . . . there's so much more we don't want to let go of."

A heavy sigh. "It is illogical to cling to such regrets." He said it not with chastisement, but with irony.

Keru narrowed his eyes. "I'm not so sure. If the mind needs time to work through them, to come to terms with them, I'd say it's illogical to force it along—just as illogical as refusing to let go when you're ready."

"A surprisingly . . . intellect-based view of grief, Mister Keru."

"I guess it comes from my time tending the symbiont pools on Trill. Mind and memories . . . that's all they are." His gaze went unfocused. "And it's hard to imagine how much loss they've known."

Tuvok nodded. "It is a universal."

Keru smiled. "But so is life, my friend. So is life."

CHAPTER FIVE

DROPLET, STARDATE 58525.3

Eviku nd'Ashelef sat atop the aquashuttle *Holiday*, having a picnic with his crewmates while watching the fish fly by.

Many of Droplet's chordates could pop out of the water, extend their long, cartilage-stiffened fins, and glide for great distances. Many had fins that could actually flap for propulsion. Eviku had catalogued a number of them today while the *Holiday* cruised a few dozen klicks behind Hurricane Spot (as the perpetual superhurricane had been nicknamed), studying the storm and its effects on the ocean in its wake. The surface cooling caused by the dense cloud cover and heavy rain caused a vertical displacement of the thermocline, promoting blooms of phytoplankton that in turn promoted a feeding frenzy. Some flying piscoids had taken to the air to avoid predators in the water, while others, predatory themselves, had come in from farther afield to pursue them or to dive after piscoids in the water. Earlier today, the crew had observed a fascinating event in which a large school of piscoids had been caught in a pincer between two predatory species: below, cuttlefish-like creatures with tentacles keratin-stiffened into multiple scissorlike blades, and above, a flock of long-tentacled piscoids with dragonfly wings. Eviku had observed this pattern before on other worlds, but this had a twist. The piscoids in the targeted school could themselves take to the air for brief moments, using their fins purely for passive lift and flapping their wide tails at blurring speed to propel themselves through the air. The small buzzfish (as Commander Vale had dubbed them) had swarmed in a bait ball that was half in and half out of the water, a writhing, glittering mass that functioned as a single entity, flowing and morphing with desperate speed like a Changeling under a phaser barrage.

Once, Eviku would have found that a thing of simple beauty, but now there was more ambivalence to the sight. The beleaguered buzzfish reminded him of Starfleet, mounting desperate action to fight off the Borg but having to sacrifice so many in hopes that some percentage of the whole could survive. He took comfort in the fact that the buzzfish shoal lived on after the feeding frenzy . . . but at what cost! He could not help but be reminded of Germu and how much he missed her. How he had never had the chance to say good-bye. Aili's close call yesterday had left him shaken, afraid of having to bear another loss.

Now that the drama had subsided, he was content to try to put those thoughts aside. He and the others sat atop the *Holiday*'s roof—which had been adapted to function as a deck of sorts—having a leisurely picnic lunch while watching the distant fireworks of a lightning storm on the periphery of the superhurricane. It was nice to be able to relax on such an agreeable planet. Not only was Droplet nice and wet, and warmer than most of Arken II, but it had a good strong magnetic field as well. Normally he had to wear his *anlec'ven*, an inverted-U headdress made of black magnetic material, to prevent the disorientation Arkenites experienced when removed from the powerful field they'd evolved in. Down here, he could go without the headdress, something he could normally do only in his quarters with their built-in field generator. He felt a certain affinity for the animal forms of this world, which also had evolved with an innate magnetic perception, according to the scans and examinations of numerous sampled species. It was a valuable aid to navigation on a world without landmarks.

It was also agreeable to share a recreational moment with his crewmates again. He'd spent too much time in those quarters in the past few months, alone with his private grief. He took some comfort in the distraction of an enjoyably banal conversation with Commanders Vale and Pazlar about last week's parrises squares finals, a recording of which had come in the last data burst from Starfleet.

But Vale trailed off in the middle of excoriating his opinion on the Izarian team's defensive strategy, staring off toward a nearby thunderhead, one of the storms on the outer edge of Spot. "What is it?" he asked, turning to follow her gaze. But he saw nothing; human eyesight was considerably better than his.

"I'm not sure." She deliberately moved her eyes back and forth, up and down. "Not just a floater in my eye. Anybody have a pair of binoculars?" she called down the hatch in a casual yet authoritative tone. She reached down, and seconds later binoculars magically appeared in her hand. She stood and searched the sky with them. "There it is. Hey, it is a floater, just not in my eye. An inflated, translucent sack, like a jellyfish, but with some more substantial components hanging from the bottom. Reminds me of an old-style weather balloon."

"May I see, Commander?" Eviku requested.

Vale handed him the binoculars. "Better look fast before it drifts inside that thundercloud. There." She tried to point it out to him; with his limited vision, it took a few moments to focus on it even with help from the binoculars' readouts.

"I see, it's—aah!" He winced as a bolt of lightning went off right in his line of sight.

"What?"

Eviku blinked, temporarily blinded. "That . . . scope needs better filters. I may need to see the doctor." The thunder arrived in the middle of his sentence. "It appears the creature's at the mercy of the wind. Getting sucked right into a low-pressure region." He was starting to see the shapes of the two women, which was encouraging.

"It doesn't seem like a very sensible design," Pazlar said. "Well, as long as a species reproduces fast enough, evolution doesn't care how self-defeating a design is."

"I wonder what it's filled with," Vale mused. "Hot air, hydrogen, helium?"

"No helium to speak of on this planet. Hot air's possible, but the mechanism for heating's hard to guess. My bet's hydrogen—that can be produced biologically."

Eviku could see Vale well enough now to recognize that she was furrowing her brow. Humans conveyed a lot of expression with their unusually flexible foreheads. "Maybe we should take the shuttle up, try to grab it before it floats into the storm. Could be doing it a fav—"

Suddenly, lightning flashed again, luckily behind Eviku this time. He turned and looked through the binoculars, only to catch the final moments of the gas bag going up in a puff of flame and vapor, while the more substantial components of the creature plummeted toward the sea.

Pazlar turned to the first officer. "About that bet—"

"No takers. Hydrogen."

The science officer grimaced. "Well, it could be methane."

TITAN

Lieutenant Eviku and Ensign Y'lira Modan stood as Deanna entered the exobiology lab. "Commander!" Y'lira said. "What can we do for you?"

"At ease, both of you," Deanna said with a smile, unsure whether they were deferring more to her rank or to her very pregnant condition. "I'm here for curiosity, not business. I'm actually getting a little bored stuck on the ship, and I just wanted to peer over your shoulders for a bit, if you don't mind. Maybe contribute in some way."

"Of course, Commander," Eviku said. "You're always welcome. Would you like to sit down?"

At first, she was inclined to brush off the invitation, but her ankles had other ideas. "Thank you," she said, gratefully easing herself into an empty seat. Near the seat was an aquarium of sorts, a bit larger and more clinical than the one in which Captain Picard had kept Livingston, his lionfish. Some kind of invertebrate creature rested on the bottom. "I think your pet is dead," she said.

"No, ma'am, just . . . inert," Eviku replied.

"What is it?"

"It's the 'weather balloon' organism Commander Vale and I observed three days ago."

She stared. "I thought that blew up."

"The gas bladder blew up," Eviku said. "The rest of the creature's surprisingly durable. Apparently it's evolved the ability to survive lightning strikes when it gets sucked into storms."

"Makes sense . . . I suppose. It seems it would be easier to avoid the storms in the first place."

"That's not the only anomaly. The surviving portion consists largely of sensory organs: sight, hearing, odor, pressure, EM fields, even infrared. And there seems to be very little to the brain that isn't devoted to the sense organs. Although it's hard to be certain with no significant neural activity, and I'd rather not dissect it."

"Well, it's at the mercy of the winds. I wouldn't expect it to have much of its brain devoted to motor functions."

"Yes, ma'am, but what does it need all those highly refined senses for if it can barely react to what it senses? Then there's the question of how they get by without any evident control over their movements. How do they reproduce if the only way they ever encounter each other is by chance?"

"Spores? Buds?"

"Maybe. In any case, Commander Vale's name for it—a weather balloon—was apt. A sac of buoyant gas with sensory equipment attached. Now if only we could figure out why a weather balloon would evolve naturally."

Deanna recalled something he'd just said. "Why don't you want to dissect it?"

"I've been keeping it alive to see if its gas bladder would regenerate after being hit by lightning. As far as I can tell from my studies, it does have that capability. But for some reason it isn't making use of it."

"Could the lightning have crippled it?"

"That was my thought, but there's no sign of damage. It's like it's deliberately not healing itself. It's essentially in a coma, absorbing minimal nutrients—just enough to maintain its physical status quo. And I can't figure out why."

Y'lira turned her large, unblinking turquoise eyes toward Deanna, who sensed uncertainty from the golden-skinned Selenean. "With respect, Commander, I'm uncertain how much you could contribute here. We're basically dealing with animals here."

"Well . . . animals have psychology too, Modan," Deanna said with a shrug. "I'm not in Chamish's league when it comes to that, but I'm happy to offer my perspective."

"We could use some," Eviku said. She sensed his usual low-level melancholy beneath the surface, but for now the Arkenite was caught up in his work. He was one of Huilan's patients; it wasn't her place to pry. "The 'weather balloon' isn't the only mysterious creature on the planet. There are other species with disproportionate sensory capability, like the bugeye piscoids. There are creatures that occupy peculiarly broad ranges, such as a genus of zooplankton that's been scanned by probes several kilometers down but has also been sampled just meters below the surface. Sea life is usually more stratified than that. We've also noted a number of species showing unusual behavior."

"Such as?"

"We've observed movements that don't have any clear motivation such as the pursuit of food or flight from predators. Indeed, there's a species of piscoid that the squales feed upon, one that actually swims *toward* them when it hears their calls."

Deanna blinked. "Seriously?"

"Yes, it's bizarre. They're bright orange, so Bralik nicknamed them 'flaming idiot fish.'" They shared a laugh. It was nice to feel humor from Eviku, though it was all too brief.

"One small molluscoid with prehensile claws has been observed in contact with numerous small creatures," he went on, "and it's hard to say what they're doing with them, since they're not just eating them. Sometimes they just seem to *move* things from one place to another. A few times we've seen a flying piscoid circling around, holding a smaller organism in its tentacles. In fact, we've seen them doing this not far from our own shuttles. It's like they're watching us—but if so, why bring other animals along for the flight?"

Deanna furrowed her brow. "Would you say these species are tool users? Like the way some animals use rocks to open shellfish and the like?"

"We've seen no evidence of that, or of nestbuilding behavior—none of the usual types of animal tool use. And these species don't have nearly large enough brains for abstract thought, not given the type of neurological structure found on Droplet."

"Certainly they show no sign of language," Y'lira added. "The sounds they make among themselves are basic—here I am, where are you, I'm large and dangerous, I'm small and submissive, food is here, danger is coming, I wish to mate, the usual." Deanna chuckled at the cryptolinguist's deadpan recital. "But some of them have been noted making odd vocal exchanges with the squales. Although the squales do most of the vocalizing."

"Does it seem like a conversation, or like some sort of dispute—the squales warning the other forms off when their boundaries are violated?"

"Hard to say, since we can't get close enough to see. But these species make sounds to the squales—and occasionally to the other animals they interact with—that they don't make among themselves. So we have no referent for what they mean."

"And does the same apply to the sounds the squales make to them?"

"The squales' vocalizations are so complex that we really can't say." Y'lira gestured at the receiver in her ear as she mentioned the squale song.

Deanna perked up. "Are you analyzing them now?"

"Yes, ma'am."

"I'd love to listen to some." She put her hands on her belly. "Plus it's good to expose a developing infant to music. It's been fascinating to sense how her emotional state responds to different musical styles. I'd love to know how she responds to squale song. If it wouldn't be a distraction, Eviku," she added.

"No, Commander. I think I'd enjoy that."

With a nod, Y'lira activated the speakers on her console. Flowing, echoing cries filled the lab, hypnotic in their complexity, uplifting in their beauty. Deanna drank them in, slowing her breathing to minimize the interference for little What's-her-name, and striving to render herself passive so as not to impose her own impressions on the little one. She was just a receiver, open to the sounds from without and the emotions from within.

But before she could get a clear read from the baby, she was startled out of her meditative state by a new sound from behind her, a sharp, staccato twittering that clearly wasn't from the speakers. Deanna opened her eyes to see Eviku and Y'lira staring at her with shock.

No, not at her—at the tank behind her. She turned. The "weather balloon" creature was not visibly more active, but there was no question that it was the source of the sounds.

"It hasn't done that before," Eviku said. He activated the tank's scanners. "But its metabolism is rising. It's coming out of its dormancy. Odd."

"You think that's odd?" Y'lira asked. "It's speaking squale!"

"A sort of pidgin squale, actually," Y'lira told the assembled department heads two hours later. "Like a very simplified version of the same catalogue of sounds."

"Are you suggesting that it was actually *answering* the squales?" Ra-Havreii asked with skepticism. Aili Lavena, who had been down on the planet but had been summoned back to the ship for this urgent briefing, was annoyed by his tone at first. But she reminded herself of the perils of jumping to conclusions.

"We're not just suggesting it," Y'lira went on. "After it stopped, we played back the squale calls again. And at the exact same moment in the playback, it began making the exact same pattern of sounds. The sequence it emitted lasted nearly ten minutes, with no overall repetition."

"And that's not all," Eviku put in. "The creature has suddenly begun to regenerate its flotation sac. And at the rate it's regrowing, it should be airborne within two weeks at most. That's after days of total inactivity, and from my analysis I'm convinced the creature could remain dormant for weeks and still do the same."

"There's only one explanation that fits what we've seen," said Pazlar, who had shuttled up with Lavena. "When we nicknamed this creature a weather balloon, we were more right than we knew. Because that seems to be what it literally is. It drifts around the sky, taking measurements with its various senses, storing what it learns. Remembering it precisely, mechanically. Eviku's scans of its neural activity—now that it has some—show its brain is tailor-made for that, almost like a digital computer."

"It gathers data until struck by lightning," Eviku said, "or maybe until some other factor causes it to descend. It floats atop the water until the squales find it. At their signal, it plays back its data encoded as sound patterns. Only then, when its data has been downloaded, does it begin to regrow its flotation sac."

"What you're saying," Riker replied slowly, "is that the squales manufactured this creature."

"That they bred it, yes."

"And probably the other anomalous species we've observed," Pazlar said. "It explains the strange behaviors that have no survival benefit. They're performing tasks for the squales. Harvesting foodstuffs, carrying things around. Even swimming into the squales' beaks when they're called. Maybe even doing more complex work. The molluscoids with prehensile digits could give the squales the fine manipulative capability they lack, explaining how they were able to achieve a lot of this engineering."

"So how did they domesticate the molluscoids in the first place?" Ra-Havreii asked. "Without the capacity to confine or handle the animals . . ."

"It wouldn't require any technology," Pazlar countered. "As long as one species could control another's movements well enough to regulate who they did or didn't mate with, then selective breeding would be possible."

"Well, how do you do that without fences or walls?"

"We did it all the time back home. Plenty of Gemworld sports depend on it."

"So the bottom line," Troi said, interrupting the building heat between them, "is that the squales are definitely intelligent."

"I have no doubt of that," Eviku said. "Not only intelligent, but technological, in a manner of speaking: capable of selectively breeding other life forms to serve as their tools."

Pazlar sighed and turned to the captain. "And they're aware of us, sir. Since the bugeye piscoids have been observed calling to the squales, I think it's a safe bet that they're like the weather balloons, and probably like those small shelled creatures we've seen being carried by piscoids flying overhead. They're probes, sir. Sensors. And they've been hovering around our away teams since day one. The squales may have been keeping their distance, but they've been watching our every move down there."

The room fell silent, except for a hushed "Oh, my God" from Christine Vale.

Finally, Eviku asked, "How does the Prime Directive apply in a case like this? Should we just . . . leave and hope no real damage is done?"

"They've been watching us for the past ten days," Pazlar said. "We're not just some sighting they can dismiss as a trick of the mind."

"But they're not a technological people," Vale put in. "Without written records, the knowledge could fade into legend."

"Don't count on that," Ra-Havreii said. "If they're anything like my people or the Alonis, they may have a means of preserving detailed oral histories and passing them on exactly. Indeed, I'd say they must have such a thing, in order to preserve the complex bioengineering skills they possess."

"We have no way of knowing how we may have inadvertently affected their society," Troi said. "We mistakenly breached the Prime Directive, but just pulling out now would be an abrogation of our responsibility. We have to try to make contact, see if there's a way to mitigate the damage."

"How do we know it will damage them?" Lavena asked. "If they've been watching us so closely, maybe they're fascinated by us. Maybe they're eager to learn."

"Then why have they been so careful to avoid us?" the captain asked gently.

"This is a world without metal, without plastic," Troi said, both answering and reinforcing her husband's point. "They've never seen anything that isn't alive. I can hardly imagine how alien we must be to them. There's no telling what kind of fear or crisis of belief we could provoke. We have to try to establish communication so we can assess the effects of our presence and try to mitigate it."

"Increase our interference to reduce its effects?" Ra-Havreii asked. "That hardly seems logical."

"There is precedent," Troi said. "On Mintaka III, when the presence of Starfleet observers was accidentally exposed to the natives, they reacted badly with a religious fervor that almost became destructive. Since the people had only fragmentary information and no understanding of what it meant, it left them confused and frightened, provoking aggression and intolerance. Captain Picard resolved the situation by making open contact and explaining our true nature. Giving them more information helped them make better decisions about how to cope with this knowledge and incorporate it into their worldview. Once they were back on their own track, of course, we left them alone again."

"The Prime Directive is about respecting other people's right to make their own choices," Riker said. "We try to avoid contact with young societies, not because they're too fragile to handle it, but because there's too much temptation for *us* to try to exploit the situation, to pressure them into believing what we want. But if they find out about us on their own, then if we try to hide or misrepresent ourselves, then that's exactly what we're doing: trying to manipulate their way of seeing things to suit our ends.

"Bottom line, we're already in a first contact situation. It's no longer a question of whether to communicate with the squales, but how. And as with any first contact, it's incumbent on us to treat them with honesty, fairness, and respect."

Vale frowned. "I'd say 'how' is the question in a more logistical sense. How do we talk to them when they've been avoiding us?"

"We haven't really been trying to talk to them," Lavena said. "Just to watch them from afar. Maybe if we let them know we're interested in talking, they'd respond. After all," she reminded the others, "they saved my life. They came to help us when we were in danger. I think that says a lot about their attitude toward other life forms."

Riker pondered her words. "I'd like you to spearhead our efforts, Aili. You're the one person among us who's already made some connection with the squales, however tenuous. And you're the one person who can live the way they do, who's most familiar to them."

"I'm glad to try, sir," Lavena told him. "But . . . I'm not a trained diplomat. I . . ." Her eyes went to Troi.

"I'll assign Counselor Huilan to assist you," Troi said, looking unhappy. "He doesn't have much experience as a contact specialist, but . . . I obviously can't go down there."

"Of course not," Riker said, discreetly touching her hand.

"Umm, Captain?" Lavena said. "If I may . . . I think it would be a good idea if . . . if you came down with us."

He looked surprised. "Why me, Ensign?"

"Well, you are an experienced diplomat . . . but also,

you're a musician. I figure if we're going to try to communicate with a species of singers . . ."

"I think she's right, sir," Y'lira said. "The squales' language relies heavily on pitch, rhythm, harmony, syncopation, and other musical elements."

"Syncopation?" Riker grinned his big, infectious grin, the same one that had won Aili over twenty-two years ago. "So they're jazz musicians?"

Y'lira's gemlike eyes just stared. "Sir?"

"Never mind." He turned to Troi. "It's tempting, but . . . the baby could come any day now. I can't be away . . ."

"Will," the counselor said. "We've always agreed, you're the captain first. Aili's right—you could be valuable down there. And if I go into labor, you're just twenty minutes away by shuttle. Go." She smiled. "I know you've been dying to."

Eagerness warred with reluctance on Riker's face, but he split the difference and settled on captainly resolve. "All right. I'll lead the away team." He turned to Ra-Havreii. "Doctor, I'd like you along as well."

It took a moment for the Efrosian engineer to realize he'd been addressed. "You'd . . . Me, sir? Wait, me . . . down there?"

"Yes."

"On the planet, you mean?"

"That's right."

"Me."

"Is there a problem, Doctor?"

"Well, sir . . . I get terribly motion-sick without a steady surface beneath me."

"We have inertial dampers in the shuttles, and Ree can give you an antiemetic."

"My people sunburn very easily . . ."

"The sun's far away and doesn't give off much UV," Pazlar told him.

"I'm a poor swimmer. Sir."

"You always did pretty well in my quarters," Aili said with a grin.

"Your quarters, my dear, are not ninety kilometers deep."

"You said it yourself, Xin," Troi told him. "The squales' language may be similar to Efrosian. Your own musical skills could prove invaluable."

"I don't doubt it, but I'd be happy to consult from the ship."

"If I'm going, Doctor," Riker said in a tone that brooked no more argument, "you're going."

"But—Very well, sir," he said with a heavy sigh.

The captain rose, signaling the end of the briefing. "Prep a shuttle," he said. "We leave at 1400."

The crew filed out, and Aili came over to Ra-Havreii. "You'll love it down there, Xin. It's so warm and beautiful . . . a very romantic setting," she added, winking at Melora.

Ra-Havreii didn't look reassured. "Maybe," he said. "But it's just so . . . *outdoors*."

Chapter Six

DROPLET

Once the *Gillespie* set down at the main floater-island base, Aili wanted to waste no time getting into the water. But Xin Ra-Havreii was less enthusiastic, hesitating even to leave the shuttle. It took a verbal prodding from the captain to get him out, and he trod gingerly across the loose soil, his eyes scanning it as if for land mines. "There, this isn't so bad, is it?" Melora asked.

"Ohh, I can feel the ground rocking beneath me." He looked even paler than usual.

Aili couldn't resist teasing him. "I thought you liked to feel the earth move."

"I prefer my metaphors less literally realized, thank you." He looked back and forth at the Selkie and the Elaysian who flanked him. "Although I must confess, the company of two of my favorite intimates could do wonders to distract me from these environs—if you'd both be inclined to cooperate."

Melora threw him a cold look. "We're here to work, Xin. Try to stay focused." She strode ahead of them.

Ra-Havreii looked after her for a bit, nonplussed. But he soon shook it off and focused on Aili. "Ah, well. All work and no play, as they say. I'm sure you and I could create sufficient distractions on our own."

Aili was tempted. Although Xin and Melora technically had an open relationship, they had been involved enough in each other that Aili hadn't shared a swim with him for months. But after a moment, she smiled and said, "I appreciate the offer, but Melora's right. I'm really looking forward to working with you on the squale language, but let's leave it at that for now, all right?" After all, Melora was her friend too, and Aili didn't want to add complications while Melora was still unsure where her relationship with the engineer stood. Aili had been the one to suggest that Melora should let Xin go, and she didn't want Melora to think she'd had any ulterior motive behind that suggestion.

Besides, Captain Riker was right behind her—also at her suggestion. She wanted him to be comfortable working with her, without their past liaison becoming an issue, and so she didn't want to give the impression that she was a potential homewrecker.

Ra-Havreii sighed. "Oh, very well. At least the work should keep me occupied. Assuming you manage to open communication."

She patted his shoulder. "Don't worry. I have some ideas about that."

Riker gave her permission to take a quick swim off the shore while he checked in with the base team. She hastened to the shoreline, and as she stripped off her hydration suit, she noticed that Counselor Huilan had arrived beside her. "Do you mind if I join you?" the diminutive blue S'ti'ach asked.

"Not at all, Counselor." She dove into the water, reinvigorated by the flow of fresh water across her gill crests. Moments later, she saw Huilan's small furred form floating above her, dog-paddling with all six stubby limbs.

Realizing something, she surfaced in front of him. He was grinning widely, his big ears perked up in pleasure. "Hold on. How are you floating? I thought you were supposed to be hyperdense or something."

The ears sagged, his big eyes looking away. "Oh. That. Umm . . ." Aili wouldn't have been able to recognize S'ti'ach embarrassment before, but she was fairly certain she had a referent for it now. "Well, yes, I do have a relatively dense bone structure—necessary for a high-gravity planet. But by the same token, you don't want a high body mass on a high-gee world—harder to move around. Plus a low-density body provides more cushioning in falls."

She didn't let the lecture distract her. "But you tell people you're heavier than a full-size humanoid!"

"Yes, well . . ." He slumped in surrender. "Look at me, Ensign. I'm small, cute, and furry. Other species have a pervasive tendency to want to pick S'ti'ach up and . . . *cuddle* us. It's embarrassing."

Aili laughed until she saw Huilan's stern glare—which made her laugh even harder. "You know I am a predator, right?" Huilan reminded her, showing his impressive array of teeth in what was not a smile.

"I'm sorry," she said, still chuckling.

"Oh, that's all right. It's not really that great a secret anyway; simple observation and reasoning should be enough to reveal it. But people tend to take what they're told at face value. It's an interesting psychological experiment to see how different people respond to the fiction." He narrowed his eyes. "Or their discovery of the truth."

"Well, far be it from me to tamper with an ongoing experiment," Aili told him. "I promise I won't tell anyone else."

"Good."

"In exchange for one quick cuddle."

Huilan growled, but acceded to her terms.

The base's equipment included a couple of small scouter gigs, courtesy of *Titan*'s industrial replicators. Aili proposed heading out in one of them, rather than the larger, more intimidating aquashuttle, to try to make contact with the squales. She advised beginning with a small party, and since Ra-Havreii was dealing with a bout of seasickness (probably psychosomatic but genuine in its effects), Captain Riker accompanied her as musical consultant for this first trip. They were joined by Huilan, who was small enough not to be intimidating.

"There's something else," she told the others as the gig carried them out toward the nearest concentration of squale biosigns. "Counselor Troi said they've never encountered unliving technology before. That must be why they were so startled by my tricorder, so wary of getting close. If I'm going to put them at ease, sir, I should go in without any technology at all."

Riker pondered. "Leaving your tricorder behind is

reasonable. But you should at least keep your combadge on. You can hide it under your clothes if you think it will disturb them."

Aili met his gaze matter-of-factly. "Captain . . . clothes are technology too."

His eyes widened for a bit before he reined himself in. Aili quashed a chuckle; human modesty was so cute. "Well . . . if you think it would make a difference . . . but I don't like the idea of you being out of communication."

"The gig's equipment includes sensitive underwater microphones, sir. At least I should be able to get a message to you, assuming I stay in range. And two-way communication should be possible through the deep sound channel, if you position an acoustic relay there. There'd be a delay, but only a few seconds' worth."

"I don't like it, Aili. You've already been attacked twice by native life forms. If you're too far for us to reach—"

"Then the squales will protect me. They've already demonstrated that. And I'll be swimming fast until I reach them—I won't be easy to catch, I promise." She leaned forward. "Please, sir. I'm willing to take the risk to earn their trust."

After a moment, he nodded. "All right, Aili. But you be careful."

She hid her annoyance behind the action of unfastening her hydration suit. She wasn't the irresponsible, juvenile creature he'd known two decades ago; she didn't need to be lectured. But she reminded herself that he didn't mean anything by it. He was the captain and it was his prerogative to worry about his crew.

Like a mother should worry about her children, she thought. *At least he has the courage to face that worry.*

Once the rubbery suit was off, she hopped into the water before slipping out of her undergarment, in order to preserve Riker's sense of propriety. Of course, in this post-reproductive phase of her life, her four breasts were about a third their former size, their nipples grown nearly vestigial and blending into the mottling of her skin. But her lower half, while a bit more padded, was still much as it had been, if she did say so herself. Best not to remind him. She had only a vague memory of their tryst—it was one of embarrassingly many—but from the way she had caught him glancing at her sometimes in their first months on *Titan*, before he'd grown accustomed to her presence, Aili was fairly confident that she'd left a vivid impression on him.

After setting up a check-in schedule with the captain—who kept his eyes firmly on her face the whole time—Aili swam off at high speed in the direction of the squale biosigns. Without a timepiece, she'd have to rely on her innate time sense, which could be tricky here. Normally she could rely on the angle of the sun to keep track of time. Though the lack of a solid surface meant the rotation rate was slightly faster at the equator than the poles, the day length was still reasonably close to nineteen hours everywhere on the planet. But subsurface currents could conceivably take her east faster or slower than the average, affecting the angle of sunlight. The check-in schedule would necessarily require a lot of leeway.

But Aili set such thoughts aside after a moment, for it was such a pleasure to be swimming free and clear in the open ocean, unencumbered by clothing. The sense of freedom, of respite from the stifling hydration suit, was delicious. She rejoiced in it, pushing herself faster and faster with her powerful long limbs. She arched her spine back and forth, bouncing in and out of the water, gaining more energy with each bounce. Finally she drove herself down several meters, then angled up and kicked with all her might, adding speed to buoyancy, the ocean's rippling ceiling plummeting to meet her. As she breached the surface at an angle, she slammed her arms down to her sides, webbed hands flat, for an extra boost.

And then she was free of the waves, a ballistic body in the empty air, sparkling droplets cascading from her flesh as she arced in free fall above the warm blue sea, twisting about her axis to take in the view in all directions. In the distance, she saw Riker in the gig, rising to his feet at the sight of her, no longer afraid to look. Reaching the zenith of her arc, she hovered for an endless instant above the sea, its surface stretching out beneath her, defining infinity . . . and then gravity had its way and the wet, welcoming blue engulfed her again, the exhilaration of flirting with the sky giving way to the joy of being once more hugged to the bosom of Mother Sea.

She made several more dives into the air as she swam, and not just for pleasure; her high, spinning leaps gave her an overhead view of the ocean, letting her see farther than she could from the surface or below. This was how Selkies hunted for fish or kept watch for predators—less of a concern now than it had once been, but still an issue, for even the Selkies had not tamed the majority of their near-global ocean, and the Federation presence was limited out of respect for their cultural autonomy. And here on Droplet, as Aili was painfully aware, the threat of predators was very real.

In the distance, to the southeast, she saw a hump of darkness in the water, a spume of turbulence. On her next leap, she saw the water settling but still foaming with a trail of bubbles. She recognized the signs: some massive predator had risen up, probably under a school of piscoids or similar creatures, its gaping mouth taking in dozens of them along with a great mass of water and air, the latter of which now drained from the edges of its maw in a torrent of bubbles. The creature would probably circle and rise again, taking several more bites from the sky before it was sated. Aili angled her course to give it a wide berth. Starfleet scientific curiosity was all well and good, but she was swimming alone and buck naked in an alien ocean, so for the moment she was perfectly happy not to learn about any more local predators.

Soon Aili began to hear familiar music echoing through the water, the successive repetitions of varying intensity indicating that the sound waves were oscillating around the deep sound channel, some waves following longer paths around the channel axis than others and taking longer to reach her ears. She swam down toward it, leaving the surface behind. She began her own tentative song; her laryngeal muscles could mimic more than humanoid speech, and now she gave her best approximation of a recurring pattern the translators had identified in the calls of the squales' various probe creatures. The computer's best guess was that it was a call for attention, a signal of readiness to communicate. But while she replicated the tones, she made sure to project it in her own voice, in hopes they would understand that her intent was to make contact rather than to deceive.

When she heard a call the computer had tentatively tagged as a response, she stopped swimming, still a hundred meters or so above the channel axis, and repeated her own declaration, waiting for the squales to come to her. But it was a bugeye piscoid that came first. She floated placidly as it swam around her, letting it see every bit of her. At the same time, she felt a series of sharp, loud clicks slicing through the water, sonar pulses taking acoustical images. Were the squales themselves generating them, or was it another species of sensor animal? Either way, she was glad she hadn't followed Riker's suggestion to hide a communicator. He was as open-minded as any human she'd ever met, but he still had his unconscious human biases, such as a tendency to think primarily in terms of sight. These sonar pulses, if the squales themselves produced them, would let them see right through her, leaving her far more naked to them than she had been to her crewmates' eyes. She calmed herself, keeping her metabolism low so as not to appear threatening. Their sonar would detect a racing heart.

The bugeye retreated, no doubt returning to give its report. She felt a murmur of squale calls, not distant but quiet, like a huddled conversation. Then for a time there was only darkness and anticipatory silence. The white noise of the ocean, with tenuous hints of movement on the edge of her awareness, possibly only the ghosts of her hopes and fears.

A faint blue light glimmered before her. At first she

thought it might be her mind playing tricks, but then it grew steadily brighter, clearer. It was some kind of bioluminescent creature, round and clear-shelled, with arcs of blue and green light chasing down the curves of its internal structure. A squale spotlight, perhaps, sent to give them a better look at her? Or maybe a beacon of some sort? Were its photophores flickering in some kind of meaningful pattern she was supposed to respond to? An intelligence test? She moved her feet gingerly, easing closer but trying not to scare it off. It continued its approach, thousands of tiny clear cilia shimmering as they caught the light, breaking it into a diffraction spectrum of blues and greens. (Red light was rarely found at these depths, since the water swallowed it up over any distance.) Now Aili could see the intricate helical twists in its internal structure, and she wondered if the squales had somehow bred that beauty into it or if it had been natural. They used bioengineering to make tools, but did they make art as well? She reached toward it, not wanting to risk damaging the fragile-seeming creature, but wanting to touch it ever so gently to ensure it was real. . . .

Then something grabbed her from behind, not gently at all. Multiple, muscular somethings that gripped her tightly and clung to her skin with dozens of small suckers. Three of them pinned her legs together and her arms against her sides, hard enough to crush the breath from her if she still had any. The fourth wrapped around her head, wrenching it back and muffling her senses, and she didn't doubt it was strong enough to snap her neck. As the tentacles dragged her downward, Aili realized the bioluminescent creature hadn't been an intelligence test but a stupidity test, and she'd tested strongly positive. How could a Selkie not remember that enticing lights in the depths, if not intended as mating signals, were used to lure in prey?

Aili was being dragged down swiftly, which was fortunate, since the tight grip of the tentacles was smothering most of her gill surfaces and she needed the rapid flow of water across the rest to keep her conscious. She felt a broad, sharp beak jabbing into her back, probing her. It confirmed that she was in the grip of a squale. The four-meter chordates were capable of greater stealth than she'd anticipated—and possibly greater aggression. That beak could tear massive chunks from her flesh. She assumed, though, that if that had been their goal, it would have happened already. For now, they wanted her alive—but she got the message from that beak that was now nipping curiously at her backside. If she tried to resist them, she was lunch.

Riker scanned the surface of the water with fading hope, wincing against the glare of the sun. New Kaferia's light was comparatively mild, but his eyes were sore from probing the ocean for hours. Leaning back in the scouter gig and rubbing the bridge of his nose, he slapped his combadge. "Riker to *Gillespie*. Anything to report?"

It was a moment before the signal came back from the aquashuttle, laden with static from the kilometers of water it needed to penetrate. *"No luck, sir,"* came Pazlar's voice. *"We've searched all around Aili's projected course and found nothing. But with the way these subsurface currents flow, she could've been taken in any direction depending on her depth."*

"Keep looking. Broaden your search parameters."

"Aye, sir. We'll find her."

The signal cut out and Riker returned to looking. Beside him, Huilan looked up from his ongoing tricorder scan and tilted his head quizzically. "She's four hours overdue. Do you think it's still likely she'll return here?"

"Without knowing what's happened," he answered tightly, "we can't rule out the possibility. We have to be here in case she does."

"Wouldn't the captain be able to do more good from the main base? Or *Titan*? Someone else could've taken your place here."

"A waste of time. We're here already; we might as well keep manning this post. Besides . . . I'm not leaving any of my crew behind again."

"I see," Huilan said, and Riker grimaced, knowing what would come after a counselor said *I see*. "Like you left the landing party behind at New Erigol? Including your pregnant wife?"

"You want me to say I feel guilty about that?" Riker said, not breaking his gaze out at the ocean. "Of course I do. I also know it was the right command decision at the time. But this is different, Huilan. There's nothing compelling me to leave. I came out here as her backup. I agreed to let her go out there naked and alone." He slammed his fist into his hand. "What the hell was I thinking? To let her risk herself like that just to ease my own conscience about a Prime Directive screwup?"

"Do you really need me to answer that?" the S'ti'ach asked.

"I'm not in the mood for the whole 'communication is worth the risk' speech right now, Counselor." He sighed. "We've lost too much lately. We all have."

In the corner of Riker's eye, he saw Huilan's big teddy-bear ears flopping as he gave a thoughtful nod. "True. None of us wants to lose any more of our crewmates—not ever, but especially not now. I suppose that explains it."

Just for a moment, Riker's eyes darted over to him. "Explains what?"

"The intensity of your concern. It almost seemed as though you have some special fondness for Aili Lavena."

"That's ridiculous," Riker said—almost instantly realizing that it had come out a lot more defensively than he'd intended. He could imagine what Huilan would make of that. True, he and Aili—the ensign—had shared a brief liaison before he'd met Deanna, but it hadn't meant anything. All right, it had been extremely memorable, but nothing to compare to the partnership of a wife as amazing as Deanna. He saw Lavena only as a crewmate now, and to all indications, she saw him the same way. There was no reason to be defensive or uncomfortable about a purely recreational experience from half a lifetime ago. If he had any "special fondness" for Lavena, it was simply nostalgic appreciation, which Deanna was fully aware of and too secure to have a problem with.

Riker realized he was acting out the whole discussion in his mind without Huilan needing to say a word. It was a habit he'd picked up from cohabiting with an empath; if he didn't pre-emptively analyze his own motivations, she surely would. *Bad enough being married to one counselor—why the hell did I let two others aboard the ship?*

But Huilan was distracted by a reading from his tricorder. "Hold on, sir . . . I'm getting something! Single life form, rising toward us . . . mass about sixty kilos . . . vertebrate!"

Riker turned in the direction Huilan pointed, straining his eyes. Soon he saw a sleek blue-green form emerge from the depths, and then Aili was on the surface, waving and swimming toward the gig. He almost reached down to pull her into the boat before remembering that she couldn't breathe for long out of the water. He just crouched down as she came up and grasped the side of the gig. "I can't tell you how relieved we are to see you, Ensign. What happened?"

Lavena related the details of her contact and abduction by the squales. "After a while," she went on, "I was completely disoriented and weakened from lack of oxygen . . . and that's when they stopped and let me go. We must have been kilometers away from my course, and very deep— so deep I'm surprised how much oxygen there was dissolved there. Too deep for any sunlight, but there were luminescent organisms there. I guess the squales need light to see too.

"Anyway, they let me go and just . . . watched me for a while. I repeated the readiness signal, and they responded and began trying to communicate with me. Or at least to test my ability to communicate, to gauge whether I was intelligent or some kind of animal."

"They've seen us with technology; how can they not know we're intelligent?" Riker asked.

Huilan replied, "To them, technology is alive. They don't know what to make of these dead metal and composite things," he added, tapping the side of the boat with his middle right fist.

"Well, I guess I managed to convince them there's more to me than a great body, since we soon moved on to establishing a baseline vocabulary. It was hard without a UT and with so little anatomy in common. And their song is so complex, I could barely follow it even when they dumbed it down for me. So I figured it made more sense to let them come to me, and I started teaching them some basic Selkie." She shrugged. "Easier to use underwater than Standard. And I figured an aquatic language would have more concepts the squales could relate to."

"Excellent call, Ensign," Huilan said.

"Thank you. But it's more to their credit than mine that they picked it up so fast. We had a pretty good pidgin conversation going within an hour. Not enough to get into abstract concepts like space exploration and alien worlds, but enough for your basic 'we come in peace, we mean you no harm'."

"And what about their intentions toward you?" Riker asked, still with steel in his voice. "Did they explain why they abducted you by force?"

Lavena paused. "As far as I could decipher it, they just wanted to make sure it wasn't a trap. That there wasn't some kind of technology or other aliens lurking nearby waiting to strike at them. They wanted to get me alone, away from all that, so they could feel safe interacting with me."

"Still, I don't see taking a member of my crew prisoner as a good way to open diplomatic relations."

"Look at it from their perspective, though," Huilan said. "If an alien materialized on *Titan*'s bridge uninvited and claimed it came in peace, wouldn't your first move be to summon security to restrain the intruder and escort it to the brig, just in case? Most first contacts begin with a modicum of distrust."

"I appreciate how you feel, Captain," Lavena said. "I was terrified when those tentacles held me. I'm still a little mad at them for being so rough and, well, grabby." Riker wasn't sure, but it looked like she was rubbing her backside underwater. "But we're so alien to them . . . I can't blame them for being on their guard. And the fact that they let me go proves they mean us no harm. And they're willing to talk with me some more. After they escorted me most of the way back here, just before they swam away, they gave me a signal to use when I'm ready to contact them again. Or maybe a signal they'll use when they want me to come back." She beamed. "So I'd say we've successfully opened diplomatic relations."

Riker gave her a smile. "No, Aili. You have. You showed great courage today, and I'm very proud of you."

Her gill crests darkened with blood—a Selkie blush. "Thank you, sir."

He cleared his throat. "Now . . . I'd appreciate it if you'd put some clothes on."

He handed down her undergarment and hydration suit, trying not to look at her or to meet Huilan's contemplative gaze as he did so.

CHAPTER SEVEN

TITAN

After returning to the ship and seeing that Lavena got a clean bill of health from Ree, Riker turned in for the evening to be with his wife and child (still in one convenient package for another few precious weeks). It was with regret that he left them the next morning, but duty had its demands.

Reaching the bridge, he was met by the new gamma-shift watch commander, Tamen Gibruch. "All systems functioning normally, sir," he said in his resonant bass-flute voice. "Surveys are proceeding on schedule."

"Very good, Tamen." The lieutentant commander was a member of the Chandir, one of the first of his unaligned species to serve in Starfleet, though Chandir civilians were often seen on worlds and stations in the Federation's rimward sectors and in former Cardassian territory. They were hard to miss, with the distinctive muscular trunks that grew from the backs of their heads and the multiple horizontal furrows that transected their wedge-shaped faces in place of the usual nose and mouth. They were often known as "Tailheads," a nickname that had initially been derogatory but that many of them had claimed as their own, a proud acknowledgment of their unique anatomy. Riker enjoyed listening to Chandir music; the cranial trunks were filled with large sinus cavities, resonating chambers to amplify their voices for long-distance communication and mating calls, and the furrows contained air passages which they could close off with muscular contraction to change the length and shape of the air column within the trunk, making their whole heads into wind instruments. Alas, when Riker had raised this subject in one of his first conversations with Gibruch, the young officer had demurred that he had little talent for or interest in music, having led a life very focused on career advancement. Gibruch reminded Riker of himself at a younger age, so serious and ambitious, so bent on getting ahead that he forgot to stop and appreciate where he was. The *Enterprise*-D—and Deanna—had cured him of that, and he hoped that *Titan* and its crew could do the same for young Tamen—not to divert him from a promising career arc, of course, but at least to help him relax and enjoy himself along the way.

For now, though, Gibruch was still focused on his report. Opening the facial furrow that served as his mouth, he said, "One matter for your attention, sir. The asteroid survey has catalogued a significant body that currently has a one-in-six-hundred probability of collision with Droplet at its closest approach in approximately fourteen hours."

Riker frowned. "That's cutting it pretty close. Why wasn't it detected before?"

"It is approaching from somewhat north of the ecliptic, sir. With our survey limited to visual observation, it takes time to catalogue all the asteroids, and our efforts have focused on the main debris disk where the highest probability of threat bodies lies. Also, its albedo is low, making it harder to detect." Riker nodded, remembering how difficult asteroid detection could be when limited to optical imaging. Earth had still been discovering new asteroids in its own backyard as late as the Third World War. And Riker recalled how Axanar had been struck by an asteroid that destroyed a major city well into their interplanetary era, due to their governments' failure to invest in adequate detection efforts.

"It was first spotted by the computer seven hours ago," Gibruch went on, "but initial probability estimates were below the threshold of concern, so it wasn't flagged." Over the past week and a half, Riker had gotten the hang of how this worked. Visual observation of asteroid trajectories was fraught with uncertainties. You could see where a body was now, but it took days or weeks of observation to narrow down exactly which direction it was moving in, creating a cone-shaped volume of potential paths it could take. The longer you observed it, the more you pinpointed its trajectory, narrowing the cone. Initially, the cones were wide enough that thousands of asteroids showed the potential to hit Droplet or *Titan*, but in most cases, as those cones narrowed, the planet no longer fell inside them and the threat could be ruled out. This asteroid's probability cone was narrow enough to be worth noting, but the odds were six hundred to one that it would end up missing the planet after all. No cause for alarm yet.

"Risk assessment if it does hit?" Riker asked.

"Minimal. Its estimated mass is high enough that it could do some damage if it hit solid ground, but here it would simply be pulverized on impact and vaporize a crater in the ocean. The impact of water rushing back into that crater would generate a series of tsunamis, but the science team tells me that those tsunamis would subside to a moderate height within a hundred kilometers or so from ground zero—and with no shallow water, they'd remain broad and gentle, giant swells rather than breaking waves. Nearby sea life would be killed by the concussion, if not vaporized in the impact, but as long as our away teams keep their distance, the wave would affect them no worse than an ordinary ocean swell down there."

Riker thought about the squales, who would not be able to evacuate the area as easily as his crew. "Could we deflect the asteroid if we had to?"

The answer came from Pava Ek'Noor sh'Aqabaa, who stood watch at tactical on gamma shift. Despite Riker's reluctance to leave his family, old habit had brought him to the bridge early, before most of alpha shift had arrived. "Yes, sir," the tall Andorian *shen* told him. "It might take a lot of tractor power, but we could deflect it successfully. The sooner we act, the easier it will be." The captain understood that easily enough; it was simple geometry. The closer it was to the planet, the larger the angle it had to be deflected by to miss it.

"Let's not act in haste," Gibruch said. "Odds are we won't have to do anything. No sense wasting ship's power without need."

"We'd have to use more power if we waited," sh'Aqabaa countered.

"But nothing the ship can't handle. And it's more likely we won't need to use the power at all." His cranial trunk curled upward to rest on his shoulder as he addressed sh'Aqabaa. Was he flirting with her? Maybe there was hope for him yet.

"Thank you both. We'll monitor the situation. I relieve you, Mister Gibruch."

"I stand relieved."

At tactical, Tuvok had now arrived for his shift and was relieving sh'Aqabaa. The *shen* headed for the turbolift slightly ahead of Gibruch. "Oh, and Commander?" he said, smiling at the Chandir when the latter turned his impressively appendaged head. "Have fun."

DROPLET, MAIN SURVEY BASE

Xin Ra-Havreii groaned as the ground—or this benighted world's fickle excuse for it—heaved beneath him once again, almost toppling him into the pool where Aili Lavena floated, working with him on mnemonic exercises to improve her translation work with the squales. Normally the prospect of a headlong dive into Aili's strong arms would have been far from unappealing, but the water level in the pool had fallen precipitately, making it a plunge of several meters. All right, admittedly there was a rather gentle polyp-shell slope with plenty of handholds between him and the drink, but blast it, he was a starship designer, not a mountain climber.

The islet he was on—one of the twenty-eight roughly disk-shaped polyp colonies that made up this flimsy pretender to the title of "land mass"—rocked back in the other direction as the ocean swell peaked and passed beneath it, bringing Aili and the water back upward, the latter almost rising to engulf him, sending him scuttling back from where he sat. The triangular pool Aili occupied was the gap between three adjacent disks, which were fused together by chains of polyps and other symbiotic species, but loosely enough that the whole structure could flex and ride the waves without breaking apart. Intellectually, he could admire the engineering solution that evolution had devised, but he would have preferred to admire it from afar.

Aili laughed as the swell passed and the base island settled down to a level pitch again—for the moment. "I've never known you to be afraid of getting wet, Xinnie."

He restrained a wince at the nickname. "I'd rather not get dragged into there by the retreating water," he said. "Really, you shouldn't even be in there, my dear. The undertow could suck you between the islets as they grind together."

She grinned, dismissing his concern. "I've been swimming my whole life, Xin. I can handle myself near shore during rough seas."

"You've never had to deal with two shores clashing together! I doubt anyone other than Jason or Odysseus has." Commander Vale, a fan of classical Earth literature, had treated the command crew to holoprograms of her ancestral world's ancient maritime myths during their three-day approach to Droplet.

"Oh, stop worrying so much! This is fun, you should try it."

"My dear, I'm seasick enough on the land."

"It could be worse," came Melora's voice from behind

him, startling him. Her elegant sylphlike frame was so lightweight, especially in her antigrav suit, that he hadn't heard her footfalls. "Just be glad the island isn't spinning like the young ones do. Now, that would be a fun ride. Just imagine the ground spinning you, twirling and twirling, the horizon rushing around you . . ." She was clearly enjoying his discomfiture, maybe even trying to make him revisit his last meal in reverse. She had a good chance of succeeding.

"Oh, Melora, don't be mean," Aili said.

"Why not? It's fun—you should try it."

Ra-Havreii rested his head on his knees and tried to distract himself with engineering. "Gyroscopic stabilization," he said.

Silence. "Uh-oh, I think I broke him," Melora said.

He ignored her. "I just figured out why the young floater colonies spin. It stabilizes them against turbulence. They resist being flipped over."

"Sorry, not quite," Melora said. "In their young, fully submerged phase, they can thrive just as well either way up. But you're on the right track."

He looked at her. "Please—enlighten me." He strove to keep the sarcasm out of his voice, for he was genuinely curious.

"The polyps have organs similar to statocysts—a type of balance organ found in many simple invertebrates. Those are sacs with a small amount of inert mass inside, surrounded by sensory hairs. When they move—"

"Its inertia presses it against the hairs on one side, letting the animal sense its direction of motion. Yes, yes."

She glared at him. "Well, the polyps have something

similar, but based on rotation. Instead of an inert mass, it's a fluid that presses against the side hairs from the centrifugal effect. It gives them a sense of direction and orientation."

"Then why, pray tell, do they stop spinning when they mature? Have you figured that out yet?"

"Sure. But you're the engineer, you tell me. Or are you too sick to think straight?"

Aili was looking back and forth between them. "Would you two like to be alone?"

But Ra-Havreii had taken the gauntlet, not wanting Melora to think he couldn't out-cogitate her on his worst day. "Well, obviously," he said, masking his embarrassment that he hadn't seen it right away, "it's the square-cube law. Only the surface shells contain live polyps, which propel the colony with their tendrils. The surface area, and therefore the number of polyps there are to spin it, rises as the square of its length. But the volume, and therefore the mass they need to propel, goes up as the cube of the length. So it becomes exponentially harder to spin as it grows."

Melora clapped slowly, sarcastically. "Very good, Doctor. So why does that lead to them rising to the surface once they mature—killing half the colony in the process?"

"Well . . ." He cleared his throat. "Naturally, they, umm . . . they need . . . something that they can only obtain *on* the surface. Nutrients to sustain their larger biomass?"

"The juveniles can float to the surface anytime they want, by extracting more oxygen into their flotation bladders. They just don't have to stay there, since they can expel it again. Why would they choose to throw away the lives of half the colony by staying on the surface permanently?"

"Especially," Aili put in, "when there's a risk that a swell could flip them over and kill the other half? Remember, they're more symmetrical when they're young." The mature ones kept growing deeper once they surfaced, naturally becoming asymmetrical since new ones were growing only on the underside. Over time, that lowered their center of mass and gave them greater stability. But Ra-Havreii realized, once Aili pointed it out, that the younger, more symmetrical polyps would be risking the entire colony when they first began their surface existence. What could be worth sacrificing half and risking all for?

"Maybe," he ventured, "by surfacing and allowing photosynthetic plants to grow on them, they gain access to a new source of nourishment?"

Melora tilted her head approvingly. "Good guess, but you're overlooking something. The polyps on top still die. The insectoids and animals that inhabit these islets do enough moving around between above and below that the live polyps underneath can collect additional nutrients from their bodies and waste, but the polyps aren't adapted to survive out of the water. Besides, it takes years, maybe decades for a surface ecosystem to develop enough to provide sufficient nourishment. So what does that leave?"

She was grinning at his inability to solve the riddle, and he racked his brain, desperate to take the wind from her sails. But he just couldn't see it. Maybe he was just too unwilling to get into the mindset that sacrifice could be acceptable. Yes, there were causes worth fighting for, but the ideal was to win the fight and come out alive. When lives were lost—like the engineers aboard *Luna* when his prototype engine failed catastrophically, like his predecessor Nidani Ledrah when his design had failed to protect her and *Titan*'s crew sufficiently from a Reman attack, like so many billions in the Federation when their technology had proven unequal to the Borg—it was a failure, a mistake, a result of inadequate tools or resources. Believing in no-win scenarios was an excuse to avoid admitting inadequacy. And only by admitting your own inadequacy—at least to yourself, no matter how much you denied it to others —could you strive harder to make sure such failures did not happen again.

But of course he was getting off the subject. A colony of floater polyps had no such profound concerns. But the one concern they did have was survival. The goal of life was to stay alive at all costs. If half had to die, there must have been some desperate need, something that would have killed them all otherwise.

"If they get too heavy to swim," he reasoned, "they would just float in place, or drift randomly. They . . . they would deplete the resources in their immediate area and be unable to travel elsewhere."

"Very good," Melora said, with less snideness this time. "But how does surfacing help them compensate for that?"

Somehow it had to bring them new food sources, but Melora had ruled out all his hypotheses along those lines. He sighed. "Why don't you just put me out of my misery and tell me already, woman?"

But it was Aili who responded. "Currents," she said, sounding like it was the most obvious thing in the galaxy. "Once they can't swim on their own, they need to rely on currents to take them to new nutrient sources—and the surface currents are stronger because of the wind."

Ra-Havreii supposed he shouldn't be embarrassed that someone who'd grown up on a pelagic planet would have more knowledge of the subject than he did. But he was nonetheless. It was so obvious. Except . . . it was *nature*. How could anyone expect him to know that? If anything, he told himself, he'd been quite brilliant to figure out as much as he had.

But try telling Melora that. The female was impossible to please lately. "Nice to see someone here's paying attention," she said with gross and deliberate unfairness. "We think they grow together into clusters so they can support more of an ecosystem, including taller trees, which let them catch more wind. As well as supplying more nutrients. Still, even with all that," she went on to Aili, essentially ignoring him now that she'd successfully proven him ignorant of one minor bit of trivia, "they still have trouble finding enough food once they get too big. So eventually the new-formed polyps grow into bubbles, or maybe buds is a better word. The buds break off and form new floaters, and eventually all that's left of the parent colony is a dead, hollow husk. Which, of course, has got its own little island ecosystem growing on top of it. And the whole cycle begins again."

"That's lovely," Aili said. "What an amazing planet. Thanks for convincing us to come here, Melora."

"My pleasure."

Another swell sent the island racing skyward, leaving Xin's stomach behind. He clung to the mossy growth on the ground beneath him until the ocean dropped him back down again. "Yes, thank you," he grumbled, clambering to his feet—*No, don't bother helping me, oh, that's right, you aren't*—and rubbing his sore back. "A veritable Endless

Sky you've brought us to. Now if you'll excuse me, I'm going back to camp to lie down." At least the camp had its own gravity plating and inertial damping field. There he could ride out the swells and feel as steady as he did aboard *Titan*—so long as he didn't open his eyes.

He had an agreeable nap, until he was awakened by Melora joining him in bed. They might not have been very fond of each other right now, but fortunately the lovely Elaysian understood that that was no reason to deny themselves the pleasures of the flesh. Indeed, their mutual annoyance with one another added a stimulating intensity to their physical passion. He rather hoped she wouldn't stop being angry at him anytime soon. At least it would make things interesting until she finally left him.

Because it was inevitable that she would leave him, wasn't it? They would have their fun and move on, just as always. Perhaps with somewhat more duration and intensity than most of his affairs, and to be cherished for that, but that was all.

But he found himself unexpectedly troubled by the prospect of its ending. So he stopped thinking of it and concentrated on the here and now, delivering a finely calibrated taunt on the subject of her pleasuring technique in order to goad the highly competitive Elaysian into proving him wrong. . . .

Three hours later, the away team's hydrophones in the deep sound channel picked up the contact signal agreed upon between Aili Lavena and the squales, coming from a location currently about thirty kilometers northeast of the main base. Aili wished the squales weren't so wary of approaching technology; she couldn't swim that distance in a reasonable time, so she would have to don the hydration suit and ride in the scouter gig again.

The captain seemed distracted when he arrived in the shuttle half an hour later. "Is everything all right, sir?" Melora asked him as he headed toward the waiting gig and its Selkie pilot. This time it would be only Aili and the captain, since Ra-Havreii was currently working with Y'lira Modan on a linguistic analysis of the sounds made by the squales' various helper species (on the theory that decoding a simpler form of the language might provide the foundation for a squale translation matrix) and Huilan had some kind of counseling emergency up on the ship. (Counselor Haaj wasn't qualified as a diplomatic officer; with his confrontational manner, that would be a good way to start a few wars.)

Riker filled them in on the asteroid detection. "It turns out to be on a collision course with Droplet after all, about seven hours away. I've ordered Commander Vale to intercept and deflect it onto a safe trajectory."

"Damn," Melora said. "Should we be preparing for an evacuation?"

"It's not that grave a risk. More an inconvenience. It'll take a fair amount of power, cutting it this close, but nothing the ship and crew can't handle."

"Sir," Ra-Havreii asked, "doesn't the Prime Directive say we shouldn't interfere in natural disasters?"

"Consider it a precaution to protect our own away teams. Besides, we're in a delicate enough Prime Directive situation already without an asteroid impact complicating things."

Aili could tell that Riker wasn't happy to have been called away from the bridge—or to be away from his wife and child—at a time like this. As they boarded the gig, she said, "Captain, I really want to thank you for agreeing to help with this. I know it must be rough to be away from your family right now."

He smiled. "It's quite all right, Aili. Counselor Troi and I both understand the demands of duty." Settling in, he started the gig's induction motor, which gave off only a quiet hum to signal its activation as the craft sped forward. Aili appreciated that; she'd read horror stories of how the crude propulsion systems of industrial-era Earth and other worlds had polluted their oceans with constant, deafening noise, making life unbearable for their denizens.

"Besides," Riker went on, "I'll get to see plenty of my little girl once she's born. After all, Deanna's the diplomatic officer—aside from these last few months, she spends more time off the ship than I do."

She smiled at him through her faceplate. "You seem excited about becoming a father."

He chuckled. "Excited is one way of putting it. To be honest, I—" He broke off. Though Will Riker was a gregarious captain, there always remained a dividing line between a captain and his crew. "Let's just say it'll be a new experience for me."

"Seems to me you've always been quick to embrace new experiences." After a second, she felt her crests flush hot inside the hydration suit's fins—that had come out with more innuendo than she'd intended. "Uh, sir."

If he caught the implied double entendre, the captain

gave no sign of it. "But you—how many children did you have again, Ensign?"

Her crests flushed deeper. "Uh, eight, sir. Three sons, five daughters."

"That many," he said, sounding impressed, though it was an average tally by Selkie standards. "After all that, you've got to have some real insights. Any pointers for the new guy on what to expect? What to watch out for?"

"I, um . . ." Aili wrung her webbed hands together, hating where this was going. Why did he have to remind her of this? Of course, it wasn't his fault; he couldn't know what a sensitive area this was for her, since she had pledged never to tell him. Twenty-two years ago, when she had seduced him in the private, sea-connected swimming pool of the Federation embassy, she had played the nervous innocent, not letting on that he was just one of many. Not letting on that she was a libertine by her people's standards, an irresponsible mother. The uninhibited sex lives of Selkies were the stuff of legend to young, libidinous starfarers; many of them didn't understand that it was only the final-phase, post-amphibious Selkies who had that freedom, that it was different for Selkies in their amphibious phase. That phase, their species' window of fertility, was only about two decades long, and Selkies were expected to raise large families. The amphibious phase was thus a time for selfless discipline and dedication to the young, with the free sensuality of their elders put on hold for the duration. Many amphibious Selkies longed for a respite from the discipline, a taste of the sexual liberty their elders enjoyed. Off-worlders, who generally didn't know better, were a favorite release valve, a chance to flout tradition and propriety without consequences. For some reason, the alien colonists who lived in Pacifica's resort towns, research bases, and the like—those who interacted enough with the Selkies to understand their culture—did not go out of their way to explain matters to offworld visitors; perhaps they felt it was the Selkies' place, or perhaps they were simply objective enough to see the occasional dalliance as a necessary release valve. Or maybe they just appreciated the heavy tourism that the Selkies' interstellar reputation brought to Pacifica.

Aili, though, had done it more than most—not just the odd, infrequent fling after several years of parenthood had left her aching for release, but hundreds of dalliances with alien males, females, and miscellanea, starting before her first child had even learned to walk on land. It hadn't been cheating in the human sense; Selkies didn't mate monogamously, and indeed rarely had more than two children with the same partner. And she didn't feel guilty about the sex itself; that was just a natural part of life to her, one she still indulged regularly. What she regretted was her negligence, indulging herself while she left her children in the care of her siblings and neighbors, making one excuse after another until she had realized that she no longer needed to pretend because everyone knew what she really was. Everyone except the offworlders who didn't understand or didn't care.

Will Riker would have cared, had he known. But to him, it had been a pleasant, harmless interlude, a brief encounter he remembered fondly. (Well, not that brief. He'd lasted most of the night, actually one of her longer affairs.) She couldn't confront him with the reality of what a sordid thing she'd involved him in. He would no doubt feel guilty, as though he'd taken advantage of her in some way. At least, it would spoil a memory that was wholesome and happy to him, and she needed at least one of them to feel that way about it.

But all she could remember now when she thought back on that night was that she'd been indulging herself while her two-year-old son was at Aili's eldest sister's home, crying and burning up from a *lekipanai* infection that kept the child up all night while his mother was off keeping Will Riker up all night. And now Will Riker was asking *her* for advice on how to be a good parent?

He was watching her expectantly, his expression so innocent, so open. What could she say to him? "There's nothing I— There's no magic formula. I don't know . . . I don't know what your daughter will be like, what challenges you'll face. Just . . . make sure you always try to do right by her. And . . . never take her for granted."

He smiled. "I never could."

Then he shook his head and chuckled. "It's hard to believe you have grown children who must be parents themselves now. It doesn't seem it's been that long since we—uh, met." He cleared his throat. "You must miss them a lot."

She stared out at the sea. "You can't imagine."

CHAPTER EIGHT

TITAN

"I've been getting complaints from the security staff, Tuvok," Deanna said, resting her hands atop her belly and striving to maintain her serenity despite the fact that her daughter seemed to be trying to kick her way out of the womb. "They don't understand why you're still conducting holodeck combat drills involving the Borg."

On the chair opposite her, Tuvok sat with his wonted erectness and cocked a brow. "I was not aware that tactical training procedures fell within your bailiwick, Counselor."

"I'm more interested in understanding why you continue to train them to fight the Borg. There are no more Borg."

"It is best to keep security personnel ready to face any threat. The Borg are the most formidable, adaptable threat Starfleet has ever faced, and thus are an excellent virtual opponent to train against."

"If you can beat them, you can beat anybody."

"Crudely put, but it approximates the principle." He took a breath. "Also . . . we have encountered groups of Borg severed from the Collective before. We do not know if all such groups were affected by the Caeliar transformation. We can never entirely rule out the possibility that some aspect of the Borg may achieve a resurgence in the future. Or that we may encounter another cyborg race developing along similar lines."

"But those are low-probability events, wouldn't you say?"

"A kilometer-scale asteroid impacting a planet a mere eleven days after our arrival there is also a very low-probability event, Counselor, even in a system as rich in asteroids as this. Yet *Titan* is currently responding to such an event. The improbable does occur."

"That's true." Deanna considered her words. "But if you want to prepare them for anything, doesn't that suggest using a wide range of different training exercises? Is there a reason you use the Borg simulation so often?"

Tuvok sighed. "You seek to elicit an admission that I am exacting a form of symbolic revenge against the Borg for the death of Elieth. I would point out, Counselor, that I am far from the only member of this crew to have lost family, friends, or colleagues to the Collective. I believe that the simulations can be cathartic for many members of my staff."

"Interesting," Deanna said—and the word was not merely the boilerplate "interesting" that therapists used to sound supportive. It genuinely was interesting that Tuvok had become comfortable enough with the idea of managing rather than repressing emotion that he would use it as a factor in his training decisions, and that he would be empathetic enough to want to offer his subordinates such a catharsis. Still . . . "That may well be. But many members of this crew suffered post-traumatic stress in the wake of the invasion. Your Borg simulations are giving some people nightmares."

She wanted to stand and walk around a bit to inject a pause in the conversation, gather her thoughts—hell, just to get the circulation back in her butt. But standing up would be such a time-consuming production that it would derail the conversation. "Tuvok, I've found that indulging anger doesn't really relieve it—more often, it simply feeds it. If you—your personnel can't be allowed to move past their rage toward the Borg, if they're made to channel and express it over and over again, it just delays their recovery."

He caught her in that no-nonsense gaze of his. "By which you implicitly mean my recovery as well."

"Yes. But both are worth considering."

For a time, the centenarian Vulcan pondered her words. "Perhaps I have . . . imposed my own needs too much on my personnel. I shall endeavor to refine my training to suit their needs better."

"I'm sure they'll appreciate it."

He gave her the look she'd come to recognize as amusement. "Obviously you have never trained under me."

But the moment was fleeting, and soon she felt the returning weight of his grief, his bitterness. "But what I choose to simulate in my own private training sessions . . . is my business, Counselor. Perhaps I am simply . . . not ready to let go yet."

Unconsciously, Deanna wrapped her arms around her belly. She could feel the gaping wound in his soul where his youngest son had been, so much like the one in her own where her daughter's unborn predecessor had lived for so tragically brief a time. She felt his frustration at his inability to protect his flesh and blood, and she understood it for reasons that had nothing to do with Betazoid senses. "Let go of what, Tuvok?" she asked. "Of futility? Of the desperate fantasy of going back and making it not happen? How do you hold on to Elieth's memory by continuing to take revenge against an enemy that no longer exists?"

"Elieth's last moments were spent defending against that enemy. His life was lost only because he chose to stay and defend others."

"To help them evacuate—not to fight the Borg himself."

"He defended in his way, as I do in mine. He gave away his life to confront the Borg. That is what I have left of him, Counselor."

"He . . . gave *away* his life? Why that choice of words?"

"Federation Standard is an imprecise language. There are many ways to convey the same concept. Is this relevant?"

"Everything's relevant in here, Tuvok."

"No. You simply try to make it so."

Hostility. Interesting. It was an almost refreshing change from the grief. "Another thing about anger, Tuvok . . . sometimes you can't let it go until you realize just who or what it is you're angry with. When it's displaced, it brings no satisfaction, no resolution."

He stared, brows furrowing. "With whom or what would I be angry if not the Borg?"

"Well, who else made a choice that contributed to Elieth's death?"

"The question is so broadly defined that there are countless possible answers. The admirals who failed to defend Deneva successfully. The Denevans who approved his employment there. Admiral Janeway for crippling the Borg's transwarp network and triggering their mass retaliation. Captain Picard for choosing not to use the Endgame program to destroy the Borg thirteen years ago. There are many other possible answers to your question."

Deanna shrugged. "We've still got half an hour. Let's consider some."

"Commander, we have a problem."

Christine Vale suppressed a wince at the fluting observation from Ensign Kuu'iut, the lanky Betelgeusian who stood beta-shift tactical. She always hated to hear those words. "Don't keep it to yourself, Ensign."

"Close-range scans show the asteroid to consist of considerably denser materials than expected. Possibly large deposits of rodinium, diburnium, indurite. Its mass is sixty-eight percent greater than previously estimated."

She sighed. "Making it sixty-eight percent harder to deflect. Or is it the square of that? I forget which."

"One-half the mass times the velocity squared," said Peya Fell, the Deltan woman at sciences. "Goes linearly with mass."

"That's something. Thanks, Ensign. Kuu'iut, can we still deflect it successfully?"

He shook his bald blue head, baring the sharp teeth in his lower eating mouth while responding through his beak-like speaking mouth. "Not by tractors alone. We'd burn out the emitters."

"And blowing it up would just leave a bunch of smaller rocks heading on the same course. Would that be any better for the planet?"

"Not much. Same amount of kinetic energy delivered, just a bit more diffusely. And given its density, the surviving chunks might still be sizeable. It might actually endanger life across an even wider area of the ocean."

Oh, great. "Options?"

The 'Geusian leaned forward eagerly. It would be just like a member of his highly competitive culture, Vale thought, to see this as an entertaining challenge to pit himself against. "We could use phasers and torpedoes to vaporize a portion of the asteroid, creating explosive thrust that would push it off course, supplementing the tractor beams. We'd have to use the beams in pressor mode, pushing in the same direction as the thrust reaction."

Vale nodded. "Do it." She had almost regretted insisting that Tuvok keep his counseling appointment with Deanna rather than supervising the deflection as he'd requested, but Kuu'iut seemed to have the matter well in hand.

In moments, the Betelgeusian had the target coordinates computed and coordinated with Ooteshk at the conn, who moved *Titan* into position, reversing thrust until the ship was keeping station with the asteroid. "If my gamble pays off," Kuu'iut said, "a phaser strike and two quantum torpedoes in that central fissure should blow off a fairly large chunk or two, providing some extra reaction mass. I'm boosting shields in case of blowback."

"We're not here to gamble, Ensign," Vale reminded him. "I want the surest thing you can give me."

"Aye, ma'am," the 'Geusian said, but he sounded like he was humoring her. "Engaging tractor beams in pressor mode." On-screen, a false-color overlay made the beams visible, a tight cone of lavender rays extending to make contact with the asteroid. Vale idly wondered why Starfleet imaging technicians generally chose blue or purple shades to represent gravitational phenomena.

"Deflection . . . point oh six arcseconds per minute," Ensign Fell reported after a moment. "Point oh eight," a few moments later.

"That's below projections," Kuu'iut said, "even accounting for its density."

"Beam status?" Vale asked.

"Full power is being delivered. But it's not having its full effect."

"Boost tractor power to compensate. How long can the emitters run at overload?"

Kuu'iut's clawed fingers danced across the console as he replied. "At this level, thirty-eight minutes. It should be sufficient."

"Deflection rate rising to . . . point one two," Fell reported in an incongruously seductive lilt.

"Still below projections."

"Internal temperature and radiation readings beginning to rise," the Deltan went on. "Something may be absorbing some of the beam energy, transforming it into radiant energy rather than kinetic."

"Something like?"

Fell tilted her smooth, elegantly contoured head. *Bald,* Vale thought in passing. *There's a look I haven't tried.* "Readings could be consistent with sarium or yurium."

Vale recognized them as elements that could store and channel energy. "Could that affect the use of phasers, Kuu'iut?"

"Not materially. As long as I boost the power as with the tractors."

She turned to Tasanee Panyarachun at the engineering console. "Have engineering stand by to deliver extra power, if needed."

"Aye, ma'am," the dainty Thai woman answered.

"Phasers and torpedoes ready," Kuu'iut said. "We're in the window, ma'am."

Vale gave a curt nod. "Fire."

A red beam lashed out, another enhanced image, though less so than the tractors. It struck the fissure perfectly, and a cloud of vaporized rock erupted around the impact site. Two bright torpedoes followed it a moment later, detonating inside the pit the phasers had carved. There was no sign of the chunk breaking off as Kuu'iut had predicted. "Temp and radiation spiking!" Fell called after a moment. "Some kind of internal surge —"

"Feedback pulse along the tractor beam!" Panyarachun cried.

Kuu'iut's corvine cry almost drowned her out: "Detonation! Brace for impact!"

Vale raced to the command chair to strap herself in as power surges ripped through the ship, jumping breakers, blowing circuits. The lights flickered and died, and the consoles danced with St. Elmo's fire, though luckily the new-generation wave guides woven into the material channeled the energies through the walls and away from the crew. But that was small comfort when *Titan* rocked under a chain of rapid-fire collisions, hitting so hard it felt like the whole asteroid had struck the ship. Vale was sent flying before she reached the chair.

"Tuvok!"

The lights were gone, only the emergency illumination remaining, but it was enough to let Deanna see that the Vulcan was sprawled motionless on the floor beneath the office table, his head coated in something dark and glistening. She couldn't see color, but she knew it was green. "Oh, God." She struck her combadge. "Medical emergency, Counselor Troi's office!" *Maybe emergencies*, she thought as she felt her insides heave and she vomited up her last meal onto the carpet. She couldn't tell through the inner turbulence if the baby was still kicking. "Sickbay, acknowledge!"

Nothing. "Computer!" She began dragging herself toward Tuvok. "Where are you, you stupid computer?" But that voice, the one that reminded her so maddeningly of her mother, remained silent. "Somebody!" she yelled. "We need help in here!"

Finally she reached Tuvok and began pulling him toward the door. Her muscles, overtaxed from months of service as a walking baby carriage, strained from the exertion. It felt like that wasn't all she was straining. "Dammit, Tuvok, wake up! Help me out here! I'll leave you here if I have to!"

Now her own voice was starting to remind her of her mother's, in attitude if not in timbre. *So be it,* she thought. *Lwaxana Troi's sheer cussedness got her through the occupation of Betazed in one piece. And kept her baby boy alive.* She'd never been more glad to be that woman's daughter.

Finally she reached the door, which shuddered halfway open—better than nothing. Forcing it the rest of the way, she channeled her mother's sheer vocal volume and began screaming for help.

"Report," Vale tried to say as the emergency lights kicked in, but her own emergency power hadn't fully engaged yet. She gathered herself and managed to get out something others could hear. "Somebody report!"

"Shields and main power . . . down," Panyarachun said between groans. "We're drifting."

"Casualties?"

"Internal communications are damaged," Dennisar reported from the security station. The hulking Orion hardly seemed shaken up at all. "Internal sensors unreliable. Most of us are alive, at least, but I can't pinpoint exact numbers."

"Commander!" Fell turned to catch Vale's eye. The left side of that gorgeous Deltan face had been badly bruised. "Intense radiation from the asteroid. With shields down . . ."

"Say no more. Evacuate the bridge. Dennisar, please tell me the alert system is working."

"Initiating radiation alert now," he called. The computer began intoning the alert, advising all personnel to evacuate the outer sections of the ship.

"Fell, get to sickbay. The rest of us will reconvene in engineering."

"I'm fine," the Deltan insisted as the crew began leaving through the emergency ladder. "I can manage the pain."

"Peya, you could have a concussion. And this ship doesn't lack for science officers. That's an order."

Fell lowered her head. "Aye, Commander."

By the time the bridge crew reassembled in engineering, with the Syrath astrophysicist Cethente filling in as science officer and with Ranul Keru taking over from Dennisar as security officer, internal power and communications had been restored. Weapons, propulsion, and shields were still down, though, as were inertial dampers—whose failure was why the debris from the asteroid had inflicted such a damaging blow. *"The good news,"* came Doctor Ree's reassuring growl from sickbay, *"is that we have no fatalities."* Vale was profoundly relieved. They'd lost too many to the Borg—she couldn't tolerate losing any of her crew to some hunk of rock. *"There have been a number of concussions and fractures, all under treatment. Commander Tuvok sustained both, and Counselor Troi suffered a herniation in pulling him to safety. Both should recover in a few hours. The baby suffered minor impact trauma, nothing serious. No radiation sickness reported yet; I'm sending Nurse Kershul around to administer hyronalin shots to key personnel, beginning with you."*

The crew took a moment to absorb the news. The chamber was disturbingly silent with the warp core down; the ship was operating on fusion power. "Can anyone tell me yet what happened?" Vale asked.

Cethente's wind-chime voice sounded underneath the vocoder-generated translation of its speech. *"Further analysis shows that the asteroid contained sizeable pockets of bilitrium and anicium in addition to yurium,"* the Syrath said. Its tentacles stretched out from under the wide dome of its saucerlike upper body, atop which an array of sensory bulges glowed a pale green as it studied the readings those tentacles brought up on the consoles. A radially symmetrical being whose body tapered below the dome into a fluted trunk with a diamond-shaped bulge on the underside and four arthropod legs extending from just above the bulge, Cethente was able to "face" its console and its crewmates simultaneously. *"All these substances can store large amounts of energy and channel them explosively. Bilitrium in particular is a rare energy amplifier; it cannot create energy, of course, but it can concentrate the energy of a reaction and release it in a tighter, more intense pulse."*

"So it took the energy of our weapons and tractors and threw it back in our faces."

"Those of you who have faces," Cethente replied. *"Actually I found the energy surge rather appetizing."*

Vale blinked, reflecting on how poorly Federation science understood Syrath anatomy. Cethente looked so fragile in construction that it seemed it should have been shattered by the impact, but the asexual astrophysicist was probably the most durable member of the crew, a semicrystalline life form evolved on a Venus-like world of hellish temperatures and pressures.

"Status of the asteroid?" Vale went on.

"Still on an impact trajectory with Droplet. The explo-

sion was not sufficiently directional to achieve the desired course change."

Nurse Kershul arrived, beginning to deliver the hyronalin shots to the crew. Vale thanked the Edosian after receiving her shot and asked, "So what are our options? Can we repair the tractors and weapons in time to try again?"

"Unlikely," said Mordecai Crandall, the thin-faced human ensign commanding engineering in Ra-Havreii's absence. "We've got, what, five and a half hours to impact? It will probably take most of that to get the warp core and shields back. Unless you want us to shift priorities."

Vale shook her head. "No, shields have to come first." The bulk of the ship could protect the crew against the radiation for only so long, and she needed to get them all back to their stations if they were to function at peak efficiency. "Other options, people?"

"The shuttles," Panyarachun said after a moment. "What if we jettisoned their warp cores and detonated them against the asteroid?"

"Negative," Cethente said. *"The bilitrium would amplify that even worse than the phasers and quantum torpedoes. It's particularly effective at concentrating and blue-shifting the gamma-ray energy of an antimatter reaction. No, thank you,"* it went on, apparently speaking to Kershul now, though it was hard to tell without a head it could turn. *"It would have no more effect on me than the radiation."*

"But Tasanee may be on to something with the shuttles," Keru said. "What if we use them to push on the asteroid? No energy beams to destabilize it further, just sheer brute force. Could their engines push it far enough to miss Droplet?"

"There's a problem there," Crandall said. "The energy surge fried the hangar bay's force field and power systems. We can't open the doors, and we'd lose a fair chunk of atmosphere if we did. And we'd need radiation suits to work in the hangar under these conditions—it would slow repairs."

"What about the captain's skiff?" Keru said. "Is the *La Rocca* in working order?"

Crandall checked a console. "Some system damage, mostly to sensors, com arrays, transporters. But it was powered down, so its main systems are still intact. It would need a few swapouts, but it could be ready to go in . . . two hours?"

"I want it sooner, Crandall. Top priority along with shields. That skiff may be all we've got." Vale sighed. "What about communications? Can we use the shuttles' systems to contact our teams at Droplet, let them know what's happened?"

"Not through this interference," Kuu'iut said.

"But they have a shuttle monitoring us optically from orbit," Cethente chimed. *"They should have observed the event by now, and should be able to determine fairly soon that the asteroid's course has not materially changed."*

"Will they be all right?" Panyarachun asked.

"Probably, as long as they stay far enough from the impact site," Vale said. "But I can't say the same for the squales. They may be in for major loss of life if we can't fix this."

Keru moved in closer and spoke softly. "Chris . . . technically the Prime Directive says not to interfere in natural disasters on pre-warp planets. And impacts like this probably happen on Droplet more often than on most worlds. We didn't cause this, and we may even have made it worse."

"Maybe, Ranul. But we've already disrupted their lives enough without meaning to. Besides, we're already committed. If we stop now, then hundreds, maybe thousands of squales could die because of our choice to stop. That's as bad as if we'd chucked the asteroid at them ourselves."

"I can accept that," Keru said. Then he leaned still closer. "Just between you, me, and the warp core, I think it's crazy to let people die because we're afraid of damaging their culture. I'm always happy to find a loophole around that part of the Directive."

"No comment," Vale said, though her smile belied it. "But there's more. Theory says our people should be safe so long as they keep their distance. But theory's only as good as the data plugged into it. We didn't know about that bilitrium and anicium. This system keeps throwing surprises at us." Her gaze turned outward. "Who knows what else we might have overlooked?"

DROPLET

Ensign Lavena had actually managed, after hours of cajoling, to persuade the senior members of the squale pod (for that seemed to be their basic social unit) to approach close enough to the scouter gig that they could meet Riker and converse with him directly, with Aili interpreting between English and Selkie. Normally Riker's combadge translator could do that; without a translation matrix for squale, it would default to the language of the next nearest individual, Lavena. But Aili had recommended against that, for the squales would be uneasy with a technological mediator. He had the gig's systems and all their equipment powered down or on standby.

Even so, the squales had approached only reluctantly, the chromatophores in their skin blushing a mottled blue, camouflaging themselves in an instinctive fear reaction. Aili had done a fine job reassuring them, but some deep-rooted anxiety remained. Riker tried to imagine how inanimate matter would seem to beings who had never encountered stone or metal. It was hard to understand why their reaction was so extreme. Even living things had inert components, such as the shells of the floater polyps and the local arthropods. He would have thought that at least a few of the squales might show enough curiosity to want a closer look, but Lavena couldn't coax them to come closer than a few meters. In the name of diplomacy, Riker finally stripped down to swim briefs and paddled out from the gig a short distance, trailing a length of line behind him so he wouldn't be separated from it by a powerful swell or other unexpected event. Even on a leash, it was not normally a wise idea to leave a boat untended; he would have preferred it if Huilan or Ra-Havreii could have been along too. But the gig was a catamaran design, able to remain afloat even if capsized. Plus, this was Lavena's element; if something untoward did occur, he trusted her to get him safely back to the gig.

Riker did his best to try to participate in the language lesson that followed. The squales needed to hear from him directly, at least enough to establish his authority, so he needed to use what Selkie he remembered, plus what Lavena helped him brush up on, to get his ideas across. But airborne Selkie was a different dialect than aquatic Selkie. "Umm, that's not the problem," Lavena said when it seemed he wasn't getting through. "The squales have a keen grasp of sound patterns and linguistic structure—the dialect difference doesn't bother them. And they can hear fine out of the water," she finished, seeming reluctant to say it.

"My accent's that bad, huh?"

Her crests flushed. "I don't know if accent is the word. More a matter of pitch and rhythm . . ."

He sighed. "I wish I had my trombone. I'm not much of a singer."

Once past the usual "We come in peace" material, Riker tried to get across the idea of *Titan*'s exploratory purpose and their intense curiosity about this world and the squales' remarkable technology. He had observed, both in first contacts and dating, that it usually helped break the ice to show interest in the other party and get them talking about themselves. And since the squales had been monitoring the away teams from afar with their living probes, Riker assumed they were an inquisitive people as well, despite their oddly inflexible fear of inanimate technology. He hoped to connect with their species through that common interest in discovery.

Besides which, he hadn't thrown the Prime Directive completely out the window. Getting the squales talking about themselves was a good way to avoid revealing too much about the galaxy beyond.

But at this stage, there was little that he or Lavena could ask coherently about the really intriguing questions: how the squales bred their living tools, how the planet's life got enough minerals to survive. They were only able to establish the basics. The squales lived in pods of flexible size and composition, not unlike Earth cetaceans. Some pods consisted of mothers and their young offspring, others of adolescents banding together under the tutelage of unrelated adult males. Although it was more complicated than that. For one thing, like many Dropletian chordates, the squales had four sexes, two that were roughly male (in that they only donated gametes) and two that were hermaphroditic, exchanging gametes with each other and both bearing and raising young. (Pazlar's people theorized this was a hedge against mutation; with four copies of each chromosome, defective genes would be overridden by the majority. Given the frequent infall of asteroids rich in heavy, potentially toxic elements, it was a valuable adaptation.) The squales seemed amused when Riker and Lavena explained that the two of them represented the whole range of biological sexes their respective species possessed. (He didn't tell them about the Andorians for fear of looking deficient in comparison.)

For another thing, the pods seemed to be organized around more than just age and sex. Riker got the impression that different pods specialized in different tasks or fields of study. Indeed, Lavena seemed to think that the pod interacting with them was actually an aggregate of two or three pods, given its size and the factionalism she occasionally sensed among them. At the very least, some of the older "males" seemed to take a more wary, defensive stance than the others, reminding Lavena of a security detail shepherding a team of science officers.

The squales lived all over Droplet, though primarily in

certain zones, presumably those where the most nutrients were concentrated by the currents. They had ways of cultivating food, mainly breeding livestock like the so-called flaming idiot fish, but also farming some sort of seaweed, or so Lavena interpreted it. They were actually able to create the stable economic surplus necessary for building a civilization, to have the resources and leisure for large-scale activities beyond survival. But how did that civilization manifest? They had no cities; where were their breeding farms, their schools, their galleries? Was it even meaningful to think in those terms when dealing with a civilization whose environment was perpetually fluid, in more than one sense of the word? What seemingly natural formations on, or below, the surface of Droplet were actually organized and managed in ways that *Titan*'s crew had not been able to discern?

Sadly, the conversation was interrupted when Riker's combadge activated and Melora Pazlar's voice sounded from the gig. The squales reacted badly, retreating several meters down. As Lavena followed to calm them, Riker swam back to the boat, clambered aboard, and hit the badge, which was still attached to his uniform. "Riker here."

"Captain, we . . . trying to reach you," came the staticky reply. *"Bad news."*

Once he'd been briefed, he swam down far enough to get Lavena's attention and signal her to come over. "What is it, sir?"

"Our observation shuttle reports that *Titan* failed to deflect the asteroid. There was an explosion of some sort, and we lost contact with the ship."

"Oh, no."

"They're picking up reflections from *Titan*—it's still in one piece. But judging from the way the ship's moving under the asteroid's gravity, it's nearly twice as massive as we thought, and it's still on course for Droplet, impact in under five hours. We have to assume the ship won't be able to prevent the impact. I've sent two of the shuttles to assist *Titan*, but we need to get back to base camp, batten everything down."

"Sir, we can't go now! We have to warn the squales! Tell them to evacuate the impact site!"

"I'd like to, Aili, but can you suggest how? We can only estimate the impact zone, and how do we even describe it without any fixed geography?"

"Please, sir, let me try. Can you get me a projection of the impact zone?"

"I'll ask Pazlar."

The impact zone would be some forty degrees east of the dawn terminator and a similar amount south of the equator. Riker suggested that Lavena describe it as the near edge of the equatorial storm belt in the region that would be halfway between sunrise and noon when the impact came in roughly a third of a local day. It was inexact, but she would urge them to evacuate as broad an area as possible.

Riker gave her a good hour to try before calling her back. "I fear we've lost their trust, sir," she said. "First we break our promise to avoid using technology, then I come back making dire warnings and telling them where they're forbidden to swim. The 'security' squales didn't react well. I think they interpreted it as a threat. They took charge of the conversation, took up intimidating postures, and questioned me pretty harshly. The 'science' squales raised some protests, but they were argued into silence. I think most of them are younger than the others. I just couldn't get through, sir."

"Ra-Havreii's proposed an alternative," he told her. "We drop a probe at the impact site, one that emits a loud, continuous klaxon—loud enough to be painful to any squale staying in the danger zone. It should force them to evacuate."

"That seems cruel, sir."

"I know, I don't like it. I was hoping it wouldn't be necessary, but we don't have time to try to get through to them now. Hopefully after it's over, they'll recognize that we acted to help them."

"At least let me go back down to tell them what we're going to do. Otherwise they'll take it as an attack."

And the security pod might just retaliate against two small bipeds out in a lonely boat in the middle of nowhere. "Try your best, Aili. But be careful. You should take a phaser —"

"No, sir," she said emphatically. "They'd never listen then."

"They won't even —" *Know what it is,* he had been about to say. But if the security pod was already on the defensive, she could bring a bicycle horn and they'd fear it was a weapon. "Just be careful. We need you more than anybody on this mission."

"Right, sir. No pressure." She vanished into the murk.

He gave her until the three-hour mark. When he ducked his head underwater, he could still distantly hear her voice, faint but distinctive against the counterpoint of squalesong, so he knew she was alive and well. But he couldn't call her back, and he couldn't wait for her any longer. He ordered Ra-Havreii to deploy the underwater klaxon.

With the speed of sound in seawater around a kilometer and a half per second, give or take, Riker estimated it would take under fifteen minutes for the sound to reach his location. Maybe sixteen minutes later, Aili shot to the surface. "Help me into the boat, quick!" He pulled her in, and she sank weakly onto the deck. Riker realized she was exhausted; she would have been out of breath if she still breathed. He began helping her into her hydration suit. "Never mind that, get the motor running. As soon as I heard the clamor of squale calls from the deep sound channel, I knew the beacon must've been deployed. . . . I lit out of there just before the security goons tried to grab me again. We've got moments, and I don't know if fear of tech will stop them this time."

Riker moved back to activate the engine, but then he looked around him. "I think it's too late, Aili. We're surrounded."

"And by two pods' worth. I think they called in another security team."

Luckily, the squales that ringed the gig seemed content with a blockade for the moment. "They're wary, sir, but I don't think they want to hurt us. They're just protecting themselves."

Lavena spent a futile half-hour singing to them in Selkie, trying to reason with them. Meanwhile, Riker contacted the *Gillespie* and requested backup, figuring a shuttlecraft would be sufficient to frighten the squales away. But before the shuttle arrived, Pazlar contacted him. *"The klaxon's gone down, sir. The squales sent some kind of large, armored creature to intercept and wreck it. They're returning to the area."*

Riker sighed. "Go back and try again. Stay as long as necessary to get the message across."

"But sir, what about you and Aili?"

"We should be able to ride out the shock waves safely at this distance. Those squales can't."

"Aye, sir. Gillespie *out."*

Lavena, floating in the water again, looked up at Riker. "I just hope they appreciate what we're doing for them when this is over."

"So do I, Aili."

"Well, maybe *Titan* will come through and deflect it after all."

Riker looked skyward. He could feel Deanna's presence through their empathic link, even at this distance, but she seemed distressed, maybe even hurt. He prayed their baby was all right. "Let's hope so."

CHAPTER NINE

TITAN

When the two shuttles from Droplet arrived at *Titan*, which was still coasting along with the asteroid, Vale immediately assigned them to help the captain's skiff in its attempt to thrust the asteroid off course. The big rock's trajectory was changing, but with aching slowness. The *La Rocca* was built for diplomatic functions and recreation, not for power, and the engines and shields of *Ellington II* and *Marsalis* had been rigged for aquashuttle mode. All told, it finally became evident that the asteroid's course could not be changed enough; at most, they had made its angle of entry shallower. That might ameliorate the impact to some degree, but not enough to spare the Dropletian lives down there.

So with less than an hour to go, Vale proposed a last-ditch plan. "We didn't want to blow it up for fear that might do more harm than good," she told the staff, back on the bridge now that the shielding was restored. "But we can't prevent the harm anyway, so maybe blowing it up is the only option we have left. We've seen how well those bilitrium deposits can amplify an explosion—maybe we should be using that to our advantage."

She proposed a variation of Panyarachun's earlier suggestion: instead of trying to detonate shuttle warp cores against the surface of the asteroid, they would position the antimatter canisters from two shuttles as close as possible to the largest and deepest bilitrium deposits they could reach. "With luck, it'll amplify the blast enough to turn that thing to rubble, and most of it will burn off in the atmosphere."

"The problem there," said Cethente, *"is that the intense radiation still emanating from the asteroid would render our sensors useless."*

"Not all of them," said Chief Bralik, who'd been called in to consult on the geology. "I can rig a good old-fashioned gravity sensor. It can find the parts that match the density of bilitrium. Just like everything else in this system, it's just a case of going back to the way they did it in the old days."

Vale nodded. "All right. Do it."

SHUTTLECRAFT *MARSALIS*

Within twenty minutes, Bralik had beamed over to the *Marsalis* with her gravity sensor. As soon as that had been accomplished, *Titan* began thrusting away on impulse, falling behind the asteroid, both to gain distance from the explosion and to decelerate for orbital insertion. Under

Bralik's supervision, Ensign Waen piloted the shuttle into the fissure blown by the previous explosion. The Ferengi cast her eyes about at the rock formations that glittered in the shuttle's spotlights. "A fortune in transuranics, and we're about to blow it up," she lamented.

"Plenty more where that came from," the Bolian pilot said, tilting her smooth blue head to glance at Bralik. "Literally." She furrowed her faintly striped brow. "Do you think this will protect the squales?"

"I think, young one, that sometimes you have to do *something* even when the odds are that it won't bring you any profit. Because then you can at least say you tried."

Waen did not look comforted. "Is that a Rule of Acquisition?"

"No, dear. It's a rule of getting by."

Bralik's console beeped, and she checked the readout. "Density readings consistent with a large bilitrium deposit at three forty-eight mark twenty," she announced. "A second deposit beyond the opposite wall, maybe sixty meters deep. Close enough." She tapped in a few calculations, sent the result to Waen. "Place the canisters at these coordinates."

"Got it, Chief."

A moment later, Bralik felt the shudder of canister ejection, then a low hum as the tractor beam engaged and moved the canister into position. "Careful!" she called as she noticed the beam spreading a bit beyond the canister. "We've seen what can happen when this rock drinks up tractor energies."

But before she even finished, an energy discharge arced between the walls of the fissure, conducted through the residual rock vapor from the earlier explosions. Some mineral deposit must have had a residual charge still stored, just on the threshold of eruption. The discharge triggered a new explosion, and debris pelted the shuttle. "Shields holding," Waen called. "Canister's still intact."

"Don't count your latinum yet, honey! Look!"

The walls were moving. The fissure was collapsing in around them.

TITAN

Vale watched in alarm through the viewscreen static as the asteroid began crumbling apart in slow motion, the fissure closing to trap the *Marsalis*. "Get them out of there!" she called, not caring how.

"No transporter lock," Kuu'iut called. "The radiation."

"Vale to *Ellington*. Can you tractor them out before the fissure finishes collapsing?"

"We're working on it," came Olivia Bolaji's voice. *"Waen's heading for the exit. We're trying to shore it up with our tractors."*

Vale watched tensely as the shuttle's beams strained to hold apart the massive chunks that were slowly crashing together. Energy discharges flashed inside the closing fissure, clouds of rock vapor bursting out and splashing over the shuttle's shields. Finally, the *Marsalis* scraped its way past the rock walls and out into space, nearly sideswiping its sister shuttle. "Both shuttles, back to the ship, now! Kuu'iut, what's happening?"

"The asteroid is breaking into three large pieces. They're still in contact, but no longer physically joined—just resting against each other. But they're shifting."

"As soon as the shuttles reach a safe distance, blow the antimatter."

"The canisters might not stay in range of the bilitrium."

"All the more reason not to hesitate!"

"Aye, ma'am. Shuttles are at minimum safe distance—detonating."

At least the detonator signal was strong enough to pierce the radiation; the explosion that erupted from inside the asteroid was satisfyingly brilliant and violent-looking through the static. The asteroid blew out into an expanding cloud of dust, and Vale gave a tentative sigh of relief.

But then Kuu'iut gave his somber report. "Not enough contact with the bilitrium. The explosion was unconcentrated, much of the energy lost to space." As the dust began to clear, Vale saw that the asteroid was still in only three very large chunks, huddled fairly close together though drifting slowly apart and tumbling separately.

"Any way to blow those into smaller pieces?"

"Weapons are still down—and we need what power and maneuvering we have just to make orbit. And the shuttles don't have the power." It clearly galled the competitive Betelgeusian to admit defeat, but that didn't stop him. "I'm sorry, Commander Vale. There's nothing more we can do."

———

SHUTTLECRAFT *GILLESPIE*

Melora Pazlar gazed at the sensor readings on the shuttle console in horror. Not only had *Titan* failed to prevent the impact, but . . . "Pazlar to Riker," she called. "The angle of impact has changed. The rock's not coming down where we put the klaxon!"

"Not that they were willing to evacuate the area anyway," Ra-Havreii said. The squales' big bruisers had destroyed their second klaxon as well. Pazlar wasn't surprised that trying to scare them out of a particular place had just made them more determined to stay there. It was downright humanoid of them.

"And it's worse, sir—the impact zone's a lot closer to you now. You've got to get out of there! Head west as fast as you can! We're coming to get you, but we may not get there in time."

"Make best speed, Commander. The squales aren't letting us go anywhere, and I'm reluctant to use force on them."

"Captain, you may have to. A stun beam won't kill them."

"I'll keep that in mind. Riker out."

Melora turned to Xin. "Is there anything else we can do?"

He sighed. "Not unless you have a containment field big enough to hold sixty billion cubic meters of water, a tractor beam strong enough to lift it all, and a transporter powerful enough to beam out any squales it contains before flying it into the asteroid's path to vaporize it before it hits the ocean. Oh, and a death wish."

"Sorry," she said without humor. "Fresh out."

"Good," Xin said. "Because spending the rest of my life with you was *not* on my agenda."

Melora glared, hurt and angry that he would hurl such a barb at a time like this. But then she turned back to her instruments, pushing it aside. Maybe he was petty enough to dwell on their personal issues when a disaster was going on, but she was going to focus on what was important.

Damn him.

Ra-Havreii was rather relieved that his suicidal plan had not been technically viable; that way he didn't have to feel guilty about not wanting to sacrifice his life for a few hundred dexterous calamari. To be sure, he appreciated the intricacies of their language and was impressed with their technical achievements, but it wasn't as if their civilization was about to be destroyed. Ra-Havreii had seen that happen multiple times in the past year and a half, had just recently had it nearly happen to his civilization; so however insensitive it may have seemed, he couldn't entirely build up as much horror about this as he saw on Melora's face.

What troubled him more, though, was the pain on her face at his unthinking words, the tears she blinked away as she forced herself back to work. He'd assumed she felt the same way he did, that she would take the comment in stride as playful banter. Or had he? Either way, he was sorry if he'd caused her genuine pain, but in the long run it was for the best that she cast aside any fantasies of commitment. His words had been inappropriate, but only in the sense that they both had far more important things to concentrate on.

It was an awesome spectacle when the asteroid chunks finally drilled into Droplet's atmosphere some ten minutes later. Melora had taken the shuttle up into the tenuous outer fringes of atmosphere to avoid the effects of impact, planning to dive back down to retrieve Riker and Lavena. Ra-Havreii's eyes were glued to the aft sensor display as the first chunk cut a fiery swath through the atmosphere at startling speed and then became a blinding fireball at the bottom of its dive. When the light faded, an enormous cloud of pulverized and vaporized rock and water was expanding into the air, with one long pillar of dust streaming out beyond it, sucked up into the tunnel of vacuum the asteroid had carved into the atmosphere. Spectacularly, the second chunk came in just behind it, colliding with the outcoming chimney of dust and splashing it outward. A string of brilliant flashes strobed through the dispersed pillar, a mix of lightning within the dust and explosions as the force of the impact vaporized parts of the asteroid and detonated its heavy elements. The third, smallest chunk came in close on their heels, vanishing from view before the light of the second impact, and then creating its own smaller blast of light seconds later. Then there were only the turbulent clouds of dust and vapor spreading through the atmosphere at multiple levels, billowing out from the disrupted vacuum chimneys.

It would have been beautiful, Ra-Havreii thought, if he hadn't been in that exact spot less than half an hour earlier. As always when he had a close brush with death, he found himself dwelling on what might have happened, his keen mind letting him imagine it all in vivid, clinical detail. It would have been quick this time, perhaps taking him before he even realized it. His whole brilliant life cut off in its prime, with so many problems unsolved, so many ambitions unrealized, so many regrets . . .

"Melora?"

"Mmm?"

"I love you."

It was a moment before he realized she was staring at him, which in turn led him to realize what he'd just said. Had that really come out of his mouth?

"I love you too," she said, and that confirmed it.

Their hands clasped, and they turned back to monitoring the impact.

DROPLET

The squales remained deaf to Lavena's desperate pleas until the horizon lit up with a series of bright flashes. "Now do you believe us?" Riker called. Not waiting for the unlikely event of an answer, he decided to take advantage of their confusion, bringing the gig's motor to full power and running the distracted blockade as soon as she was back in the boat. He had to swerve between two squales' tentacles, but the creatures were taken by surprise and made only a token effort to snatch at the boat.

"Can we get far enough in time?" Lavena called over the rush of the waves as she pulled her hydration suit back on.

"No way of knowing. But if we're too close now," he admitted, "that's not likely to change. I'm basically trying to gain enough speed to ride the wave." He threw her a glance, noting her unease. "Wish you could just dive down and swim away?"

"With that shock wave hitting me? I'm safer in the air."

"Don't be so sure. There's going to be a hell of a hot wind blowing our way—and that's after the atmospheric shock wave hits. Try to cover your ears."

Lavena looked worried. "Captain . . . if storm winds can kick up heavy waves . . . then what . . ."

"Say no more," he said, pushing the engine to its limits. *So much for riding the tsunami.*

The airborne shock wave came first, thunder pounding into them with the force of a phaser barrage. He almost lost control of the boat. He wasn't even sure when the noise passed, for the ringing in his ears was nearly as deafening (not literally, he prayed, though that was the least of his worries). Within a few minutes, he felt the first surge of hot wind from behind. "Here it comes!" he cried, barely hearing himself. He looked back and saw a turbulent wave racing toward them, spanning nearly half the horizon and looming higher and higher as it drew near. And it would just be the first. "Brace yourself!" he cried. He hoped that at the right time he'd be able to angle the boat sideways, to ride along the swell lengthwise like a surfer.

But he didn't have a chance. Darkness loomed over the boat, darkness that hauled back and kicked the whole gig into the air, and the next thing he knew, he was in the water, turbulence spinning him, disorienting him. The roaring noise tore into his head, pummeled his body like fists. A cloud of red billowed out from over his eyes. Trying to right himself, he saw the gig well out of reach and being carried farther along the front of the swell. But it was inverted, empty. A moment later he thought he saw Aili's form flailing in the water, unwieldy in its hydration suit. He thought her hands were clamped to her ears, but he couldn't be sure. He couldn't hold on to any perception, any thought, for more than an instant before the roaring washed it away. He couldn't hold on to . . .

Breath . . .

Knocked from his lungs on impact . . . He tried to stop his body from gasping for air, but it was already too late . . . water choked him . . . choked his thoughts . . .

Imzadi!

TITAN

"Will!"

Deanna jerked awake, knowing she was in sickbay, but she was somewhere else too. In the water, drowning . . .

"Counselor, what is it?" Tuvok was in the next bed, looking at her sharply. He understood the bond she had with her husband, knew her cry was no nightmare.

"Will's in danger, on the planet. We have to . . ."

Ree had arrived, his fearsome hands closing gently on her shoulders as she tried to rise. "Easy, Counselor. I advise against undue strains."

"Will's in danger," she repeated. "Tell the bridge."

The ship shuddered, and Deanna's heart raced, still on edge from the explosions before. "I fear we are in some danger as well," the doctor said. "Our maneuvering ability is limited, and we are currently in the outer atmosphere and attempting to remedy the situation."

"But Will . . ." His voice was gone, an echoing void remaining.

She felt a surge of terror, of grief, of despair. She knew it wasn't fully hers—a pang went through Tuvok at her words, touching a deeper well of empathy than he would ever admit to—but she couldn't help it, couldn't focus her perceptions to discern between loss of consciousness and loss of everything. She could only feel dread certainty that Will was dead, as her child was dead . . . *my last child* . . . no, her first, the baby was still in her and silently wailing in resonance with her emotions . . . not born yet and already she knew grief . . . *Imzadi!*

"This is no place for an unborn child," Ree growled, bringing her awareness outside herself again. The doctor was agitated, his breath rasping, his yellow eyes darting ceilingward as the ship continued to shudder. "This is insane, letting infants face perils such as these! We have to do something."

Contrary to his earlier actions, he began helping Deanna to her feet, cradling her against his large, strong saurian frame. "Come with me, please, Counselor. We must get your child to safety."

She let him lead her, her mind and spirit numb, until she realized Tuvok was blocking the exit. "Doctor Ree. Where are you taking her?"

"Away from this ship of death! Away from this vile system!"

"Doctor, you are behaving irrationally. I suggest you release her."

"So you can keep her here? Keep her child in danger? Stand aside!" Matching actions to words, Ree flung the Vulcan into the wall as though he were a toy.

Nurse Ogawa rushed over to Tuvok, checking him, crying, "Ree, please, stop this! What are you doing?"

"Do not interfere, Alyssa! Nothing is as important as protecting this baby. *Nothing*." The last was a predatory snarl, and Ogawa quailed in fear of her friend.

But when Ree dragged Deanna out into the corridor, draping her over his back as he launched into a run, she heard dainty footsteps following after and Alyssa's breathless voice calling, "Ogawa to bridge! Send security . . ."

Tuvok had just been dazed, and Doctor Onnta was on hand, so Alyssa Ogawa had grabbed a medkit and headed after Ree and Counselor Troi at the best speed she could manage. Perhaps there was a personal bias involved; Troi had been a colleague of hers on the *Enterprise* for years, a bond that wasn't easily broken, and Ree had been a good friend and trusted senior officer for over a year and a half. But there was obviously something wrong with the Pahkwa-thanh CMO that might threaten Troi and her baby. Personal or not, Alyssa saw her choice as a simple matter of triage.

After calling security, she quickly lost sight and sound of Ree. But from his rantings, it was clear he would be trying to leave the ship, even the whole system. That meant he was heading for the shuttlebay.

No security fields sprang up to stop Ree along the way; that system must still be down, like so many others. Ogawa caught up to him only because he was delayed by a security team. The team was headed up by Lieutenant Feren Denken, a large Matalinian male whose right arm was a biosynthetic replacement for the original lost during *Titan*'s

first mission. His religious beliefs had forbidden the use
of prosthetic limbs, threatening to end his security career;
but Counselor Troi had persuaded him to consider the possibility that *Titan*'s multiculturalism could go both ways,
and that maybe there was room in his beliefs for interpretation. Captain Riker had helped by getting an old friend
of his, then-Captain Klag of the *I.K.S. Gorkon*, to put in a
good word. Klag had also lost an arm in combat and had
been persuaded to accept an allograft from his deceased
father, in defiance of any number of Klingon beliefs and
traditions. His example had persuaded Denken to study his
scriptures and realize that his reading of them had been too
self-directed; he could better defend the integrity of the living by restoring his full capability to preserve numerous
other lives.

But even with two good arms—the new one perhaps
better than the old—Denken was no match for a determined Pahkwa-thanh, even one weighed down by a pregnant, struggling Betazoid. Ree's heavy, rigid tail swung
around and smashed Denken into the corridor wall, and
Ogawa winced at the sound of a probable rib fracture. "I
suggest you have that seen to promptly," Ree told him.

Taking advantage of the distraction, Balim Cel, a pur-
ple-haired Catullan woman, leapt onto Ree's back and attempted a Catullan neck pinch—actually more a sort of
temporary psionic shock induced by touching the thumbs
to the base of the skull. But it didn't work on Pahkwa-
thanh, or maybe Cel just had the anatomy wrong, since
she went flying too, skidding to a stop before Ogawa's feet.
"Please, stay out of my way!" Ree growled. "You threaten
the child!"

"I threaten *you*, Doctor!" It was Pava sh'Aqabaa, whose phaser was drawn. "Now put the commander down so I can shoot you, throw your fat tail in the brig, and talk this out reasonably."

"No need to be *rude!*" the doctor snarled, knocking the phaser aside faster than Ogawa could see and striking Pava down with a sweep of his large, elongated muzzle. "Apologies, but I cannot spare the time!" he called back as he resumed his flight down the corridor. "Alyssa, see to them, will you?"

"We're fine!" Denken gasped. "Go after them! Do . . . something."

Alyssa hit her combadge. "Ogawa to transporter room. Beam the security team at this location directly to sickbay." She looked them over briefly before resuming the chase. *Sorry, but I have two other patients to take care of. Maybe three.*

But there was one thing she had to take care of first. Tapping her combadge as she ran, she called, "Ogawa to Noah Powell."

"Noah here," came the reply after a moment. *"Mom, are you all right?"*

"I'm fine, honey. I wanted to make sure you were okay."

"I'm not hurt, Mom. We're with T'Pel—Totyarguil and me. He was crying, but she calmed him down. She's good at that."

"That's good."

"Mom? You sound like you're running."

"I'm . . . pretty busy right now, Noah."

"I understand. You probably have people to take care of. You should go do that."

Her eyes stung. "I appreciate it, sweetheart. You keep yourself safe, okay? I love you."

"You too, Mom. See you later."

"I promise, honey. Ogawa out."

She wanted to say more, but there was no time. Ree had led her to the shuttlebay, and she caught up with him at the entrance of the *Horne*: *Titan*'s new *Flyer*-class heavy shuttle, a midsized craft based on the *Delta Flyer* design created by the crew of *Voyager*. Ree confronted her at the hatch, apparently having already strapped Deanna in. "Stay out of this, Alyssa! I will do whatever I must to protect this child."

Despite Ree's fearsome dinosaur-like aspect and predatory habits, Alyssa had never once been afraid of him—until now. For the first time, she looked into his eyes and knew that he could kill her without hesitation.

But she had patients—she couldn't hesitate either. She met his gaze evenly and held up her medkit. "If you're going to deliver her safely, you need a nurse," she said in a voice remarkably free of tremolo.

Holding her gaze for a moment, he then stepped back and let her in. Her thoughts were of Noah as she entered; she hated herself for leaving him. But he was in good hands, and he was wise beyond his years. He would understand.

If I come back, she answered herself. *If I don't . . . if he has to go through that again . . .* She forced the thought down. *Well, I'll just have to make sure I come back.*

She saw that Ree had torn out the pilot's seat to make room for his large, nonhumanoid frame. "Make sure she is secured in the aft compartment," he said as she entered. "Our departure is likely to be turbulent."

"Can you prevent the launch?" Vale demanded.

Keru's heavy fingers worked his console. "The systems are still too damaged, but I may not have to. The door mechanisms are still . . ." He broke off as a faint shudder went through the deck.

"Report!" Vale snapped.

"That was the shuttlebay depressurizing. He shot his way out. He's clear."

Vale knew that *Titan* would be in no condition to go to warp for days. "Send the shuttles after it."

"The *Horne*'s the fastest shuttle we have," Keru said. An indicator on his console bleeped, and he looked down at it and sighed. "And it's just gone to warp."

At times like this, Christine Vale hated Will Riker for fast-tracking her into a first officer's post. It was so much easier when she was just a lieutenant waiting for Riker and Captain Picard to make the decisions and tell her what to do. They made it look so easy.

But now, half her ship's systems were failing, its orbit was unstable, the ship's CMO had just abducted the captain's wife and unborn child, and the captain himself was missing in a planet-sized ocean with no safe harbors. Which absolutely urgent crisis took priority over the others?

No—Vale knew that wasn't the problem. The priorities were actually quite clear. Living with them would be the hard part.

"We must go after them." It was Tuvok, just back to the bridge from sickbay and still looking rather shaky. She doubted Onnta had released him voluntarily, but only Ree had ever been able to keep him in sickbay when he was determined to leave. Obviously not an option now. "Ree must stop somewhere, sooner or later. He is seeking a safe haven in which to deliver the child. He cannot do that while piloting a shuttle at high warp. Once he stops, we can catch him."

In fact, Tuvok's sentences were not delivered in a single block like that, but interpolated between Vale's rapid-fire orders to the engineering and repair crews, squeezed in when she paused for breath. Sure, every instinct in her body, as a woman and former cop, was screaming at her, *Save that baby at all costs!* But she had three hundred and fifty other lives depending on her right now, including two other children, one not even old enough to walk. And those three hundred and fifty lives needed their captain.

"We need the shuttles to search for Riker and Lavena," she told him when she could spare a moment. *Titan*'s sensors would be useless even if they weren't damaged; the impact had sent a shroud of dust and vaporized ocean spreading over the planet, and the minerals in the dust still blocked sensors as well as they ever had, an effect made even worse by the intense static charges in the cloud. And the haze made optical imaging from orbit useless as well.

"What about the captain's skiff?" Tuvok pressed.

"Its drive and shields were overtaxed in the deflection effort. It couldn't handle warp, and could never go fast enough if it could."

"It does not need to. Assign it to the search for the captain and let me take a shuttle after Troi and Ree."

She realized he was right; the *La Rocca*'s engines

would not be unduly taxed by a planetary search-and-rescue effort, and what shields it had left could handle wind and residual radiation better than high-velocity space debris. "I'll send a team in the *Armstrong*," she said. "But not you. Get back to sickbay."

"I am fine. Merely dazed."

"No offense, Tuvok, but after all that's been done to your head in your career, I'm not willing to take chances after you got it slammed into a wall."

He moved closer, lowering his voice. "Commander, I need to go."

"Look, I understand that you of all people need to protect that child right now —"

"It is more than that." She was startled that he didn't deny his emotional stake in this. But then, he was in no more mood to waste time than she was. "From what I . . . perceived, I believe Ree's irrational behavior was somehow triggered by Commander Troi's extreme fear of losing her child, coupled with her perception of the danger to her spouse. And . . ." He looked away for a moment. "She was counseling me just before this. I believe her fears were amplified by my own . . . experience of loss. I am partly responsible for what has occurred. I must take responsibility for resolving it."

"Tuvok —"

"*Please*, Commander."

She had reservations about his objectivity, but she had no time to argue. Besides, maybe a Vulcan who admitted his own emotions to himself and spent every moment working to manage them would be more objective about them than most Vulcans, or humans, for that matter. At least, she was satisfied to pretend for now that that made sense.

She nodded. "Go. Bring them back safe." She caught his arm, halted him as he started to depart. "Including Ree—if you can."

His eyes showed nothing but determination. "If circumstances permit."

Chapter Ten

"It's been thirty-six hours," Keru told the others in the observation lounge, fighting the weariness in his voice. "All available shuttles have searched the area as thoroughly as possible, above and below the surface. All we found is the capsized, empty skiff." He took a slow breath. "We've dropped hydrophone probes, sending out hailing signals to catch Lavena's attention or hear her calls if she's down there trying to reach us. But the ocean's still too disrupted from the impact to have a stable deep sound channel. Even so, the squales don't appreciate the noise pollution—they've been knocking out the hydrophones."

"What about . . . what about the squales?" asked Kuu'iut, filling in as tactical officer in Tuvok's absence. "We know they've interceded when our people were in trouble before. Could they have taken them somewhere?"

So many absences, thought Vale. It was odd looking around the table and seeing Kuu'iut sitting there for tactical, Huilan filling in as diplomatic officer, Onnta representing medical . . . *and me. I shouldn't be in the big chair. Not this way.*

"Where?" Pazlar countered. In contrast to the past few months, she and Ra-Havreii were sitting as far apart as possible and hadn't even looked at each other since entering. Even they weren't the same anymore. "We've imaged every floater and seaweed island within a thousand kilometers of the skiff's location," the Elaysian went on. "The squales couldn't have taken them that far in that amount of time. And they would've had problems of their own after that impact."

"And that's something we have to face," Vale said. She understood the crew's desire to see a miracle happen; it wouldn't be the first time such a thing had occurred. She shared their hope, their refusal to give up on the captain and Lavena. But as acting commander of *Titan*, she couldn't let her crew dwell on scenarios they could do nothing about. "We've done all we could to find our people . . . and we'll keep looking for as long as we can." It wouldn't be easy, with the shroud of dust and haze still blinding orbital scans. The thorough survey Pazlar had mentioned had been achieved only through the efforts and exhaustion of many shuttle pilots, determined to find one of their own and their captain as well. "But we're not the only ones hurting. We couldn't prevent the impact, but maybe there's something we can do to mitigate its damage."

"It's possible we already did, just slightly," Pazlar said, her voice subdued. "Normally in an impact event, the vacuum chimney effect sucks a great deal of the dust into the stratosphere, where it can linger for months, blocking the

sun and cooling the planet. But because we broke the asteroid into pieces, the successive impacts disrupted the chimney effect, and so the majority of the dust was splashed out
into the lower atmosphere, and it's already precipitating
out. The sky should clear within weeks."

"But what about all those heavy radioisotopes suddenly
injected into the biosphere?" Onnta asked. "We could be
seeing mass die-offs as a result."

Chamish, the ecologist, answered the Balosneean
doctor. "Actually that does not seem to be a concern.
Keep in mind that impacts of this type are relatively
common on Droplet. The biota have evolved sophisticated methods of DNA repair that protect them against
radiation damage and heavy-metal poisoning, at least in
limited amounts."

"And this stuff is dense," Pazlar said, "so it's sinking
pretty quickly—or rather, the water that it dissolves into is
sinking quickly. If there's any cause for concern, it's that all
that surface water suddenly sinking might disrupt circulation patterns, drag nutrients out of reach of the life that
needs them."

"But presumably the biosphere has adaptations to that
as well," Chamish said.

"Maybe. In any case, the stuff that's radioactive—or
still charged with residual energy from our weapons and
tractors—is sinking pretty quickly out of the inhabited levels of the ocean. It should settle down all the way to the ice-
seven mantle, or at least the hypersaline layer just above it.
It shouldn't be a lasting problem for the biosphere."

"Can we assume that?" Vale asked. "The whole reason
this planet is a mystery is that metals somehow remain in

the biosphere even though they should sink out of it like you say."

"But most of them do—hence the hypersaline layer."

"But is it enough? We shouldn't assume anything. We need to continue to observe the situation on Droplet."

"With respect, Commander," asked Kuu'iut, "shouldn't our priority be to pursue Doctor Ree and Counselor Troi?"

"In what, Ensign?" Ra-Havreii asked. "I can't repair the engines any faster just because it would be convenient."

"Tuvok's team has that matter in hand," Vale said. "Until we can get *Titan* up and running, our job is to stay here and monitor the situation on Droplet. And . . . to continue the mission of exploration that Captain Riker set for us. That Aili Lavena threw herself into with her whole being—literally. That's what we owe them. To keep looking for them . . . but also to keep looking at Droplet on their behalf.

"Because that's what we do. We explore. Sometimes it seems pointless, trivial. But let's remember, people, it was our pure exploration that found the Caeliar and saved the whole damn Alpha Quadrant. And . . . and Beta. You guys from Beta know what I mean." She cleared her throat. As a motivational speaker, she needed practice. She would've rather left it to Riker. "So let's get out there . . . and get the job done."

SOMEWHERE ON DROPLET

A sensation of warmth is the first thing to impinge upon his consciousness. Warmth, and a gentle pulsing sound . . . or is it a feeling? Is it from without or within?

Where is without? He tries to open his eyes but fails. Or is it that his eyes are open but there is no light?

He seems to be totally immersed in fluid. A part of him feels alarmed, tries to struggle, but his muscles do not obey. Besides, he has no trouble breathing. Indeed, to some deeper part of him this feels perfectly natural.

How did he get here? What came before? Noisy, turbulent memories clamor distantly, impinge on what little awareness he has, flash at him uncomfortably before dispersing back into the miasma of his mind. He barely thinks. All he knows is that he inhabits a warm, dark, pulsing place immersed in life-giving fluid.

Now why does that feel so familiar?

And why does it remind him of the cry echoing in his mind?

TITAN

"Hey! You know we don't like malingerers on this ship."

Eviku opened his eyes to see Doctor Bralik standing alongside his sickbay bed, wearing a crooked-toothed smile to offset her teasing words. "So you better get out of that bed and get back to work soon," she went on.

"Doctor Onnta says I still need another day of rest," he said.

"Aww, rest is no way to get better! Rule of Acquisition Number Sixty-three: 'Work is the best therapy—at least for your employees.'"

"Bralik, please . . . if you are trying to amuse me, I am not in the mood."

"I'm trying to get you back on your feet and doing science. Nothing to cheer you up like solving a problem." The Ferengi gave a sad smirk. "Well, most of the time. I just got my biggest problem solved, but it's hard to be happy about it, because it was the asteroid that solved it for me. Rule One Sixty-two: 'Even in the worst of times, someone turns a profit.'"

Eviku raised his head, curious despite his mood. "What do you mean?"

"Why this system has so many asteroids and so few large planets for its metallicity. It's all those explosive elements—bilitrium, anicium, voltairium, yurium. They can absorb energy from the accretion process, or from sunlight, until it triggers explosions that blow apart the accreting masses. So you end up with a reduced rate of accretion overall, giving you smaller planets and more leftover debris. Simple as that."

"I see," Eviku replied. "Well, I'm glad you solved that."

"That's it?" Bralik asked after a moment. "Don't deafen me with your cries of enthusiasm."

"What do you want from me?" he asked, with more weariness than heat. "I said I was glad."

"Ev, you haven't been glad about anything for months. What's been going on with you?"

He stared at her. "After what happened months ago, can you really ask that?"

"I know, I know. We all suffered in the invasion. But the rest of us have faced it, talked it out, worked through it. We're moving on. But you just keep it bottled up, whatever it is. Don't you think you'd feel better if you told somebody about it?" She gestured at her largish ears. "Ferengi are famous for being good listeners, you know."

"It is . . . a gracious offer, Bralik. But I really would rather not talk about it."

Setting her jaw, she loomed over him. "I could quote a whole passel of Rules of Acquisition at you about why you'd be better off letting it out. The only way to prevent that is to tell me."

He almost laughed in spite of himself. But it wasn't his laughter he was worried about. "I haven't told anyone because . . . it's embarrassing. It seems so petty."

"Ev, you're obviously grieving for somebody. That can't be petty."

"But I didn't lose a mate or a son or a mother or . . . anyone like that."

"I'm listening," she said, crossing her arms.

He sighed. "It was . . . Germu. My *wadji*."

"What's a *wadji*?"

"My . . . pet. A small furred mammal native to Arken. She had such beautiful fur, so many colors . . ." He was silent for a moment. "I left her with my brother on Alrond when I went on this mission. I hated to be without her . . . we were so close. *Wadji* are a self-sufficient breed, often aloof, but she was so affectionate when the mood struck her. I felt honored that she would bless me with that. But *wadji* cannot stand being cooped up in small spaces, so I had to leave her behind."

"What happened? I assume your brother survived . . ."

Eviku nodded. "When the Borg attacked Alrond and the evacuation was called, Germu . . . escaped in the turmoil. My brother lost his grip in the push of the crowd, and she fled for some safe hiding place, no doubt—she never did well with strangers. I don't blame my brother—he almost missed the evacuation shuttle searching for her. He did everything he could." He lowered his head. "The whole planet . . . its entire surface was rendered lifeless. Germu . . . Oh, she was so beautiful."

A moment later, he felt Bralik's hand on his shoulder. "It's nothing to be ashamed of, Ev. You loved her."

"But so many others are mourning families, cities, whole worlds that were lost. To tell them I am mourning for a pet and claim my grief is comparable with theirs . . . it seems arrogant."

"Hey. It doesn't matter what they think. It doesn't even matter if they disapprove. She was a part of your family, as much as anyone. Just because she couldn't talk or count latinum doesn't mean your pain is any less meaningful. Don't be ashamed that you loved her."

Eviku couldn't hold the tears back any longer. They poured out of him for a time he couldn't measure. When it was over, he didn't feel particularly healed or cleansed, but there was a sense of release, as though a sealed door had finally broken open, letting in fresh air.

"Thank you, Bralik," he finally said. "You're very understanding."

"Hey. I grew up on a world where females were treated as little more than pets. So I guess I have a soft spot for underappreciated creatures. It's nice that you loved her so much." Her hand rested atop his. "I bet you gave her a very happy life."

"I tried to." He was quiet for a time. "But I will never get past the fact that she died alone."

"Hey—like you said, she was self-reliant. She made her own choice. Maybe it didn't turn out well, but she owned her own life at the end. I admire that." She sat on the side of his bed, still clasping his hand. "I bet I would've liked the gal. Why don't you tell me about her?"

So he began to speak of Germu and her antics, and soon he was laughing even as he wept.

HEAVY SHUTTLECRAFT *HORNE*

Doctor Ree had locked Deanna and Nurse Ogawa in the *Horne*'s aft compartment, nominally for their safety, and had only come back intermittently over the past two days to check on the health of mother and child before returning forward. It had given the two women little chance to reason with Ree, but plenty of time to talk and figure things out. "We understand why you're doing this," Deanna told the doctor as soon as he entered for one of his periodic checkups.

"Try not to talk," he advised. "You need to conserve your energy."

"Doctor," Alyssa said, "lying around like a lump and losing muscle tone won't make delivery any easier for her. You know that."

"She is also recovering from an injury. Remember who is the doctor here."

"You're not thinking like a doctor right now, Ree," Deanna said. "You're thinking like a Pahkwa-thanh male. In your species, the males do the main work of guarding the eggs, isn't that right?"

"That is our privilege," he conceded. "Which is why you should trust that I have your baby's best interests in mind when I advise you to be quiet and rest." There was an edge in his voice as he spoke.

Deanna swallowed, but kept on despite her visceral fear. "There are those fierce protective instincts of a Pah-kwa-thanh male. You're in guardian mode, Ree."

"That is unlikely, Counselor. I am obviously not the father of your child. And Alyssa," he went on without turning, "I would advise you to put the hypo down and return to where I can see you. I would regret having to do anything to you that I do not have the facilities to mend."

Alyssa quickly complied, but said, "Ree, we're just trying to help you. You have to see that you're behaving in an . . . extreme manner."

"Warranted by extreme circumstances."

"No," Deanna said, keeping her tone gentle. "Triggered by extreme emotion. It started when we were in sickbay, when I felt Will . . . was in danger." She knew he was still alive; she could feel it in the core of her being. And she wouldn't even entertain the possibility that it was wishful thinking. "I feared losing him, and it triggered the memory of my grief at losing our first child, nearly losing this one. It was amplified by my awareness of Tuvok's grief at losing a son.

"Somehow, my overwhelming fear for the safety of my child must have affected you, triggered an intense surge of paternal instinct—the instinct that evolved to protect your young from predators even larger and fiercer than you.

"But you must realize that we aren't on the Pahkwa-thanh homeworld. That those instincts don't apply here."

"On the contrary, Counselor. Space can be far more dangerous than my homeworld at its most primitive." He completed his scans, seeming satisfied with the results. "And you forget—I have no empathic sensitivity."

"Just because most Pahkwa-thanh don't have active psi abilities doesn't mean your brains don't have the potential to act as receivers. A strong enough telepathic projection can affect even non-psionic species. I've seen it happen," she said, though patient confidentiality kept her from specifying the late Ambassador Sarek and the effects of his Bendii Syndrome—while sheer embarrassment kept her from mentioning the similar chaos her mother had inadvertently sparked on Deep Space 9 that one time. "And maybe your species' latent potential makes you especially sensitive."

She reached out to touch his arm, to appeal to his reason and mercy. But he grabbed her wrist tightly and turned it over, peering at her hand. Satisfied that it was empty, he released it. As Alyssa hurried to check her arm for damage, Deanna gasped and said, "No tricks, Ree. Please, you have to believe us. You're not thinking clearly. Your hormones are out of control. You have to take us back to *Titan*, for all our sakes."

"With respect, Counselor, you give me no reason to trust you. You have already used one distraction to try to attack me. Now you try to lull me off my guard, to prepare me for the next hand that will have a hypo in it." He loomed over her, his sharp-toothed snout hovering over her neck. "And you wheedle and plead to be taken back to a ship where your child would be in constant danger. *Your own child*."

After an alarming, Damoclean moment of silence,

Ree turned his attention to Alyssa, who reflexively backed against the wall. "And you . . ." He let out a small growl. "You should know better. Sympathy with a patient is well and good, but you must not let it compromise your medical judgment."

Controlling her fear, Alyssa met his eyes and said, "My child is on that ship too, Doctor. And I know my place is there, with him. Please, Ree. Let's all go home."

"Were that true, you would never have left him. You made your choice, Alyssa." He returned to the hatch, saying, "Neither of you attempt to trick me again." He went through the hatch, then paused, turned his head, and added, "Please."

Once the hatch locked behind him, Alyssa slumped, and Deanna sat up to put a comforting arm around her. "He . . . almost forgot to be polite," the nurse said. "He must be furious."

"Worse," Deanna told her. "He's becoming paranoid— seeing any attempt to question his judgment as a threat against my daughter's safety."

Alyssa turned to her, great sorrow in her lovely dark eyes. "I don't think any of us are very safe right now."

DROPLET

The first thing Riker sensed was the sound of a gentle surf against a sandy shore. Opening his eyes, he saw that he was lying on a beach, gazing out at a calm, placid ocean which pulsed against the shore under the impetus of the morning breeze. The boldest waves pushed their way up to within inches of his arm, and he could almost feel the coolness of the water.

He realized he could also feel the shore beneath him bobbing with the larger waves.

Remembering where he was, Riker shot to a sitting position, bringing on a bout of dizziness. He lowered his head, and realized he was nude. His hand reflexively went to his chest—no combadge. He twisted his head sharply back and forth, scrambled to his bare feet, and made an intensive search of his immediate environs, but no combadge, uniform, or any other equipment was in sight.

His eyes went skyward. He knew *Titan* would be searching for him—if it was still in any condition to do so. The last he remembered, the ship was damaged, and he had no idea how badly. But if they had any means at all to do so—

No. The sky was thick with clouds and a lurid red haze. *Dust and vapor from the asteroid*, he realized. *And sensors had enough trouble before.* Any search would have to be visual, from the shuttles. There were probably nitrogen oxides up there too, eroding the ozone layer. Given his lack of coverings, it was fortunate that Droplet's sun was relatively distant and low in ultraviolet emissions.

He brushed the sand off his skin and turned his attention to the floater islet he occupied. It was obvious on first glance that he was the only sizable life form present. Hell, there weren't even any trees or shrubs, just a smattering of mosses and grasses of various sizes. *And no flint, no rock—how can I start a fire?*

Riker ran the few dozen meters to the islet's highest point—about as high above sea level as his midriff was above the ground—and scanned the sea out to the horizon. Nothing but ocean was visible in any direction. Floaters were usually found in clusters, but this one was all by itself. That smacked of the artificial. *The squales—they saved me, but now . . . why have they brought me here?* He remembered their hostility just before the impact. It occurred to him to be very concerned for Aili Lavena. What kind of prison might they have for her—if she'd even survived?

Warning himself against jumping to conclusions, Riker decided to test the most immediate possibilities first. Striding to the edge of the islet, he waded out into the shallows and circled its perimeter, periodically swimming down below the edge to see if Lavena might be somewhere on the underside.

But less than halfway around, his muscles began to cramp. He cursed himself for a fool, realizing that he didn't know how long it had been since he'd eaten. And his muscles were stiff, weak, as though they hadn't been used in days. He tried to force his body to take him back to shore, but just then a large swell hit and lifted the islet, the currents sucking him underneath it. He grabbed hold of the coraloid tendrils, probed for a crack, desperately hoping he could break his way through to a pocket of air. But the shell material would not budge, and he felt himself weakening. . . .

After that was a montage of vague perceptions as he faded in and out of consciousness—a warm body against his, a rippling of feathery blue membranes, the shock of air hitting his face again, the ground rocking beneath his back once more. Returning to full consciousness, he turned his head to see Lavena crouched over him. She had no hydration suit, and indeed was as nude as he wa—

Clearing his throat, he sat up and folded his legs before him. "Ahh, Ensign. I, umm, appreciate the rescue."

She giggled, and seemed immune to the resultant glare. "It was my pleasure, Captain. And don't worry, it's nothing I haven't seen before. More or less."

"Ensign, remember your Starfleet decorum," he told her. She lowered her head at his chastisement, kept her eyes averted as he retreated behind a stand of tall grasses nearby. In turn, she waded out into the shallows and lay on her side to submerge her gill crests, which had begun to shrivel a bit as the water drained out from between their filaments. He managed to break a blade of grass free with some effort, testing its strength and flexibility. *I can do something with this.* "Report," he ordered, raising his voice to compensate for distance. "How long have you been conscious?"

"A few hours, sir. Long enough to discover I can't swim too far without squales coming to stop me."

"They're holding us prisoner?" he asked, pausing in his efforts to tear more blades free.

Lavena propped herself partway up, considering. She was far enough out that most of her crests remained submerged—along with most of her other anatomy, which was a comfort to Riker. "I think it might be . . . protective custody. The deep sound chatter is angry. Hundreds died in the impact, and a valuable feeding ground or something was destroyed. Most of the squales blame us. But the research pod that made contact with us is keeping us safe . . . at least until the others decide whether we deserve punishment."

Riker sighed. "Our equipment? Our clothes?"

"All scuttled, sir. They didn't want any part of it. It's . . . well, probably getting a lot more compact now," she said, pointing down toward the bottom of what might as well be a bottomless ocean.

"That figures. They couldn't at least have left me my swim briefs?"

"Sir . . . with respect, they *did* save our lives. I think . . . they even gave us medical care somehow. I remember . . . being enclosed in a warm fluid. Something . . . pulsing, like a great heartbeat. I asked the squales about it, and they said something about . . . tending to life."

"I remember the same thing," he said. "I'd thought it was just . . . I didn't know." An atavistic memory of his mother's womb? Maybe an empathic connection with his unborn daughter? *Deanna* . . . He reached out to her by reaching within. He couldn't get any response, any clear sense of her presence. But he believed he could still feel a basic awareness of their connection. She was alive; he was sure of it. But somehow she couldn't communicate with him. She could be injured, or very distant—but why would she be so far away?

"I think there must be even more to their bioengineering than we thought, sir," Lavena said. "I was pretty banged up when I was knocked from the skiff, but I'm almost fully healed now."

Riker remembered bleeding from his head. His hand went to his forehead, felt around—there was only the barest hint of a scar. "Normally I'd be fascinated," he said.

"But right now I'd rather be in *Titan*'s sickbay." He fought off another wave of dizziness. "Make that the mess hall."

"Oh!" Lavena cried. "Hold on, sir, I'll get you something to eat."

She was gone before he could stop her, no doubt foraging on the underside for something that was edible raw. Riker knew from the crew's reports that Dropletian biochemistry was reasonably compatible with human, although lacking in mineral nutrients. It would tide him over for a few days, at least. He didn't plan to be here that long.

By the time Lavena returned, Riker had successfully woven the grasses into a thong-type garment that covered him nearly as well as his briefs had. Lavena seemed even more amused by this than she had been when he was naked, though she struggled to keep her amusement in check. Wanting her attention elsewhere, he asked, "Did the squales tell you anything about the rest of our teams? Other survivors?" He was unsure if all the teams had been evacuated in time, though most would probably have been safely out of range.

Lavena shook her head. "I asked, but they won't tell me anything. I don't think they want us talking to anyone else. When I dove to the deep sound channel, the security pod intercepted me, made sure I didn't make any loud noises. We're not only in custody, we're in a communications blackout." She looked up at him. "I'm . . . a little nervous about what that might mean for our future."

"I'm more worried about the rest of our people," he told her. "You said this faction of squales is protecting us from the anger of the others."

"The research pod, at least, yes, sir. I think it's because they've established at least a tenuous relationship with us—with me. And the security pod is going along because, well, they're on the same team for the duration, I guess."

He met her dark-eyed gaze. "So who's going to protect everyone else?"

Chapter Eleven

SHUTTLECRAFT *MARSALIS*

Tamen Gibruch stared out at the endless ocean outside the *Marsalis*'s forward port, so unlike the wide, arid savannas of Chand Aad, and yet so similar in some ways. Here, as everywhere, life vied for survival, embracing every possible strategy—predation, social cooperation, flight, concealment—whatever it took to gain a march over oblivion. That, Gibruch reflected, was the impetus that drove *Titan*'s crew now, in their unrelenting search for a captain and chief pilot who were probably crushed to paste at the bottom of the ocean. Even when failure was nearly certain, they never gave up. It was a quality Gibruch admired, and one he had seen in Starfleet many times, most of all during the Borg invasion. They may not have had anything growing from the backs of their heads save hair and the odd gill crests or spines, but in their own way, Starfleet people had trunks.

But the instinct for survival drove the life of Droplet

as well, and in recent days it had compelled the squales to overcome their timidity and swim closer to the aquashuttles, facing them down threateningly, restricting their movements (at least in the water) beyond the floater colony they'd made their base. They hadn't attacked yet, still keeping a moderate distance, and Gibruch suspected they might retreat if pressed. But Commander Vale wasn't ready to test that, feeling they had been antagonized enough.

Instead, Gibruch's team was assigned to make one more effort to communicate with the squales. Y'lira Modan had taken over Lavena's role of spokeswoman, brushing up her Selkie for the task; but her dense body structure made her a poor swimmer, so she was relying on hydrophones and submerged speakers, something the squales did not appreciate. It was not going well. Apparently this was a pod consisting of hermaphroditic "mothers" and their children, rather than one specializing in research or governance (if they had governance; the science staff was still uncertain of that). It wasn't the ideal type of pod to try to communicate with, but it was what they had at the moment. Huilan had volunteered to go out into the water and try his luck; but Gibruch was reluctant to send out the bite-sized counselor under current conditions. In the three standard days since the impact—nearly five Dropletian days—the animal life of the planet had been agitated, aggressive.

"Don't worry," Huilan told him. "I can take care of myself. At worst, you can keep a transporter lock on me and beam me to safety."

"I admire your determination," Gibruch said. "But my duty is to keep you safe."

"Our duty is to find the captain and Lavena, if we can.

And to try to make amends for our mistakes here. We can't do that without talking to the squales."

"That may have to wait," Y'lira told them, listening to her earpiece. "I'm picking up chatter from the squales. It sounds like a predator alert."

"Confirmed," said Eviku at the science console. "I'm picking up something approaching the squale pod. It's big."

Soon Eviku was able to call up a magnified image on his screen. He had been right about the creature's size; it read as over ten meters long. A low-slung, brick-brown shell bulldozed through the water like a boat that had capsized and hadn't realized it. Behind a heavy, nasty-looking prow, the shell presented a rough, bumpy surface like a magnified crab carapace. Right at the waterline in front were numerous glints suggesting tiny cabochon eyes. Behind the creature, the water roiled in slithering shapes, suggesting multiple vertical fins beneath the surface.

"The squales are forming a defensive circle," Eviku reported, "protecting their young." A pause. "Now the two largest hermaphrodites are—yes, they're heading toward the creature. They're going to intercept it!"

"Underwater sensors?" Gibruch asked. "What do they reveal of the creature's underside?" He strode over to view the sensor feed. To his mind, eye and scanner comple-mented each other.

"Tentacles," Eviku reported, interpreting the roiling, confused image. "Looks like hundreds of wiggling ten-tacles, pushing it forward. Several . . . roughly triangular tailfins. And two thick tentacles coming out of the front, several meters long." His voice was tense, agitated. Gibruch was surprised; he hadn't known Eviku long, but had come to think of him as a reserved, level-headed officer.

"They're not slowing down," said Olivia Bolaji from the pilot's seat. Gibruch looked out the window; now he could see firsthand as the largest of the squales and the dreadnought creature barreled toward a head-on collision. If anything, the dreadnought was picking up speed.

The entire audience winced as one at the mighty impact. Gibruch felt the sinus cavities tighten in his trunk as a bloom of bright vermilion stained the sea. "My God," came Bolaji's whisper as the dreadnought trundled forward, carelessly sloughing off the wounded squale's bulk to push on with its attack.

As the underwater sensors showed, the second squale dodged a head-on crash, swerving around to slam its tail into the monster's side. The dreadnought fishtailed, as it were, but quickly steadied and swung to meet its foe. "It's bringing in the tentacles!" Eviku exclaimed.

The squale dodged with all the speed its bulk allowed, barely evading the first ropy limb; but the second brushed its flank and the squale went into convulsions, throwing the surface into turmoil. "I'm picking up electrical discharges!" Eviku reported. "Look at the voltage!"

Normally, Gibruch would have taken him to task for the imprecise and overly emotional report. But Gibruch was too caught up in the drama as the dreadnought wrapped both limbs about the squale, sending a still greater shock into its body. The tentacles managed to hold their grip despite the thrashing they induced. The water warped and crumpled under the onslaught of the squale's throes, obscuring the scene from view. But before long, the turmoil subsided, revealing the squale motionless, burned, showing the unique limpness of death despite the water's buoying.

And then the dreadnought moved in to feed. No one much cared to witness that. "What's the status of the other squale?" Gibruch asked after a pause.

Another pause followed before Eviku responded. "It's alive, but bleeding severely. The . . . the others seem to be . . . yes, they're gathering around it. I suppose the predator is focused on its kill, so they're getting their wounded away."

"Commander?" the pilot spoke up. "They're heading roughly in our direction."

"Don't make any sudden moves. I don't think they'll collide with us."

"Yes, sir."

"Are you sure, Commander?" Eviku asked, still un-wontedly nervous.

"Calm yourself, Lieutenant," the Chandir replied, opening a sinus cavity in his trunk to add more resonance and authority to his voice. "Given the way the life on this world recoils from technology, I'm sure we have no cause for concern."

As the diminished pod made haste to clear the scene, the crew spontaneously fell into a respectful silence. The pod left behind a thinning wake of blood that spread until it touched the hull of the *Marsalis*. It seemed symbolic to Gibruch, as though saying that all life is joined at the pith and that the life and death of one being will touch all others sooner or later, though worlds divide them.

And then the shuttle lurched, knocking everyone to the deck, and Gibruch instinctively knew that that baptism of blood had passed beyond mere metaphor. The second dreadnought had been drawn by the bouquet of blood spreading through the sea. Mistaking the shuttle for another squale, it had slammed its thick, battering-ram prow into the side, knocking the vessel into a drifting spin. The clang reverberated so loudly through the water that every squale for kilometers around must have looked up from what it was doing and thought, "What was *that*?!"

The dreadnought recoiled, the unexpectedly hard skin of the shuttle having given it a once-in-a-lifetime opportunity to experience a headache. But that apparently just made it mad, and it whipped its tentacles around the portside hull, trying to deliver a fatal shock. The insulated hull kept its current from getting a foothold, but it went on trying with mindless determination. "No cause for concern, sir?" Eviku snapped.

"Belay that, Lieutenant," Gibruch ordered. Still, he didn't want to take any chances. "Bolaji, take us up."

"My pleasure," Bolaji replied. But it was a struggle to get the shuttle into the air; the leviathan held on relentlessly. Bolaji had to kick in enough power to lift the whole creature out of the water, yet still it clung, mindless in its frenzy. Soon he felt a tremble and a surge of speed, telling him the dreadnought had fallen away, and the sensors confirmed it. But there was still a thick tentacle adhering to the forward port by its suckers. The creature's own weight had torn it free.

"I . . . I don't understand," Eviku said once the shuttle had gained some altitude and he had regained greater calm. "It's not normal for predators to be so reckless. Their survival depends on being fit and intact. Sacrificing a limb like that, even after it should have known we offered no nourishment . . . what could drive it to that?"

"I don't know," Gibruch said. "But until we find out, I think going out swimming on this planet is definitely a bad idea."

ELSEWHERE ON DROPLET

If there's one good thing about this captivity, Aili Lavena reflected on more than one occasion, *it's that I get to do plenty of swimming.*

Indeed, she could hardly do otherwise; without a hydration suit, she couldn't function out of the water for long. Of course there was more oxygen in the air, but her gills needed water between their countless tiny filaments to function; otherwise the filaments would clump together and have too little exposed surface area to absorb sufficient oxygen. Out of the water, her membranes could only hold their moisture for a few minutes before shriveling up.

Which made it somewhat awkward to interact with Captain Riker—although she recognized that he would feel even more awkward if she could be up there on the islet with him, having no clothes of any kind. She'd declined to wear the kind of woven-grass garment he sported, stating that it would probably not hold up to the amount of swimming she had to do; besides, she imagined it must itch terribly, though she felt no urge to seek confirmation from him.

It was hard for Riker, she knew, being stranded on that little saucer of land with nothing to do, virtually no tools or resources to make anything with, virtually no food to forage for. He could swim reasonably well for a human, of course, and sometimes joined her in gathering food from beneath the floater or simply swimming for exercise. But he couldn't last without air any longer than she could last without water. And he was still weak from his injuries; he seemed to have gotten hurt worse than she had in the tsunami, or else he was healing more poorly for some reason.

She kept him company as best she could, but there was only so much they could talk about: Academy stories, navigation problems, music, the Pacifican yacht races, the most tasteless Borg jokes they could think of. They both shied away from more serious topics, such as what might have become of *Titan* or what their chances were for rescue—and of course they avoided talking about their past.

So, truth be told, Aili was relieved to spend the bulk of her time either foraging for food or conversing with the squales. Luckily the members of the research pod were still interested in continuing the language lessons—although she soon realized that was because they still wished to interrogate her about the asteroid impact and her people's role in it. She was saddened that they shared the defender pod's mistrust of her. Indeed, when the lessons first resumed, she hadn't felt so fortunate, for one of the defender squales had grabbed her bodily again and kept her under close, intimidating guard at all times. She was pretty sure it was the same pseudo-male that had restrained her before, and she was starting to think of him as "Grabby." But over the past few local days since then, once it had become clear she was eager to participate in the conversation, the researchers had grown more comfortable with her and talked Grabby and his team into keeping their distance.

Well, "comfortable" might not have been the word. Aili

had noted that all the squales were acting more tense and agitated over the past few days. She had soon discerned that they had reason, when the defender squales guarding the perimeter came under attack from a school of large chordate predators with broad, delta-wing fins, not unlike the rays of Earth but with long, scissorlike double beaks bracketing a flexible, prolapsing maw that shot out to engulf what the beaks severed. Grabby lost a tentacle and another defender lost a tailfin before the rest of the pod closed in and harried the scissor-rays off, firing bursts of intense concentrated sound to stun them. Aili was tempted to consider Grabby's fate poetic justice, but she couldn't bring herself to take pleasure in such a serious amputation and couldn't help but be moved by the way his fellow defenders held and comforted him and the other injured male as they took them away for, presumably, medical treatment. She wondered if it would involve the womblike things she and Riker had apparently been placed in. But when she asked about it, the squales declined to answer.

The next day, Aili had found herself under attack from a large molluscoid that used its long, narrow conical shell to thrust at her like a jouster's lance. Only quick reflexes saved her from being impaled, but she lost part of one gill fringe before two of the younger research-pod squales arrived and assailed the creature, crushing its shell and tearing out and consuming the innards. It was hard to be unambivalently grateful after seeing that, but she reminded herself it was simply the cycle of nature.

Those same two squales began spending an increasing amount of time with her, taking the lead in the language lessons. These two pseudo-males—one each of the two roughly masculine sexes—were apparently fairly new apprentices in the research pod, having left their maternal pod less than a Dropletian year before, and they were still rich with the open, inquisitive spirit that drove squales of their age to seek apprenticeships, often going through several specialist pods before settling on a preferred career. They watched with fascination as she swam, taking note of how her alien form functioned in the water, carefully examining the details of her body. She did her best to cultivate their curiosity, guiding the conversation toward a mutual exchange of knowledge, offering them a share of the food she harvested, even engaging with them in play. One or two adults always hovered nearby, ready to strike if she attempted anything untoward, but they allowed the young ones their freedom to engage her. *What was the game Commander Vale mentioned when we were prisoners of the Hreekh? Are these the "good cops" I'm supposed to open up to?* If so, that was fine, since she was here to be open.

Aili dubbed her young friends Alos and Gasa, after two of her younger siblings. But it turned out they were not related, or even part of the same specialist pod. What she'd thought of as the research pod was actually an aggregate of two. As Alos and Gasa explained, the squales had no pods specializing in studying newly encountered species, for they had long since catalogued all the species in the sea and air and domesticated many of them. (Aili wondered how long that would have taken; an ocean was vast, but Droplet's fairly uniform ocean had more limited biodiversity than would be found on a planet whose seas were subdivided by land masses. And there was always the possibility that their knowledge was not as pervasive as they assumed.) So two specialist pods had combined their efforts. Alos was apprenticed to a pod that studied astronomy, using specially bred flying chordates and balloon jellies as probes that recorded visual information and encoded it into echo-location-like impulses. Gasa's apprenticeship was with an animal-management pod specializing in interactions with their world's more intelligent nonsquale species, making them the closest thing Droplet had to experts in inter-species communication or diplomacy. This was the first time those two pods had collaborated, and the two young-sters were enjoying the exchange of ideas, perhaps more so than the elders, who were more set in their ways.

But Aili soon discerned that even Alos and Gasa were as much on edge as the rest of the squales. If anything, they seemed to find her presence comforting, for she was the one being they knew who wasn't suffering from the general anxiety. When she asked them what was troubling the squales, their answer was confusing: the Song, they said, was out of tune. Or so she interpreted it. Alos and Gasa tried to explain the concept, but it was difficult for them to communicate some of the ideas they apparently took for granted.

So they took the matter to their respective pods' dominant males, essentially the lead scientists. Aili dubbed the leader of the astronomy pod Melo, after Melora Pazlar, while the leader of the animal-management pod got the nickname Cham, after the ecologist Chamish. The two of them discussed the issue and decided to call in more specialists. Periodically, pods of squales would aggregate into temporary superpods of hundreds of members for feeding or mating purposes. When the combined contact pod (as

Aili began to think of it) drifted near an area rich in pis-coids and joined with other pods for the feeding frenzy, the members of the contact pod persuaded an elder hermaph-rodite—apparently a spiritual leader of sorts—to break away from her pod for a time and give Aili some spiritual instruction.

According to Alos and Gasa, there was a fair amount of tension during the frenzy, with many in the other pods seeing the offworlders as a threat and wanting them dealt with aggressively. A couple of members of the defender pod had even defected to other pods, persuaded by their arguments. Some of those in Cham's pod had come close, the young ones told her; since they were closely attuned to the animal life of Droplet, they were deeply troubled by the distress of their fellow creatures. Cham, being a stolid and conservative sort who disliked divergence from the proper order of things, had been unhappy with the idea of their defection, but could not really disagree with their reasons. But Melo and his astronomers had taken the offworlders' side. Melo was elderly, but that had not made him hide-bound; if anything, a lifetime of studying a purely abstract science had made him something of a dreamer. He and his like-minded podmates were enthralled by the discovery of life from beyond the sky and had sung eloquently of the great insights they might be able to gain from them. This had brought around the potential defectors from Cham's pod, and it had also persuaded the Matron, as Aili dubbed the spiritual leader, to come meet Aili and discuss squale beliefs with her.

"They believe in something called the Song of Life," she explained to Riker once she'd sorted out the Matron's lessons to her own satisfaction. As usual, he was seated at the shoreline of the floater, with her lying on her side in the shallows just beyond. "Everything is song to them. They sing to the world, and it sings back to them. The song and its reflections define the world, make it real, give it form and substance."

"Echolocation," Riker interpreted. "They perceive their world by sending out sonic pulses and listening to the echoes."

She nodded. "To them, that's just part of the greater Song. They sing to find food. They sing to find other squales to sing with, to mate with, to make new squales. They sing, and other species listen and obey.

"Even the universe is a song to them. As they see it, there's the World Below, the World Between, and the World Above. That's the hypersaline depths, the regular ocean, and the air. And they're all overtones of a deeper fundamental, the core of the world."

She smiled as she tried to recapture the beauty with which the Matron had sung it to her. The World Between was the physical realm, the world of waking; the World Above was the realm beyond the physical, the world of sleep. Squales would regularly visit the World Above through sleep, sustaining their spirits as the air sustained their bodies. In squale as in English, "spirit" was kin to "respiration." However, no squale could remember one's sojourn Above upon waking. At most, one remembered dreams, which were distorted reflections of the waking world, like the rippling reflections the surface of the sea cast back below. Like Selkies, they slept with only half the brain at a time, retaining enough awareness to respond to threats; so in their dream state they straddled the World Between and the World Above, just as they did when they swam at the surface.

But just as the motions of the surface told of the weather above, so the nature of one's dreams bespoke the conditions in the World Above, providing spiritual guidance—with plenty of room for interpretation, of course. A large percentage of deep sound channel communication was devoted to oneirocriticism, as the meanings of squale dreams were debated back and forth. There was no dogma in squale beliefs; they enjoyed a good argument too much.

As for the World Below, that was the realm of death, where all living things sank eventually, inexorably. But they did not believe the spirit belonged there; its nature, when freed from the flesh, was to rise into the World Above, as gases escaped from a decaying body and bubbled upward as the body sank below.

"But the World Below is alive to them too, somehow," she said. "It's part of the Song, a deeper level than ours— theirs. Somehow it's more . . . real. I guess because the Song is what creates reality, to them."

"In the Beginning was the Word," Riker said. "And the Word became flesh."

"Sir?"

"The Bible, from Earth. The Gospel of Saint John. The term he actually used was *Lógos*—a pretty remarkable Ancient Greek word. It means not just a word, but the concept underlying it, the act of reasoning itself . . . maybe a few other things besides. In the beginning was *Lógos*, and *Lógos* was the Creator, and the act of creation, of all things."

Lavena smiled. She'd always been impressed by Rik-

er's eclectic knowledge, the product of his insatiable curiosity. "Squale beliefs are a lot like that," she agreed. "But
there's something more I'm still not getting. The squales
. . . somehow they don't see themselves as creating the
Song, but participating in it. It comes from inside them,
but outside them too. Maybe it's more fundamentals and
harmonics, the same thing having multiple layers."

She smiled in recollection. "Even the way the
Matron sang it to me was layered. She took me down to the
ri'Hoyalina—the deep sound channel. The sea's stabilized
enough since the impact that the channel's mostly working
again. She let me listen in to the global dialogue, and made
her song harmonize with its shifting melodies and echoes.
I think she was using the channel's ambience as an analogy
for the Song. The greater melody that they're all part of."

Riker had perked up when she mentioned the long-
range acoustic channel. "Did you listen for calls from
Titan while you were there?" They had both concluded that
the crew would use hydrophones in the DSC to listen for
Lavena's calls. On this world, with its sensor interference
and vast stretches of empty ocean, the channel was the best
way to search over large areas.

She nodded. "They even let me call out to them. But I
think it was because they knew somehow I'd get no answer.
As if *Titan* . . ." She couldn't finish the thought.

"You were saying?" Riker prompted. "About the Song
and why they're agitated?"

"Yes, sir. What they're telling me is that the asteroid
strike . . . it's disrupted the Song somehow. Not just their
communication channel, but the deeper Song that ema-
nates from the World Below. Its . . . timbre has been altered.

Discord has been added. And that's throwing the world out of joint."

Riker furrowed his brow. "They think that's why the Dropletian life is getting so agitated? That there's some kind of annoying sound putting them on edge?"

"No," she said, shaking her head. "At least, I don't think so, sir. It's more like the squales think of themselves and the other species as parts of the sound . . . as living notes that are being played wrong."

He was silent for a while, absorbing her words. "But how could the asteroid strike be affecting them? Asteroids hit this planet all the time." He fidgeted, shifting his weight. "Maybe they're just on edge because we're here. Something strange and alien comes to their world, and then an asteroid hits . . . it's making them afraid of what might happen next. And so they imagine the Song is out of tune."

"But that doesn't explain the other animals reacting the same way."

"Are they really? Or does it just seem that way to the squales who are already on the alert for trouble?"

"But the attacks —"

"Aili, you were attacked twice in your first week here."

She conceded the point with a tilt of her head. "Hmm . . . I suppose the asteroid dust settling in the water is changing the salinity, affecting the circulation . . . shifting the nutrient balance. Even the DSC still has some areas that don't have service restored yet, so to speak. So the normal cycles of the ocean are out of joint in a lot of ways. That could be what's disorienting the animals, putting them on edge." She leaned back and stretched, and Riker felt the need to look off at the horizon for a moment. "But try telling them that. Even some of the squales in Cham's pod, and most of the defender squales, are still convinced we caused it all by coming here, that we threw off their Song with our discordant alienness. Some of them are genuinely curious to learn about us, especially the astronomers. But a lot of the pod members are studying us because they hope it will reveal what we've done to their world and what they can do to fix it. And it sounds like a lot of squales around the world agree that we're the problem."

"But it didn't begin until the asteroid struck."

"Which happened less than two weeks after we arrived. They don't believe in coincidences. In music, everything's interrelated." She leaned forward again. "And remember, sir, they have aerial probe creatures bred for astronomical observation—and they're better at it than we imagined. They were actually able to detect *Titan* interacting with the asteroid before it hit." She shook her head. "To many of the squales, that's proof positive. I'm having a hard time changing their minds. I think Alos and Gasa believe me, but they're just apprentices and they also want to trust their mentors."

"You're doing the best you can, Aili," Riker told her with a gentle smile. "I have every confidence in you."

"Thank you, sir." His approval warmed her. Yawning, he rose, excused himself, and wandered up to the bed of mosses he'd made to take a nap—something he was doing a lot lately, with little else to occupy him.

But Aili occupied herself by enjoying the view as he walked away. His body really hadn't changed that much in twenty-two years—not as slender as before, perhaps, but then neither was she, having developed a thicker layer of body fat for insulation once she'd gone fully aquatic. Yes, he was her captain, and he was married. But she'd been alone on this planet for days now and she had appetites that were going unslaked. So she saw no harm in indulging in a private fantasy now and then.

Besides, we may be here for a while, she found herself thinking. *What if* Titan *never comes back? What if Will and I have to live out our lives here?* She contemplated him as he lay down to sleep. *Would that really be so bad?*

For him, maybe. She knew he'd miss his wife and daughter terribly, not to mention his career and his ship. But he was an adaptable man. And as for herself, Aili realized that there was little she would miss. Even confined by the squales, she felt more at home here, more free and vital, than she ever had in her life. She already thought of Alos and Gasa as friends, and she believed she could win the other squales over in time. They were dangerous when they had to be, but she felt they were a noble people, gregarious, inquisitive, wise, even quite beautiful. And all they knew of her was what she showed them here, with none of the stink she carried in the oceans of her homeworld. She could have a fresh start here, without having to seal herself inside a skintight prison surrounded by searing air. So she had to admit, although there were members of *Titan*'s crew she would miss, she would not be unhappy to live out her life on Droplet.

And if Will Riker had to live it out with me? Well, a girl has needs. And he would certainly need someone to comfort him.

She spent a pleasant hour imagining the details of that

comfort. It was just a fantasy, of course. But Aili knew there was a chance it could become reality, and she could live with that.

TITAN

It was Eviku who finally figured out what was driving the life forms of Droplet to their increasingly erratic, aggressive behavior. "I realized that I felt a similar anxiety myself when I was on the planet," he told Vale and the others gathered in the conference room. "At first I assumed it was because of my . . . well, my fears for the captain and Ensign Lavena. But then I realized that there was a direct correlation between how close I was to Droplet and how anxious I felt. And it struck me that Arkenites have something in common with Dropletian life forms."

"Your magnetic sensitivity," Vale realized, her eyes going to the black magnetic headdress he wore to maintain his equilibrium.

"Yes. We had assumed the Dropletian animals' magnetic sense was used primarily for navigation. But what if it has some influence over their behavior as well?" He went to the viewscreen and pulled up a cross-section graphic of Droplet and its magnetic field. "According to our readings, the planetary magnetic field has been subtly altered since the impact. This is because the field has two sources. In addition to the core dynamo that creates the field, the hypersaline layer at the base of the ocean generates a saltwater dynamo effect that enhances and modulates the field. The interaction of the two dynamos creates an oscillation of sorts, a regular fluctuation like a, well, a sort of heartbeat for the planet."

"Or a musical beat," Ra-Havreii said. "From what we know of the squales, they perceive the world in very musical terms."

Vale's eyes widened. "So they could be constantly aware of this magnetic pulsing in their heads? Like a . . . a rhythm track for their lives?"

"More than just a rhythm," Eviku said. "The way the field patterns fluctuate as the saltwater dynamo undergoes convection, thermal changes, and so forth produces modulations and variations on top of the basic rhythm."

"Like modulations in pitch, variations in intensity and duration," Ra-Havreii added, smiling now. "A perpetual song underlying their whole existence—a song without sound."

And I get annoyed enough having a song stuck in my head for more than a day or two, Vale thought. But then, if she'd lived her whole life with a song in her head, she'd probably take it for granted.

"Incidentally," Eviku went on, "we now think that's why the squales have been so reluctant to come near our technology. It wasn't just fear of the unknown; the EM fields emitted by our vessels and devices may have been causing them discomfort. Or perhaps simply drowning out the song."

"I have a team working with Life Sciences on finding a way to damp their emissions," Ra-Havreii said.

Eviku called up graphics of the field parameters in the wake of the impact event. "But the song appears to have changed recently. It's all those exotic dissolved minerals and dust sinking down to the hypersaline layer. Minerals that still carry a substantial residual charge of energy from our attacks on the asteroid."

"And not just the solar or kinetic energy these compounds usually absorb," Pazlar elaborated. "Nadion energy from the phasers, gravitons from the tractor beams, thoron and subspace radiation from the quantum torpedoes, gamma, x- and m-rays from the antimatter blast. It's a potent cocktail. And as more and more of those energized remnants descend into the dynamo layer, their exotic emissions disrupt the magnetic field."

Vale frowned. "So . . . the planet is singing off-key?"

"In a sense," Eviku said. "It creates a dissonance. Imagine if you had to listen to music whose pitch had been flattened and whose timbre was turned into a high-pitched whine. With periodic bursts of noise as pockets of asteroid debris discharge."

Oh my God, they're listening to bagpipes. "So the chaos down there . . . it's our fault. If we'd just left well enough alone . . ." She exchanged a look with Keru.

But he would have none of it. He met her gaze evenly and asked, "So what can we do to fix it?"

Pazlar went on as Eviku resumed his seat. "First we need to evaluate the condition of the dynamo layer in more detail. Our scans from up here just don't get enough resolution."

Vale stared. "From up here? You mean we need to dive down there." The Elaysian nodded. "Melora, the pressure's over a hundred thousand atmospheres! We don't have anything that can withstand that."

"Don't we?" Keru asked. "Remember that ocean in

space Tuvok told us about, the one *Voyager* encountered? As I recall, their *Delta Flyer* dove down a good six hundred kilometers. This ocean's only ninety."

"The pressure in the Monean ocean was relatively low," Pazlar said, "or else most of it would've been allotropic ice like Droplet's mantle. Its core generators gave off just enough gravity to hold the sphere together, not so much that the pressure would crush the generators themselves. The Moneans relied on artificial gravity in their ships and habitats." She turned to Vale. "And even despite that, with pressures of *only* a few thousand atmospheres, the *Delta Flyer's* shields could barely withstand the pressure differential. And they had it easy. The kind of energies that are at play down inside Droplet could disrupt any shuttle's shields and integrity systems."

Vale threw her a glare. "So you're telling me that the thing we have to do can't be done."

Pazlar's brow ridges shot up defensively. "I'm working the problem, okay?"

Ra-Havreii leaned forward. "The key is differential. The external pressure is less of a problem if the internal pressure is as high as possible."

"Right," Pazlar said without meeting his eyes. "The higher the pressure we can achieve inside the craft, the less field energy we'll need to counteract the rest. It's the same principle that's been used by deep-sea divers for centuries."

"But wouldn't the pressure eventually get high enough to crush their lungs, no matter how high the air pressure is?" Vale asked.

"There's precedent from pre-force-field days—divers

immersing themselves in an oxygenated fluid. It let them dive much deeper."

"I'm sorry, no." It was Doctor Onnta, representing medical in Ree's absence. The Balosneean leaned forward and shook his golden-skinned, downy-feathered head. "That would only work up to a thousand atmospheres or so. At that point, humanoid enzymatic processes begin to break down. Increase that to tens of thousands of atmospheres, and cellular lysis occurs—the cell walls themselves burst under the pressure. None of us could survive that."

Vale looked back to Pazlar. "Would a thousand atmospheres internally be enough?" she asked, knowing the answer.

"Not even close," Pazlar confirmed.

"So if we get the internal pressure high enough to protect the diving vessel, anyone inside it would be turned to jelly." She sighed. "Can we rig a remote probe?"

"Too much interference. We couldn't control it or guarantee it would function at all."

"So do we have *any* options?"

The Elaysian paused before answering. "There's one. I hesitate to bring it up because it's not a sure thing, and it would put one of my people at risk." Vale just waited until she went on. "But we do have one person aboard who evolved in a high-pressure environment."

"I should clarify," Se'al Cethente Qas said to its senior science officer and first officer, *"that Syr's surface pressure is less than two hundred standard atmospheres. You are speaking of a pressure nearly a thousand times greater."*

"But Syrath biology isn't as affected by pressure as

ours," Melora Pazlar told it. "And even most humanoids can survive a pressure a thousand times normal, with sufficient preparations and time to acclimate."

"Simulations show your life processes should not be critically affected by the pressures believed to exist in the upper range of the hypersaline layer," Doctor Onnta said.

"Believed to exist?" Cethente replied. But it was more amused than alarmed. Pazlar and Onnta were right; unlike the fragile protein-based chemistry on which their bodies depended, Syrath anatomy was far more robust, based upon piezoelectric crystal "cells" in a liquid silicate solvent, with genetic information encoded structurally in chains of dislocation loops and electrically in stored potentials, rather than chemically in nucleic acids.

"I know we're asking you to take a chance, Cethente," Vale said. "And I know it's somewhat outside your area of expertise. I could order you to do it; in fact, I probably will if I have to, because it's the only way to fix this mess. But you deserve to have a chance to volunteer."

The astrophysicist pondered the decision carefully. It was incapable of the fear that the humanoids probably assumed it was feeling. Syrath were hard to damage and nearly impossible to kill—permanently, anyway. It wasn't something they revealed to other races without need, not wishing to earn their envy. They might not have been physically indestructible, but their neural information was encoded in the same ways as their genetic information and distributed just as widely through the body; indeed, they were both facets of the same thing. Any sizeable intact part of a Syrath's body, even if "dead" for weeks, could regenerate in the proper growth medium into a new Syrath with the same basic personality template. True, many memories would be lost, even most if the surviving portion were small enough; but Syrath saw that as a way of getting a fresh start, sparing themselves the tedious sameness of immortality. So while they weren't reckless with their lives, preferring to avoid the inconvenience of dying, the Syrath had simply never evolved the capacity for mortal fear.

Still, Cethente recognized there was cause for concern here. It could survive most anything, but if the diving vessel Ra-Havreii's engineers were designing failed, Cethente could be trapped in the ocean depths forever. Its body might be crushed if it sank to where the pressures were sufficiently deep, or it might simply be buried slowly, encased in the hot allotropic ice of the planet's mantle. Either way, Cethente would be risking a death far more permanent than any of its previous three—and probably far more prolonged and unpleasant, though it could only remember the two less severe ones.

Of course, there was an option, though it would come as something of a shock to the others. It only needed to have a portion of its physical structure survive and be returned home in stasis, and the essence of Se'al Cethente would survive in a new form, and with a new thirdname. It would lack most of its memories of *Titan* and its discoveries, which would be a grave loss; but at least part of Cethente would live on.

"Tell me, Doctor Onnta," Cethente chimed before making its final decision, *"how easy would it be for you to reattach my legs if I had them removed . . . ?"*

CHAPTER TWELVE

DROPLET

It had begun to rain the day before, a matter of some discomfort for Riker, who had insufficient means to build a shelter. Aili felt somewhat guilty about being unaffected by the downpour, aside from being able to enjoy the soothing sound of the rainfall and a slightly less saline flavor to the water—though the rain brought a faint metallic tang all its own, for it was still precipitating asteroidal debris out of the atmosphere. Aili was also concerned that if the rain kept falling and diluting the water at the surface, Riker's floater islet would lose some of its buoyancy and subside a little, leaving him more vulnerable to the high swells being kicked up by the growing wind—swells that often drenched much of the floater's land surface despite the way it bobbed with them.

It would have been a matter of enough concern had Riker been at his peak, but he had been growing increasingly weak over the past few days. "It's this mineral-poor ecosystem," Riker had deduced once his weakness had become impossible to deny. "I'm not getting enough iron, calcium, you name it. And it didn't help that I was injured, lost a lot of blood. The squales couldn't give me enough of what I needed to recover, even with whatever miraculous biotech they used."

Lavena looked skyward. "What about the asteroid dust in the rain?"

Riker threw an ironic glance toward the clouds. "That might help a bit, but it's got too *much* heavy metal to be good for me. Although the malnutrition will probably get me long before the metal poisoning does. Unless we get back to *Titan*."

Aili felt guilty again. As natives of a pelagic world, Selkies had evolved to get by with a less mineral-rich diet than humans, so she was less affected than Riker. Still, she would suffer nutritional deficiencies as well if she had to stay here long enough.

But the immediate concern now was the weather, and she went to the squales to ask if anything could be done for Riker. As it happened, the squales already had plans to move them, because the weather problem was more severe than she had realized.

Riker's eyes widened when she relayed the news. "The hurricane? *The* hurricane?"

She nodded. "Spot, in all its glory. We're drifting into its fringes."

"Please tell me there's a way to navigate this island," he said. "Or have it towed."

"Actually, you can say good-bye to the island, sir. We're being relocated. I asked if they could arrange for better accommodations, but right now they're pretty insistent about just getting us out of here."

Riker looked around the tiny speck he inhabited with no trace of nostalgia in his eyes. "How do they plan to do that?"

But soon enough, the answer presented itself. An object of some sort became visible in the distance, drawing toward them as though being towed. Once it came close enough, it became evident that it was a flat, disklike creature with a tall stem of some sort rising from the center, almost like a raft of some kind. Cham, Gasa, and some of their podmates were accompanying it, towing it into range. Cham sang to her that it had been obtained from another pod—he called them "life-makers"—through some kind of trade she did not understand (and that Cham seemed less than happy with—or maybe he was just offended at having his talents wasted on shepherding such an unintelligent tool-creature). Aili swam out to investigate, singing thanks to them, and clambered onto it to test its stability. It held her weight easily. It was flexible and bouncy like a waterbed, and made of a soft membranous material. She could barely keep her footing, and hastily knelt on the surprisingly warm surface. She examined the vaguely translucent membrane visually and probed it with her hands, and realized she was sitting on a large inflated organism, reminiscent of one of the gas jellies that were common on this world, but with a tougher skin and no sign of any stings, at least on top.

Aili dove back into the water to replenish her oxygen and examine the creature's underside. Indeed, there were no stings or tendrils, to her relief. There didn't even seem to be any means of propulsion—just a keel-like protrusion along the bottom. But that mastlike growth on top made her wonder.

Riker was in no condition to tarry, so she helped him over to the raft. His grass thong, grown sodden and rotted from the rain, fell apart before he reached the raft, leaving him with no protection once he climbed onto it. Squeezing his eyes shut, trying to stay calm, Riker asked, "Now what?"

"I think it's a sailboat," Aili told him. "On Pacifica there are some jellies that have sails of sorts, letting them travel by wind. I think Earth has similar creatures."

Gasa swam over to her and guided her around the sail-jelly, showing her a set of loops that she soon discerned were a harness, allowing her to ride the craft with her gill-crests mostly immersed but her head above water to speak to Riker. Once she was in place, another squale—one she didn't recognize, perhaps a visitor from the "life-maker" pod—emitted a clear, precise sound. Immediately, the sail began to unfurl, and in moments it was pulled fully taut and catching the wind. The sail-jelly began to move under the wind's impetus, and in moments another squale call came and the sail moved, adjusting its angle, altering the creature's course. "The damn thing's domesticated," Riker murmured.

"More than that," Aili said. "I think they designed it for us. I can't figure why else it would have these loops for me."

"In just a couple of days? How is that possible?"

Aili asked Gasa and the new visitor, but all they would tell her was, *"Later."* But there was an overtone of uncertainty, as though her young friends were unsure their elders would let the offworlders in on the secret.

So there was nothing to do but lie back and enjoy the ride. Riker sighed. "What is it with us and jellyfish vessels?" he wondered.

"It is threatening to become a trend," Aili replied, chuckling.

But Riker couldn't sustain good humor for long. Although the sail-jelly was tacking away from the hurricane, they were still being steadily rained on. Riker pressed himself against the jelly's surface, getting what warmth he could from it, but he was shivering before long. After a moment's deliberation, Aili climbed up onto the raft alongside him. "Sir . . . let me." She lay down behind him and spooned her body against his, sharing her warmth.

"Ensign," he replied through chattering teeth, "this is not appropriate."

"Letting my captain freeze to death isn't appropriate."

"You'll suffocate."

"The rain will keep my gills wet. At least for a while."

"No. Really, I can't."

"Please, Will," she said, using his given name in an attempt to reassure him. "Just relax. It's nothing to be afraid of." She slid her arms around him, pressing herself closer to share her warmth. "We've been a lot more intimate than this before."

He pulled himself away, turning to face her, though keeping his knees up modestly—not soon enough to hide how he was responding to her, though. "I'm a married man, dammit. How dare you?"

"What?!" she exclaimed. "Sir, I'm just trying to keep

you warm! If anyone's feeling anything sexual, it's you!" she said, nodding toward the proof.

"You expect me to believe that? I've seen the way you've been looking at me and smiling since we ended up here."

"Because I think it's so silly that you feel you have to hide from me!"

"I'm your commanding officer and I love my wife!"

She knew they were miscommunicating. She sometimes forgot that many humans perceived all nudity as sexual, regardless of context. That part of it was a simple cultural misunderstanding, and Riker's weakened condition wasn't doing wonders for his judgment or patience. But she was past caring about any of that. He'd struck a far deeper nerve. "Is that what you really think of me, Captain? That I'm nothing but a hedonist? That I can't be trusted to act responsibly? Do you really have so low an opinion of me?"

"I only expect you to act according to your culture. And that's fine, for you. Just leave me out of it, that's all. It's different for me."

"You think I can't understand commitment because I'm a Selkie?" She let out a frustrated growl, lowering herself far enough off the side to replenish her oxygen. "You damn offworlders! We're all just a bunch of libertines to you, aren't we? Just like Argelius or Risa, but more exotic. Wetter." She felt a twinge of guilt at the mention of Risa, which had been thoroughly devastated by the Borg. But she was too angry to take it back. "You come to our world to take advantage of us and you never bother to learn just what it is you're exploiting. You think that just because we're Selkies, we're all alike, all free and uninhibited no matter which phase we're in."

"What are you talking about?" Riker shot back. "You certainly weren't inhibited back when you were amphibious. Not that night at the embassy, anyway."

"And it never occurred to you that *that was the problem?!* All you brilliant Starfleet explorers, didn't you ever think about the implications of a life cycle with less than two decades of fertility?"

He shook his head at the seeming non sequitur. "I know you have large families while you can."

"Yes! Yes. And who the *iesat* do you think is raising those families while we're off having crazy uninhibited sex all the time, hm? Did it never occur to you that responsibility and hedonism don't exactly mix?"

She'd vowed never to let him know what he'd been a part of, not wanting to burden him with her guilt. But she no longer cared. She told him the whole thing: how only the mature aquatics were free to indulge themselves; how the amphibious were expected to be responsible; how recreational sex was a selfish thrill they sought, pairing with offworlders because they didn't know and wouldn't judge. "Because you're all a bunch of hypocrites," she told him. "You don't bother to figure out that you're facilitating something improper and irresponsible. Easier for you to pretend we're all just like the full aquatics, because then you can take advantage of our negligence and convince yourselves it's a celebration of cultural *kyesh*ing diversity!"

"Is that so?" Riker fired back, as angry as she was now. "*You* choose to neglect your family responsibilities and that makes it *our* fault? Well, tell me something, Ensign Lav-

ena. If your dalliances with offworlders are such a source
of shame to you, why did you join Starfleet? You certainly
haven't found it repulsive to sleep your way through a quarter of my crew! Perhaps the lady doth protest too much!"

She wanted to strike him. But on some level she remembered that he was weak and miserable . . . and he wasn't
the one she was truly angry at. But she was angry enough
to swim away and leave him shivering. He wouldn't accept
her warmth anyway, and right now neither of them could
stand to be together. So she let Alos cradle her gently in his
strong tentacles and carry her the rest of the way.

PLANET LUMBU (UFC 86659-II)

Administrator Ruddle was eager to get home. The latest round of debates would be starting any *gryt* now,
and the canal ferry didn't have a radio. Ruddle would
probably miss the beginning of the coverage. But the sooner
she could finish up her hospital business for the day and
get out the doors, the more of the debate she could par-
take in.

Not that Ruddle fancied herself any great philosopher.
She could barely follow the intricacies of the ideas the
combatants expounded upon—the origins of the cosmos,
the gradations of corporeality, the multiplicity of worlds,
the dynamics of poetry. But she did have a vested interest
in knowing whether Lirht would remain ruled by the Cafmor or be ceded to the Regent of Kump. Those Kumpen
had notions of medical ethics that Ruddle had no desire
to see implemented here at Hvov Memorial—unless, of

course, she could be persuaded of their worth by sufficiently eloquent debate.

But then, that was the major bone of contention being hashed out in tonight's debate. In principle, the war of words had already ended, and the Regent was claiming victory. But the Cafmor and the Lirhten Council rejected the claim. It all came down to an issue Ruddle felt more qualified to comprehend: was the winner in a debate the one who proved one's case more thoroughly and substantially, as Lirhten believed, or the one who adhered more skillfully to the traditional rhetorical form, as Kumpen held to be true? No doubt the Regent had debated beautifully, improvising in perfect twelvefold stanzas without a single syllable stressed out of place. No doubt his use of traditional formulas and invocations had been flawless. But the Council was led by reformists who held that the traditional elevation of form was shallow and decadent, that a leader needed to prove actual knowledge and practical ability, not just mastery of conventional formulas. The Cafmor's arguments had been more informed, more weighted with facts and deduction; but to the Kumpen authorities, that was irrelevant, for her form had been so sloppy and informal that they perceived it as an insult to the Regent himself.

The question Ruddle was dying to hear tested, therefore, was: How would the respective voters decide who won the debate about which set of standards for debate were more valid, when they would be judging that debate using different standards? The recursion involved was dizzying, and Ruddle was mentally assembling a couple of stanzas about it to amuse her cousins with.

Of course, it wouldn't be amusing if the debates broke

down entirely, for then the Regent might actually send in troops. Ruddle wouldn't put it past those Kumpen. It would certainly make things busier at the hospital. Why, lives might even be lost. The thought preoccupied her as she compiled the fatality record for the day. None of the deaths today had been due to violence, but deaths from disease and accident were still all too common, even with the new antibiotic medicines—medicines that a Kumpen regime would force them to give up in favor of homeopathy and spiritual healing, no doubt.

As a result of her morbid mood, Ruddle was extremely alarmed when a loud roaring sound came from outside, accompanied by cries of panic. She rushed to the ambulance lot out front, following the ruckus, pushing past the people who were fleeing inside. She expected to see the worst, some kind of war machine from Kump, maybe an airship delivering troops.

What she saw instead was . . . undreamt of in her philosophy. An angular object of some sort, smaller than an airship but not by much, was descending from the sky, making a roaring, whining noise as it did so. Bright, multicolored lights, even more vivid than the electrics that had replaced gaslights during Ruddle's adolescent years, shone from the object, half-blinding her. What she could make out of the object's shape was bizarre, its contours alien to her experience. "Where did it come from?" she cried to an orderly who was heading inside, grasping his arm.

"Out of the sky! Like a spirit-wain!"

"Don't be absurd! There's a rational explanation for this!"

"I'll be happy to debate that, ma'am," the orderly told

her, "some other time!" He pulled free of her grip and retreated within.

Ruddle had to admit, she could understand the perception of this thing as a spirit manifestation. It had an eldritch quality to it, she realized as it slowly settled to the ground. The way it crushed the *gwik* when it landed left no doubt that it was heavier than air, yet still it had been able to hover without any visible propellers and only the stubbiest of winglike protrusions. Perhaps her childhood beliefs in the spirits deserved another examination after all.

The noise and wind from the bizarre craft subsided, and Ruddle dared to step forward and take a closer look. It was larger than she had estimated, intimidating in its looming bulk and arrowhead contours. And did she catch a glimpse of some massive form moving inside? It was hard to see through the transparent portion mounted on the high upper surface of the hull.

But then a hatch opened on the side—*sliding* open under its own power, as though with a will of its own. Maybe the craft did indeed have its own spirit. Ruddle ducked behind a tree, though it afforded little cover.

Then *it* emerged. It was huge, terrifying—a massive golden-brown *thing*, walking on two legs but with a long, horizontal body and heavy tail like an *elkruh*. But unlike an *elkruh*'s gentle blue-furred countenance, this thing's head was as long and angular as the craft it had emerged from, its enormous mouth filled with countless razor-sharp teeth. Ruddle was too frightened to move.

As the monster came out farther, Ruddle realized it was carrying another creature on its back. This creature was built more like a person, even a female, except it was a giant—Ruddle estimated it was nearly half again a real woman's height—and had no evident *clarfel* below the chin. She (the pronoun seemed reasonable enough to use) also had a pronounced belly, almost like a pregnant woman.

Another giantess emerged behind the monster, walking under her own power. This one was roughly the same size but with no abdominal bulge; still no *clarfel*, though. She placed a hand on the other giantess's flank, perhaps to stabilize her on the monster's back, though it reminded Ruddle of a doctor's gesture of comfort to a patient. The walking giantess held something in her hand that gave off lights and a high warbling sound, waving it in the direction of the other giantess and studying it intently as though it were some magic talisman. Was this how spirits tended each other's illnesses? Or was she reading too much of her own experience into something truly unknown?

The hideous, toothed monster had been looking around the ambulance circle, and now its eyes locked on Ruddle. She jumped, and as it began to stride toward her, she scrambled backward, hoping to retreat into the hospital. But she promptly backed into the side of an abandoned ambulance. And there was no time to try to get inside the cab before the monster reached her. Terror overwhelming her, she sank to the ground, her back against the ambulance's large middle wheel. She prayed to every spirit she'd stopped believing in as the monster loomed over her and opened its slavering maw.

"I am Shenti Yisec Eres Ree of *Titan*," the monster said. "Take me to your obstetrics wing."

Even at his most aggressive, Deanna observed, Ree managed to maintain the politeness that the Pahkwa-thanh cherished—that, indeed, they needed as a people to defuse potential conflicts before they became violent. Instead of roaring and threatening the diminutive, scarlet-skinned hospital staffers into assisting him, he addressed them in a level voice and cast his demands as courteous requests—yet made the underlying threat clear with his body language. ("Amazing what one can accomplish with a civil word and a smile," Ree liked to joke while displaying his alarming array of teeth. Right now, though, he was employing the implied principle in earnest.)

"Think about what you're doing, Ree," she said to him as he carried her into the hospital's maternity ward, the terrorized Lumbuans hastening to make the preparations he'd demanded. She glimpsed other nurses and orderlies carrying newborn Lumbuan babies to safety, something Ree was willing to allow so long as the needs of his own "patient" were met. "You swore an oath to uphold the Prime Directive."

"I have a higher obligation, Counselor," he told her. "And your reminder would carry more weight if not for recent events on Droplet."

"That was unavoidable. This is a wanton violation of noninterference. Why come here? Why not a warp-capable people?"

"The nearest warp-capable species are either nonhumanoid or prone to belligerence. Lumbuans, aside from their size, are similar enough to you for their child-care facilities to be suitable, and unlikely to present any threat to the child. More advanced facilities would have been preferable, but they have the essentials, and we can supplement with Alyssa's kit and the *Horne*'s replicator."

Deanna noted with some satisfaction that the Lumbuan facilities included a birthing chair, which was her preference, although it would be a bit snug for her. However, for the moment, Ree insisted she lie down in one of the ward's smallish beds and rest. Ogawa moved to her bedside and ran a scan on the baby's vitals. But her eyes darted to the window as the sound of alien sirens came from outside, drawing nearer. "They've called in the police," she said sotto voce. "I hope they're as nonviolent as Ree says."

"That's what our survey last month suggested. They're a philosophical people, preferring debate over physical conflict." Still, Deanna reflected silently, even a normally peaceful species could be dangerous when terrified. And *Titan* had not been able to survey this society as thoroughly as she would have liked; Vidra Tabyr, the new Ithenite petty officer from engineering, had been the only one small and humanoid enough to go among the Lumbuans in disguise. Tabyr had done her best, but she had not been trained for the task. Most of what the crew had learned about Lumbu had come from orbital scans, stealth probes, and monitoring of their radio-band communications, which were still in an early, audio-only stage. Deanna took some comfort in their limited telecommunications and crude motor vehicles, hoping that it would minimize the exposure of this culture to the knowledge of alien life—and delay the response of this nation's military, which was rarely used but currently on high alert due to ongoing tensions with a neighboring state.

"Ree, think about this," Deanna said when the doctor came back from securing the doors. "Peaceful or not, those police officers out there see us as a threat, and they will do what they feel they must to defend their people. My baby and I are not safe here. You must take us away from here."

"There is no time. You are too close to term. You could deliver at any time. As for the authorities, I will not allow them to harm the child." The fierce gleam in his eye intimidated her, and her throat constricted.

But she calmed herself and found her voice again. "If you inflict violence on them, matters will only escalate. Hostage situations rarely work out well for the captors. And they will see me as a captor, as a threat."

Ree whirled to the Lumbuan ward nurses who cowered in a corner. "You! If you would please tell me what you see here," he said, pointing to Deanna.

"A . . . a pregnant giantess?" one of the male nurses managed to say.

The doctor smiled. "Very good. And pray tell, how do your people feel about babies?"

"They . . . are precious to us. Please, I have a young son at home, he needs me!"

Ree strode closer and spoke in a low growl. "Is this true?"

"Yes! I swear! His mother died last year!"

The Pahkwa-thanh lifted the nurse by his collar and carried him to the exit. "Then go. Make sure the police understand there is an unborn child in this room . . . and that I will devour anyone who brings the slightest harm to it. Then go to your son and keep him safe."

He unsealed the door long enough to toss out the nurse. One of the younger female nurses straightened up and said, "I—I have a son too! And two daughters! Just babies!"

Ree's head whirled to transfix her in his gaze. "You've

never been pregnant in your life," he told her after a moment. His head lunged forward, jaws gaping, and Deanna almost screamed. But in a second, it was over—the doctor's jaws were clamped shut just in front of the nurse's nose, and her own scream trailed off as she sank to the floor, wetting herself. "Be grateful I need a staff familiar with your equipment," he told her. "But keep in mind that your value is contingent on your cooperation. I trust my . . . point . . . is made?" The nurse nodded, unable to speak. "Very good." He turned to the other nurses. "Help her clean up, will you, please? This *is* a hospital."

Deanna's fear had triggered a surge of adrenaline, which she chose to use by getting angry; maybe confrontation would help where reason had failed. "This whole situation is ridiculous! Look at yourself, Ree! What do you expect to accomplish here? What kind of caregiver leads an expectant mother into a hostage situation where the people you depend on for help have to be terrorized into compliance? Is this really your idea of how a Pahkwa-thanh male cares for a child?" Alyssa looked at her in shock, subtly shaking her head. But Deanna knew that she was the one person Ree would not harm, so long as the child was still inside her.

But her words had no effect. "Calm yourself, Counselor. We don't want to place the dear child under any stress."

"You're creating the stress, Ree! Why can't you see that?"

Ree came closer, taking her hand. He was suddenly in full Reassuring Doctor mode. "Have faith, Deanna. I have decades of experience as a specialist in obstetrics. Your child is in safe hands with me."

She studied him. Was there more motivating him than an instinctive response to her projected fears? "It's important to you to believe that, isn't it?"

"Nothing matters more to me than the well-being of a child."

"You have so much devotion to children."

"Profoundly."

"Then why have you never had any of your own?"

His hand twitched atop hers; luckily he filed his claws, or the mild scratches she sustained would have been far worse. He looked away. "My . . . professional commitments have not allowed me the time."

"But you have had offers?" He remained silent. "No, you haven't, have you? Come to think of it, don't Pahkwa-thanh females generally prefer their males somewhat larger and more robust than you?"

He fidgeted. "My strengths are in the mind," he declared. "They are just as valuable."

"But are they as valued?" She softened her voice. "It's not your fault if they never appreciated you. Never gave you the chance to prove what a devoted father you'd be.

"But now you have that chance. Your chance to be the strong, aggressive, masculine one. Your chance to be the father figure you've wanted to be all your life. It must be a very rewarding feeling."

"My only reward will be the safe delivery of your daughter. And her continued safety thereafter."

"Do you intend to watch over her the rest of her life? You've made your point, Ree. You've proven your commitment to her safety. You've proven your worth as a protector. You don't need to take this any further."

Suddenly his snout was in her face, his hot breath ruffling her hair. "Proven my worth? Says the female who called me ridiculous? You've seen that I don't appreciate being lied to, Counselor. It's intensely impolite. Be as angry with me as you like, but do not deceive me or attempt to interfere with my efforts to protect your child. As you have heard, I will not tolerate lack of cooperation." He lowered his head, eyes locking on hers while the front of his jaws hovered over her neck. "Your child is able to survive on her own now. I suggest you do not make yourself superfluous to her well-being."

As she looked into his eyes, Deanna realized she had miscalculated. Ree's concern for the child's safety did not necessarily extend to her mother. But what terrified her, even more than the implied threat to her own life, was another thought: once the child was delivered, how did she know Ree would let her keep it?

CHAPTER THIRTEEN

TITAN

T'Pel looked up from the poem she was composing as Noah Powell came into her quarters, where he had been staying since his mother—and T'Pel's husband—had departed the ship nearly five standard days before. "Greetings, Noah," she said. "How was your afternoon with Commander Keru?"

"It was acceptable," the boy said, his tone devoid of affect.

T'Pel lifted a brow. "Has there been any news pertaining to your mother?" Logically, if there had been, T'Pel would have received word pertaining to her husband as well. Yet there was occasional value in human conversational gambits such as asking questions whose answers were known—at least when conversing with humans. The status of Nurse Ogawa had weighed heavily on the ten-year-old boy these past several days, so T'Pel had striven to be receptive to his concerns on the issue.

"No, there has not," the boy said, still evincing no emotion.

"I see. And how do you feel about that?"

Noah endeavored to cock an eyebrow at her, though the other one went partway up along with it. "I feel nothing."

"Indeed?"

"There is nothing I can do to alter the situation. So it would be illogical to expend emotional energy upon it."

T'Pel rose from her console and crossed her arms. "You are attempting to emulate Vulcan behavior in the belief that it will insulate you from your current emotional distress."

Noah frowned at her. "I thought you'd like—approve of that. You were the one who told me it was illogical to worry."

"That is a misinterpretation, Noah. I said that it would be illogical to dwell unduly upon your fears. But those fears are perfectly natural for you to experience."

"Well, maybe I don't want to experience them anymore. If you can do it, why can't I?"

"It is not that simple. Come." She moved to the couch and sat; a moment later, Noah followed, though he kept a formal distance. "Noah, the Vulcan way is a lifelong path of discipline and self-examination. If you chose, after careful consideration, to dedicate yourself to pursuing that path, I would not disapprove—so long as your mother gave *her* approval. But it takes many years of immersive training to discipline oneself to the point that one's emotions can be successfully managed and partitioned from one's everyday decision-making. It requires a careful and gradual reorientation of the cognitive process, for it is not the natural way for a humanoid mind to function.

"You do not have that training, Noah. Your emotions are an integral and normal part of your psyche. So a sudden attempt to lock them away and deny their influence upon you can only do you harm. The feelings will not be managed, only ignored."

She met his gaze squarely. "You say you do not wish to experience your current fears as to your mother's well-being. Is that your only motive? Or is there some other emotional experience you are hoping to avoid?"

By now, Noah was struggling to maintain his façade of detachment. "I went through that once . . . with my father. And I hardly knew him. If . . . if Mom doesn't come back . . . I don't want to feel that."

T'Pel was silent for a time, gathering her thoughts. "I understand. But if that were to happen . . . even a fully trained Vulcan could not avoid experiencing the grief. Grief is too powerful an emotion to wish away. It is a transformative experience. No matter how ideal your control . . . the grief is there. Vulcan discipline does not erase that."

She lowered her eyes, gazing at her folded hands upon her lap. "Indeed, in some ways, it makes the process of dealing with grief more . . . intense. More difficult. Because we must master it within ourselves—confront it directly in meditation and . . . negotiate with it until we find a way to make peace with it. It requires great strength and self-control.

"In some ways, I believe, the human way must be easier. For you can share your grief with others . . . turn to them for comfort and release."

After a moment, T'Pel saw Noah's small hand clasp her own. "I didn't know. I know it's been hard for Mister

Tuvok to get over losing your son . . . but I thought you . . . I didn't know you had to go through that. I'm sorry."

"There is no cause for regret, Noah. My son's life, as well as that of my daughter-in-law, carried great value. They deserved the acknowledgment of my grief, even if it was a private experience. I regret their loss, but I do not regret grieving their loss. It was necessary—and proper."

She saw that Noah's eyes had grown wet, and realized it was necessary to modify the course of this discussion. "I see that you are no longer attempting to deny your emotions," she said. "That is good. But remember—we have no reason to believe your mother will not return safely. In all likelihood, this discussion will prove to be purely hypothetical."

The boy studied her. "So . . . you're not worried about Mister Tuvok?"

"He and I have been separated for far longer than this," T'Pel told him. "Our longest separation was seven years, when he was aboard *Voyager* in the Delta Quadrant. Two years, six months into that time, my husband was officially declared dead, and was not discovered to be alive until seven months thereafter. I have already been through the experience of grieving for him. It is not an experience I wish to repeat.

"However, it also established a precedent. If my husband was able to stay alive for seven years in the Delta Quadrant and return to me, then I have little cause for concern in the current instance."

Noah smiled. "Me too, T'Pel. If Mister Tuvok's anywhere near as smart as you, my mom's gonna be fine."

DROPLET: THE DEPTHS

It took the engineers a day to design, replicate, assemble, and test the diving pod for what the crew had already dubbed "Cethente's Descent." It was a perfect sphere for uniform compression, and in fact was designed to be somewhat compressible so that the interior pressure could increase along with the exterior, minimizing the differential that its structural integrity field would have to resist. Also to that end, the interior was filled with a dense fluid not unlike Syrath growth medium, which would serve to sustain Cethente throughout the dive. The control cradle was designed to be snug against the underside of Cethente's dome, so that it could use its tentacles—the most vulnerable parts of its body—to operate it without needing to expose them to the full pressure. Cethente, whose legs were now being kept in medical stasis, had needed assistance to be lowered into the cradle, but once securely in place, the Syrath actually felt more comfortable than it would if it had needed to fold up its long legs somewhere in the bathysphere. Cethente was not concerned by the amputation; Onnta had assured it that the limbs could be reattached without difficulty, and even if they could not, a few weeks in genuine growth medium would suffice to regenerate them. Cethente only preferred reattachment because, for one thing, it was more convenient, and for another, it didn't want that extra set of legs potentially growing into a clone of itself. In those rare cases where separate pieces of an injured or dead Syrath were simultaneously regenerated into whole beings with the same core personality, it proved difficult for two beings with equal claim to the same identity to coexist civilly. Dying was easy; comity was hard.

Once Cethente was secured in the pod, it was towed by shuttle down to the surface and released. As soon as it was given the go-ahead, Cethente turned off the antigravs that gave the pod buoyancy, allowing it to sink more swiftly than a humanoid could endure, though still slowly enough to give Cethente's body time to acclimate to the rising pressure. Odds were that it would be unharmed, but why take chances? The slower descent was easier on the pod as well.

It soon became clear just how shallow the veneer of life was on this world. After just the first kilometer, barely over one percent of the way to the solid mantle, all sunlight was gone, even to Cethente's wide-band optics, and far fewer living things were coming in range of the pod's sensors—only a few scattered, bioluminescent organisms. And they rapidly thinned out over the next few kilometers. Without sunlight, life could only consume other life to survive; but the constant "marine snow" of organic detritus that descended into this realm, the remains and discards of the more abundant creatures dwelling above, was progressively consumed along the way, growing sparser and sparser. And so the life became sparser as well. (Cethente reflected that it would not want to live if it had to consume the remains of other organisms to do so, rather than subsisting on radiant or geothermal energy and the occasional absorption of mineral compounds. It didn't understand how its crewmates could tolerate it, even when the consumables were created in a replicator. Luckily, without a digestive tract, Syrath were incapable of nausea.)

By about a dozen kilometers down, the ocean had become virtually barren. The sensors registered only one exception: a particular genus of zooplankton, microscopic animal life. It was sparsely distributed, but still the only life to exist in any abundance at all down here. Cethente was no biologist, but it believed it was odd to find plankton at these depths, with no sunlight to sustain it. True, the sensors showed that the plankton was in a dormant state, alive but conserving what little energy it had. *Conserving it for what?* Cethente wondered. *And why are they down here at all if they cannot function here?*

Cethente could not share these questions with anyone except the bathysphere's log recorder, for the EM interference and the sheer intervening mass of water made communication with *Titan* impossible. It logged its observations into the recorder, but soon it ran out of things to say. For long minutes, the realm outside was unchanging, save only for a steady increase in pressure and a gradual brightening of the magnetic field patterns emanating from below. There was nothing to do, nothing to perceive. *So much of the universe is empty,* the Syrath reflected. *Life exists only in tiny portions of it. Even on planets whose surfaces seem so lush and rich with life, scratch below the surface and you find immense volumes of emptiness.* Cethente knew the emptiness of space was unimaginably more vast, but it was more difficult to perceive that as one raced through it at high warp speeds, hurrying through it to avoid facing it. Especially on a ship with hundreds of other beings of numerous different types, surrounding one with life. And as an astrophysicist, he was able to think of the universe in terms of vast scales, abstract and removed from life. But down here, alone, drifting slowly through the emptiness, facing it on a scale that was smaller and more comprehensible, it was easier to appreciate how vast the cosmos actually was in proportion to living things. *Is this why we so rarely visit ocean planets?* Cethente mused. *Not only because they are barren, but because their depths frighten us?* Syrath had little fear of nonexistence, but to exist without input or companionship—that was terror.

Cethente's time sense slowed in response to the sensory deprivation, and it entered the meditative state that was its species' closest analog to sleep. An unknown time later, it was roused by several changes in its environment. One was that the magnetic field patterns dancing across its sensory nodes were resolving and growing brighter. Another was that the pod's descent was beginning to slow. The third, related to the second, was that the readouts in the control cradle were registering an accelerating increase in water density. It was a myth that water was incompressible; it was merely difficult to compress, requiring hundreds of atmospheres of pressure to make a significant difference in its density. But that point had been reached at about the same depth where total darkness had fallen, and the density had been increasing at a slow but exponentially rising rate ever since; this comparatively sudden increase had to be from some other cause.

The other thing that affected water density, Cethente recalled from its daylong crash course in oceanography, was salinity, the ratio of minerals dissolved in the water. Checking its depth and taking a few more scans, Cethente confirmed that it was nearing the hypersaline layer, the saltwater dynamo whose contamination was altering the planet's magnetic chorus. Cethente took a moment to "listen" to the magnetic field, although to the Syrath it was more like tasting; the field patterns did seem slightly dissonant, tinged with more exotic energies, though Cethente found it bracing rather than disquieting. *Must be a flesh thing,* it reflected.

The interface between the upper ocean and the hypersaline layer was not a sharp divide. The two layers had separate convection currents, keeping them from mixing too extensively, but there was a gradual transition from one to the other, more like the distinction between two layers of an atmosphere or a stellar interior than between two strata of rock, say. Nonetheless, the pod was slowing as the water around it grew denser and more buoyant, and once it was confident it had become sufficiently immersed in the dynamo layer, Cethente set the antigravs to give the pod neutral buoyancy, halting its descent. The Syrath set the sensors to maximum gain, and opened its own senses as well—the same senses that had allowed its species to develop an advanced knowledge of astrophysics while living on a perpetually clouded world.

Both sensory suites soon revealed the same thing: Cethente was not alone down here. It could sense smaller surges and pulsations in the magnetic field, isolated, seemingly random, yet oddly purposeful. It had the flavor of life to it. The sensors confirmed it: the dynamo layer was inhabited!

"Remarkable," Cethente said into the log recorder after studying the scan results. *"This is an order of high-pressure life —barophiles, the computer calls them—completely unlike what is found on the surface. They are evolved for pres-*

sures that would destroy protein-based life. They are very dense, solid creatures, made of pressure-resistant shapes: spheres, toroids, cylinders with rounded ends. They have no internal voids, no pockets of lower density to give them buoyancy. They use hydrofoil surfaces, fins, to give themselves lift. They seem to ride the convection currents, which implies they can survive being swept down near to the deepest, highest-pressure regions of the dynamo layer."

Cethente took the time to collect samples of a few small creatures, beaming them into the sample chamber, for the pressure-resistant design of the pod allowed for no hatches to draw them through. After a few minutes of analysis, it went on. *"Instead of normal cell walls, they have microskeletons made of silicate spicules. Down here, the heavier elements are sufficiently concentrated to allow this. The spicules are intricately interlocked in a tight but flexible framework. It reminds me of plant biology on Syr."* "Plant" was a rough analogy, but it would do. *"They appear to be magnetosynthetic, feeding on the field energy of the saltwater dynamo. Their biochemistry is based on molecules that are sturdy enough to withstand these pressures and temperatures, but would be inert under normal conditions. Intriguingly, this includes clathrates of carbon and heavier elements—ice-seven crystals actually serving as part of their biology."* This did not come as a complete surprise; Cethente was near a depth where it was possible for that allotrope of ice to form, though salinity, temperature, and other factors affected its formation and survival. At this depth, the water was fully liquid, but farther down it would grow increasingly slushy, a gradual transition from the liquid ocean to the hot-ice mantle below. Apparently when the creatures followed the convection currents down to the deeper levels, they fed upon the clathrates—ice-crystal lattices holding other types of atoms or molecules caged within them—and made use of the elements and compounds thus obtained, including the ice crystals themselves as a structural material. No doubt this was a major source of the silicates and other heavy elements constituting their biology; although the hypersaline layer was itself rich in these substances compared to the ocean above, the clathrate layer atop the mantle would be richer still, for that was where the infalling debris from space would eventually settle, accumulating more and more over billions of years.

"Is this how the heavy elements are kept in play in the ecosystem?" Cethente asked after summarizing this. *"These barophile life forms bring them up from the mantle . . . but then what? How do they get from here to the surface? Convective mixing does not seem enough."*

Cethente watched the barophiles for a while longer, enjoying the intricate dance of light across their surfaces, though it doubted this was a light that its humanoid crewmates could see. *"They emit magnetic pulses in complex patterns,"* it reported, *"apparently a form of communication. The translator detects nothing indicative of intelligence, though. But it is beautiful music. I wish you could experience this."*

But as it continued to travel through the dynamo layer, sinking deeper to where the barophilic life was more abundant, Cethente found that it was not all so lively and beautiful. It began to encounter dead creatures drifting in the convection currents, slowly sinking coreward before being latched onto by other creatures that pierced their bodies with stingers and began sucking out their internal fluids, making them crumple and crack under the pressure. Other creatures were weak and apparently ill, their magnetic calls feeble and distorted. Some were acting erratically, swimming aimlessly or striking out at anything that moved near, whether a prey species or one of their own kind. *"They have been poisoned,"* Cethente reported after bringing the pod closer to a cluster of them for a more detailed scan. *"I read the same nadion and subspace energy signatures as in the asteroid dust. It is sinking here, being consumed by these animals, and it is disrupting their magnetosynthetic processes and their magnetic senses. It is at once starving them and deranging them."*

But Cethente had drawn too close. Not having the instinct for mortal fear, it sometimes acted with insufficient caution, especially when in the throes of curiosity. It had been so caught up in observing these animals' hyperaggressive behavior that it had not considered how they would react to the pod's proximity. Cethente was shaken in its cradle as the creatures began to batter at the pod, stabbing at it with their stingers. They were made of sturdy stuff, less sturdy than the pod's SIF-reinforced duranium hull in absolute terms, but enough to put added strain on a hull and integrity field that were already pushed to the limits by the sheer weight of seventy kilometers of ocean overhead. Deciding it had gotten enough scans for now, Cethente turned the antigravs to full, causing the pod to shoot upward.

A few of the creatures managed to cling to the pod somehow, perhaps by magnetic adhesion. Some fell away as the bathysphere soared upward, but two proved exceptionally persistent, hanging on for dear life and jabbing at the hull with blind ferocity. They were on the upper surface of the pod, perhaps held there by the water pressure itself. But as the pressure and temperature fell, as the magnetic energy sustaining them grew more attenuated, their movements weakened and tapered off. Cethente did nothing to prevent the animals' deaths; after all, they were dying already, and at least this way it was quicker.

Eventually, the creatures' bodies burst open, the pressure outside their bodies too low now to contain the pressure within. At this depth, they might as well have been in vacuum—though the pressure was still beyond the maximum amount that protein-based life could withstand. *"Remarkable,"* Cethente said. *"Two totally different biospheres sharing a single planet, but they might as well be on entirely different worlds. There seems to be no way they can ever interact physically. So how can the heavy elements in the deep biosphere be returned to the surface biosphere?"*

But it had another reaction that it chose not to record for its crewmates: astonishment and pity at the sheer fragility of non-Syrath life forms. *If they were more like us, they would not have lost so much to the Borg. But then, they lose everything, in time. Their whole existence must end in tragedy.*

Cethente was philosophical about it, though. After all, for the same reasons Syrath lacked mortal dread, they also lacked any deep sense of grief. It understood regret at losing something valuable, but to a Syrath, even the loss of life memory was a growth experience, a chance for a fresh start. Excitement at new possibilities always overcame regret before long. That was why it was able to live among these fragile beings, even knowing their existence was doomed.

Not that they would ever know it felt that way, of course. Syrath maintained their enigmatic reputation for very good reason.

DROPLET: THE SURFACE

Riker's new floater-islet sanctuary—or prison—was somewhat larger and more comfortable than the previous one. It had some larger palm-like growths with wide, round leaves that the plants could apparently angle into the wind to serve as sails. Aili wished Eviku or even Kekil were here to tell her why a tree would evolve this ability. Was it simply to maneuver out from under clouds or away from storms, or was it more symbiotic, the palms actually helping the floater colonies navigate to nutrient-rich areas so that the palms could in turn draw more nourishment from the islets? She could ask Cham or Gasa, but the elder squale reacted to her frequent questions with impatience and the younger might not know. Besides, she missed her crewmates.

For now, though, all that mattered was that the leaves provided Riker with some covering and warmth. There was also a depression holding enough fresh rainwater to sustain him, and a small cave burrowed into the islet by some tool-creatures of the squales, apparently used to store surplus food, but now largely cleared out to serve as a shelter for the weakened human. Some remnants of the surplus seaweed had been left at the base of the cave to rot, its decay producing some warmth for Riker's benefit, although he clearly did not enjoy the smell. Aili asked the squales if they had anything that could potentially start a fire, perhaps some creature secreting chemicals that generated heat when mixed, but they had little familiarity with the concept. On a world like this, pretty much the only thing that could start fires was lightning, but the high humidity of the air near the ocean surface conducted charge too well for any large voltage differential to build up, so most of the lightning on Droplet was cloud-to-cloud, except in cases where an ocean swell surged exceptionally high.

Riker's condition was growing steadily worse. He was weak, fatigued, suffering occasional tremors, and he was having difficulty keeping food down and keeping fluids in. It made Aili feel somewhat guilty about fighting with him, but that guilt was smothered by her continued anger at his assumptions about her. She didn't want his health to suffer further, but she wasn't inclined to speak civilly to him beyond what was necessary between an ensign and her commanding officer.

The ideal solution to both problems was a return to *Titan*—assuming the ship and its crew were still intact, still able to help them. Aili asked Alos to take her to Melo so she could plead her case, on the theory that the astronomy-pod leader would be the one most sympathetic to the off-worlders (aside from Alos and Gasa, who lacked the authority Melo held). She explained to the aged squale that neither she nor Riker could survive on Droplet in the long term. But Melo denied her request, and Aili soon recognized that there was an apologetic tone to his song; his denial was cast, not so much in terms of what the squales would not do, but in terms of what they *could* not do. "What do you mean?" Aili demanded in Selkie. "Is there anyone else left? Are the others like me still on . . . in the world at all?"

The two astronomer squales exchanged a private communication for several moments, flashing intricate color patterns to one another on their carapaces. Then they sang to the others nearby at a speed that outraced her tenuous understanding of their speech. The squale language was polyphonic and incredibly intricate, with multiple channels of information being conveyed at once in parallel. Even at slow speed, she could only follow a fragment of it.

But when Melo finally sang to her in Selkie again, his reply was simple: *"Not for Aili."*

"What does that mean?" Aili pleaded.

"That is a mystery we have not solved."

She winced. Either the contact pod was being kept out of the loop for some reason, or . . . she didn't know what. Sensing her distress, Alos stroked her with a tentacle and told her not to worry, assuring her that they would take care of her.

"You can't," she tried once more to explain to them. "Your food cannot sustain me for long. It can sustain Riker for far less time. It lacks things we need. We are different from you, from the other life that lives here."

Once the astronomers understood her concern, they promised to discuss the matter with the biologists. Finally, after hours of squalesong she could not follow, Aili was approached by the visitor from the life-maker pod, a mature male she had nicknamed Eres, after Doctor Ree's third name.

"There is a way the two from World Beyond can be made well," Eres sang. *"Your Song is out of harmony, in key unlike our own. But keys may be transposed. Though our own Song is in discord, it still sustains our life, more so than your metallic theme. Perhaps, indeed, transposing you would end the dissonance, and bring the Song of Life back into ancient harmony."*

Aili struggled to parse the poetry, but the ideas were too strange to her. Was Eres actually proposing some kind of biological transformation? She knew the squales believed the Song of Life created the world and all things in it. It followed that they defined biology as an aspect of the Song. But even with the squales' exceptional capacity for animal breeding, how could they transform a living individual?

Eres was reluctant to reveal the answer to an alien; Aili was reminded of a priest defending a sacred mystery from exposure to heathen eyes. But Alos and Gasa took her case, debating eloquently that she deserved the opportunity to make an informed decision. The squales were an open society, necessarily so in an ocean where sound could travel so far and wide that secrets were difficult to keep (although the squales' color-changing skin gave them an avenue for private discourse at close range). All matters were debated openly in the *ri'Hoyalina* forum and decided through democratic consensus. It was part of their basic beliefs, Alos reminded his elders, that all sapient beings had the right to informed self-determination.

Finally, Eres agreed that Aili should be shown the answer to her questions. But Aili consulted with Riker before agreeing to go. The meeting was awkward, but necessarily brief due to the limited time she could spend on dry land. "I don't like it," he said. "We shouldn't separate too far."

"I know they'll keep me safe. And their helpers will tend to you while I'm gone, if you need anything."

"Marvelous," he muttered. "Cared for by woodland creatures. Just like a storybook."

She wasn't sure if he was being sarcastic or becoming delirious. But then he nodded and said, "Go." And that was all. Deciding she couldn't afford to linger, she raced back to the water.

The trip took most of the night, even with the large, strong Eres holding Aili in his tentacles and swimming at top speed. As local dawn broke, they entered an area where the squales kept their farms and breeding facilities, one of several such complexes which were centralized to be more defensible. As she drew near the first farm, she initially thought it was just a large kelp bed. But she soon realized it was far too regular. It was a vast, floating lattice on which the kelp grew like ivy on a trellis. By catching a swell and swim-leaping out of the water, she was able to get an overhead view, revealing it to be an enormous fractal spiral like a sunflower blossom. The lattice was itself alive, made of a woodlike material; below the spiraling surface, a series of branches grew straight down, evenly spaced so as to make light and nutrients available equally to all the plants. Several small species of animal coexisted with the kelp, serving as "farmhands" under the supervision of a large aggregate pod of farmer squales. As Eres explained, a couple of species gobbled up parasites and organisms that fed upon the kelp; others devoured "weeds" that happened to take root upon the lattice. Animals of a harvester species

used their hard beaks to break off lengths of the kelp, carrying it up to the surface in their tentacles and transferring
it to flying chordates that carried it away, no doubt to storage caverns like the one now sheltering Riker. The flight
presumably helped dry the kelp, prolonging its shelf life.

Soon they came upon a variant of the farm lattice organism, this one with a second spiral framework down below,
forming an enclosed cage. Fast-swimming, dangerous-
looking squale-related animals with fearsome beaks
patrolled its perimeter. Here, Eres rendezvoused with the
others in his "life-maker" pod, who had been alerted to
his arrival hours ago by *ri'Hoyalina* telecommunication.
The pod passed Aili through the defense cordon and let her
examine the woodlike columns that formed the cage. They
were made of a material considerably harder than normal
wood, though presumably hollow enough for buoyancy.
Aili suspected that they had used a lot of their limited
metal reserves to supply this organism with its structural
strength.

The columns were arranged in a precise pattern, forming a complex maze. Using their keen sonar as well as
firsthand memory, and with Aili clinging to Eres's back,
the squales navigated the maze, finding the spaces wide
enough to admit them but taking care to avoid the deceptively clear-looking paths which would lead to dead ends.
Aili realized that a maze made of broomsticks was far
more treacherous than one made of walls; at least in the
latter there was no ambiguity about what was an opening
and what was not. But here, openings abounded, and the
constantly shifting parallax made it devilishly difficult to
tell which ones were really the clearest. As the pod wound

through the perimeter, they passed a few small animals that struck Aili as being quite at the end of their ropes.

Aili wondered how they got larger organisms into this facility if need be. But before she could ask, they cleared the maze into a zone of clear, still water, shielded from wave action by the surrounding lattice. At the heart of the clear zone, she saw what it was that the squales were protecting so carefully.

The core mass of the organism, floating in the center of the lattice, was easily the size of Earth's largest extinct whales. From that mass extruded over two dozen stems, or trunks, or limbs, each of which led to a bluish oval pod. Some of the pods were irised open at one end like the petals of a flower. They came in various sizes; the smallest, of which there were several, were about a meter long, while the largest one could accommodate a small humpback whale. The majority of the pods seemed to be just right for the squales, though. The stems were complex, with numerous veins of various sizes and tints weaving among each other.

The core mass itself pulsed with life. Its structure was startlingly complex, a mélange of colors, textures, and contours, seeming as dazzlingly sophisticated in an organic way as *Titan*'s control consoles. Multiple valves pulsed and peristalted, taking in water, expelling bubbles of gas; while at least one orifice was hungrily sucking in a supply of food being shoveled like coal by a small, dextrous helper species. It made sense that the organism would need a rich and steady fuel supply. It certainly seemed busy enough, pulsing and throbbing and exhaling vapors unknown.

But most of all, it was *singing*. And its squale tenders sang back to it. It was an interspecies chorus, liturgy and antiphon, builder and tool conversing in a common tongue. Rich, complex chords, elaborate phrases recurring, being repeated back and forth, sometimes changing from one statement to the next. The mathematical perfection of Bach or T'Lenye meeting the improvisational energy of Riker's beloved jazz musicians.

Aili took some time to make sense of what she'd seen, seasoning her analysis with the occasional answer from the squales. It was a machine, she reasoned. It took in a living sample and analyzed its genome, probably using enzymes like those that zipped, unzipped, and assembled nucleic acids. Somehow, that information was converted into sound, a melody with the notes A, C, G, and T, the four component bases of the genetic code. What the life-smiths sang back were instructions, modifications to the genes and protein structures; those changes were probably made through the action of further enzymes. This could be used for healing, and indeed many of the attached oval pods held squales who were being treated for injuries inflicted by the other frenzied species of this world. Eres led her to one pod and sang a tone that caused it to iris open partway, far enough for her to see a squale inside. After a moment, she recognized it as Grabby, the defender squale who had lost a tentacle days before. Now that tentacle was almost fully regrown!

Aili remembered the perception of a womblike environment that both she and Riker had experienced after the asteroid strike, and realized that they must have been placed in these "lifepods" (as she mentally dubbed them) for treatment of their injuries. But as Grabby's rapid regeneration showed, the lifepods were capable of far more than that. Eres confirmed this, singing that the lifepods could also be used to make more fundamental changes, transforming creatures at the cellular or even genetic level.

Now she understood what the lifesmiths were proposing. Using this remarkable technology, they could modify Aili's and Riker's biochemistry to be compatible with Dropletian life, able to survive with fewer minerals in their diet. Even if *Titan* never found them, they would be able to live out their lives here on this world.

But there was a danger, as Eres explained. A transformation this drastic would alter their bodies on the cellular level. This would include the neurons in their brains. Their memories would be affected as a result—not so much lost as blurred. They would still retain their identities and knowledge, but certain details of their former life would be hazier, as if more distant in time.

But if they underwent the change a second time, Eres warned, the effect on their memories would be exacerbated. They would lose too much memory of their past, their identities. If Aili and Riker underwent this change, they could never go back.

Aili knew that Riker would never accept that. His conviction that he would be reunited with his wife and child was unwavering. And in the wake of their recent argument, given what he thought about her intentions toward him, he would not be receptive to the suggestion coming from her.

But what about me? She found the lifesmiths' proposal did not instill fright or despair in her. On the contrary, she felt more at home here on Droplet than she ever had anywhere else. And she couldn't share Riker's certainty that there would be any rescue from *Titan*. For that matter, after her fight with the captain, she wasn't sure how welcome she would be aboard *Titan*—or how willing she would be to continue serving under a commander who didn't respect her.

Or was it really her own lack of self-respect she was feeling? The argument had dredged up memories she wasn't proud of. *Maybe losing some of those memories wouldn't be so bad,* she thought. *It would be like . . . being reborn. Starting over with a clean slate.*

Maybe the song of my life is out of tune, she reflected. *And not just biologically. Maybe getting "transposed" is just what I need.*

But thinking in terms of the squales' Song of Life brought her a different perspective. To them, everything that happened in life was a part of the flow and rhythm of the Song. Every event was a note in a greater symphony, progressing from what had come before. True, there could be dissonance, but that was a part of music too, tension leading to an inevitable resolution.

What if everything that's happened in my life was part of a bigger purpose? she wondered. The way she had rejected her family's example and become self-indulgent and irresponsible, which had led her to seduce countless visitors from space and alienate her from her own people, which had pushed her to leave Pacifica, which had brought her to Starfleet Academy on a quest to become responsible at last, which had put her aboard *Titan* and led her here to Droplet . . . maybe all of these events were notes in the cosmic song, the requirements of harmony arranging the melody of her life, inexorably guiding her to this point. *Maybe this is where I'm meant to be.*

But what about the captain? she asked herself. *He would never believe that for himself.*

But the bottom line was, they might very well have no choice. Whether or not Riker could be happy with that, Aili knew that she could.

And if it came to that . . . maybe she could help bring him around.

CHAPTER FOURTEEN

LUMBU

By the time Tuvok's team arrived in the UFC 86659 system, Ree and his captives had been on the surface of Lumbu for nearly twenty-one hours, evidently besieged within a local hospital in the nation-state of Lirht. Once Ellec Krotine had tapped into the signal leakage from the city's land-line audio communications system to listen in on the local authorities, Tuvok reflected that it was fortunate the Lumbuans were a people predisposed to philosophy and discussion above action. Even now, more than a local day into the crisis, the police commander on the scene, her chief, and their mayor were still locked into an involved debate over the best way to negotiate with an alien monster—with sidebar discussions about whether Ree's origin was extra-planetary or paranormal, and what either possibility might reveal about the nature of existence. If anything, the mayor seemed more interested in capturing Ree and the women in order to interrogate them on the meaning of life and the truth of the cosmos than in ending the immediate threat Ree posed to the hospital staff. As for the siege commander, she seemed content to try out new negotiation tactics indefinitely so long as no imminent mortal threat to the hostages arose, and if anything seemed to be quite stimulated by the intellectual challenge. *Admirable in principle,* Tuvok thought, *but somewhat paralyzing in a crisis. Luckily, that works in our favor.*

On the negative side, the police chief was rather eloquently arguing the position that this incident was too ontologically important for city officials to handle and that federal assistance should be sought. While news of the incident had been reported by wire to the national news services, it was apparently not being taken seriously in the absence of concrete evidence. The Lirhten military was monitoring the reports in case they were proven legitimate, but was currently on alert due to tensions with a neighboring nation-state and had not assigned the situation a high priority. Had this world been a generation more advanced, with the capacity for live video broadcasting, the situation would have been rather worse. However, the police chief was proposing that photographic evidence and eyewitnesses be flown by propeller-driven aircraft to the regional capital in order to persuade the government to supply soldiers, diplomats, and philosophers to address the crisis. If that happened, it would worsen the Prime Directive violation. If Tuvok could end this situation while it remained isolated and leave no physical evidence behind, the incident would likely become a local legend and have no global effect. But if a major government gained proof of alien life, the contamination would be far worse.

Moreover, given the current tensions between Lirht and its neighbor, dividing the attention of the Lirhten military could weaken their position and lead to the conquest of their nation. It would probably not be a very bloody conquest, but it would be a major political change caused by a Starfleet presence on the planet, and that was unacceptable.

The police chief was close to winning the debate, leaving Tuvok no choice but to act. "Rig the warp core to emit a magneton pulse," he ordered Krotine, whose years aboard an S.C.E. vessel had given her more engineering experience than the others on his team. "It should be sufficient to knock out the power systems citywide and prevent them from summoning outside help."

"But what about the hospital?" Ensign Hriss asked. "What if Counselor Troi needs that power?"

"The hospital should have an emergency generator," he told her. "Failing that, Starfleet equipment should be unaffected."

"And if the hospital does shut down," Chief Dennisar opined in his deep voice, "maybe that will make Ree abandon the place, come out in the open."

"Unlikely," Tuvok told the hulking Orion. "Doctor Ree is a resourceful individual, and he clearly feels the hospital is the safest place for his patient. He will adapt rather than retreat."

"Predators don't like taking unnecessary risks," Hriss observed; as a predator herself, the Caitian spoke from experience. "They tend to retreat when faced with unexpected opposition."

"As a rule, yes. But I believe Ree is in the paternal

guardian mode of a Pahkwa-thanh male. In that mode, the survival of the child overrides individual safety. His instinct will be to stand his ground."

Just as Elieth stood his ground to protect the people of Deneva, he thought. *Just as I would have stood my ground to protect him . . . if only I could have.* He understood very well how Ree thought right now. And he would be just as ruthless in protecting Counselor Troi and her child, if Ree forced him to.

"Emitting the pulse," Krotine announced. Outside the viewport, Tuvok saw the city lights flare and go dark. Moments later, faint lights returned at a few key facilities with emergency power, including the hospital below.

"Take us down," Tuvok said. "Can we get a transporter lock on any of our personnel?"

Krotine shook her cherry-tressed head. "No, sir. There's a jamming field being generated by the heavy shuttle. We can't beam in either."

"Very well. Douse all external lights and bring us in as stealthily as possible. We shall make our way on foot."

TITAN

"The situation is worse than we thought," Melora told Vale and the others in the observation lounge.

"Naturally," Vale said. "Because things have just been going *so* well this week."

Melora waited, but rather than saying more, Vale nodded, signaling her to continue. "It turns out the barophilic life Cethente discovered in the saltwater dynamo layer has more influence on the life up above than we initially thought," the science officer went on. "In two ways. First, it turns out that a lot of the subtle patterns we read in the dynamo layer's field were actually generated by the barophiles' communication. It's the disruption to the barophiles' life cycle, caused by the exotic radiation in the infalling asteroid dust, that's altering the planetary magnetic field, and that's what's stirring up the surface life." It was odd to start referring to the oceangoing life of this planet, even that living in the deeps kilometers down, as "surface life." But a world like this forced one to redefine one's parameters.

"Symbiosis," Keru observed with a touch of Trill irony. "The life up above is feeling the pain of the life below."

"You're more right than you know, Ranul. There's a deeper symbiosis as well." She moved to the wall screen and called up an image of several tiny arthropod forms, magnified thousands of times. "These are bathyplankton—the deep-sea zooplankton that Cethente sampled in the intermediate layers of the ocean, even deeper than we'd sampled them before. As you'll recall, we were wondering why they would exist at such depths when there's no sunlight or food to sustain them. Well, Eviku and Chamish figured that out."

She altered the display to show the creatures alternating between two modes. "It turns out the bathyplankton have a dual biochemistry. Their life functions are based on two distinct types of organic molecules. One is the ordinary type found in the surface life and most carbon-based life forms. The other is the type found in the barophiles. At low pressures, normal life processes operate and the barophile molecules are inert, just part of their structural bracing, which is why we didn't register the bathyplankton's dual life cycle before. Near the surface, they consume organic nutrients and use photosynthesis to store solar energy—making them as much phytoplankton as zooplankton.

"But eventually, if they don't get eaten, gravity and convection currents pull them into the depths. As they sink further, their normal enzymes stop working, and they fall dormant. But then, when they get down to the dynamo layer, the pressure and temperature become great enough for their barophile biochemistry to become active."

"But how do they stand the pressure down there?" Ra-Havreii asked.

It was practically the first thing he'd said to her since the shuttle. Fortunately, Melora didn't have to respond directly to him. She called up a cross-section graphic, pointing to an array of small, glassy spindle shapes within them, and addressed the group. "They have an internal skeleton of silicate spicules. Up top, the spicules are loosely distributed, giving them some additional structural strength but leaving them fairly flexible. As they descend, they're compressed further and further, the spicules coming together into a tight, geometric array that braces them against the pressure. As with the pure barophiles, the silicate framework contains and directs their molecular machinery the way cell walls do in our kind of life."

"That's fascinating, Commander," Vale said, "but how does it connect the barophiles to the surface life?"

"Sorry," Melora said. It was easy to get caught up in the wonder of this. "The critical thing is what the bathyplankton do once they're down there. They feed on the metals and heavy elements that are part of the saline layer's biosphere, the residue given off by the barophiles."

"Which they in turn consumed from the clathrates in the mantle," Onnta said.

"Exactly. And once they've stockpiled on metals, they swim upward until they reach the interface with the normal ocean. Then they spread fins that let them catch convection currents that carry them back up to the surface. The barophile life functions fall dormant, they drift upward, and finally their normal life functions engage again."

Vale's eyes widened. "And once they're up there, being plankton, most of them end up getting eaten by bigger critters."

Melora nodded. "Except enough of them survive to reproduce and start the cycle over again."

"But they're how the metals get back up from the mantle to the upper ocean. They're what makes it possible for life to exist on the surface."

The Elaysian couldn't help grinning, despite the gravity of the situation. "An entire biosphere, a whole sentient civilization—it wouldn't exist without these tiny, invisible creatures. Chamish suspects the barophile biosphere evolved first, driven by the energy of the magnetic dynamo, and that these bathyplankton somehow developed the ability to spread up to the ocean surface and take advantage of a new energy source, sunlight. Maybe they initially relied on some kind of organic molecules that could function well at intermediate pressures and marginally at surface pressures, and eventually replaced them with molecules better suited to surface life. Finally some of them evolved into forms that lived permanently on the surface and lost their extraneous barophile compounds, and the rest of the surface biosphere evolved from those."

"But what matters," Vale said, "is that the surface life depends on the barophile life for its survival."

"Yes, ma'am."

"And the barophile life is dying."

"Yes, ma'am."

"Because we thought shooting an asteroid would be a helpful thing to do."

"Well . . . we did mean well."

Vale sighed. "What exactly will happen if we don't fix this?"

"Gradually, more and more of the barophiles will die. They'll sink to the mantle, and there won't be enough surviving barophiles to bring up enough clathrates. That'll lead to a crash in the bathyplankton population, and that'll leave the surface life with progressively worsening metal deficiencies. Meanwhile, with the magnetic field patterns permanently disrupted, the surface life will continue to behave erratically or have difficulty performing necessary tasks. Remember how on Earth, many cetaceans would beach themselves and die because the noise from human ocean vessels confused and blinded their echolocation sense?" Vale nodded, looking embarrassed. "It's a similar principle. There's no telling how much the Dropletians' navigation, mating cycles, and so on could be thrown off by this. It could endanger whole species even without the excess violence this is producing among the sea life.

"In time, the contamination will dissipate; the dust will either use up its exotic charges in the dynamo layer or will sink to the mantle, get locked in clathrates, and dissipate its charge into the ice. The surviving barophile life will recover, and there will probably be enough dormant bathyplankton left to resume the nutrient exchange with the surface. But not before there's major loss of life on the surface, possibly even a mass extinction."

Vale shook her head. "So with a few phaser shots and two torpedoes, we kill a whole biosphere. That's efficient."

"Don't forget the antimatter canisters," Melora replied, earning a glare.

"What about the squales?" Xin asked. "Could their biotechnology protect them?"

"If anything, I'd say it makes them more vulnerable," she shot back. "They're dependent on so many other species that I doubt they could weather an extinction event. Not without enormous loss of life, at any rate."

There was a pause before Vale spoke. "Just for the sake of argument . . . if Riker and Lavena are still alive down there, somehow, what are their chances?"

Melora shook her head. "They'd succumb to metal deficiencies before this became an issue. If they managed to escape the crazed predators."

Vale glared at her. "Somehow, that's not very comforting."

LUMBU

The landing was fairly rough, since Krotine brought the *Armstrong* in on antigravs for the last few hundred meters.

They made a water landing in one of the city's wide canals and secured the shuttle under a bridge; luckily, travel through this portion of the canal was blocked by two large ferries at either end, both unable to move with their electrical systems and lights burned out from the pulse. In all likelihood, the shuttle would remain undiscovered for a few hours, at least.

It took the team half an hour to reach the hospital on foot, using tricorders on proximity scan to avoid encountering any Lumbuan citizens. Fortunately, Ree's jamming field did not prevent tricorder operation, enabling the team to scan the hospital's structure and determine an optimal stealth entry route. It was difficult for a Vulcan, a Boslic, a Caitian, and an Orion, all giants by Lumbuan standards, to make their way through the police perimeter undetected; but Tuvok had decades of experience at stealth and his teammates were well-trained. Hriss in particular was able to move with the soundlessness of a felinoid predator, but the lithe Krotine was nearly as light on her feet. Dennisar had a harder time of it, particularly since it was difficult for him to squeeze his bulk through Lumbuan doorways. Had Tuvok known that this world would be Ree's destination, he would not have picked Dennisar for the team. But it could not be helped now. As Dennisar attempted to squeeze through a narrow maintenance passage into the hospital, he inadvertently produced a noise that drew the attention of a police officer guarding the perimeter. But Tuvok was able to waylay her with a nerve pinch before she could catch a clear sight of them or raise the alarm.

Finally they reached the corridor outside the maternity ward, where three Lumbuan guards stood, one at each of the entrances. They all kept as far from the actual ward as possible while still keeping it in sight; no doubt Ree had demanded that they keep their distance. It made it easier to pick them off one by one; Tuvok took one down with a nerve pinch while Hriss ambushed another and injected him with a tranquilizer that would leave no traces detectable to Lumbuan science.

But Tuvok's guard let out a moan before she fell to the floor, and that drew the attention of the third guard, who came running with his weapon drawn. "What have you done?" the guard asked, his voice trembling. "What are you?"

"Your colleagues are unharmed," Tuvok told him. "The same will hold for you if you do not interfere with us."

"You—you're another giant. Another monster."

Tuvok raised a brow. "What leads you to that conclusion, sir?"

"Why . . . your size. Your color. And . . . Great Anam, you have no *clarfel*!"

"So are these the qualities that define a Lumbuan?"

The guard thought it over. "Well . . . some of them."

"But are they not mere appearances? And cannot outward appearance be deceptive?"

More thinking. "I suppose. My supervisor says I appear unintelligent. For that matter, so does my wife. And she appeared warm and loving when I married her," the guard added, speaking more to himself now.

"Then, as an intelligent man, you must know better than to take outward perceptions at face value. What you see could be a dream or a hallucination."

"Oh, no." The guard shook his head. "I'm not falling

for any Solipsist casuistry. That's Kumpen talk, and I'm as loyal as they come."

Tuvok realized he had overreached himself. "Very well. I will stipulate that I am objectively real. Even so, the standards you employ for defining me as not Lumbuan are still in question. Is it your external attributes that define your identity? Or is it your intellect? Your self-awareness? Your ability to communicate?"

"Well, that's what I always say," the guard replied slowly.

"Excellent."

"Though come to think of it, I just say that because it's what my wife thinks. And that's appeal to authority, right? Which is a fallacy. Besides, she's not here, is she?" The guard raised his gun again. "Me, I've always been a believer in the appeal to force."

Luckily, Tuvok had distracted the guard long enough for Hriss to come up behind him and inject another dose of tranquilizer. "I thought you had him on the ropes for a moment there, sir," the Caitian told him.

"Thank you, Ensign. Unfortunately, membership in a philosophically driven society does not guarantee an inquisitive spirit." He sighed. "I believe I now understand the human saying that one should avoid entering into a battle of wits with an unarmed opponent. Especially one who is armed in a more literal sense."

Tuvok made his way to the maternity ward doors, which were sealed off from within. His team came in behind him, phasers at the ready. "Doctor Ree!" he called. "This is Commander Tuvok. Please respond."

"Tuvok!" The voice was Troi's. But before she could say

anything more, the doctor's raspy, sibilant voice emerged.

"Welcome to Hvov Memorial, Commander," Ree said. "I'm afraid I can't invite you in. Counselor Troi's contractions are arriving closer together. I believe first-stage labor is imminent, and I must keep my patients safe. I assume you and your companions have weapons, and that cannot be tolerated. If you'll please wait outside? Outside the hospital, that is. I imagine the local constabulary would gladly extend their hospitality. They've been trying to get me to accept their invitation all day."

"Doctor. I understand why you are doing this. You feel compelled to protect the baby. I can assure you we all share that priority. I give you my word as a Vulcan that I will allow no harm to come to the child."

"Forgive me, Commander, but that offer would be more credible if your identity as a Vulcan were more stable."

Tuvok suppressed a wince. "Then I give you my word as a father."

"A father who cannot keep his own children safe?"

That was an even lower blow. Ree's outward courtesy masked a vicious streak in more ways than one. And if he was trying to anger Tuvok, he was coming close to success. "Can you guarantee that you can keep the child safe?" Tuvok replied with some heat.

Something heavy slammed against the door. Tuvok could see the shape of Ree's elongated head through the frosted glass, his rapid breaths fogging it further. "You doubt me too? That is my *purpose!* I don't care what you or anyone else thinks—I will not let anything happen to this child! Not again!"

Tuvok's eyes widened. Processing this new information, he began to arrive at a deeper understanding of the situation. "Doctor Ree. I would like to speak to Counselor Troi."

"You may not enter."

"I believe she can hear me from here. I wish only to speak. You may listen."

Ree gave an uncertain growl. "Very well. But briefly."

"Tuvok? I'm here," came Troi's voice. "Alyssa and I are all right."

"I am pleased to hear it," he called. "Counselor, do you have an understanding of what has precipitated the current situation?"

After a moment, Troi said, "Yes. Ree's in guardian mode. My fear for the baby triggered it."

"Exacerbated, no doubt, by my own enduring grief. I apologize for my role in this."

"It's not your fault, Tuvok. I'm the catalyst here."

"But does it not seem to you that the effect should have worn off by now?"

There was a pause. Tuvok could sense her uncertainty, her fear of saying the wrong thing with Ree listening. This close to term, her hormones were intensifying her empathic projections. "After all," he went on, prompting her, "with the imminent threat to your child gone, should not the impetus for his . . . protectiveness have subsided as well?"

She responded slowly. "I . . . assumed it was my anxiety at being held hostage that was feeding back onto him."

"Except that the one thing he has surely made quite clear to you is that he will not harm your child. Have you not, Doctor?"

"It is my highest priority. The counselor is aware of that."

Troi gave a heavy sigh. "He's talked about nothing else for days."

"As though," suggested Tuvok, "he has something to prove to you?"

Silence filled the ward for a time. Troi's emotions were ambiguous. "Tuvok, what are you saying?" she finally asked.

"The fact is, Doctor Ree did not save your first child, did he?"

"It was a spontaneous miscarriage!" Ree cried. "There was nothing I could do. I had no warning."

"But you did have warning, early in this child's term. You determined that she would die and might kill the counselor in the process."

"Yes."

"Counselor Troi. I would like you to answer my next question. What did Doctor Ree suggest as the solution?"

He felt her anger at him for dredging this up. "He wanted to terminate the fetus."

"Which you refused."

"Yes!"

"You could not bear to lose another child."

"Yes!"

"And you hated him for wanting to kill the child."

"I—no. No, Ree, I understood."

"Did you?" Tuvok demanded, letting his own emotions color his voice. "Could any parent truly accept such a suggestion with total equanimity?"

"But the baby's fine now. The Caeliar saved her."

"Despite Ree's best efforts to ensure her termination."

Ree's growl sounded from the other side of the door, disquietingly close. Next to him, Tuvok could see Hriss's fur standing on end. "Commander, you are agitating my patient. I advise you to end this."

But Tuvok was relentless. "It is not just your fear for your child that is influencing Ree. It is your fear of *him*. Subconsciously, you resent him for letting one child die and threatening another. As long as that resentment is within you, you are projecting it onto him. Filling him with the perception of himself as a potential child-killer."

"*No!*" Ree cried.

"Yes, Doctor! You prove my point. Do you see, Counselor? To his instincts as a Pahkwa-thanh male, that is intolerable. He is driven to prove himself a worthy caregiver—to prove to you and to himself that he will not let your child down again. As long as your resentment is still inside you, he cannot be free of it—and you cannot be free of him."

He felt her struggling with it, denying it. "No, Tuvok. No, Ree, I don't resent you. It was months ago."

"It was no longer ago than the death of my son," Tuvok told her. "And that still burns in me as fiercely as ever. That is why I understand the anger and blame you must hold within yourself. Because when a parent loses a child, we need to blame someone. We need to blame the person responsible for their loss."

He paused, having trouble controlling his voice. This was difficult for him. But it had to be done. "You yourself told me, Counselor . . . we cannot let go of our anger until we identify its real target. I know now what you were trying to get me to confess. That I . . ." He glanced over at his team, reluctant to expose himself to them like this. But he saw only trust and support in their eyes. "That I blame Elieth for his own death. That I am angry at him for making the choice that took him from me. Angry at him for causing his mother to endure loss.

"I am ashamed of myself for feeling that. But you sensed it in me, and knew it was important that I face it. If that is so, then you must do the same. As long as we are in denial about our anger, neither of us can let it go."

He was breathing hard, as though he'd just sprinted up a mountain. He could feel her turning inward, searching her soul. But for a time, there was no sound. He wasn't sure if he'd done any good. If not, he had humiliated himself in front of his team for nothing.

But then he felt a hesitant pat on his shoulder. He glanced back to see Krotine there. "Whether it works or not, sir," she whispered, "that was the bravest thing I've ever seen."

Deanna wept at the surge of emotion coming from Tuvok as he confessed his anger. The flavor of it was agonizingly familiar. She remembered how Counselor Haaj had elicited a similar confession from her, months ago: that she was angry at her first child for leaving her. That she had been afraid to admit it, to face it, because it made her feel horrible about herself. But Haaj had helped her understand, as she had tried to help Tuvok see in turn, that it was a natural, forgivable part of the grieving process.

Yet now Tuvok forced her to confront the possibility that she had not exorcised all her anger after all. Even as she drank in his catharsis, she was compelled to look inward and examine her own soul.

Ree was coming toward her, hands spread placatingly. "Counselor . . . Deanna . . . please. You must know I have your child's best interests at heart."

"Yes," she told him, her voice rough, its tone warning him to stop. "I know that. But there's what I know, and there's what I feel.

"You can't know, Doctor. You try so hard to prove yourself, to go through the motions of a caregiver. But you've never had a child, never lost a child of your own. You can't imagine what that does to a parent. Even just once. And to be told it has to happen a second time . . .

"God, yes, I was angry. Angry at you. Angry at the baby for leaving me alone again. Angry at Will, angry at myself for letting it happen to another child. Angry at the whole damn universe for putting me through this!"

Ree had lowered his head. "I thought . . . you had forgiven me."

"So did I. But that pain, it stays with you. And the anger. And the fear.

"The fear, Doctor. Do you have any idea? You *attacked* me. Back on New Erigol, you told me you wanted to end my baby's life, and then you attacked me. You *bit* me!"

"I injected you with venom to slow a life-threatening hemorrhage."

"That doesn't change how it *felt*, Doctor! You joke about how dangerous you are, tease others about their fear of you, but you can't imagine what it's like to feel like your prey!

"My God, Doctor!" she went on, her voice growing louder with each sentence. "How could you think I could *ever* trust you to care for my child after that? How could you imagine you could *take me hostage*, terrorize a whole hospital, and somehow prove to me my baby will be safe with you?!"

"I *will* keep her safe! Always!"

"*No!*" she screamed. "You can't have her! I won't let you take my baby from me!" This was not the hysterical rage she had met him with in her delirium on New Erigol. This was the self-possessed fury and determination of a loving mother. "This is *my* child, and I will give birth to her where I wish, raise her how I wish. And *I* will keep her safe, Ree. Safe from anyone who would hurt her—safe from anyone who would take her from me. Including you!"

For a long moment, Ree was silent, gazing downward, breaths rasping slowly in and out. She couldn't tell if he was chastened or furious; her own emotions were too chaotic at the moment, her hormones on overload. Finally, he raised his head. "Counselor . . ."

But at that moment, her insides convulsed and she felt hot wetness spilling onto her thighs. "Oh, my God," Alyssa gasped. "Doctor, her water just broke."

The contraction worsened, growing more painful until she moaned aloud. "It hurts!"

Alyssa was at her side. "You're too tense. You need to breathe, Deanna." She glanced over at Ree, who stood taut, ready to act, but keeping his distance. "Deanna, you need the doctor."

Once the contraction subsided, she met his eyes, trying to control her breathing. "The baby is mine," she said.

"Yes," he replied.

"You know how I feel now."

". . . Yes."

She held his gaze. "Do your job, Doctor. Prove yourself."

His tension eased. "Yes. Thank you, Counselor."

As he moved forward, a throat cleared. The Lumbuan nurses had come forward, the senior nurse at the head of the group. "We can assist," she said. "Doctor."

Ree studied them. "You would help a monster?"

The senior nurse fidgeted. "Monsters have babies too, it turns out. And we help babies."

"Very well," he said, not wasting time. "Prep for delivery and begin sterilizing the necessary equipment."

The nurse paused. "Is there anything . . . different . . . I need to know about?"

"Nothing of substance. Your experience should serve."

"Counselor!" Tuvok called from outside.

"Tuvok!" Deanna called back. "The baby's coming! You can come in!"

"I appreciate the invitation, but I must decline. According to our signal intercepts, the local police have discovered the officer we incapacitated upon our entrance, and are preparing to storm the facility in response."

"Tuvok, don't let them get near her! Protect my baby!"

"That is what we all wish, Counselor. We shall protect her. You have my word."

"Yes," Ree said. "We will all protect her."

"I know," Deanna said. Right now, they all shared a single priority: the safe delivery of the child inside her.

But what would happen afterward?

CHAPTER FIFTEEN

TITAN

Ra-Havreii was surprised when Melora came to see him in engineering. "Commander," he said with wary civility.

"Commander," she replied. "I, ah, need your help." His brow rose, and she continued. "Cethente and Kesi have developed a particle field that can neutralize the disruptive charge in the asteroid dust. We've exposed samples of the dust to the field and achieved a total dissipation of the stored energy."

"Excellent," he said. "What's the problem?"

"Deployment. *Titan*'s main deflector can project the field from orbit to deal with the dust in the stratosphere, but reaching the deep ocean is another matter."

"Yes, I see," he said, speaking over her last word. "The most practical way would be to replicate a series of deep-sea probes that can descend to the dynamo layer and permeate it with the field. The techniques we used on Cethente's pod should serve to protect them from the pressure."

Melora stared. "But that would take hundreds of thousands of probes. The dynamo layer has a volume of over thirty billion cubic kilometers, and the field can only penetrate so much water!"

"The probes can move through the dynamo layer, each one covering a fair swath over time."

"But they might only last a few hours each at those pressures."

"Yes, we'd need redundancy. But we could make do with maybe a thousand. The industrial replicators should be up to it. And we can always harvest the asteroid field for extra raw materials."

"Deploying a thousand probes would take every available hand we could spare! It'd take days!"

"Have you got a pressing appointment somewhere else? I'm sure Commander Vale would be happy to leave this world to its doom so you don't have to be inconvenienced."

Her gaze hardened. "Oh, don't start with me now, Xin. This isn't the time."

"*I* am being entirely professional. Unlike you, we Efrosians have the knack for objectivity toward our sexual liaisons."

"Says the man who said he loved me!"

Everyone close enough to hear—meaning everyone in engineering, for she had said it rather loudly—turned to stare at them. Refusing to acknowledge their distraction, Ra-Havreii pulled the Elaysian into his office, her light build and antigrav suit making her almost weightless. She didn't resist, though. Once they were in private, he pointed angrily and opened his mouth. "I—"

After a moment, she crossed her arms. "You?"

"Well, you said it too."

"I did."

"It was the heat of the moment. The distress. Look, we really should get back to these probes—"

"Xin, what are you so afraid of?"

There was no hostility in it. Her emotional armor fell before his eyes. This proud, defensive woman had left herself vulnerable to him by choice. In response, he felt his own guard falling away. "Isn't it obvious?" he said.

"That we love each other?"

"Yes! I—I never expected that to happen. I don't know how to deal with it. I'm not ready for . . . for that."

She frowned. "For what, Xin? I thought Efrosian men didn't form commitments."

"Well, no, it's— Just because we don't pair-bond for child-rearing doesn't mean we don't form emotional bonds. We just consider them something separate from parenting. An Efrosian female has the support of her entire community in raising her children. That can include male lovers, although generally not the seed donor." He shrugged. "Our society evolved in difficult conditions, with a limited population. That made it necessary for males to father each child with a different mate, to maximize gene pool diversity. It's a matter of necessity. It doesn't mean we're incapable of emotional commitment."

Melora was silent for a time. "So are you saying . . . you want to commit with me?"

"No! I mean . . . I don't know. Don't you?"

"Is that what you think?"

"You said you love me."

"I do."

"And your people . . . you *do* commit."

"Usually," she confirmed.

He tried to think of something clever to say, but all that came out was, "I'm afraid to. I don't think I'm ready."

Melora took his hand and smiled. "What makes you think I am?"

His eyes widened. "But . . . what we said . . ."

She nodded. "I love you. You love me. Isn't that enough?" She moved closer. "We've been fighting because we've both been afraid of the same thing: that being in love meant having to escalate things, to make a commitment. But why mess with a good thing? If we're both happy just . . . being together, having good times together, then why can't that be what love means to us?" She kissed him. "This ship is all about embracing different ways of living and being. So why force ourselves to conform to some set of expectations about what being in love requires? Let's make it what *we* want it to be."

He thought it over for a few moments, then nodded. "All right. Let's do that." He felt relief wash over him. They were comfortable together again, and that was what he wanted most of all.

"Great." She smiled. "I love you, Xin."

He kissed her, taking his time. "I love you, Melora." After a moment, he let her go, fidgeting a bit. "I . . . suppose we should get back to work on those probes."

She blinked a few times and cleared her throat. "Uhh, right. Right behind you."

They both took a moment to gather themselves, then came back out into engineering, totally professional, their eyes daring the crew to be anything else. But then Melora moved close and spoke softly. "You know . . . if most of the crew's going to be down on Droplet, covering the planet's surface systematically . . . maybe we'll find the captain and Aili while we're at it."

He nodded. "I'm sure we'll all be looking."

After all, there was more than one kind of loving relationship. And Captain Riker and Counselor Troi deserved to have theirs restored.

DROPLET

By now, Aili herself was starting to feel the effects of malnutrition. She was weakening, unable to swim as far without needing rest. She knew matters must be far worse for Riker at this point—and would get far worse for her before long.

We can't rely on Titan *finding us,* she thought. *The lifepod transformation may be our only hope.* If anything, she was starting to look forward to the prospect of beginning a new life with the squales. She felt she had grown close to Alos, Gasa, Melo, and others in the contact pod, and knew she would be safe with them. And she enjoyed their company—enjoyed communing with aquatic beings who didn't judge her (at least not by the same standards she used in judging herself). The squales were a beautiful people, and even their most idle conversation was a symphony. She would gladly spend the rest of her life mastering the intricacies of their song.

As for her more carnal needs, the squales were rather

casual about sex play, not unlike aquatic Selkies, and she was sure she could engage in some interesting experimentation with them. But she would be better off having another humanoid to keep her company.

The thought made her feel guilty, but a part of her countered, *It's a matter of cruel necessity. The change would take weeks; even if* Titan *is still up there looking for us, we'd be out of their reach long enough for them to give up. And there'd be no going back anyway. The only way to save Will's life might be to let the others think we're dead. And then we'd have to learn to . . . live together. We'd need each other . . . like it or not. He'd hate me for a while, but he'd have to come around.*

But she didn't want him to wake up and find that this had been done to him. That would make it far harder for him to adjust—or to forgive her. Better if she could persuade him to accept the change willingly. She quailed at the thought, knowing how he would react. *Oh, how I wish he spoke better Selkie. Then the squales could be the ones to convince him.*

She had no choice, though. As much as she would have preferred to avoid it, Aili had to be the one to convince Riker to stay here—to abandon his family and spend the rest of his life here with her. *So much for not making him think I'm a homewrecker.*

Aili put it off as long as she could, rehearsing what she could say, trying to figure out how to cast the argument in the most convincing, unselfish terms possible. Eventually, though, her own fatigue and nausea convinced her that Riker couldn't afford to wait much longer. So she went to his islet, still having no idea what to say.

When she reached the islet, though, Riker failed to respond to her calls. Bracing herself, she climbed out onto the solid surface and jogged to Riker's cave.

She gasped when she saw him. He lay sprawled, unmoving save for tremors, his breathing shallow. "Captain!" she cried, running to his side. At her touch, he moaned, but that was all. He was burning with fever. She registered an unpleasant smell; gingerly pulling his leaf-blankets aside, she saw that he was lying in his own filth, unable to move enough to tend to his basic needs. Two of the squales' helper creatures were nearby, but they were agitated, keeping their distance. Aili realized the disruption in the Song was throwing them off, preventing them from fulfilling their duties. The others must have wandered off or perhaps been taken by predators.

Aili winced in sympathy at the sight of Riker, and though her kind did not shed tears, she keened for him. She cradled his head in her lap, stroking his hair. "Sir, can you hear me?" she said softly. "There's a way to save you. Please, I need to tell you about it."

But he gave no response beyond another feeble groan. Aili's first thought was to take him to the squales. She pulled at him, trying to lift him up enough to lead him to the water. He was practically a dead weight, but swimming kept her strong and he'd lost several kilos, so she was able to pull him mostly upright and drag him forward, his weight on her shoulders.

When she reached the shore, however, she didn't summon the squales. Instead, she simply lowered Riker into the water to cool his fever and cleanse his skin of sweat and other things. She hurried back inland to get some fresh water from the small pond, soaking it up in a spongy leaf. (*Idiot! You could have brought him here!* she thought, before responding to herself, *Idiot! And foul his drinking water?*) Returning to Riker, she dribbled it into his mouth. Once he'd been rehydrated, she used the leaf to clean him. It was embarrassing to do this with her captain, but it was nothing she hadn't dealt with many times with her eight children. Though at the time, she had retreated from such duties whenever she could finagle a relative into taking them over for her.

But not now. At first, she wasn't sure why she was tending to Riker in this way instead of letting the squales remake him and remove the need. But the more she tended to him, the more she understood. "I'm sorry, Captain," she told him as she wrapped him in new leaf-blankets, this time near the shore so she could stay close. "Sorry I left you to go through this alone. I was selfish, and childish." The truth was, she *couldn't* simply fob him off onto others as she had so often done with her own children. She'd been the one to let him deteriorate into this state. And so it was her responsibility to help him through it.

And so she took care of him. Over the next several hours, she kept him hydrated, fed him what he could keep down, wiped away what he could not, kept him wrapped in leaves to stay warm, changed his leaves, and cleaned him when the need arose. When he awoke halfway, he ranted in delirium about being locked in a pit in the darkness. He screamed curses at "Kinchawn," and Aili realized he was flashing back to an ordeal on Tezwa before his promotion to captain. The curses soon gave way to pleas; he begged to be allowed to see his wife and his baby girl. "My girl," he sobbed. "Deanna! I'm with you! Please, tell me you know I'm with you. I should be there, I should . . . hold . . . hand . . . be there to . . . see her . . . come out . . . help you . . . I'm sorry!" He broke down sobbing, and Aili held him and stroked his hair. She eased him closer to the water, lay with her back to it, her gills trailing in the shallows, so she could continue to comfort him.

Why did I ever run away from this with my own children? she found herself wondering. *Why did I think I couldn't do this?* She had rarely felt such a sense of purpose. Rarely been so fulfilled.

In time, Riker became lucid again—still weak, but able to respond coherently. "Thank you" was the first thing he said to her.

"I'm sorry" was the first thing she replied.

"Unhhh . . . forget it." He tried to roll around to face her. She helped him to sit up at the water's edge and stepped back a few paces to crouch in the shallows, resting on the submerged outer curve of the islet, while she faced him. "What's . . . the situation?" he asked her.

She filled him in on the basics, including the squales' offer. "I see," Riker said when she was done. "You think we should take it?"

Aili lowered her eyes. "I did. But not now."

"Why not?"

It was several moments before she spoke. "You remember what you asked me before? Why I joined Starfleet if I was so ashamed of my affairs with offworlders?"

He showed no confusion at the non sequitur, perhaps simply being too weak to muster it. "Uh-huh."

"I always told myself it was about responsibility. That

it was a way to make up for being so irresponsible as a mother. I'd used the galaxy as a distraction from my duties, so maybe giving something back to the galaxy would even the scales. Or something like that."

"But that's not it?"

She gave a small shake of her head. Again, a long silence preceded her next words. "When I was young . . . my sister Miana was out swimming with our mother and Miana's father when . . . she was taken by a sea predator. Such things still happen on Pacifica . . . even with modern technology, an ocean is a big, wild place, hard to tame. It's one reason we need such large families."

"I'm sorry."

"So was I. And I was angry. I loved Miana so much, and I blamed Mom for letting her die. For not protecting her like she was supposed to." She winced at the memory of the pain in her mother's face as she'd cursed her—the grief, as strong as her own, that she'd ignored. "So as I grew up . . . when she tried to teach me the values of good parenting that are so important to amphibious Selkies . . . I didn't find it credible, considering the source. I tuned them out, rebelled against her lessons. Miana's father left, of course, and other fathers came and went, but I wasn't willing to trust any of them either.

"I didn't even want to become a mother, but I'd tuned out my parents' lessons in responsible sex too, so I kind of ended up getting parenting thrust upon me. And I wasn't ready. I didn't know how to cope. And . . ." She leaned back in the water, immersing more of her gills—in essence, taking a deep breath before going on. "And I was afraid. I didn't admit it, but I was afraid of being just as bad a mother as I thought my own was. I didn't trust myself to take care of my children. So I retreated. As often as I could, I left my kids in the care of relatives, friends, anyone. And I lost myself in the kind of self-indulgence we're supposed to save for our aquatic phase—that's supposed to be a well-earned reward for two decades of devoted parenting. I played, I danced, I drank, and I had sex with aliens who didn't know our customs or didn't care."

Riker studied her. "Why have more children, then?"

"Because I couldn't completely get away from my social obligations. And because I preferred taking the easy way out. It was easier to go along with the pressure to take more mates and then foist the babies off on family than to try to stay unattached." She smirked. "Besides, I liked sex with Selkie men too. I attracted a lot of desirable partners. My affairs with offworlders made me seem alluringly experienced . . . mature. And some men like 'bad girls.'

"And maybe, eventually, it became about trying to mend my reputation. I got tired of being the butt of everyone's gossip and dirty looks, wanted to prove I could do the respectable thing. But I still didn't trust myself to be a good mother, so I still ran from my responsibilities."

"So is that why you left?" Riker asked. "To get away from everyone's judgment?"

She shook her head. "All I had to do for that was wait for my amphibious phase to end. Aquatics lead the kind of uninhibited life I was already leading on land. They don't judge much."

Riker's eyes widened. "You mean you left before you . . . changed?" He gestured to indicate her current physiological state.

"Not long before. A couple of years. And it could've come on me at any time."

He narrowed his eyes, discerning what lay behind her words. "You wanted to leave Pacifica before it happened."

She nodded. "I told myself I'd be bored as a mature aquatic. It would just be more of the same thing I'd been doing for twenty years, but with less variety and less . . . spice. Because it would be normal and accepted. No more 'bad girl', just blending in with the group. We call it a *sepkinalorian* . . . I think the closest Standard concept would be a face in the crowd, except it's more of a party than a crowd. I liked to joke to myself that it was a kind of drudgework, a 'job' I was happy to have avoided.

"But really, I guess I didn't think I deserved the life of a mature aquatic. I hadn't earned it. They wouldn't have judged me, but I was judging myself, whether I admitted it or not."

"So you cast yourself out of paradise."

She tilted her head. "You could say that. I signed up with Starfleet, and I told everyone it was so I could give something back, make up for my selfish life. I even convinced myself.

"But I think I understand now—I was still running away. Leaving home was a way to avoid facing the real root of my problems. To avoid facing my mother . . . and my memories."

She straightened in the water. "Sir, I really am happy here. The squales have offered me something that would be an amazing adventure, and I'm grateful to them for that. But . . . it would still be running away. Hiding from my responsibilities.

"Well, I'm not going to do that anymore, sir. You're my captain, and I have a duty to you. If you're convinced *Titan* and Commander Troi are still out there, then I trust you. And we just have to make sure we find them and get you back together with your family." She lowered her eyes. "It's too late for me to get back the time I lost with my children. I'm not going to let you lose out on yours."

Riker gave her a slow, heartfelt smile. "Thank you, Aili."

LUMBU

"She's beautiful," Nurse Mawson said as Deanna cradled her newborn daughter in her arms.

"Even without a *clarfel*," Nurse Hewton added, but Mawson shushed him.

The delivery had been very smooth, ironically an anticlimax after all the melodrama leading up to it. Deanna's Caeliar-restored physique had proved robust enough to handle the delivery with relatively little difficulty; the intense exertion of labor had been more euphoric for her than painful. Ree had done his part with total professionalism, but there really hadn't been much he needed to do. As for Tuvok and his team, they had frightened off the local police with little difficulty; a few phaser stuns and a few roars from Hriss and Dennisar had been enough to overwhelm their courage.

And now she had the most beautiful creature in the universe in her arms, and the only way she'd be happier was if Will had been here to see it. But she knew, deep in her soul, that he was alive, and during the arduous euphoria of the birth, she had felt his essence touching her, reaching out to her. It had been distant, the barest thread, and the psychologist in her recognized that the perception could have been a memory, a hope, a piece of herself reflecting him. But her heart *knew*.

Now that matters were calm, Deanna found her gaze turning to Ree. Tuvok was now in the room, standing near Ree, watching him carefully. Alyssa had subtly interposed herself between Ree and the baby, just in case. It was unimaginable that her dainty frame could slow him for even a second, but there she stood nonetheless, and it was very reassuring.

"Doctor?" Deanna asked, not needing to put the next thought into words: *Now what?*

Ree made a noise akin to throat-clearing. "Ah. Counselor. Yes." Another rumble. "I, um . . . Upon reflection, it seems I have been somewhat . . . overzealous in my protectiveness. I . . . seem to be thinking more clearly now." He gave a convulsive shake of his head. "I had not realized guardian mode was so . . . intense."

"It may not be, as a rule," she told him, sensing his sincerity and giving Tuvok a subtle nod to that effect. He remained wary, however. "What I was broadcasting to you . . . my anger, my resentment . . . it must have been difficult for you."

Tuvok raised a brow. "Then you believe that releasing your repressed anger has brought about a resolution?"

She gave a wry grin. "It's never that simple, Tuvok. I . . . have a lot to talk out with Ree yet, and a lot to work out within myself. Honestly, it may have been my euphoria from the delivery," she said, gazing down lovingly at her daughter, "that counteracted the effect. Or maybe the sheer intensity of the experience overloaded Ree's empathic reception."

"Or maybe," Ree said, looking as sheepish as a raptor could, "you simply shouted some sense into my thick head. There can be value in rudeness . . . when wielded judiciously. Counselor, I am so sorry."

"Ohh, let's not start that again," she urged him.

Mawson tentatively reached out and stroked the baby's hand with a finger. Deanna smiled at the diminutive nurse. "Do you have a name in mind?" the Lumbuan asked.

"Well . . ."

"Excuse me," Tuvok said. "Now that matters are in hand, we should not linger. The local military may arrive at any time. And we have caused enough disruption to this world."

"Oh dear," Ree said. "That's right. I've violated the Prime Directive rather badly, haven't I?"

"Indeed. I shall have to place you under arrest and take you back to *Titan* for a hearing."

"Tuvok," Deanna protested, "he wasn't responsible."

"That, my dear Counselor, is for the hearing to decide," Ree said. "The commander is quite right."

As Krotine and Hriss helped Deanna to her feet (all while valiantly resisting the urge to coo and dote over the baby, as her empathic senses told her), Nurse Mawson said, "Are you taking her back to the spirit world?"

Deanna studied her. "Is that what you think we should do?"

Mawson puffed her *clarfel* in embarrassment. "It's not

my place to advise spirits on their ways. But we mortals are no proper caregivers for her kind. Best to keep the veils up between the worlds, I say."

The new mother smiled. "Thank you, Mawson. We're grateful for all your help. But we'd appreciate one more favor."

The Lumbuan nodded sagely. "A spirit encounter should be a private thing. Isn't that right?" she said sternly to the others, who nodded obediently.

Tuvok and his team led the others out into the halls, making their way to the exit. Dennisar had placed Ree in arm restraints and was watching him closely, though there was nothing to be done about the doctor's mighty tail except to trust in his cooperation. Deanna could tell from his outward, drooped posture and his inward emotions that he was still abashed and concerned about the consequences of his Prime Directive breach. "I don't think we've done any lasting damage to this world, Ree," she reassured him. "As you heard, many of them still have a strong belief in animism. They'll just accept us as a spirit manifestation of the kind they already believe in."

"But spirits appearing in the flesh?" Krotine asked. "Having babies in their hospitals? Isn't that a little more concrete than usual?"

"Animists see spirits within every aspect of nature," Deanna told her. "To them, a river or a tree is an embodied spirit. This won't be that profoundly different to them."

"But many Lumbuans are of a more skeptical bent," Tuvok said. "Belief in spirits is not universal. Might not our presence shift the balance toward a revival in animist belief?"

"Maybe. But if we leave without tangible evidence, it will just be a few dozen people's testimony added to a whole world's ongoing philosophical dialogue. And Mawson and her nurses will probably help confuse the issue. These are a people who relish debate and are slow to come to a consensus." She smirked. "I wouldn't be surprised if many of the eyewitnesses ended up getting persuaded that they imagined what they saw."

"That may be more difficult than you think, Counselor," Tuvok said.

"Well, anyway, they've got more immediate concerns, with the future of their nation at stake. This will probably fade from public attention before long."

Ree said to Tuvok, "Commander, if we can get to a suitably private place, I can remotely shut down the jamming field and have us beamed to the *Horne*. We can then beam your team back to your shuttle and depart together."

"An excellent suggestion, Doctor. However, we have one more loose end to resolve. The locals have photographic documentation of our presence."

Tuvok and his team began discussing how to track down the photographs and retrieve or destroy them without detection. Deanna tuned them out, trusting them to get the job done. Right now, the baby in her arms was her entire universe.

CHAPTER SIXTEEN

DROPLET

Once she was sure Riker could manage without her, Aili swam back out to the squales, determined to extract some answers about the status of her crewmates. She realized now that she hadn't pressed the issue hard enough before, perhaps because she'd been enjoying the escape too much. It was an error she was determined to remedy.

It took a while, but Aili finally managed to ask the right questions. "Are my people still in the ocean?" had initially brought the same answer from the members of the contact pod: *"Not for Aili."* Alos and Gasa had accompanied the answer with chorused assurances that they were here for her now. Once her song had been transposed, they sang, she could join their choir.

"It's not like that for us," she told them. "We don't change pods as easily as you. We want our old pod back."

"That's clear enough," Cham sang in harmony with Gasa's refrain of comfort. *"But they are silent to the found-*

lings' ears. *We cannot change their ways; for that, we need to comprehend.*"

"Change their ways?" Aili pressed the issue. Did that mean they were still on Droplet after all?

With further questioning, she confirmed the impression Cham had given. Once she understood, she rushed to the surface to give the news to Riker. A little hope would do wonders for him right now.

"We've been assuming they were holding us prisoner," she said. "That if *Titan* was still here, the squales were unwilling to return us to them."

Riker nodded. "Hostages," he said weakly. "Or guinea pigs."

"At first, that was probably true. They didn't know what to make of us and were being cautious. But they've come to trust us now. A lot of other squales still blame us for the crisis, but the contact pod understands we meant no harm. But when they wouldn't reunite us with the others, I was afraid that maybe *Titan* had been destroyed by the asteroid, or had written us off for dead and abandoned us."

"I know Deanna's alive," he said, more to himself than to her.

"Yes, sir. And *Titan*'s still here. The squales confirmed it."

"So why wouldn't they tell us before, if we weren't their prisoners?"

"The thing is," she said, "the squales are always in touch with each other. The deep sound channel lets them communicate with squales thousands of kilometers away—or relay messages through other squales to communicate with any other squale, anywhere on Droplet. They're as connected as we are with our combadges. It's slower, but they can hear about anything happening anywhere on the planet within six hours.

"So they just take it for granted that keeping track of every member of your species is a natural ability of intelligent beings. And so they assumed we had the same ability.

"So when *Titan* didn't come to retrieve us, it never occurred to the squales that they didn't know where we were. They assumed that, for some alien reason, our people had abandoned us."

"Wait a minute," Riker said. "They knew we didn't know where the others were. Wasn't that a clue?"

"They pretty much assumed it took mutual cooperation. If you call out to someone and they don't answer, you can't tell where they are."

"But wouldn't they have heard you if you gave out any such calls?"

"I'm an alien," she said with a shrug. "They don't know what strange ways we may have for staying in contact with our people. But it just never occurred to them to consider that we couldn't. They take the ability as much for granted as—well, as water. This is their first alien contact," she said in their defense. "They don't know what assumptions they need to unlearn."

He still wasn't convinced. "Our people must have looked for us. Sent out shuttles."

"They knew our people were looking for something. Some of them suspected it was us, since we were silent inside the healing pods. But once we were released and our people still didn't come for us, they didn't know what to think."

Riker nodded. "So now that they understand?"

"I think they'd be happy to reunite us, sir. Since we won't go through the change, it's our only chance. They don't want us to die."

"Even the ones who blame us for ruining their Song?"

"They just want us to leave so their world can be pure again."

He perked up. "Then they'll help us find *Titan*?" he asked, his voice strengthening. Aili had been right; the news had been nourishment in itself.

"They're waiting for me now," she replied with a smile. "We just need to dive to the deep sound channel and start asking around, track down the nearest crew from *Titan*. It shouldn't be more than a few hours."

For the first time in days, the familiar Riker grin was on his gaunt face. "Then you'd better get started, Ensign. That's an order."

She beamed back. "Aye, Captain."

Xin Ra-Havreii wished Aili Lavena were still around. Not only because he missed her and feared for her survival, but because he wasn't entirely sanguine about his own at the moment.

All of *Titan*'s available shuttles were spreading out planetwide to initiate the probe deployment, after depositing further crews with their own probe allotments on the main floater-island base and other floater colonies across the planet; by following the currents, they would be able to cover a wide swath of Droplet's surface and drop probes at regular intervals, turning the floaters into additional "vessels" at *Titan*'s disposal. Vale herself was supervising from the main base; she had brought Ra-Havreii with her to oversee the first drop. He had demurred that he was more a man of theory than execution and that Lieutenant Tylith or Ensign Crandall could supervise the deployment effectively. But Vale had wanted him there for his communication skills, to try to inform the squales that the aliens seemingly invading their world and dropping hundreds of large technological devices into its depths were acting in their best interests.

And so here he was, out in the middle of the open sea in a tiny scouter gig, facing down a pod of angry squales and trying to negotiate with them in Selkie, a language he had studied recreationally but had limited fluency in. Aili, he reflected, would be so much better for this on every level. At least they had been willing to listen to her.

This pod, however, didn't seem to be in the mood for listening, despite the new EM dampers on the gig and equipment. It was a largish pod, nearly two dozen members, and thus presumably was aggregated from several smaller pods, banded together for mutual protection. Many of the squales were scarred or missing limbs. They seemed to be swimming in rather a hurry for a region several hundred kilometers south of the main base, a heavily defended location containing multiple large spiral structures that appeared to serve an agricultural function. Normally, Ra-Havreii wouldn't have dreamed of getting in their way. But this was the first pod that had passed near enough to the base to engage with.

But they were too angry, too embittered by the growing turmoil of their world. They didn't deign to respond to his

Selkie entreaties in kind, but Y'lira Modan had deciphered enough of their own language by now to get a rough idea of their response. "They say we corrupt the sea by being here," she told Ra-Havreii from her seat behind him in the gig, studying her tricorder. "They object to our fouling the sea with any more of our devices."

He sighed. "Yes, I could've guessed that. The fact that our devices are more squale-friendly now hasn't changed their opinions, has it?"

"Apparently not, sir."

"Of course not," he muttered. "They've made up their minds." Tapping he combadge, he called Vale at the base. "Commander, we're not getting anywhere here, and we don't have time to keep going in circles. I say just deploy the first probe. At least we explained first, whether they listened or not. Once they sense the magnetic field healing and the biosphere calming down over the next few days, maybe they'll realize we were telling the truth."

"Are you sure that's a good idea?" came Vale's voice.

"I think we're beyond having the luxury of good ideas. It's what we've got."

"Strangely, I can live with that. Okay, we're deploying the first probe."

Naturally, it didn't prove that easy. According to the reports Ra-Havreii received from the base camp, as soon as the probe was released from the floater island, sensors showed a pod of squales racing to intercept it. They must have been ready for this, since they managed to catch it within a minute and proceeded to carry it to a barren, dead floater islet on the outskirts of the cluster, pushing it up and out onto the surface.

"I think they've made their point," Vale said. *"So you'd better make ours again."*

Feeling set upon, Ra-Havreii tried again. He explained to them why the planet's magnetic field was causing them discomfort and how the probes would repair the problem. He promised them that *Titan*'s crew would gladly leave their world alone once the balance had been restored. He offered them medical help to tend their wounds, assuring them that *Titan*'s medical facilities could provide treatments they would find miraculous. Oddly, Y'lira reported that they reacted to that with amusement.

Finally, he lost his patience. "The simple truth," he intoned in awkward Selkie, "is that you can't stop us. You can't prevent all our probes from descending. And what do you plan to do with the ones you catch and hold on the surface? Everything on this world sinks eventually, you know!"

Y'lira stared at him. "Doctor, I'm unfamiliar with this style of diplomacy."

So am I, he silently confessed. But he was fed up with catering to their technophobic superstition. "Just let us do this," he told them. "You're only hurting yourselves and wasting your effort by trying to stop us."

"Uh . . . Doctor?"

"Don't worry, Modan," he said, switching back to Standard. "I know what I'm doing."

"Doctor!" Y'lira shoved her tricorder in front of him. Its proximity scan showed several new shapes coming in from a distance. Several very large shapes.

"Doctor," came Vale's voice from the main base, *"we're detecting multiple large creatures moving in. Eviku*

says they're the same armored things the squales used to destroy our warning klaxon before."

"They're moving in on us, too," Ra-Havreii told her. "I think we'd better get out of here."

"Agreed."

But that was easier said than done. The gig was surrounded by squales on all sides, in the center of a circle some thirty meters wide. "Oh, no. What do we do?"

"Could we ram one of them?" Y'lira asked.

"They're heavier than the gig. We'd come to a rather abrupt stop and end up either in the water or in the tentacles of the next squale over. And I'd rather not kill any of them while the others are in a surly enough mood to begin wi—" He broke off, gazing westward.

"Commander?" Y'lira said.

A large ocean swell, a good dozen meters high, was approaching the gig from beyond the circle of squales. "I think I see a way out. Brace yourself."

The swell soon reached the circle of squales, lifting the ones on the western side higher and higher into the air. The squales took it in stride (or in stroke), remaining in formation despite the warping of the circle. But as soon as the crest of the swell had passed under the squales on the western edge, Ra-Havreii gunned the gig's engine and drove west at maximum acceleration. The gig rose up the slanted surface, using it as a ramp, and shot into the air as it crested the swell. The gig's arc carried it clear over the squales, though Ra-Havreii could swear he heard and felt a tentacle slap against the rear of the hull. After a stomach-wrenching moment in free fall, the gig splashed down hard. Ra-Havreii banged his elbow and his teeth slammed together

painfully. But at least they were free of squale encircle-
ment. Not letting up on the throttle, he veered on course
for the main base. As much as he hated the floater island, it
was the closest thing to a safe haven on this planet now.

Any further thoughts were driven from Ra-Havreii's
head by the immediate need to vomit. He managed to get
his head over the side before it came, which was small
comfort as his entire digestive tract seemed to be trying
to force itself out through his mouth for a good minute to
come. When his heaves became dry and finally subsided,
he gasped in exhaustion for a while, then looked back and
croaked, "There, you damned squid. How's that for con-
taminating your precious ocean?"

But then the water bowed up around a large, dark form,
and a sharp armored prow cleaved out through the middle
of it, tentacles writhing beneath the bow wave as it drove
toward the gig. Ra-Havreii instantly turned back to the controls and pushed the throttle to its limit. "Y'lira to Vale," he
heard the Selenean saying. "We need assistance."

*"Sorry, but we've got our hands full right now. They're
attacking the whole island."*

It turned out that Aili had misinterpreted the pod's intentions slightly. When they took her down to the deep sound
channel, it wasn't just to search randomly for a team from
Titan. To her surprise, the squales brought her to a device
she recognized as one of *Titan*'s hydrophone probes. Melo
explained that many probes had been blaring noise into the
ocean following the asteroid impact, and that most had been
destroyed to clear the lines of communication. Aili asked,
a bit heatedly, whether it had occurred to any of them that

the probes might have been an attempt to make contact. Most had not, Cham replied; inanimate objects were so foreign to them that they had not thought to associate them with intelligent communication. Members of his own pod and some others had considered that the probes might have been analogous to their own engineered helper species, but Cham himself had dismissed the notion, unable to accept that something inanimate (a concept they had needed to coin a new word for) could communicate like a living being. And the majority of squales participating in the global discussion had shared his opinion.

"But they would have called our names," Aili insisted. "You must have heard the sound."

Melo acknowledged that some patterns vaguely similar to the names "Riker" and "Lavena" had been heard in the probe chatter, but Cham objected that overall they were too different. Apparently it was an argument they had had before, with Cham and the majority of squales convincing those like Melo that they had imagined the similarity, reading a pattern into randomness because they had wished to find one. Listening to the debate, Aili discerned that the squales perceived the emissions of a speaker differently from those of a living voice. Perhaps the output from the speakers was missing too many ultrasonic overtones, although it sounded to her as though they perceived some additional components not present in humanoid speech. Aili guessed that it might have been the probes' EM emissions; from the way the squales described the source of the Song of Life, she was coming to suspect that it had some connection to their ability to sense the planet's strong magnetic field.

In any case, Melo went on, the contact pod had intercepted this probe and figured out how to deactivate it, preserving it for study. The elderly squale was quite proud of his apprentices, Alos included, for having the courage to approach the disquieting object and the insight to shut it down. Aili suspected it had been as much luck as insight, but that didn't stop Melo from gloating to Cham that his team's preservation of the object had not been a waste of effort after all.

Aili gave Melo a huge hug, grateful to him for the spirit of curiosity that had led him to preserve the probe intact. At the limited speed of sound through this huge ocean, she'd assumed it would take hours to summon help, and Riker's condition was tenuous as it was. But assuming there was a receiver close enough to pick up this probe's signals through the interference, then help could be on the way in minutes.

Finding the controls, Aili activated the probe. The squales writhed in discomfort and retreated, and she sang apology to them. Soon, they came to rest at a safe distance, and she turned back to the input. "Lavena to anyone who can hear me. Repeat, this is Ensign Lavena calling anyone from *Titan*. Do you read?"

Even with the base's inertial damping field on maximum, Christine Vale could feel the ground shuddering beneath her feet as the sharp-prowed leviathans rammed into the floater island over and over. The squales clearly meant business now, even attacking the island itself, and Vale was coming to realize that even this, the largest, most stable piece of "land" on the planet, was still a small, impermanent thing.

Beyond the field perimeter, though she couldn't feel it, the cluster of linked floaters was rocking and warping like the ground during an earthquake as the icebreakers (as Vale had dubbed the creatures, wondering if they might actually have been bred for that purpose but not really caring at the moment) assailed it from multiple sides, including below. The squales were directing them purposefully, aiming them at the joins between the outer floater segments, the weakest points. She watched in shock as one segment broke free under a decisive blow and spun away. It was listing, taking on water through a gouge that a misplaced blow had left in its side. Closer to Vale, outside the base's field perimeter, the small crustacean- and insect-like creatures that dwelled atop the island were retreating inland, along with other creatures that normally lived below but had climbed to the surface to flee the bombardment.

Sorry, folks, she thought, *but I don't think going inland will be much of a defense. They'll tear this whole thing apart to get to us.* And the force field would be small comfort if the icebreakers managed to hull the floater beneath her feet and sink it, base and all.

Hell, at least that way some of the probes will get sunk. Vale had ordered the crew to proceed with the deployment, despite the fact that doing so would subject them to squale attack. A choice between saving themselves and saving this world was no choice at all. But so far, success had been minimal. Only a few probes had avoided capture and beaching, and many of those were damaged or off course from glancing blows. At this rate, the percentage that reached the dynamo layer would be too low to make a difference. But they had to keep trying.

She struck her combadge. "Vale to *Titan*. Any luck with those transporters?"

"Commander, this is Torvig," came the reply. *"We're unable to boost the confinement beam sufficiently to ensure a safe transport. I have an idea how to get around the problem, but Mister Radowski is resistant."*

"Radowski?" Vale called, knowing the lieutenant would be beside Torvig in the main transporter room. "What's the problem?"

"Commander. He wants to rebuild one of the confinement beam emitters into a wormhole generator."

"Not a wormhole per se, ma'am. More of a subspatial catenation."

"Torvig, what the hell—" She took a breath. "Ensign, even if your . . . theory is sound, how long do you estimate it would take to rebuild and test the emitter? In practical terms?"

She heard the little purring hum Torvig often made when mulling over a problem. *"Given current crew allocation, I'd say . . . about three weeks, ma'am. Assuming success on the initial test."*

"Do you perceive a snag in your proposal, then?"

A pause. *"Ah."*

"Ah. Do you have any *useful* ideas?" You had to love Torvig, but his enthusiasm for his wild hypotheses often blinded him to their practical flaws, and at times it took some prodding to get him focused on the same consensus reality as everyone else.

"Is retrieval by shuttle still not an option?"

"The shuttles are needed to deploy the probes. We have to try to get *some* of these probes past the squale blockade."

"Hrrmmm . . . An orbital phaser barrage around your position?"

"I'll keep it in mind, Ensign. Keep thinking about how to boost the transporter—*before* we run out of island down here. Vale out."

The island shuddered again, and a treelike stalk a few segments over snapped and fell over. *It may come to using phasers,* she thought. But she was reluctant to give the order. After all, she was the invader here, and her crew had done enough damage to this world. Ship's phasers could be set on stun, but the effect was unreliable. A hand phaser had feedback sensors that could calibrate the beam strength and duration to the target's metabolism to keep the effect nonlethal, but that kind of feedback wasn't possible from orbit. That was why Starfleet policy discouraged the practice. Besides, given the squales' unusual sensitivity to energy fields, Vale couldn't be sure that even a stun charge wouldn't have a more serious effect on them. Even firing to frighten them off might be a bad idea. *Hell, the way things are going, it'd probably just make them madder.*

As Vale heard the now-familiar sound of another floater segment being broken away behind her, she almost missed the hail on her combadge. *"—salis to Vale. Come in!"*

She tapped the badge. "Olivia? Is that you?"

"Yes, Commander!" Bolaji, calling from the *Marsalis*, sounded excited. *"You need to hear the signal we just picked up! I'm patching it in."* A pause, then: *"Go ahead, Ensign."*

A moment later, Vale's's annoyance at the distraction vanished when she heard: *"Lavena to Vale. Do you read me?"*

Her heart raced. "Holy shit, Aili, is that you?"

Laughter. *"Oh, Commander, thank the Deep! I'm here, I'm fine. Captain Riker is alive, but he's very ill. We need a rescue shuttle right away. He's on a floater not far from my position."*

"Bolaji? How close are you to Lavena?"

"About six minutes, ma'am."

Under the circumstances, they could certainly spare the delay. "Permission granted to divert from probe deployment to retrieve the captain."

"Aye, Commander! Diverting to retrieve the captain!" came Bolaji's immediate reply.

Another voice intruded on the channel. *"Aili, is that really you? Ah, Ra-Havreii here!"* From the background noise, he was still in the scouter gig, heading toward the base at top speed. Vale wondered if the base would provide any refuge for him by the time he arrived.

"Xin! It's good to hear your voices, all of you."

"Aili, we could really use your diplomacy right now. We're under attack from the squales!"

"What? Why? What did you do?"

"Wha—what the hell do you mean, what did we do?! We're only trying to save their whole damned planet, and they're showing their gratitude by trying to kill me!"

"Hello, superior officer here!" Vale shouted. "Listen, Aili. Are you on good terms with the squales?" It stood to reason, if she and Riker were still alive.

"Some of them, Commander."

"Well, it's a start. Ra-Havreii's right, we're having a diplomatic meltdown of the potentially fatal variety, and I don't just mean for us. Listen—"

———

As Vale spelled out the immediate threat to her crew-mates and the larger threat to Droplet in a few terse sentences, Aili absorbed it with growing dismay. She understood perfectly why the squales were so afraid and angry, so she could not blame them for their actions. But if they couldn't be made to understand the truth, their own fear would doom them.

And Aili Lavena was the only one who could make them understand. Only she knew them well enough to make the case in terms that would hold meaning for them. The fate of this entire world rested on her voice.

Why me? an old, familiar part of her asked. *I can't handle this. There must be someone else.*

But that impulse was quickly damped. Aili was done running from responsibility. She'd always done more harm than good that way.

"Acknowledged," she told Vale. "I'll talk to them. All of them. But I have to leave the probe. I need the squales' help, and they can't stand being close to it."

"We can damp the EM fields now. We can drop more probes, get your message out quicker."

"It won't work, Commander. They don't hear speakers the same way as voice. I need to do this the natural way. Through the *ri'Hoyalina*—the deep sound channel. It will take a few hours, but it's the only way."

After a brief pause, Vale said, *"Do it. We'll hold out as long as we can."*

"Acknowledged, Commander. Good luck. And . . . take care of the captain."

"We will, Aili. Good luck to you too—for everyone's sake. Vale out."

Aili swam toward the squales and began singing, loudly enough to reach the whole contact pod. She had to persuade them to help her, for not enough of the squales knew her language, and her voice alone could not carry far enough through the *ri'Hoyalina*. Expressing her gratitude for all their help, she pleaded with them to help her one more time, and help save their world in the process.

They were reluctant, though. By now, the first reports were reaching them through the long-range channel—songs of fury from squales elsewhere on the planet, battling the perceived invasion of their world. Aili's voice had to outweigh that angry chorus, and it was hard. The defender squales went on their guard, like troops reacting to a declaration of war, and counseled against doing anything to help the offworlders. Alos and Gasa came to Aili's defense, but Cham argued them down, scoffing at the notion that dumping lifeless, alien things into the World Below, the very source of the Song, could heal it rather than harming it worse. Aili hoped Melo would come to her defense again, but the elderly pod leader seemed uncertain, more comfortable with abstract science and philosophy than concrete political decisions.

Still, Aili pleaded with them. *"You know me,"* she sang, using Selkie but approximating their musical idiom as closely as she could. *"You have saved my life, and his, so many times. You're podmates to me, all of you. Would I betray you now?"*

"The others . . ." Cham began.

"They're the same as me. They'd do no willing harm. And listen," she said, calling their attention to the news of battles from distant fronts. *"They would give their lives to*

mend the harm they've done. To save your people, even if you kill them in return.

"You know me. You, of all the squales, have touched another world, and felt its Song. Through me. Your sister. Trust what you have heard. Trust me, if no one else. I only ask you, help me sing!"

Alos and Gasa swam to her side. *"We shall,"* they sang in chorus. *"She is our podmate. Our responsibility! Must students teach our mentors now where obligation lies?"*

"Your duty's to the Song!" Cham intoned.

"And that's the duty that we serve! All things are voices in the Song; they play their destined parts. Aili and we, converging here, as discord finds its peak—might this not be the key that will resolve the Song again?"

The two young squales told Aili to sing her case to the world; they would amplify it for her if no one else would. The defender squales swam forward, but Cham interceded; despite his distrust of Aili, he was angered that they would threaten to turn on podmates. Taking a chance that she would not be stopped, Aili began to sing in Selkie, as loudly as she could. The boys joined her in harmony: Gasa repeated her Selkie words, mimicking her voice as perfectly as any amplifier, but adding strength so it could carry further; while Alos sang the squale translation as a counterpoint. A humanoid might have been confused, but the squales normally communicated this way, in multiple parallel lines of song.

With just the three of them, her song was inadequate to carry far. But Alos and Gasa's fellow apprentices began joining in one by one, some amplifying her own words as Gasa did, others offering translations. To Aili's ears, it seemed they were not all singing the same thing, but interpreting in more than one way, offering different lines of argument at the same time.

At first, it was simply a matter of getting the squales' attention. She sang introductory verses to identify herself, to explain how she came to be here. All the world knew of her by now, of course, but they had not heard her side of it. As she sang of her origins in a different, much smaller ocean, Melo joined in, perhaps intrigued enough by the subject matter of the song to want to sing along. Even one or two of the defender squales were singing with her now. After all, Aili realized, one of the things they believed in defending was the right of all individuals to make their voices heard, whether they agreed with what was sung or not.

And that was something she could build on. *"Our mission's to explore,"* she sang.

> *"To seek out strange new worlds, new life,*
> *To go where we have never gone, and meet the*
>   *people there.*
> *We voyage in the name of peace. We celebrate all*
>   *life.*
> *Diversity combined: it's the refrain that guides*
>   *our quest.*
> *For different voices, even those that frighten us*
>   *at first*
> *Can join with ours in harmonies we never could*
>   *have dreamed;*
> *Just as your voices all combine to sing the Song*
>   *of Life—*

> *A whole that's greater than the sum, a chord of destiny."*

As she elaborated further on the theme, she heard Alos and the other squale translators begin to improvise upon it, illustrating it by the very act as well as by the words. She reflected that Riker would love the jazzy spirit of it. Together, they developed the theme that all things in the cosmos, even those that are dangerous or painful or discordant, were nonetheless harmonics of the same fundamental tone, the overarching Song that sang the universe into being. As alien as she and her companions seemed, she told them, they were still part of the same continuum of life and mind.

At this point, Cham began singing too, but not to reinforce her words. His was a counterpoint conceptually as well as musically, reminding the squales of the crisis precipitated by the offworlders. The defender squales not singing her part sang his, amplifying it to compete with hers.

Yet it wasn't truly competition, she realized. Melodically, rhythmically, even thematically, it merged harmoniously with her song rather than clashing. Cham wasn't trying to drown her out or sabotage her. He was simply adding a voice of caution to the chorus, making sure all sides were heard. In a way, Aili thought, he was even reinforcing her point: even dissenting voices could be part of a single song. An argument didn't have to be about silencing or sabotaging the opposition; it could be a cooperative act, a way to participate in seeking a resolution to a conflict. Cham wanted the other side to be heard, but only to facilitate a healthy debate.

And maybe, she realized, to give her an opening to

address his concerns. *"I understand your fear—your dread of losing all you have,"* she sang. *"That dread is known to us, more so than you could ever dream."*

Aili dug deep down in herself, calling on her memories of the ordeal the Federation had faced at the hands of the Borg. She reached for all the emotions she'd buried away at the time and since: terror for the survival of herself, her ship, her world; grief at the deaths of friends and crewmates; shock, anguish, and sheer incomprehension at the devastation of entire worlds, the elimination of entire civilizations from the cosmos. She knew the squales could not comprehend the events, but she sang to them of the emotions—emotions she'd never let herself face this directly. It was painful, harrowing, and her voice often faltered, but her squale chorus compensated, making her vocal distress a part of the music. When she could not go on, their singing trailed off into a long, sustained chord, a dirge for the dead. It gave her time to gather herself before she went on.

> *"Like you today, we faced the end of our entire*
> *world.*
> *We could have bowed to panic, helped to tear*
> *that world apart.*
> *Instead, we let our fear inspire us all to stand as*
> *one.*
> *To join in greater chorus, even with our enemies,*
> *And sing a louder, richer song than any could*
> *alone—*
> *A harmony that won out over chaos and discord,*
> *Resolved the darkest movement in our cosmic*
> *symphony,*

> *And let us start anew, transposed into a brighter*
>   *key."*

But something was still missing. Aili didn't feel she'd sold it enough; Cham's counterpoint was still present, his skeptical melody creating an unresolved chord. The Borg invasion, the loss of worlds—however movingly she sang, it was too abstract for them. As drained as she was, there was one more corner of her soul she had to bare for them.

> *"Still, there is loss, I know. My grief will be an*
>   *overtone*
> *In every joyous song to come. For they'll be*
>   *incomplete.*
> *They'll lack a certain voice that I will never hear*
>   *again.*
> *Miana, sister, lost when I was but a little girl."*

She told them of Miana, of how she had blamed her mother for her death, turning her grief into rage in order to avoid facing it. She faced it now as she never had before. Despite her emotional and vocal exhaustion, she pushed on.

> *"In all my songs thereafter, Void has sung one of*
>   *the parts.*
> *But Void must not become the loudest singer in*
>   *the song,*
> *As it became for me. I feared the loss and pain so*
>   *much*
> *That I became the cause of loss and pain to my*
>   *own kin."*

She confessed it all, not hesitating to make herself unsympathetic. Her purpose could not be served by anything less than brutal honesty. And she needed to drive home the theme of how fear could become a self-fulfilling prophecy. By singing of how her own fear of hurting her children had cost her a loving family life, she hoped to underline how their panicked efforts to protect their world would bring just the opposite result.

> *"We act in fear because we wish to change the*
> *course of Fate,*
> *Believing we can stop the surge of oceans if we*
> *try.*
> *But if we swim against the Song's inexorable*
> *flow,*
> *We may just smash ourselves upon the shores of*
> *death and pain,*
> *Destroyed by our misguided fight against that*
> *very doom.*
>
> *"There is no shame in fear, unless we let it make*
> *us deaf.*
> *We've all known fear and loss; we need to heed*
> *each other's song*
> *And add the voice the other lacks, fill in the*
> *aching void—*
> *Not swim alone in fear until we lose our very*
> *selves.*
> *Together, we can bring the Song back into*
> *harmony."*

She wasn't sure it was enough; she was afraid it was hokey, sentimental rubbish. And her voice was raw and failing; she couldn't imagine it sounded very pretty to the squales.

But she must have poured her soul into it, for she could hear a change in the squale chorus. Cham's counterpoint had modulated, synchronizing with her part of the song and allowing the chord to resolve at last. It was his way of showing that she'd won him over.

And beyond, in the ri'Hoyalina, the squalesong was changing too. There had been mostly silence for a time, as the squales had paused to listen to her song, with only a few voices raised in protest or anger. But now, new voices were singing, repeating her own song, echoing it even as the multiple reflections of the deep sound channel echoed it, turning the song into a round, a canon. Aili realized they were passing the message along, reamplifying it for the benefit of squales farther away. She wasn't sure if that meant she had convinced them, but at least it meant they were willing to ensure she was heard. Within six hours, she knew, every squale on Droplet would have heard her plea.

But what would they decide?

Not for the first time this day, Christine Vale cursed the speed of sound for being so slow.

Sure, the idea of a layer in the ocean that allowed effectively global telecommunication simply through a quirk of water density was fascinating and elegant, but why did it have to be the layer with the lowest speed of sound instead of the highest? She was used to subspace radio making it possible to speak instantaneously with people twenty parsecs away. The notion of having to wait an hour and a half to know the results of an action being taken less than nine thousand kilometers away was infuriating.

Especially given what had been happening in that hour and a half. The compound floater had been eroded down to its last few segments around the base camp; indeed, the camp might have fallen already if not for Ra-Havreii. He and Y'lira had returned to the base an hour ago, making a daring run of the squales' blockade and driving the scouter gig clear up onto dry ground—though the Efrosian engineer had insisted that any bravery in the act had been inspired by his greater fear of remaining in the water.

Since then, he had somehow figured out a way to conduct a structural integrity field through the organic shell material of the floaters, making them far more resistant to the icebreaker creatures' attacks. But it took a great deal of power and couldn't be maintained for long. And it had the unfortunate side effect of making the remains of the island more rigid, no longer flexing with the constant swells of the ocean. More than one segment had snapped off under its own weight when too much of it had been suspended out of the water, overstraining its connections to its neighbors beyond what the SIF could bear. The squales had seemed puzzled by the change at first, but now had modified their attacks to take advantage of it, waiting for swells and then sending the icebreakers in to strike sidelong at the bases of the suspended floater segments.

"I never imagined myself saying this," Ra-Havreii told Vale as they and Keru watched a segment adjacent to the base rock and twist under just such a bombardment, "but the island can't take much more of this."

"Aili, come on," Vale muttered through clenched teeth, knowing that whatever Lavena had attempted was already completed by now. They were out of comm range of the surviving hydrophone, without the *Marsalis* to relay through the interference, so there was no way to get a status report. The shuttle had ferried the captain back to *Titan* and had then suffered an ill-timed engine failure, the delayed result of an attack by one of the electric-tentacled dreadnought creatures; and replacement parts were slow in coming as long as the ship's industrial replicators were in full-time probe-making mode. The shuttle was on its way back down to evacuate the base, but there was no guarantee Bolaji would make it in time. At least Vale could take comfort in the knowledge that Captain Riker was alive and safe. *One way or the other, I won't have to be the one giving orders for much longer.*

"Commander, come quick!" It was Ensign Evesh, calling from the sensor shed. "You need to hear this!" she cried.

Vale jogged over to the waving Tellarite, while Ra-Havreii remained at his equipment, trying to keep the SIF from burning out just a while longer. Keru stayed on guard, watching the icebreakers closely, phaser at the ready in case defensive measures failed. The islet shuddered and heaved beneath her feet; the inertial damper field had been cut to minimum to boost the SIF. She was getting seasick.

But music was coming from Evesh's console—a chorus of squalesong combined with Selkie, the translator rendering the latter for her ears and filtering out the echoes. "Diffraction leakage from the deep sound channel," the sensor tech explained. Vale listened for a while and was moved; even after serving with Aili Lavena for a year and a half, she had never learned this much about her.

"But did it work?" Vale asked as the islet shuddered again. "Are they listening?"

"They must be," Evesh said. "They're relaying the sound forward."

"Okay, but the sound I want to hear is the one that calls off the damn icebreakers!"

Evesh stared. "Would you recognize that if you heard it?"

Vale glared back. "Context is everything, Ensign." The ground shuddered again. "Case in point."

"Understood, ma'am."

"Oh, no," Ra-Havreii called.

"Oh, no?" Vale called back. "That's *not* a sound I want to hear, Doctor!"

"Oh, no."

"Doctor!"

"The field's going. I can't stop it."

The ground heaved, knocking them both over. Keru somehow managed to keep his footing, though just barely. "Oww . . . don't tell me, the dampers too?"

"The whole field assembly! I told you this would happen."

"Then that means . . ." She looked up and saw the Cerenkov sparkle as the deflector dome around the base decohered and died.

"It means I should've stayed in my nice safe lab at Utopia Planitia. That it should come to this . . . dying out here in this desolate waste . . ."

"Hold it together, Doctor."

"I should've known I'd be killed by *nature*!"

She grabbed him by the front of his uniform. "Would you rather be killed by a pissed-off Izarian?"

He cleared his throat. "Ah. Apologies, Commander. What are your orders?"

She clambered to her feet. "Vale to *Marsalis*. What's your ETA?"

The response was barely audible through the static. *"Ano . . . lve minutes, Co . . . der. . . . ld on."*

The ground jerked forward three meters and left her behind, landing her on her behind. "Easy for you to say," she groaned.

Rising only into a crouch this time, she drew her phaser. Keru caught her gaze and nodded, raising his weapon as well. Ra-Havreii's eyes widened. "It's come to that, then?"

"I'm afraid so, Doc."

"Do you think they'll even penetrate those shells?"

"It's what we've got."

He nodded. "I understand." He drew his own phaser and waited.

And waited.

It took a few moments for Vale to realize the ringing in her ears was from the sudden silence. She scanned her surroundings. The icebreakers were veering off, wending their way through the detached floater segments as they retreated from the remnant of the islet.

Evesh staggered out of the sensor shed, breathing hard. "They're singing a new sound pattern. Part of it is a single Selkie word. 'Yes.'"

Vale closed her eyes and lowered her phaser. *Yes. Thank you, Aili Lavena. Thank you for everything.*

CHAPTER SEVENTEEN

TITAN

Riker climbed out of bed as Christine Vale entered, despite the attempts of Doctor Onnta and Nurse Kershul to keep him down. He was still weak, but he was tired of being off his feet, even if they would only support him for a few moments. "Any word on Deanna?"

Vale shook her head. "Not yet, sir." His heart fell. "But the news from the surface is good."

"The probes are being deployed?"

"Yes, sir. Lavena did an amazing job getting them past their fears. They're letting us drop the probes—in fact, they're even helping. It's amazing—they've already figured out the deployment pattern we're using, and they're offering ways to improve it, based on their knowledge of the deep-sea currents. They may mythologize it, but I think they probably have a better scientific understanding of Droplet's depths than we do. And Cethente's actually *been* there."

"Oh, yes, I heard about that. Is it back in one piece?"

"All four legs are reattached and healing nicely," Onnta said. "Cethente should be back on regular duty within two days."

"Good, good." Riker looked back to Vale. "Aili didn't come back with you?"

She shook her head, which was still tinged midnight blue. "She still needs to stay as an interpreter. But she asked me to send her best."

He smiled. "She already gave me that. And more."

After a moment, he realized the others were giving him a very strange look. "I . . . I didn't mean that the way it sounded!"

"Oh, of course, sir," Vale said. "I'm sure you were completely professional while you were naked together for nearly a week."

"Hey, I had a thong! Unhh . . ." He suddenly felt dizzy, his feet giving way under him.

Vale was there, catching him and easing him back into the bed. "Uh-huh. Well, like the old punch line says, the thong is over but the malady lingers on."

He stared at her. "I don't remember. Were you always this sarcastic?"

She sighed. "Consider it a defense mechanism. This has not been a good week to be the one making the big decisions. I'm really glad to have you back, sir. Really glad."

He smiled. "Thank you." Then he cleared his throat. "Then . . . could you do me a favor?"

"Of course, sir."

His eyes went to the top of her head. "I am . . . really sick . . . of the color blue."

She laughed. "I'll get on it right away, sir."

"When you can spare a moment."

DROPLET

It took two days to finish replicating and deploying all the probes, and another half a day before the squales began reporting that the dissonance was fading from their magnetic Song of Life. The Song was not fully restored yet, since it would take time for the dying barophiles to heal and the population to replenish itself. The Song would be subdued for a time, and might even be changed once it returned, since the attrition of some species in the dynamo layer might allow other, faster-reproducing species to gain an edge, altering the "orchestration" of the Song. But the squales saw the Song as an evolving thing, and were confident they and their fellow Dropletian life forms would keep up with the changes. When he came back down to Droplet, Riker told them they had the spirit of true jazz musicians.

"And you were amazing too," he told Aili when he was reunited with her. "I've heard the recording. . . . I never knew you could sing like that."

"Neither did I, sir," she said from where she floated in the water, next to the scouter gig where he sat. She still hadn't donned any clothing, choosing to "go native" as much for the squales' comfort as her own; but she now wore a field-damped combadge on a choker around her neck, at least. He still wished she'd put something on, but over the past week, he'd come to associate the sight of her nudity with experiences that were less than pleasant, so it evoked no stirrings in him anymore. "But I guess after living with the squales for a time, learning to think and communicate like them, I couldn't help but improve my singing."

He studied her, sensing something beneath her words. "Ensign . . . are you thinking of staying here?"

Her mouth hung open. "Oh, sir. No."

"But the squales . . . they've essentially adopted you into their pod, haven't they?"

"Yes, but . . . pods change members all the time. It's like a family in a lot of ways . . . but it's really more like a crew. And I already have one of those." She smiled. "My responsibility is to *Titan*, and to you. I wouldn't run away from that. I'll stay here as long as you need an interpreter, an ambassador. But then I'm going back to the conn." She winced. "Back to living in that damn hydration suit."

He smiled down at her. "Maybe there's a way to make the suit more comfortable. How about adding a pin?"

She tilted her head. "A pin, sir?"

Riker nodded. "A small, round gold pin with a black circle in the middle. To go next to the solid gold one on the collar."

The Selkie gaped. "Sir?"

"Aili, you just saved a planet. People who save planets get to be lieutenants."

She was speechless for a moment. Then she grinned. "Well, it's about time!"

"It certainly is. I—"

"Gillespie to Riker. Come in."

Riker looked up, though the shuttle was not in sight.

It had been on *Titan* at last report and wasn't scheduled to return; it must have come down to relay a message. "Riker here."

"We've just heard from the Horne *and the* Armstrong," came Ensign Waen's voice. *"They're coming in, sir, all hands safe and well. And Commander Troi says there's an extra passenger she wants you to meet."*

TITAN

As soon as the shuttles had landed, Riker raced inside the *Horne* and into its aft compartment to see Deanna. The sight of her with their daughter in her arms was the most extraordinary thing he'd ever seen. He felt whole in a way he never had before.

He embraced her softly for a long time, the baby between them. She offered her to him without a word, and his arms cradled the tiny girl with great delicacy and care, though it felt like the most natural thing in the world. Her big black eyes looked up at him with awe to match his own.

"*Imzadi*," he said. "Look what we did."

"Mm-hmm. We did good."

"I am so sorry I wasn't there," he told them both, shaking his head.

His wife stroked his cheek. "You were, *imzadi*. I felt you." She nodded at the child. "Something tells me she felt you too."

His eyes went away from the baby for the first time since he'd first seen her, moving to Deanna. "How much empathy do you think she'll have? Only a quarter Betazoid . . ."

"Hey. Don't sell the Troi genes short. Remember, this is a daughter of the Fifth House. An heir to the Sacred Chalice of Riix."

"And let's not forget the Holy Rings of Betazed," Riker added in a mock-bombastic voice, wiggling his daughter's tiny hand as it clutched reflexively at his thumb. He frowned and glanced back at Deanna. "Really? I never thought of that. We get *the* Holy Rings of Betazed?"

She gave a sheepish grin. "Don't get excited. There are fifty thousand of them. Half the families on the planet are heirs to them."

"Fifty *thousand*?"

Deanna shrugged. "The ancient Betazoids were a very holy bunch."

"Captain." It was Tuvok, coming back from the cockpit. "Commander," he added, then nodded formally to the child, to Riker's great amusement. "It is gratifying to see you reunited."

"Thank you, Tuvok. I want to thank you for everything you did to keep my family safe."

"I did my duty as a Starfleet officer, Captain. However, I consider this particular duty to have been an honor as well."

"Oh, Tuvok, you old softie." Deanna grinned. "The fact is, Will, he went above and beyond. And I don't think you'll be hearing any more complaints about his performance. Isn't that right, Tuvok?"

The Vulcan closed off somewhat, but he had a serenity about him that Riker hadn't seen since Deneva was destroyed. "I stand ready to serve, Captain."

But just then, Deanna let out a giggle as if she were sharing some private joke with Tuvok. "Well, go on, show him."

"Show me what?"

Tuvok handed him an isolinear chip. "A video recording of the birth, from my tricorder."

Riker's eyes widened, along with his grin. "Tuvok! You took baby pictures?"

"I monitored the event as a security precaution. To ensure the safety of mother and child."

Yet Riker could see the gleam in Tuvok's eye, a sense of gratification that he could allow a fellow father to witness the birth of his first child. "Thank you," he said, and he could swear he saw the faintest hint of a smile on the Vulcan's face in reply.

Growing serious, Deanna said, "Speaking of which . . . Doctor Ree would really like to talk to you, Will."

They went out into the shuttlebay, where Nurse Ogawa and her son were in the middle of a joyful reunion, holding hands and telling each other about their respective experiences. Keru and T'Pel stood near them, basking in the warmth of the scene. T'Pel's eyes widened at the sight of her returned husband, and though she and Tuvok only exchanged a simple nod, Riker believed he'd gotten to know them well enough to see the mutual relief and love beneath the surface.

The scene wasn't entirely happy, though. Nearby, Ree stood in restraints, surrounded by the security team. Riker came forward to meet him, still cradling the baby. Ree looked at him in surprise. "You . . . trust me to be near her?"

"Why not, Doctor? You delivered her." Deanna had shared everything she thought and felt about her experience through their empathic link. He knew they were in agreement on this. "There still needs to be a hearing, but it's just a formality. I understand why you did what you did."

"I stole your pregnant wife. Attacked a security team. Hijacked a shuttle."

"And you did it all to protect my little girl. Do you have any idea how reassuring that is, Doctor? To know that anyone who wants to hurt this child will have to get past the most dangerous and relentless member of my crew to do it?" He took Ree's shackled manus in his hand and shook it. "Thank you, Doctor Ree. Now don't ever do that again."

Ree gave a formal, heartfelt bow, then let Tuvok and the security team lead him away.

Deanna was by his side. "Does he really have to be in the brig?"

"Regulations," Riker said. "We'll have the hearing as soon as possible, I promise. But if anything, I think maybe he needs this. He's obviously very guilty about what he did—I think he wants to feel he's paid his dues."

"Hey. Who's the psychologist in this family?"

He beamed. "Family. We're really a family now." He admired his daughter a while longer.

Then he furrowed his brow. "I think we're forgetting something."

"What?"

"I don't think the young lady and I have been formally introduced."

Deanna nodded. "Oh. A name. I wanted to talk with

you about that." She huddled up against him, stroking the baby's head. "We've all lost so many people this year. You and I lost the one that would've been her brother or sister. I want to name her in honor of someone we knew far too briefly. A friend whose life was cut short much too soon . . . because she tried to save mine." She whispered the name in his ear.

He smiled. "I like it. In fact . . . I think there's someone else lost too soon that I'd like to commemorate. In honor of this world, and the one who saved me from going too soon."

"The repairs are almost complete," Vale reported to the command crew. Riker looked around the conference lounge, pleased to see the whole group reunited again. Even Lavena was finally back aboard and back in her hydration suit—fidgeting like crazy, but visibly glowing with pride at the new pip on her collar. "When they rebuilt this ship, they built her to last. Even after all the damage we took, the spaceframe is as solid as ever and all systems are virtually good as new. We should be ready to set course to our next destination within the day," the first officer continued. "Whatever we decide that destination will be."

"That's it?" Lavena asked. "After all this, the relationship we've built with the squales, we're just going to up and leave? There's still so much we can learn about them, and they about us."

At Riker's side, Deanna leaned forward. T'Pel was taking care of the baby so the two of them could both attend the briefing, though he knew Deanna was just as eager to get back to their daughter as he was. For now, though, she was the ship's diplomatic officer again. "Aili, we're all very grateful for the job you did with the squales," she said. "It was a remarkable piece of diplomacy. I'm glad to know we have someone who can fill in for me when I'm busy with parental obligations." A chuckle went through the room, though Lavena didn't join in. "But the Prime Directive is clear. Just because interference has happened, that isn't a license to keep interfering. We have to minimize the interaction as much as possible, just as we did on Lumbu."

"But that isn't fair to them! The squales are scientists and explorers just as much as we are. They have an intense curiosity about the universe, and we've just opened the door to a whole new realm of it."

"Then we need to let them build on that knowledge at their own pace," Christine Vale countered. "We don't do them any favors by giving them knowledge they aren't ready for yet."

"Who says they aren't ready? Just because they don't have warp drive?" Lavena laughed. "Look at what the squales have accomplished. They have a biotechnology far more advanced than our own—and they've developed it all, built an advanced technological civilization, without metal, without stone, without even having hands! Can you imagine how long that took? They're a much older civilization than yours or mine. They had genetic engineering before your species even learned to domesticate animals. And in a lot of ways, they're a more advanced civilization than ours. Is it fair, is it even meaningful, to use warp drive alone as the only benchmark for whether a civilization is 'advanced enough' for contact?"

"It is not the only benchmark," Tuvok put in. "However

advanced their technology may be, the squales responded to our arrival with aggression and xenophobia."

"It's not like we didn't give them reason. Our devices were hurting them from the moment we landed. And we should've left well enough alone with the asteroid."

"And there's another reason, Aili," Deanna said. "The Prime Directive is as much about our lack of readiness as theirs. It's about keeping us from being incautious in a contact situation. The squales are very, very alien. Who knows how else we might clash with the best of intentions?"

Lavena straightened. "Then doesn't that make this a symmetrical issue? What gives us the right to make the decision unilaterally? Shouldn't we at least give them a say, let them decide if they think *we're* ready for further contact?"

"I think she's right," Riker said. "This is their world. And we've done enough harm trying to make decisions on their behalf. The Prime Directive exists to keep us from imposing our will on other races, but unilaterally deciding to deny them further contact can be just another way of imposing our will."

"But do we have the right to reinterpret the Prime Directive?" Vale asked. "If the rules are going to be changed, isn't that for Starfleet Command and the Federation Council to take up? There's a reason why the Directive uses space travel as its standard. It says something about a species' readiness to accept the idea of being part of a larger cosmos, their curiosity about other forms of life, their ability to reach out to them. However advanced the squales' biotech may be, the idea of space travel is totally new to them. It could be generations before they're ready to cope with it."

Suddenly Lavena wore a knowing smile beneath her suit visor. "Commander, I think you should come down to Droplet. There's something Melo mentioned to me that I really think you should see."

Lavena's invitation extended to Riker, Ra-Havreii, and Pazlar as well as Vale. Christine was uneasy about leaving the ship without both its command officers, but Riker assured her that they would be safe in squale . . . tentacles. She wanted to convince the captain to stay behind, continue recuperating, and spend time with his family, but she could tell that Lavena's little secret had fired his curiosity and nothing would stop him.

Their destination was one of the woodlike lattice structures that the squales used as secure facilities. They found that the top spiral of the lattice had been bred to fold open in response to a vocal command, irising out in an intricate, flower-petal pattern that was beautiful and stunning to see on such a scale.

The aquashuttle wouldn't fit in there, of course, so the visitors donned scuba gear to dive in—all save Lavena, who went in nude save for a combadge choker and wrist tricorder. Hardly regulation, but everyone except Ra-Havreii seemed to be taking it in stride. They were accompanied by Melo, the leader of the astronomy pod Lavena had bonded with, and by another pod leader from a bioengineering group, but not the one Lavena and Riker had dealt with before. Reportedly this pod specialized in breeding life forms devoted to meteorological and astronomical research, such as the "weather balloon" creatures that had first tipped the crew off to the squales' sentience.

Lavena had dubbed this squale Anidel after a famous astronomer from her world.

Once Vale dove into the water and her vision cleared, the object of their journey came into view. It was a large conical structure, over four meters high. Its surface was a honeycomb lattice of hard, whitish material, the holes filled with a smooth translucent substance. It tapered to an elongated spire at the top, and four large fins were evenly spaced around its lower perimeter. It reminded Vale of the silica shell of a protistan organism she'd once seen under a microscope. Beneath the conical "shell" bulged four large spheroids, with pulsing tubes leading into them from parts unknown.

"What is it?" asked Riker. But the squales remained silent. "Lieutenant?"

It took a moment for Lavena to realize he was talking to her. "I'll tell you if you order me, sir . . . but I think they want you to figure it out for yourselves."

It was hard to tell through the scuba mask, but Vale was sure Riker was grinning. "I enjoy a challenge. Commander Pazlar?"

Melora had been glancing at the squale Lavena had named in her honor, or perhaps glaring. She had initially been flattered to learn that Lavena had named a pod leader after her, until Lavena had demurred that they had little in common beyond profession—with Melo being much more good-natured. Now, the Elaysian refocused on her work, bringing her wrist tricorder to bear. "The shell is of a dense organic polymer of some kind."

"The clear parts of the shell seem to be a polymer resin," Ra-Havreii added a few moments later.

"The interior appears to be filled with the same oxygenated fluid used in the lifepods," Melora reported.

Riker swam up and gazed through the translucent ports. "It's hollow, all right. No sign of internal organs—maybe in the lower part. And there seems to be . . . algae growing on the inner surface." He played his helmet light over it. "It's green. . . . Photosynthetic?"

"Yes," Pazlar confirmed.

"The creature has an interesting nervous system," Ra-Havreii reported. "The wattage is surprisingly high. You could power a light panel with it, which is more than you can say for the humanoid brain."

Vale swam to the upper portion, which bulged out slightly before tapering to the spire. The honeycomb cells were smaller here, and she realized they spiraled down, growing larger as they went, as in many natural shell formations. But there was a discontinuity in the shell pattern. "There's some sort of valve here—several plates of that dense polymer that seem to open outward. Maybe 'hatch' is a better word."

Melora's eyes were wide under her scuba mask. "Are you thinking what I'm thinking?"

"Don't tempt me," Vale answered.

"What do you mean?" Ra-Havreii asked.

"Melora," Vale went on, "what can you tell about the pods at the bottom?"

The science officer swam down to scan them. "They're made of a more flexible biological material, but they're still very thick-skinned. I think . . . yes . . . they seem to be designed to contain fluids under very high pressure, complete with interior baffles. These conduits seem to be for filling

the tanks. . . . Must use peristalsis to build up pressure."
She looked to Lavena. "Do we have to guess what they're
for, or will you tell us that?"

"Well, once they're fully grown," Aili said after a brief
exchange with the squales, "two will be filled with oxygen
and the other two with hydrogen."

"My god," Vale whispered, gazing at the conical shape
of the object.

"What is it?" asked Ra-Havreii, still not seeing it.

Vale's response was preempted by Riker's awed laughter. "This is fantastic!"

"Will someone tell me what it is?"

Still laughing, Riker crowed, "It's a baby space capsule!"

For millennia, Anidel sang to the offworlders, the squales
had been exploring their world, seeking to quench their
bottomless thirst for knowledge. Using living probes
adapted from existing life forms, they had explored the
depths of their native sea and the seemingly endless reaches
of the sky.

But then they had found the sky was not endless after
all. Over centuries, they had evolved their aerial probes to
rise higher and higher, to survive ever greater cold and ever
thinner air. They gained an understanding of the vast, frigid
emptiness between bodies in space, but this did not terrify
them any more than the emptiness of the air in comparison
to the water. After all, their own World Between was as
good as vacuum to the creatures of the World Below, the
dynamo layer. That was a realm even the squales had not
developed the means to reach, for it was impossible for

their biotechnology to function there. The void of space seemed far more attainable in comparison.

And so they had studied and learned for centuries. They had derived the laws of gravity by watching the motions of the planets. They had studied the stars, learning much from them about the nature of light. Ultimately they had become aware of the invisible forms of light and developed instruments to study them. A living nervous system was a ready-made radio antenna.

Thousands of years ago, before humans or even Vulcans had ventured into space, the squales had sent forth the first capsule like this. But outside Droplet's magnetic field, away from the Song of Life, the squales had been disoriented and impaired. The unfamiliar field of the system's star and the emissions of the exotic elements in the debris disk had caused them discomfort. They had decided they could learn enough about the emptiness through astronomical observation, and had turned their attention back to exploring the profundities of their ocean and improving their biotechnology.

But now, Melo said, the arrival of visitors from space had inspired his pod and others in related disciplines to revive their ancient space program, recreating the design from their extraordinary racial memory. As an echolocating species, they perceived three-dimensional shapes in terms of sound patterns, and could literally speak the form of an object in detail. And they had an eidetic recall for sound patterns, keeping the "blueprints" alive in oral memory. Anidel's team had needed to fill in certain details degraded over time, but it hadn't proven too difficult to deduce what was needed.

The key difference, Anidel sang, came from a study of *Titan*'s field-neutralizing probes. Their design had given the squales some ideas for how to use the capsule's nervous system to generate a field that would compensate for the effects of extra-Dropletian travel on squale neurology. They had wasted no time incorporating these insights into the design of this capsule, which would be over ten meters high when fully grown in a week or so. *"Our thanks to you,"* Anidel sang, *"for giving us the final key we need to bring this ancient dream again to life."*

Once they surfaced again, it was some time before Vale could speak. "I owe you an apology, Aili. And them. This is . . . Tell Anidel I am truly humbled. I think maybe we're the ones who have the most to learn here."

"She understands," Aili told her. "They pick up languages very fast."

"Okay, okay. Don't rub it in."

Riker chuckled. "To be fair, it's only the equivalent of a Mercury capsule," he said. "They're a long way from warp drive."

"Technologically. Not conceptually. Hell, Will, we've seen living creatures with warp capability. If it hadn't been for their dependence on the Song, they might've been the ones visiting our planet, a few thousand years ago."

"Isn't that a reason to leave them alone, then?" Riker asked. "Let them develop their own technology in their own direction, instead of using ours?"

Vale glared. "I hate it when you play devil's advocate." Taking a slow breath, she went on. "Of course that's what we should do. Hell, something tells me they wouldn't tolerate anything else. But that doesn't mean we can't . . .

keep them in the loop. We could recommend that the Federation open diplomatic relations. Just the occasional visit. With slipstream drive, that should be more feasible in a few years. And not just for the squales' benefit. We could learn a lot from them about biotechnology, medicine . . ."

"Hmm, something tells me they wouldn't take too well to the Federation's policy against genetic engineering."

"It never hurts to have a contrasting opinion. And like the Denobulans and Choblik, they seem to have adjusted to their enhancements pretty well."

Riker studied her. "You've really come around, haven't you?"

"Well, I didn't have the chance for as much close contact with them as you did. They are an impressive bunch of people." She lowered her head. "Especially for not blaming us for what happened."

"Hey. Don't blame yourself, Christine. You made a mistake, but you went above and beyond to fix it. The squales see that, and so do I." He clapped her shoulder. "You did a fine job, Commander."

"Thank you, sir." She frowned. "Although wouldn't 'below and beyond' be more accurate here . . . ?"

EPILOGUE

HVOV MEMORIAL HOSPITAL, PLANET LUMBU

Nurse Mawson was glad to see things getting back to normal at the hospital. Not only was Administrator Ruddle due back from her rest cure soon, but the city was growing calmer with the war fears dying down. The Cafmor had done a fine job in the last round of debates, restating her position in the finest, most elegant traditional forms and thereby undermining the Kumpen challenge to her victory. Many Kumpen were crying foul, insisting that she had been coached, but the Cafmor had proven a subtler point: by making the same argument in traditional rhetorical structure that she had in more informal words, she had implicitly demonstrated that the form was irrelevant, undermining the Regent's position enough that a majority of voters in both countries had declared the Cafmor victorious. So Lirht was safe now, and so was Kump, for what would the Lirhten want with that arid, mountainous waste anyway? All they had there were dilithium crystals, and what good were those?

And then there was the other thing. But Mawson and her fellow maternity nurses had little to say about that. And those who'd chosen to speak of it had soon learned there was little gain in doing so, for the government, the press, and the public were satisfied to chalk it up to mass hysteria, the people's fear of a looming war manifesting in visions of spirits and monsters. Mawson and her nurses knew better, but they were content to communicate it in knowing looks and shared laughter. In years to come, they might get together and speak of it in reminiscence, maybe privately debate the true origin of the giant men and women and the scaled monster with the hands of a surgeon. For now, they were content to absorb the experience in their own thoughts. For Mawson, it had reaffirmed a faith she had begun to question in these uncertain times, this age of electricity and factories and motor carriages, when nature and the spirit world seemed more distant than they had in her childhood. Now she had confirmation that the spirits were there, and that they had children and loved and protected them just as people did. That reassured her, inspired her to put more passion into her work. But she also knew that the spirits had their own lives to lead, that people could not rely on them to interfere in mortal affairs—that it was up to people themselves to find their own solutions to their wars and plagues and so forth. That the only guidance the spirits could offer was by example. But these spirits had proven to set a fine example—after a rocky start, to be sure, but imminent childbirth tended to do that to people.

As Mawson left the hospital for the night, she looked

up at the stars and wondered if the giant baby and her mother were happy.

DROPLET, STARDATE 58590.2

The capsule ascended on a pillar of wind.

Borne aloft on a thermal by huge, transparent balloons—related to the weather-balloon creatures and bred specifically for this purpose—the fairy-castle rocketship rose toward the tenuous reaches of the sky. When it had risen as far as it could go, a spark from its supercharged nervous system would fire its rockets, sending it . . .

Well, not far, Will Riker thought as he watched its ascent. The squales were nowhere near far enough along to get into orbit, since it had been less than two weeks since they'd begun the project, even if their ability to build on ancient knowledge accelerated the program considerably. This was merely a propulsion test, but it was a historic enough event that Riker had accepted the squales' invitation to remain at Droplet until after the launch.

"Lovely weather for it," Deanna said, and he lowered his eyes from the diminishing speck of the capsule to gaze upon her. She lounged beside him on a floater-islet beach, while Natasha Miana Riker-Troi nursed at her breast.

He smiled. "Beautiful scenery indeed."

"Oh, you."

"I just wish it could last." He stroked Tasha's head, but she remained focused on slaking her appetite. "We came so close to losing each other."

"We have before," Deanna told him. "And we will

again. But we have a good crew, and I have faith that they'll always bring us back together. Back to this . . . the three of us."

"Sir?" It was Lavena, swimming up into the shallows. Two squales were behind her; Riker couldn't tell them apart, but he suspected they were her young friends. "They're ready."

"I think it would be diplomatic," Deanna said, "if we joined them in the water for the occasion. After all, they're extending their first toe into a new sea."

"But the view is better here."

"A few meters won't make any difference to the view. Besides, it's even more humid here than it was in the holodeck. I'm dying for a swim," she said, meaning it this time.

Shrugging, he acceded to her wishes. They stayed in the shallows, with Deanna keeping the baby close but letting the water bear much of her weight. But they knew Tasha would be safe so long as the squales surrounded them. Indeed, the squales seemed intrigued by the child, coming up close, extending their tentacles to touch her with great delicacy, and flashing color patterns that Riker imagined were the squale equivalent of doting baby talk.

But soon the big event came. Riker could see little more than a sustained point of light and a distant streak of white vapor, but that was enough to tell him the test was successful. Eventually, the remote roar of the rocket reached his ears. He knew that *Titan* was monitoring the event with full sensors, that Vale and the others on the bridge were seeing it in rich detail, preserving the image for history. Riker would enjoy reviewing that in time. But there was a greater wonder in being here with the squales themselves, experiencing this first step as they did, without any machines—any unliving machines—in the way.

As the distant roar faded, Riker turned back to his own first step into new seas. Tasha was splashing around, making little cooing noises that sounded like enjoyment. He met Deanna's eyes, and she sensed his impression and nodded. "She likes the water," she confirmed. "She's curious about the new environment. Yes, that's my girl, isn't it? My daring little girl, all ready for adventure!"

"Just like her namesake," Riker said.

"Like her father," Troi replied. "She's going to be quite the explorer, this one."

Yes, Riker thought as he saw the tiny child testing her abilities, stretching her arms feebly toward the flickering squales as though eager to quest into the unknown. *This one will go boldly.*

Appendix

Who's who on the *U.S.S. Titan* in *Over a Torrent Sea*

Captain William T. Riker
(human male) commanding officer

Commander Christine Vale
(human female) executive officer

Commander Tuvok
(Vulcan male) second officer/tactical officer

Commander Deanna Troi
(Betazoid-human female) diplomatic officer/senior
counselor

Commander Xin Ra-Havreii
(Efrosian male) chief engineer

Lieutenant Commander Shenti Yisec Eres Ree
(Pahkwa-thanh male) chief medical officer

Lieutenant Commander Ranul Keru
(unjoined Trill male) chief of security

Lieutenant Commander Melora Pazlar
(Elaysian female) senior science officer

Lieutenant Commander Tamen Gibruch
(Chandir male) gamma shift bridge commander

Lieutenant Commander Onnta
(Balosneean male) assistant chief medical officer

Lieutenant Alyssa Ogawa
(human female) head nurse

Lieutenant Eviku Ndashelef
(Arkenite male) xenobiologist

Lieutenant Kekil
(Chelon male) xenobiologist

Lieutenant Chamish
(Kazarite male) ecologist

Lieutenant Se'al Cethente Qas
(Syrath asexual) astrophysicist

Lieutenant Huilan Sen'kara
(S'ti'ach male) assistant counselor

Lieutenant Pava Ek'Noor sh'Aqabaa
(Andorian *shen*) gamma shift tactical officer

Ensign Aili Lavena
(Pacifican "Selkie" female) senior flight controller

Ensign Torvig Bu-kar-nguv
(Choblik male) engineer

Ensign Mordecai Crandall
(human male) engineer

Ensign Tasanee Panyarachun
(human female) engineer

Ensign Peya Fell
(Deltan female) relief science officer

Ensign Vennoss
(Kriosian female) stellar cartographer

Ensign Y'lira Modan
(Selenean female) cryptolinguist

Ensign Zurin Dakal
(Cardassian male) sensor analyst

Ensign Evesh
(Tellarite female) sensor technician

Ensign Olivia Bolaji
(human female) shuttle pilot

Ensign Waen
(Bolian female) shuttle pilot

Ensign Kuu'iut
(Betelgeusian male) relief tactical officer

Ensign Hriss
(Caitian female) security guard

Chief Petty Officer Bralik
(Ferengi female) geologist

Crewman Ellec Krotine
(Boslic female) security guard

T'Pel
(Vulcan female) civilian child care specialist

Noah Powell
(human male) civilian, son of Alyssa Ogawa

Acknowledgments

As always, thanks go to Marco Palmieri for commissioning this novel and initiating the *Titan* series. I'm indebted to those who have come before me, including Andy Mangels, Mike Martin, and Geoffrey Thorne, and to those who offered advice on the manuscript, including Kirsten Beyer, Keith R.A. DeCandido, William Leisner, and David Mack. The President Bacco quote that opens the novel is from *Destiny: Lost Souls* by David Mack. President Bacco was created by Keith R.A. DeCandido, as was Admiral Masc (mentioned in "The Ceremony of Innocence Is Drowned" in *Tales of the Dominion War*) and the Alrond colony (from *A Singular Destiny*). Information on Arkenites comes from the FASA and Decipher role-playing games. Thanks to Theodore Sturgeon for inspiring Lumbuan linguistics, and to the *Freefall* webcomic for inspiring Doctor Ree's philosophy on the power of smiles.

The concept of an ocean planet as depicted herein was proposed in 2003 by Marc J. Kuchner and Alain Léger (independently), with Léger coining the name. I am indebted to their papers on the subject: Kuchner, "Volatile-Rich Earth-Mass Planets in the Habitable Zone" (*The Astrophysical Journal Letters* Vol. 596, 10 Oct. 2003, pp. L105–L108) and Léger et al., "A New Family of Planets?

Ocean Planets" (*Icarus* Vol. 169 Iss. 2, June 2004, pp. 499–504), for providing the basic information I needed to create Droplet. For more detailed calculations of Droplet's size and internal structure, I relied on Christophe Sotin et al., "Mass-radius curve for extrasolar Earth-like planets and Ocean planets" (*Icarus* Vol. 191 Iss. 1, 1 Nov. 2007, pp. 337–351). More details were provided by "Ocean planets . . . soon" on the Crowlspace.com blog, February 4, 2007. Hal Clement's novel *Noise* provided useful information on the meteorology of a world without land masses. Martin Chaplin's *Water Structure and Science* webpage at www.lsbu.ac.uk/water/ was helpful for determining the behavior of water and ice under extreme pressure. The University of Rhode Island's *Discovery of Sound in the Sea* page at www.dosits.org/ helped fill in details about the deep sound (or SOFAR) channel. For the effect of extreme pressure on biology, I am indebted to Anurag Sharma et al., "Microbial Activity at Gigapascal Pressures" (*Science* 22, Vol. 295 No. 5559, Feb. 2002, pp. 1514–1516) and Christoph Hartmann and Antonio Delgado, "Numerical Simulation of the Mechanics of a Yeast Cell under High Hydrostatic Pressure" (*Journal of Biomechanics* Vol. 37 Iss. 7, July 2004, pp. 977–87). Aspects of Cethente's biology were suggested by Jean Schneider, "A Model for a Non-chemical Form of Life: Crystalline Physiology" (*Origins of Life* Vol. 8 Iss. 1, April 1977, pp. 33–38).

This book is dedicated to and informed by the memory of my cat Natasha, who passed away on June 20, 2008, at the age of 17. I've lived with many cats over the years, but she was very special to me, one of the greatest sources of joy in my life. She is deeply missed.

About the Author

Christopher L. Bennett is the author of two previous works of *Titan* fiction, the novel *Star Trek: Titan: Orion's Hounds* and the short story "Empathy" in the *Star Trek: Mirror Universe: Shards and Shadows* anthology. He has also authored such critically acclaimed novels as *Star Trek: Ex Machina*, *Star Trek: The Next Generation: The Buried Age*, and *Star Trek: The Next Generation: Greater Than the Sum*, as well as the alternate *Voyager* tale *Places of Exile* in *Myriad Universes: Infinity's Prism*. Shorter works include *Star Trek: SCE #29: Aftermath* and *Star Trek: Mere Anarchy: The Darkness Drops Again*, as well as short stories in the anniversary anthologies *Constellations* (original series), *The Sky's the Limit* (TNG), *Prophecy and Change* (DS9), and *Distant Shores* (VGR). Beyond *Star Trek*, he has penned the novels *X-Men: Watchers on the Walls* and *Spider-Man: Drowned in Thunder*, and is also developing original science fiction novel concepts. More information, original fiction, and novel annotations can be found at http://home.fuse.net/ChristopherLBennett/.